CALCULATING
GOD

NOVELS BY ROBERT J. SAWYER

*Golden Fleece**
Far-Seer
Fossil Hunter
Foreigner
*End of an Era**
The Terminal Experiment
Starplex
*Frameshift**
Illegal Alien
*Factoring Humanity**
*Flashforward**
*Calculating God**

*published by Tor Books

(Readers' group guides available at www.sfwriter.com)

ANTHOLOGIES EDITED BY ROBERT J. SAWYER

Tesseracts 6 (with Carolyn Clink)
Crossing the Line (with David Skene-Melvin)
Over the Edge (with Peter Sellers)

CALCULATING

GOD

ROBERT J. SAWYER

TOR®

A TOM DOHERTY ASSOCIATES BOOK

NEW YORK

CALCULATING GOD

Copyright © 2000 by Robert J. Sawyer

This book is printed on acid-free paper.

Edited by David G. Hartwell

Book design by Victoria Kuskowski

A Tor Book
Published by Tom Doherty Associates, LLC
175 Fifth Avenue,
New York, NY 10010

www.tor.com

Tor® is a registered trademark of Tom Doherty Associates, LLC.

Library of Congress Cataloging-in-Publication Data

Sawyer, Robert J.
Calculating God / Robert J. Sawyer.—1st ed.
p.   cm.
"A Tom Doherty Associates book."
ISBN 0-312-86713-1
1. Human-alien encounters—Fiction.   2. Life on other planets—
Fiction.   3. Toronto (Ont.)—Fiction.   4. God—Proof—Fiction.
I. Title.
PR9199.3.S2533 C35 2000
813'.54—dc21   00-027662

First Edition: June 2000

Printed in the United States of America

0   9   8   7   6   5   4   3   2   1

AUTHOR'S NOTE

The Royal Ontario Museum really exists, and, of course, it has a real director, real curators, real security guards, and so on. However, all the characters in this novel are entirely the product of my imagination: none of them are meant to bear any resemblance to the actual people who currently hold or in the past have held positions at the ROM or any other museum.

For

Nicholas A. DiChario

and

Mary Stanton,

who were there for us

when we needed friends the most

ACKNOWLEDGMENTS

Sincere thanks to my lovely wife, Carolyn Clink; my editor, David G. Hartwell, and his associate, James Minz; my agent, Ralph Vicinanza, and his associates, Christopher Lotts and Vince Gerardis; Stanley Schmidt, Ph.D., the editor of *Analog* magazine; Tom Doherty, Jynne Dilling, and Linda Quinton of Tor Books; Harold and Sylvia Fenn, Robert Howard, Suzanne Hallsworth, and Heidi Winter of H.B. Fenn and Company; Marshall L. McCall, Ph.D., Department of Physics and Astronomy, York University, Toronto; John-Allen Price; Jean-Louis Trudel; and Roberta van Belkom. Beta testers for this novel were the Reverend Paul Fayter, historian of science and theology, York University; Asbed G. Bedrossian; Ted Bleaney; Michael A. Burstein; David Livingstone Clink; James Alan Gardner; Richard M. Gotlib; Terence M. Green; Howard Miller, Ph.D.; Ariel Reich, Ph.D.; Alan B. Sawyer; Edo van Belkom; and Andrew Weiner. Special thanks to those fine folks who let me bounce ideas off them in the "Robert J. Sawyer" section of the SF Authors Forum on CompuServe (accessed with the CompuServe command "Go Sawyer"). I also gratefully acknowledge the financial support of the Writing and Publishing Section of the Canada Council for the Arts, which provided me with a travel grant to assist me in attending the World Science Fiction convention in Melbourne, Australia, while I was finishing this novel. Finally, thanks to my father, John A. Sawyer, for letting Carolyn and me repeatedly borrow his vacation home on Canandaigua Lake, where much of this book was written.

COMPLETE FOSSIL SKELETONS ARE RARELY FOUND. IT IS PERMISSIBLE TO FILL IN MISSING PIECES USING THE RECONSTRUCTIONIST'S BEST GUESSES, BUT, EXCEPT FOR DISPLAY MOUNTS, ONE MUST CLEARLY DISTINGUISH THOSE PARTS THAT ARE ACTUAL FOSSILIZED MATERIAL FROM THOSE THAT ARE CONJECTURE. ONLY THE AUTHENTIC FOSSILS ARE TRUE FIRST-PERSON TESTIMONY OF THE PAST; IN CONTRAST, THE RECONSTRUCTIONIST'S CONTRIBUTIONS ARE SOMETHING AKIN TO THIRD-PERSON NARRATION.

> —*Thomas D. Jericho, Ph.D., in his introduction to* Handbook of Paleontological Restoration *(Danilova and Tamasaki, editors)*

I know, I know—it seemed crazy that the alien had come to Toronto. Sure, the city is popular with tourists, but you'd think a being from another world would head for the United Nations—or maybe to Washington. Didn't Klaatu go to Washington in Robert Wise's movie *The Day the Earth Stood Still*?

Of course, one might also think it's crazy that the same director who did *West Side Story* would have made a good science-fiction flick. Actually, now that I think about it, Wise directed *three* SF films, each more stolid than its predecessor.

But I digress. I do that a lot lately—you'll have to forgive me. And, no, I'm not going senile; I'm only fifty-four, for God's sake. But the pain sometimes makes it hard to concentrate.

I was talking about the alien.

And why he came to Toronto.

It happened like this . . .

The alien's shuttle landed out front of what used to be the McLaughlin Planetarium, which is right next door to the Royal Ontario Museum, where I work. I say it used to be the planetarium because Mike Harris, Ontario's tight-fisted premier, cut the funding to the planetarium. He figured Canadian kids didn't have to know about space—a real forward-thinking type, Harris. After he closed the planetarium, the building was rented out for a commercial *Star Trek* exhibit, with a mockup of the classic bridge set inside what had been the star theater. As much as I like *Star Trek,* I can't think of a sadder comment on Canadian educational priorities. A variety of other private-sector concerns had subsequently rented the space, but it was currently empty.

Actually, although it was perhaps reasonable for an alien to visit a planetarium, it turned out he really wanted to go to the museum. A good thing, too: imagine how silly Canada would have looked if first contact were made on our soil, but when the extraterrestrial ambassador knocked on the door, no one was home. The planetarium, with its white dome like a giant igloo, is set well back from the street, so there's a big concrete area in front of it—perfect, apparently, for landing a small shuttle.

Now, I didn't see the landing firsthand, even though I was right next door. But four people—three tourists and a local—did get it on video, and you could catch it endlessly on TV around the world for days afterward. The ship was a narrow wedge, like the slice of cake someone takes when they're pretending to be on a diet. It was solid black, had no visible exhaust, and had dropped silently from the sky.

The vessel was maybe thirty feet long. (Yeah, I know, I know—Canada's a metric country, but I was born in 1946. I don't think anyone of my generation—even a scientist, like me—ever became comfortable with the metric system; I'll try to do better, though.) Rather than being covered with robot puke, like just about every spaceship in every movie since *Star Wars,* the landing craft's hull was completely smooth. No sooner had the ship set down than a door opened in its side. The door was rectangular, but wider than it was tall. And it opened by sliding up—an immediate clue that the occupant probably wasn't human; humans rarely make doors like that because of our vulnerable heads.

14

Seconds later, out came the alien. It looked like a giant, golden-brown spider, with a spherical body about the size of a large beach ball and legs that splayed out in all directions.

A blue Ford Taurus rear-ended a maroon Mercedes-Benz out front of the planetarium as their drivers gawked at the spectacle. Many people were walking by, but they seemed more dumbfounded than terrified—although a few did run down the stairs into Museum subway station, which has two exits in front of the planetarium.

The giant spider walked the short distance to the museum; the planetarium had been a division of the ROM, and so the two buildings are joined by an elevated walkway between their second floors, but an alley separates them at street level. The museum was erected in 1914, long before anyone thought about accessibility issues. There were nine wide steps leading up to the six main glass doors; a wheelchair ramp had been added only much later. The alien stopped for a moment, apparently trying to decide which method to use. It settled on the stairs; the railings on the ramp were a bit close together, given the way its legs stuck out.

At the top of the stairs, the alien was again briefly flummoxed. It probably lived in a typical sci-fi world, full of doors that slid aside automatically. It was now facing the row of exterior glass doors; they pull open, using tubular handles, but he didn't seem to comprehend that. But within seconds of his arrival, a kid came out, oblivious to what was going on at first, but letting out a startled yelp when he saw the extraterrestrial. The alien calmly caught the open door with one of its limbs—it used six of them for walking, and two adjacent ones as arms—and managed to squeeze through into the vestibule. A second wall of glass doors faced him a short distance ahead; this air-lock-like gap helped the museum control its interior temperature. Now savvy in the ways of terrestrial doors, the alien pulled one of the inner ones open and then scuttled into the Rotunda, the museum's large, octagonal lobby; it was such a symbol of the ROM that our quarterly members magazine was called *Rotunda* in its honor.

On the left side of the Rotunda was the Garfield Weston Exhibition Hall, used for special displays; it currently housed the Burgess Shale show I'd helped put together. The world's two best collections of Burgess Shale fossils were here at the ROM and at the Smithsonian; neither institution normally had them out for the public to see, though. I'd arranged for a temporary pooling of both collections to be exhibited first here, then in Washington.

The wing of the museum to the right of the Rotunda used to contain our late, lamented Geology Gallery, but it now held gift shops and a Druxy's deli—one of many sacrifices the ROM had made under Christine Dorati's administration to becoming an "attraction."

Anyway, the creature moved quickly to the far side of the Rotunda, in between the admissions desk and the membership-services counter. Now, I didn't see this part firsthand, either, but the whole thing was recorded by a security camera, which is good because no one would have believed it otherwise. The alien sidled up to the blue-blazered security officer—Raghubir, a grizzled but genial Sikh who'd been with the ROM forever—and said, in perfect English, "Excuse me. I would like to see a paleontologist."

Raghubir's brown eyes went wide, but he quickly relaxed. He later said he figured it was a joke. Lots of movies are made in Toronto, and, for some reason, an enormous number of science-fiction TV series, including over the years such fare as *Gene Roddenberry's Earth: Final Conflict, Ray Bradbury Theater,* and the revived *Twilight Zone.* He assumed this was some guy in costume or an animatronic prop. "What kind of paleontologist?" he said, deadpan, going along with the bit.

The alien's spherical torso bobbed once. "A pleasant one, I suppose."

On the video, you can see old Raghubir trying without complete success to suppress a grin. "I mean, do you want an invertebrate or a vertebrate?"

"Are not all your paleontologists humans?" asked the alien. He had a strange way of talking, but I'll get to that. "Would they not therefore all be vertebrates?"

I swear to God, this is all on tape.

"Of course, they're all human," said Raghubir. A small crowd of visitors had gathered, and although the camera didn't show it, apparently a number of people were looking down onto the Rotunda's polished marble floor from the indoor balconies one level up. "But some specialize in vertebrate fossils and some in invertebrates."

"Oh," said the alien. "An artificial distinction, it seems to me. Either will do."

Raghubir lifted a telephone handset and dialed my extension. Over in the Curatorial Centre, hidden behind the appalling new Inco Limited Gallery of Earth Sciences—the quintessential expression of Christine's vision for the ROM—I picked up my phone. "Jericho," I said.

"Dr. Jericho," said Raghubir's voice, with its distinctive accent, "there's somebody here to see you."

Now, getting to see a paleontologist isn't like getting to see the CEO of a *Fortune* 500; sure, we'd rather you made an appointment, but we *are* civil servants—we work for the taxpayers. Still: "Who is it?"

Raghubir paused. "I think you'll want to come and see for yourself, Dr. Jericho."

Well, the *Troödon* skull that Phil Currie had sent over from the Tyrrell had waited patiently for seventy million years; it could wait a little longer. "I'll be right there." I left my office and made my way down the elevator, past the Inco Gallery— God, how I hate that thing, with its insulting cartoon murals, giant fake volcano, and trembling floors—through the Currelly Gallery, out into the Rotunda, and—

And—

17

Jesus.

Jesus Christ.

I stopped dead in my tracks.

Raghubir might not know the difference between real flesh and blood and a rubber suit, but I do. The thing now standing patiently next to the admissions desk was, without doubt, an authentic biological entity. There was no question in my mind whatsoever. It was a lifeform—

And—

And I had studied life on Earth since its beginnings, deep in the Precambrian. I'd often seen fossils that represented new species or new genera, but I'd never seen any large-scale animal that represented a whole new phylum.

Until now.

The creature was absolutely a lifeform, and, just as absolutely, it had not evolved on Earth.

I said earlier that it looked like a big spider; that was the way the people on the sidewalk had first described it. But it was more complex than that. Despite the superficial resemblance to an arachnid, the alien apparently had an internal skeleton. Its limbs were covered with bubbly skin over bulging muscle; these weren't the spindly exoskeletal legs of an arthropod.

But every modern Earthly vertebrate has four limbs (or, as with snakes and whales, had evolved from a creature that did), and each limb terminates in no more than five digits. This being's ancestors had clearly arisen in another ocean, on another world: it had *eight* limbs, arranged radially around a central body, and two of the eight had specialized to serve as hands, ending in six triple-joined fingers.

My heart was pounding and I was having trouble breathing. *An alien.*

And, without doubt, an *intelligent* alien. The creature's spherical body was hidden by clothing—what seemed to be a single long strip of bright blue fabric, wrapped repeatedly around the torso, each winding of it going between two different limbs, al-

18

lowing the extremities to stick out. The cloth was fastened between the arms by a jeweled disk. I've never liked wearing neckties, but I'd grown used to tying them and could now do so without looking in a mirror (which was just as well, these days); the alien probably found donning the cloth no more difficult each morning.

Also projecting from gaps in the cloth were two narrow tentacles that ended in what might be eyes—iridescent balls, each covered by what looked to be a hard, crystalline coating. These stalks weaved slowly back and forth, moving closer together, then farther apart. I wondered what the creature's depth perception might be like without a fixed distance between its two eyeballs.

The alien didn't seem the least bit alarmed by the presence of me or the other people in the Rotunda, although its torso was bobbing up and down slightly in what I hoped wasn't a territorial display. Indeed, it was almost hypnotic: the torso slowly lifting and dropping as the six legs flexed and relaxed, and the eyestalks drifting together, then apart. I hadn't seen the video of the creature's exchange with Raghubir yet; I thought that perhaps the dance was an attempt at communication—a language of body movements. I considered flexing my own knees and even, in a trick I'd mastered at summer camp forty-odd years ago, crossing and uncrossing my eyes. But the security cameras were on us both; if my guess was wrong, I'd look like an idiot on news programs around the world. Still, I needed to try something. I raised my right hand, palm out, in a salute of greeting.

The creature immediately copied the gesture, bending an arm at one of its two joints and splaying out the six digits at the end of it. And then something incredible happened. A vertical slit opened on the upper segment of each of the two front-most legs, and from the slit on the left came the syllable "hell" and from the one on the right, in a slightly deeper voice, came the syllable "oh."

19

I felt my jaw dropping, and a moment later my hand dropped as well.

The alien continued to bob with its torso and weave with its eyes. It tried again: from the left-front leg came the syllable *"bon,"* and from the right-front came *"jour."*

That was a reasonable guess. Much of the museum's signage is bilingual, both English and French. I shook my head slightly in disbelief, then began to open my mouth—not that I had any idea what I would say—but closed it when the creature spoke once more. The syllables alternated again between the left mouth and the right one, like the ball in a Ping-Pong match: *"Auf" "Wie" "der" "sehen."*

And suddenly words did tumble out of me: "Actually, *auf Wiedersehen* means goodbye, not hello."

"Oh," said the alien. It lifted two of its other legs in what might have been a shrug, then continued on in syllables bouncing left and right. "Well, German is not my first language."

I was too surprised to laugh, but I did feel myself relaxing, at least a little, although my heart still felt as though it were going to burst through my chest. "You're an alien," I said. *Ten years of university to become Master of the Bleeding Obvious . . .*

"That is correct," said the leg-mouths. The being's voices sounded masculine, although only the right one was truly bass. "But why be generic? My race is called Forhilnor, and my personal name is Hollus."

"Um, pleased to meet you," I said.

The eyes weaved back and forth expectantly.

"Oh, sorry. I'm human."

"Yes, I know. *Homo sapiens,* as you scientists might say. But your personal name is . . . ?"

"Jericho. Thomas Jericho."

"Is it permissible to abbreviate 'Thomas' to 'Tom'?"

I was startled. "How do you know about human names? And—hell—how do you know English?"

20

"I have been studying your world; that is why I am here."

"You're an explorer?"

The eyestalks moved closer to each other, then held their position there. "Not exactly," said Hollus.

"Then what? You're not—you're not an invader are you?"

The eyestalks rippled in an S-shaped motion. Laughter? "No." And the two arms spread wide. "Forgive me, but you possess little my associates or I might desire." Hollus paused, as if thinking. Then he made a twirling gesture with one of his hands, as though motioning for me to turn around. "Of course, if you want, I could give you an anal probe . . ."

There were gasps from the small crowd that had assembled in the lobby. I tried to raise my nonexistent eyebrows.

Hollus's eyestalks did their S-ripple again. "Sorry—just kidding. You humans *do* have some crazy mythology about extraterrestrial visitations. Honestly, I will not hurt you—or your cattle, for that matter."

"Thank you," I said. "Um, you said you weren't exactly an explorer."

"No."

"And you're not an invader."

"Nope."

"Then what are you? A tourist?"

"Hardly. I am a scientist."

"And you want to see me?" I asked.

"You are a paleontologist?"

I nodded, then, realizing the being might not understand a nod, I said, "Yes. A dinosaurian paleontologist, to be precise; theropods are my specialty."

"Then, yes, I want to see you."

"Why?"

"Is there someplace private where we can speak?" asked Hollus, his eyestalks swiveling to take in all those who had gathered around us.

"Umm, yes," I said. "Of course." I was stunned by it all as I led him back into the museum. An alien—an actual, honest-to-God alien. It was amazing, utterly amazing.

We passed the paired stairwells, each wrapped around a giant totem pole, the Nisga'a on the right rising eighty feet—sorry, twenty-five meters—all the way from the basement to the skylights atop the third floor, and the shorter Haida on the left starting on this floor. We then went through the Currelly Gallery, with its simplistic orientation displays, all sizzle and no steak. This was a weekday in April; the museum wasn't crowded, and fortunately we didn't pass any student groups on our way back to the Curatorial Centre. Still, visitors and security officers turned to stare, and some uttered various sounds as Hollus and I passed.

The Royal Ontario Museum opened almost ninety years ago. It is Canada's largest museum and one of only a handful of major multidisciplinary museums in the world. As the limestone carvings flanking the entrance Hollus had come through a few minutes before proclaim, its job is to preserve "the record of Nature through countless ages" and "the arts of Man through all the years." The ROM has galleries devoted to paleontology, ornithology, mammalogy, herpetology, textiles, Egyptology, Greco-Roman archaeology, Chinese artifacts, Byzantine art, and more. The building had long been H-shaped, but the two courtyards had been filled in during 1982, with six stories of new galleries in the northern one, and the nine-story Curatorial Centre in the southern. Parts of walls that used to be outside are now indoors, and the ornate Victorian-style stone of the original building abuts the simple yellow stone of the more recent additions; it could have turned out a mess, but it's actually quite beautiful.

My hands were shaking with excitement as we reached the elevators and headed up to the paleobiology department; the ROM used to have separate invertebrate and vertebrate paleontology departments, but Mike Harris's cutbacks had forced us to consolidate. Dinosaurs brought more visitors to the ROM than

ROBERT J. SAWYER

did trilobites, so Jonesy, the senior invertebrate curator, now worked under me.

Fortunately, no one was in the corridor when we came out of the elevator. I hustled Hollus into my office, closed the door, and sat down behind my desk—although I was no longer frightened, I was still none too steady on my feet.

Hollus spotted the *Troödon* skull on my desktop. He moved closer and gently picked it up with one of his hands, bringing it to his eyestalks. They stopped weaving back and forth, and locked steadily on the object. While he examined the skull, I took another good look at him.

His torso was no bigger around than the circle I could make with my arms. As I noted earlier, the torso was covered by a long strip of blue cloth. But his hide was visible on the six legs and two arms. It looked a bit like bubble wrap, although the individual domes were of varying sizes. But they did seem to be air filled, meaning they were likely a source of insulation. That implied Hollus was endothermic; terrestrial mammals and birds use hairs or feathers to trap air next to their skin for insulation, but they could also release that air for cooling by having their hair stand on end or by ruffling their feathers. I wondered how bubble-wrap skin could be used to effect cooling; maybe the bubbles could deflate.

"A" "fascinating" "skull," said Hollus, now alternating whole words between his mouths. "How" "old" "is" "it?"

"About seventy million years," I said.

"Precisely" "the" "sort" "of" "thing" "I" "have" "come" "to" "see."

"You said you're a scientist. You are a paleontologist, like me?"

"Only in part," said the alien. "My original field was cosmology, but in recent years my studies have moved on to larger matters." He paused for a moment. "As you have probably gathered by this point, my colleagues and I have observed your Earth for some time—enough to absorb your principal languages and to make a study of your various cultures from your television and radio. It has been a frustrating process. I know more about your popular music and food-preparation technology than I ever cared to—although I am intrigued by the Popeil Automatic Pasta Maker. I have also seen enough sporting events to last me a lifetime. But information on scientific matters has been very hard to find; you devote little bandwidth to detailed discussions in these areas. I feel as though I know a disproportionate amount about some specific topics and nothing at all about others." He paused. "There is information we simply cannot acquire on our own by listening in to your media or through our own secret visits to your planet's surface. This is particularly true about scarce items, such as fossils."

I was getting a bit of a headache as his voice bounced from mouth to mouth. "So you want to look at our specimens here at the ROM?"

"Exactly," said the alien. "It was easy for us to study your contemporary flora and fauna without revealing ourselves to humanity, but, as you know, well-preserved fossils are quite rare. The best way to satisfy our curiosity about the evolution of life on this world seemed to be by asking to see an existing collection of fossils. No need to reinvent the lever, so to speak."

I was still flabbergasted by this whole thing, but there seemed no reason to be uncooperative. "You're welcome to look at our specimens, of course; visiting scholars come here all the time. Is there any particular area you're interested in?"

"Yes," said the alien. "I am intrigued by mass extinctions as turning points in the evolution of life. What can you tell me about such things?"

I shrugged a little; that was a big topic. "There've been five mass extinctions in Earth's history that we know of. The first was at the end of the Ordovician, maybe 440 million years ago. The second was in the late Devonian, something like 365 million years ago. The third, and by far the largest, was at the end of the Permian, 225 million years ago."

ROBERT J. SAWYER

Hollus moved his eyestalks so that his two eyes briefly touched, the crystalline coatings making a soft clicking sound as they did so. "Say" "more" "about" "that" "one."

"During it," I said, "perhaps ninety-six percent of all marine species disappeared, and three-quarters of all terrestrial vertebrate families died out. We had another mass extinction late in the Triassic Period, about 210 million years ago. We lost about a quarter of all families then, including all labyrinthodonts; it was probably crucial to the dinosaurs—creatures like that guy you're holding—coming into ascendancy."

"Yes," said Hollus. "Continue."

"Well, and the most-famous mass extinction happened sixty-five million years ago, at the end of the Cretaceous." I indicated the *Troödon* skull again. "That's when all the dinosaurs, pterosaurs, mosasaurs, ammonites, and others died out."

"This creature would have been rather small," said Hollus, hefting the skull.

"True. From snout to tip of tail, no more than five feet. A meter and a half."

"Did it have larger relatives?"

"Oh, yes. The largest land animals that ever lived, in fact. But they all died out in that extinction, paving the way for my kind—a class we call mammals—to take over."

"In" "cred" "i" "ble," said Hollus's mouths. Sometimes he alternated whole words between his two speaking slits, and sometimes just syllables.

"How so?"

"How did you arrive at the dates for the extinctions?" he asked, ignoring my question.

"We assume that all uranium on Earth formed at the same time the planet did, then we measure the ratios of uranium-238 to its end decay product, lead-206, and of uranium-235 to its end decay product, lead-207. That tells us that our planet is 4.5 billion years old. We then—"

"Good," said one mouth. And "good" confirmed the other.

CALCULATING GOD

"Your dates should be accurate." He paused. "You have not yet asked me where I am from."

I felt like an idiot. He was right, of course; that probably should have been my first question. "Sorry. Where are you from?"

"From the third planet of the star you call Beta Hydri."

I'd taken a couple of astronomy courses while doing my undergraduate geology degree, and I'd studied both Latin and Greek—handy tools for a paleontologist. "Hydri" was the genitive of Hydrus, the small water snake, a faint constellation close to the south celestial pole. And beta, of course, was the second letter of the Greek alphabet, meaning that Beta Hydri would be the second-brightest star in that constellation as seen from Earth. "And how far away is that?" I asked.

"Twenty-four of your light-years," said Hollus. "But we did not come here directly. We have been traveling for some time now and visited seven other star systems before we came here. Our total journey so far has been 103 light-years."

I nodded, still stunned, and then, realizing that I was doing what I'd done before, I said, "When I move my head up and down like this it means I agree, or go on, or okay."

"I know that," said Hollus. He clicked his two eyes together again. "This gesture means the same thing." A brief silence. "Although I now have been to nine star systems, including this one and my home one, yours is only the third world on which we have found extant intelligent life. The first, of course, was my own, and the next was the second planet of Delta Pavonis, a star about twenty light-years from here but just 9.3 from my world."

Delta Pavonis would be the fourth-brightest star in the constellation of Pavo, the peacock. Like Hydrus, I seemed to recall that it was only visible in the Southern Hemisphere. "Okay," I said.

"There have also been five major mass extinctions in the history of my planet," said Hollus. "Our year is longer than yours, but if you express the dates in Earth years, they occurred at roughly 440 million, 365 million, 225 million, 210 million, and 65 million years ago."

I felt my jaw drop.

"And," continued Hollus, "Delta Pavonis II has also experienced five mass extinctions. Their year is a little shorter than yours, but if you express the dates of the extinctions in Earth years, they also occurred at approximately 440, 365, 225, 210, and 65 million years ago."

My head was swimming. I was hard enough talking to an alien, but an alien who was spouting nonsense was too much to take. "That can't be right," I said. "We know that the extinctions here were related to local phenomena. The end-of-the-Permian one was likely caused by a pole-to-pole glaciation, and the end-of-the-Cretaceous one seemed to be related to an impact of an asteroid from this solar system's own asteroid belt."

"We thought there were local explanations for the extinctions on our planet, too, and the Wreeds—our name for the sentient race of Delta Pavonis II—had explanations that seemed unique to their local circumstances, as well. It was a shock to discover that the dates of mass extinctions on our two worlds were the same. One or two of the five being similar could have been a coincidence, but all of them happening at the same time seemed impossible unless, of course, our earlier explanations for their causes were inaccurate or incomplete."

"And so you came here to determine if Earth's history coincides with yours?"

"In part," said Hollus. "And it appears that it does."

I shook my head. "I just don't see how that can be."

The alien gently put the *Troödon* skull down on my desk; he was clearly used to handling fossils with care. "Our incredulity matched yours initially," he said. "But at least on my world and that of the Wreeds, it is more than just the dates that match. It is also the nature of the effects on the biosphere. The biggest mass extinction on all three worlds was the third—the one that on Earth defines the end of the Permian. Given what you have told me, it seems that almost all the biodiversity was eliminated on all three worlds at that time.

"Next, the event you assign to late in your Triassic apparently led to the domination of the top ecological niches by one class of animals. Here, it was the creatures you call dinosaurs; on my world, it was large ectothermic pentapeds.

"And the final mass extinction, the one you have referred to as occurring at the end of your Cretaceous, seems to have led to the shunting aside of that type and the move to the center of the class that now dominates. On this world it was mammals like you supplanting dinosaurs. On Beta Hydri III, it was endothermic octopeds like me taking centrality from the pentapeds. On Delta Pavonis II, viviparous forms took over ecological niches formerly dominated by egg layers."

He paused. "At least, this is how it seems, based on what you have just told me. But I wish to examine your fossils to determine just how accurate this summary is."

I shook my head in wonder. "I can't think of any reason why evolutionary history should be similar on multiple worlds."

"One reason is obvious," said Hollus. He moved sideways a few steps; perhaps he was getting tired of supporting his own weight, although I couldn't imagine what sort of chair he might use. "It could be that way because God wished it to be so."

For some reason, I was surprised to hear the alien talking like that. Most of the scientists I know are either atheists or keep their religion to themselves—and Hollus had indeed said he was a scientist.

"That's one explanation," I said quietly.

"It is the most sensible. Do humans not subscribe to a principle that says the simplest explanation is the most preferable?"

I nodded. "We call it Occam's razor."

"The explanation that it was God's will posits one cause for all the mass extinctions; that makes it preferable."

"Well, I suppose, if . . ."—dammitall, I know I should have just been polite, just nodded and smiled, the way I do when the occasional religious nut accosts me in the Dinosaur Gallery and demands to know how Noah's flood fits in, but I felt I had to speak up— ". . . if you believe in God."

Hollus's eyestalks moved to what seemed to be their maximal extent, as if he was regarding me from both sides simultaneously. "Are you the most senior paleontologist at this institution?" he asked.

"I'm the department head, yes."

"There is no paleontologist with more experience?"

I frowned. "Well, there's Jonesy, the senior invertebrate curator. He's damn near as old as some of his specimens."

"Perhaps I should speak with him."

"If you like. But what's wrong?"

"I know from your television that there is much ambivalence about God in this part of your planet, at least among the general public, but I am surprised to hear that someone in your position is not personally convinced of the existence of the creator."

"Well, then, Jonesy's not your man; he's on the board of CSICOP."

"Sky cop?"

"The Committee for Scientific Investigation of Claims of the Paranormal. He definitely doesn't believe in God."

"I am stunned," said Hollus, and his eyes turned away from me, examining the posters on my office wall—a Gurche, a Czerkas, and two Kishes.

"We tend to consider religion a personal matter," I said gently. "The very nature of faith is that one cannot be factually sure about it."

"I do not speak of matters of faith," said Hollus, turning his eyes back toward me. "Rather, I speak of verifiable scientific fact. That we live in a created universe is apparent to anyone with sufficient intelligence and information."

I wasn't really offended, but I *was* surprised; previously, I'd only heard similar comments from so-called creation scientists. "You'll find many religious people here at the ROM," I said.

"Raghubir, whom you met down in the lobby, for instance. But even he wouldn't say that the existence of God is a scientific fact."

"Then it will fall to me to educate you in this," said Hollus.

Oh, joy. "If you think it's necessary."

"It is if you are to help me in my work. My opinion is not a minority one; the existence of God is a fundamental part of the science of both Beta Hydri and Delta Pavonis."

"Many humans believe that such questions are outside the scope of science."

Hollus regarded me again, as if I were failing some test. "Nothing is outside the scope of science," he said firmly—a position I did not, in fact, disagree with. But we rapidly parted company again: "The primary goal of modern science," he continued, "is to discover why God has behaved as he has and to determine his methods. We do not believe—what is the term you use?—we do not believe that he simply waves his hands and wishes things into existence. We live in a universe of physics, and he must have used quantifiable physical processes to accomplish his ends. If he has indeed been guiding the broad stokes of evolution on at least three worlds, then we must ask how? And why? What is he trying to accomplish? We need to—"

At that moment, the door to my office opened, revealing silver-haired, long-faced Christine Dorati, the museum's director and president. "What the devil is *that*?" she said, pointing a bony finger at Hollus.

ROBERT J. SAWYER

2

C hristine Dorati's question stopped me cold. Everything had been happening so quickly, I hadn't had time to really consider how momentous all this was. The first verified extraterrestrial visitor to Earth had dropped by, and instead of alerting the authorities—or even my boss Christine—I was sitting around with the being, indulging in the kind of bull session university students have late at night.

But before I could reply, Hollus had turned around to face Dr. Dorati; he rotated his spherical body by shifting each of his six legs to the left.

"Greetings," he said. "My" "name" "is" "Hol" "lus." The two syllables of the name overlapped slightly, one mouth starting up before the other had quite finished.

Christine was a full-time administrator now. Years ago, when she'd been an active researcher, her field had been textiles; Hollus's unearthy origins might therefore not have been obvious to her. "Is this a joke?" she said.

"Not" "at" "all," replied the alien, in his strange stereophonic voice. "I am a"—his eyes looked briefly at me, as if acknowledging that he was quoting something I'd said earlier—"think of me as a visiting scholar."

"Visiting from where?" asked Christine.

"Beta Hydri," said Hollus.

"Where's that?" asked Christine. She had a big, horsey

mouth and had to make a conscious effort to close her lips over her teeth.

"It's another star," I said. "Hollus, this is Dr. Christine Dorati, the ROM's director."

"Another star?" said Christine, cutting off Hollus's response. "Come *on*, Tom. Security called me and said there was some kind of prank going on, and——"

"Have you not seen my spaceship?" asked Hollus.

"Your spaceship?" Christine and I said in unison.

"I landed outside that building with the hemispherical roof."

Christine came into the room, squeezed past Hollus, and pushed the speaker-phone button on my Nortel desk set. She then tapped out an internal extension on the keypad. "Gunther?" she said. Gunther was the security officer at the staff entrance, located off the alley between the museum and the planetarium. "It's Dr. Dorati here. Do me a favor: step outside and tell me what you can see out front of the planetarium."

"You mean the spaceship?" asked Gunther's voice, through the speaker. "I've already seen it. There's a huge crowd around it now."

Christine clicked off the phone without remembering to say goodbye. She looked at the alien. Doubtless she could see its torso expanding and contracting as it breathed.

"What—um, what do you want?" asked Christine.

"I am doing some paleontological research," said Hollus. Surprisingly, the word *paleontological*—quite a mouthful, even for a human—wasn't split between his two speaking slits; I still hadn't figured out the rules governing the switchover.

"I have to tell someone about this," said Christine, almost to herself. "I have to notify the authorities."

"Who *are* the appropriate authorities in a case like this?" I asked.

Christine looked at me as if surprised that I'd heard what she'd said. "The police? The RCMP? The Ministry of External Affairs? I don't know. It's too bad they shut down the planetarium; there might have been someone there who would have known. Still, maybe I should ask Chen." Donald Chen was the ROM's staff astronomer.

"You can notify anyone you wish," said Hollus. "But please do not make a fuss about my presence. It will just interfere with my work."

"Are you the only alien on Earth right now?" asked Christine. "Or are others of your kind visiting other people?"

"I am the only one currently on the planet's surface," Hollus said, "although more will be coming down shortly. There are thirty-four individuals in the crew of our mothership, which is in synchronous orbit around your planet."

"Synchronous above what?" asked Christine. "Toronto?"

"Synchronous orbits have to be above the equator," I said. "You can't have one over Toronto."

Hollus turned his eyestalks in my direction; perhaps I was going up in his esteem. "That is right. But since this place was our first goal, the ship is in orbit along the same line of longitude. I believe the country directly beneath it is called Ecuador."

"Thirty-four aliens," said Christine, as if trying to digest the idea.

"Correct," replied Hollus. "Half are Forhilnors like me, and the other half are Wreeds."

Excitement coursed through me. Getting to examine a lifeform from one different ecosystem was staggering; to get to examine lifeforms from two would be amazing. In previous years, when I'd been well, I'd taught a course on evolution at the University of Toronto, but everything we knew about how evolution worked was based on one sample. If we could—

"I'm not sure who to call," said Christine again. "Hell, I'm not sure who would believe me if I *did* call."

Just then my phone rang. I picked up the handset. It was Indira Salaam, Christine's executive assistant. I passed the phone to her.

"Yes," Christine said into the mouthpiece. "No, I'll stay here.

Can you bring them up? Great. Bye." She handed the phone back to me. "Toronto's finest are on their way up."

"Toronto's finest what?" asked Hollus.

"The police," I said, replacing the handset.

Hollus said nothing. Christine looked at me. "Someone called in the story of the spaceship and its alien pilot who had walked into the museum."

Soon, two uniformed officers arrived, escorted by Indira. All three stood in the doorway, mouths agape. One of the cops was scrawny; the other quite stocky—the gracile and robust forms of *Homo constableus,* side by side, right there in my office.

"It must be a fake," said the skinny cop to his partner.

"Why does everyone keep assuming that?" asked Hollus. "You humans seem to have a profound capacity for ignoring obvious evidence." His two crystalline eyes looked pointedly at me.

"Which of you is the museum's director?" asked the brawny cop.

"I am," said Christine. "Christine Dorati."

"Well, ma'am, what do you think we should do?"

Christine shrugged. "Is the spaceship blocking traffic?"

"No," said the cop. "It's entirely on the planetarium grounds, but . . ."

"Yes?"

"But, well, something like this should be reported."

"I agree," said Christine. "But to whom?"

My desk phone rang again. This time it was Indira's assistant—they can't keep the planetarium open, but assistants have assistants. "Hello, Perry," I said. "Just a sec." I handed the phone to Indira.

"Yes?" she said. "I see. Umm, hang on a second." She looked at her boss. "CITY-TV is here," she said. "They want to see the alien." CITY-TV was a local station known for its in-your-face news; its slogan was simply "Everywhere!"

Christine turned toward the two cops to see if they were going to object. They looked at each other and exchanged small shrugs. "Well, we can't bring any more people up here," said Christine. "Tom's office won't take it." She turned to Hollus. "Would you mind coming down to the Rotunda again?"

Hollus bobbed up and down, but I don't think it was a sign of agreement. "I am eager to get on with my research," he said.

"You'll have to speak to other people at some point," replied Christine. "Might as well get it over with."

"Very well," said Hollus, sounding awfully reluctant.

The thickset cop spoke into the microphone attached to the shoulder of his uniform, presumably talking to someone back at the station. Meanwhile, we all marched down the corridor toward the elevator. We had to go down in two loads: Hollus, Christine, and me in the first one; Indira and the two cops in the second. We waited for them on the ground floor, then made our way out into the museum's vaulted lobby.

CITY-TV calls its camerapersons—all young, all hip—"videographers." There was one waiting, all right, as well as quite a crowd of spectators, standing around in anticipation of the return of the alien. The videographer, a Native Canadian man with black hair tied in a ponytail—surged forward. Christine, ever the politician, tried to step into his camera's field of view, but he simply wanted to shoot Hollus from as many angles as possible—CITY-TV was notorious for what my brother-in-law calls "out-of-body-cam."

I noticed one of the cops had his hand resting on his holster; I rather imagine their supervisor had told them to protect the alien at all costs.

Finally, Hollus's patience was exhausted. "Surely" "that" "is" "enough," he said to the guy from CITY-TV.

That the alien could speak English astounded the crowd; most of them had arrived after Hollus and I had spoken in the lobby. Suddenly the videographer started peppering the alien with questions: "Where are you from?" "What's your mission?" "How long did it take you to get here?" Hollus did his best to

35

CALCULATING GOD

answer—although he never mentioned God—but, after a few minutes, two men in dark-blue business suits entered my field of view, one black and one white. They observed the alien for a short time, then the white one stepped forward and said, "Excuse me." He had a Québecois accent.

Hollus apparently didn't hear; he went on answering the videographer's questions.

"Excuse me," said the man again, much louder.

Hollus moved aside. "I am sorry," said the alien. "Did you wish to get by?"

"No," said the man. "I want to speak to you. We're from the Canadian Security Intelligence Service; I'd like you to come with us."

"Where to?"

"To a safer place, where you can talk to the right people." He paused. "There *is* a protocol for this sort of thing, although it took a few minutes to find it. The prime minister is already on his way to the airport in Ottawa, and we're about to notify the U.S. president."

"No, I am sorry," said Hollus. His eyestalks swiveled around, looking at the octagonal lobby and all the people in it before settling back on the federal agents. "I came here to do paleontological research. I am glad to say hello to your prime minister, of course, if he wants to drop by, but the only reason I revealed my presence was so that I could talk to Dr. Jericho here." He indicated me with one of his arms, and the videographer swung to shoot me. I must say, I felt rather pumped.

"I'm sorry, sir," said the French-Canadian CSIS man. "But we really have to do it this way."

"You are not listening," said Hollus. "I refuse to go. I am here to do important work, and I wish to continue it."

The two CSIS agents looked at each other. Finally, the black man spoke; he had a slight Jamaican accent. "Look, you're supposed to say, 'Take me to your leader.' You're supposed to *want* to meet with the authorities."

ROBERT J. SAWYER

"Why?" asked Hollus.

The agents looked at each other again. "Why?" repeated the white one. "Because that's the way it's done."

Hollus's two eyes converged on the man. "I rather suspect I have more experience at this than you do," he said softly.

The white federal agent pulled out a small handgun. "I really do have to insist," he said.

The cops now moved forward. "We'll have to see some identification," said the burlier of the two policemen.

The black CSIS agent obliged; I had no idea what a CSIS ID was supposed to look like, but the police officers seemed satisfied and backed off.

"Now," said the black man. "Please do come with us."

"I am quite sure you will not use that weapon," said Hollus, "so doubtless I will get my way."

"We have orders," said the white agent.

"No doubt you do. And no doubt your superiors will understand that you were unable to fulfill them." Hollus indicated the videographer, who was madly scrambling to change tapes. "The record will show that you insisted, I declined, and that was the end of the matter."

"This is no way to treat a guest," shouted a woman from the crowd. That seemed to be a popular sentiment: several people voiced their affirmation.

"We're trying to protect the alien," said the white CSIS man.

"Like hell," said a male museum patron. "I've seen *The X-Files*. If you walk out of here with him, no regular person will ever see him again."

"Leave him alone!" added an elderly man with a European accent.

The agents looked at the videographer, and the black one pointed out a security camera to the white one. Doubtless they wished none of this was being recorded.

"Politely," said Hollus, "you are not going to prevail."

"But, well, surely you won't object to us having an observer present?" said the black agent. "Someone to make sure no harm comes to you?"

"I have no concerns in that area," said Hollus.

Christine stepped forward at this point. "I'm the museum's president and director," she said to the two CSIS men. Then she turned to Hollus. "I'm sure you can understand that we'd like to have a record, a chronicle, of your visit here. If you don't mind, we will at least have a cameraperson accompany you and Dr. Jericho." The CITY-TV guy surged forward; it was quite clear that he'd be happy to volunteer for the job.

"But I *do* mind," said Hollus. "Dr. Dorati, on my world, only criminals are subject to constant observation; would you consent to someone watching you all day long as you worked?"

"Well, I—" said Christine.

"Nor will I," said Hollus. "I am grateful for your hospitality, but—you, there," he pointed at the videographer. "You are the representative of a media outlet; allow me to make a plea." Hollus paused for a second while the Native Canadian adjusted his camera angle. "I am looking for unfettered access to a comprehensive collection of fossils," said Hollus, speaking loudly. "In exchange, I will share information my people have gathered, when I think it is appropriate and fair. If there is another museum that will offer me what I seek, I will gladly appear there instead. Simply—"

"No," said Christine, rushing forward. "No, that won't be necessary. Of course, we'll cooperate any way we can."

Hollus turned his eyestalks away from the camera. "Then I may make my studies under terms that are acceptable to me?"

"Yes," she said. "Yes, whatever you want."

"The government of Canada will still require—" began the white CSIS man.

"I can as easily go to the United States," said Hollus. "Or Europe, or China, or—"

"Let him do what he wants!" shouted a middle-aged male museum patron.

"I do not mean to intimidate," said Hollus, looking at one of the federal agents and then the other, "but I have zero interest in being a celebrity or in being forced into narrow passages by documentarians or security people."

"We honestly don't have any latitude in our orders," said the white agent. "You simply have to come with us."

Hollus's eyestalks arched backward so that his crystal-covered orbs looked up at the mosaic on the Rotunda's domed ceiling high above, made up of more than a million Venetian-glass tiles; perhaps this was the Forhilnor equivalent of rolling one's eyes. The words "That all men may know His work"—a quote, I'm told, from the Book of Job—were arranged in a square at the dome's apex.

After a moment, the stalks came forward again, and one locked onto each of the agents. "Listen," Hollus said. "I have spent more than a year studying your culture from orbit. I am not fool enough to come down here in a way that would make me vulnerable." He reached into a fold of the cloth wrapped around his torso—in a flash, the other CSIS man had his gun in his hand, too—and pulled out a polyhedral object about the size of a golf ball. He then scuttled sideways over to me and proffered it. I took it; it was heavier than it looked.

"That device is a holoform projector," Hollus said. "It has just imprinted itself with Dr. Jericho's biometrics and will only work when in his company; indeed, I can make it self-destruct, quite spectacularly, if anyone else handles it, so I advise you not to try to take it from him. Further, the projector will only work at locales that I approve of, such as inside this museum." He paused. "I am here by telepresence," he said. "The actual me is still inside the landing craft, outside the building next door; the only reason I came down to the surface was to supervise the delivery of the projector that Dr. Jericho is now holding. That projector uses holography and micromanipulated force fields to give the impression that I am here and to allow me to handle objects." Hollus—or the image of him—froze for a few seconds, 39 as if the real Hollus was preoccupied doing something else. "There," he said. "My lander is now returning to orbit, with the real me aboard." Some people rushed outside through the museum's glass-doored vestibule, presumably to get a glimpse of the departing ship. "There is nothing you can do to coerce me, and there is no way you can physically harm me. I do not mean to be rude, but contact between humanity and my people will be on our terms, not yours."

The polyhedron in my hand issued a two-toned bleep, and the projection of Hollus wavered for a second, then disappeared.

"You'll have to surrender that object, of course," said the white man.

I felt adrenaline coursing through me. "I'm sorry," I said, "but you saw Hollus give it directly to me. I don't think you have any claim to it."

"But it's an alien artifact," said the black CSIS agent.

"So?" I said.

"Well, I mean, it should be in official hands."

"I work for the government, too," I said defiantly.

"I mean it should be in *secure* hands."

"Why?"

"Well, ah, *because*."

I don't accept "because" as an argument from my six-year-old son; I wasn't about to accept it here. "I can't turn it over to you—you heard what Hollus said about it blowing up. I think Hollus was quite clear about how things are going to be—and you gentlemen do not have a role. And so," I looked at the white guy, the one with the French accent, "I bid you *adieu*."

ROBERT J. SAWYER

3

I t had started eight months ago with a cough.

I'd ignored it. Like an idiot, I'd ignored the evidence right in front of me.

I'm a scientist. I should have known better.

But I'd told myself it was just a result of my dusty work environment. We use dental drills to carve rock away from fossils. Of course, we wear masks when doing such work—most of the time (we remember to put on safety goggles, too—most of the time). Still, despite the ventilation system, there's a lot of fine rock dust in our air; you can see the layers it leaves on piles of books and papers, on unused equipment.

Besides, I first noticed it in the sweltering heat of last August; an inversion layer had been hanging over Toronto, and air-quality advisories were being issued. I thought maybe the cough would stop when we got away from the city, got up to our cottage. And so it seemed to.

But when we came south again, the cough returned. Still, I'd hardly noticed it.

Until the blood came up.

Just a bit.

When I blew my nose, there had been blood in my mucus often enough in winter. Dry air will do that. But this was the sultry Toronto summer. And what I was producing wasn't mucus; it was phlegm, kicked up from deep in my chest, maneuvered off the roof of my mouth with the tip of my tongue, and transferred to a tissue to get rid of it.

Phlegm, flecked with blood.

I noted it, but nothing similar happened for a couple of weeks. And so I didn't give it any further thought.

Until it happened again, late in September.

If I'd been paying better attention, I would have noticed my cough getting more persistent. I'm the head of the paleobiology department; I suppose I should have done something, should have complained to the guys in Facilities about the dry air, about the mineral dust floating around.

The second time there was a lot of blood in my phlegm.

And there was more the next day.

And the day after.

And so, finally, I had made an appointment to see Dr. Noguchi.

The Hollus simulacrum had left about 4:00 in the afternoon; I normally worked until 5:00, and so I walked—*staggered* might be a better term—back to my office and sat, stunned, for a few minutes. My phone kept ringing, so I turned it off; it seemed that every media outlet in the world wanted to talk to me, the man who had been alone with the alien. I directed Dana, the departmental assistant, to transfer all calls to Dr. Dorati's office. Christine would be in her element dealing with the press. Then I turned to my computer and began to type up notes. I realized that there should be a record, a chronicle, of everything I saw and everything I learned. I typed furiously for perhaps an hour, then left the ROM via the staff entrance.

A large crowd had gathered outside—but, thankfully, they were all up by the main entrance, half a block away. I looked briefly for any sign of the spaceship landing that had occurred

ROBERT J. SAWYER

earlier that day; there was nothing. I then hurried down the concrete steps into Museum subway station, with its sickly yellow-beige wall tiles.

During rush hour, most people head north to the suburbs. As usual, I rode the train south, right down University Avenue, around the loop at Union station, and then up the Yonge line all the way to North York Centre; it was hardly the direct route, but it ensured I'd get to sit all the way. Of course, my condition was obvious, so people often offered me seats. But unlike Blanche DuBois, I preferred not to have to depend on the kindness of strangers. As usual, I was carrying a Zip disk with work-related files in my briefcase, and I had some article preprints I wanted to read. But I found myself unable to concentrate.

An alien had come to Toronto. An actual alien.

It was incredible.

I thought about it throughout the forty-five-minute subway ride. And, as I looked at the myriad faces around me—all colors, all races, all ages, the mosaic that is Toronto—I thought about the impact today's events would have on human history. I wondered if it was Raghubir or I who would end up being mentioned in the encyclopedia articles; the alien had come to see me—or at least someone in my position—but his actual first conversation (I had taken a break to watch the security-camera video) was with Raghubir Singh.

The subway disgorged many passengers at Union, and more at Bloor. By the time it was pulling into North York Centre— penultimate stop on the line—there were seats for all who wanted them, although, as always, some riders, having endured most of the journey standing, now disdained the empty chairs as if those of us who had scored a place to park our behinds were a weaker breed.

I exited the subway. The walls here were tiled in white, much easier on the stomach than Museum station. North York had been a township when I was born, later a borough, then a city in its own right, and, at last, in another fiat of the Harris government, it had been subsumed with all the other satellite burbs into the expanded megacity of Toronto. I walked the four blocks—two west, two north—from North York Centre to our house on Ellerslie. Crocuses were poking up, and already the days were getting noticeably longer.

As usual, Susan, who was an accountant with a firm at Sheppard and Leslie, had gotten home first; she'd picked up Ricky from his after-school daycare and had started cooking dinner.

Susan's maiden name had been Kowalski; her parents had come to Toronto from Poland shortly after World War II, via a displaced-persons camp. She had brown eyes, high cheekbones, a smallish nose, and an endearing little gap between her two front teeth. Her hair had been dark brown when we'd met, and she kept it that way thanks to Miss Clairol. In the sixties, we'd both loved the Mamas and the Papas, Simon & Garfunkel, and Peter, Paul and Mary; today, we both listened to New Country, including Deana Carter, Martina McBride, and Shania Twain; Shania's latest was coming from the stereo as I came in the door.

I think more than anything, I enjoyed that: coming home to the stereo playing softly, to the smell of dinner cooking, to Ricky bounding up the stairs from the basement, to Susan coming down from the kitchen to give me a kiss—which is precisely what she did just now. "Hi, hon," she said. "How was your day?"

She didn't know. She hadn't heard. I knew that Persaud, her boss, had a rule against people playing radios at work, and Susan listened to books-on-tape in her car. I checked my watch; ten to six—it hadn't even been two hours since Hollus's departure. "Fine," I said, but I guess I wasn't quite suppressing my grin.

"What are you smiling at?" she asked.

I let the grin flourish. "You'll see."

Ricky arrived just then. I reached down, tousled his hair. It was blond, not unlike mine had been when I'd been his age; a nice coincidence, that. Mine had turned brown by the time I was a teenager, and gray by the time I was fifty, but I'd managed to keep almost all of it until a few months ago.

Susan and I had waited to have a child—too long, it turned out. We'd adopted Ricky when he was just a month old, young enough that we got to give him his name: Richard Blaine Jericho. Those who didn't know sometimes said Ricky had Susan's eyes and my nose. He was a typical six-year-old—a bundle of skinned knees, scrawny limbs, and stringy hair. And he was a bright kid, thank God. I'm no athlete, and neither is Susan; we both make our livings with our brains. I'm not sure how I would have related to him if he hadn't been smart. Ricky was good natured and took well to new people. But for the last week or two there had been a bully beating him up, it seemed, on his way to school. He couldn't understand why it was happening to him.

I could relate to that.

"Dinner's almost ready," said Susan.

I headed to the upstairs bathroom and washed up. There was a mirror above the sink, of course; I made an effort not to look in it. I'd left the bathroom door open, and Ricky came in after me. I helped him wash his hands, inspecting them when he was done, and then my son and I went down to the dining room.

I've always had a tendency to put on weight, but for years I've managed to control it by eating properly. But I'd recently been given a booklet. It said:

> If you can't each much food, it's important
> that what you *do* eat is nutritious. It should
> also contain as many calories as possible. You
> can increase your calorie intake by adding
> butter or margarine to your food; mixing
> canned cream soups with milk or half-and-
> half cream; drinking eggnogs and milkshakes;
> adding cream sauce or melted cheese to

vegetables; and snacking on nuts, seeds,
peanut butter, and crackers.

I used to love all those things, but for decades I'd avoided them. Now, I was supposed to eat them—but I didn't find them the least bit appealing.

Susan had grilled some chicken legs coated with Rice Krispies; she'd also prepared green beans and mashed potatoes, made with real cream, and for me, a small saucepan full of melted Cheez Whiz to pour over the potatoes. And she had made chocolate milkshakes, a necessity for me and a nice treat for Ricky. It was unfair, I knew, for her to have to do all the cooking. We used to take turns, but I couldn't face it anymore, couldn't face the smell.

I checked my watch again; it was just coming up to six. We had a family rule: although the living-room TV was easily visible from the dining room, it was always off during meals. But tonight I made an exception: I got up from my place at the table, put on the *CityPulse News at Six,* and let my wife and son watch, mouths agape, as the home videos of the alien ship landing and the footage the videographer had shot of me and Hollus played.

"My God," Susan kept saying, her eyes wide. "My God."

"That is *so* cool," said Ricky, looking at the wild, hand-held shots the videographer had taken in the Rotunda.

I smiled at my son. He was right, of course. This was way cool, as cool as it gets.

ROBERT J. SAWYER

E arth's various leaders were not pleased, but the aliens seemed to have no interest in visiting the United Nations, the White House, the European parliament, the Kremlin, India's parliament, the Knesset, or the Vatican—all of which had immediately extended invitations. Still, by early the next day, there were eight other extraterrestrials—or their holographic avatars—on Earth, all of them Forhilnors.

One was visiting a psychiatric hospital in West Virginia; he was apparently fascinated by unusual human behavior, especially severe schizophrenia. (Apparently, the alien had first appeared at a similar institution in Louisville, Kentucky, but had been dissatisfied with the level of cooperation he was receiving, and so had done precisely what Hollus had threatened to do at the ROM— he left and went to a more accommodating place.)

Another alien was in Burundi, living with a group of mountain gorillas, who seemed to have accepted him quite readily.

A third had attached himself to a public defender in San Francisco and was seen sitting in on arraignments.

A fourth was in China, apparently spending time with a rice farmer in a remote village.

A fifth was in Egypt, joining an archeological dig near Abu Simbel.

A sixth was in northern Pakistan, examining flowers and trees.

Another was seen variously walking around the sites of the old death camps in Germany, scuttling through Tiananmen Square, and visiting the ruins in Kosovo.

And, thankfully, one more had made himself available in Brussels to speak with media from all over the world. He seemed to be fluent in English, French, Japanese, Chinese (both Mandarin and Cantonese), Hindi, German, Spanish, Dutch, Italian, Hebrew, and more (and managed to mimic British, Scottish, Brooklyn, Texan, Jamaican, and other accents, depending on whom he was speaking to).

Even so, no end of people wanted to speak with me. Susan and I had an unlisted phone number. We'd gotten it a few years ago after some fanatics started harassing us following a public debate I'd had with Duane Gish of the Institute for Creation Research. Still, we had to unplug our phone; it had started ringing as soon as the item appeared on the news. But to my surprise and delight I managed to get a good night's sleep.

The next day, there was a huge crowd outside the museum when I emerged from the subway around 9:15 A.M.; the museum wouldn't be open to the public for another forty-five minutes, but these people didn't want to see the exhibits. They were carrying signs that read "Welcome to Earth!" and "Take Us With You!" and "Alien Power!"

One of the throng spotted me, shouted and pointed, and people started moving my way. Fortunately, it was only a short distance from the staircase leading up from the subway to the ROM's staff entrance, and I made it inside before I could be accosted.

I hurried up to my office and placed the golf-ball-sized holoform projector on the center of my desk. About five minutes later, it bleeped twice, and Hollus—or the holographic projection of him, at any rate—appeared in front of me. He had a different cloth wrapped around his torso today: this one was a salmon color with black hexagons on it, and it was fastened not with a jeweled disk but a silver pin.

"I'm glad to see you again," I said. I'd been afraid, despite what he'd said yesterday, that he'd never come back.

"If" "it" "is" "per" "mis" "able," said Hollus, "I" "will" "appear" "daily" "about" "this" "time."

"That would be absolutely terrific," I said.

"Establishing that the dates for the five mass extinctions coincided on all three inhabited worlds is only the beginning of my work, of course," said Hollus.

I thought about that, then nodded. Even if one accepted Hollus's God hypothesis, all that having simultaneous disasters on multiple worlds proved was that his God had thrown a series of hissy fits.

The Forhilnor continued. "I want to study the minute details of the evolutionary developments related to the mass extinctions. It appears superficially that each extinction was designed to nudge the remaining lifeforms in specific directions, but I wish to confirm that."

"Well, then, we should start by examining fossils from just before and just after each of the extinction events," I said.

"Precisely," said Hollus, his eyestalks weaving eagerly.

"Come with me," I said.

"You have to take the projector with you, if I am to follow," said Hollus.

I nodded, still getting used to this idea of telepresence, and picked up the small object.

"It will work fine if you place it in a pocket," he said.

I did so, and then led him down to the paleobiology department's giant collections room, in the basement of the Curatorial Centre; we didn't have to go out into any of the public areas of the museum to get there.

The collections room was full of metal cabinets and open shelving holding prepared fossils as well as countless plaster field jackets, some still unopened half a century after they'd been brought to the museum. I started by pulling out a drawer containing skulls of Ordovician jawless fishes. Hollus looked them over, handling them gently. The force fields projected by the holoform unit seemed to define a solidness that precisely matched the alien's apparent physical form. We bumped into each other a few times as we negotiated our way down the narrow aisles in the collections room, and my hands touched his several times as I passed him fossils. I felt a static tingling whenever his projected form contacted my skin, the only indication that he wasn't really there.

As he examined the strange, solid skulls, I happened to comment that they looked rather alien. Hollus seemed surprised by the remark. "I" "am" "cur" "i" "ous," he said, "about" "your" "concepts" "of" "alien" "life."

"I thought you knew all about that," I replied, smiling. "Anal probes and so on."

"We have been watching your TV broadcasts for about a year now. But I suspect you have more interesting material than what I have seen."

"What have you seen?"

"A show about an academic and his family who are extraterrestrials."

It took me a moment to recognize it. "Ah," I said. "That's *3rd Rock from the Sun*. It's a comedy."

"That is a matter of opinion," said Hollus. "I have also seen the program about the two federal agents who hunt aliens."

"*The X-Files*," I said.

He clicked his eyes together in agreement. "I found it frustrating. They kept talking about aliens, but you almost never saw any. More instructive was a graphic-arts production about juvenile humans."

"I need another clue," I said.

"One of them is named Cartman," said Hollus.

I laughed. "*South Park*. I'm surprised you didn't pack up and

ROBERT J. SAWYER

go home after that. But, sure, I can show you some better samples." I looked around the collections room. Off at the other end, going through our banks of Pliocene microfossils, I could see a grad student. "Abdus!" I called.

The young man looked up, startled. I waved him over.

"Yes, Tom?" he said once he'd reached us, although his eyes were on Hollus, not me.

"Abdus, can you nip out to Blockbuster and get some videos for me?" Grad students were useful for all sorts of things. "Keep the receipt, and Dana will reimburse you."

The request was strange enough to get Abdus to stop looking at the alien. "Um, sure," he said. "Sure thing."

I told him what I wanted, and he scurried off.

Hollus and I continued to look at the Ordovician specimens until noon, then we headed back up to my office. I imagined that intelligence probably required a high metabolism everywhere in the universe. Still, I thought the Forhilnor might be irritated that I had to take a lunch break (and even more irritated that after stopping our work, I ate almost nothing). But he ate when I did—although, of course, he was really dining aboard his mothership, in orbit over Ecuador. It looked strange: his avatar, which apparently duplicated whatever movements his real body was making, went through the motions of transferring food into his eating slit—a horizontal groove in the top of his torso revealed through a gap in the cloth wound around it. But the food itself was invisible, making it look like Hollus was some extraterrestrial Marcel Marceau, miming the process of eating.

I, on the other hand, needed real food. Susan had packed me a can of strawberry-banana Boost and two leftover drumsticks from yesterday's dinner. I downed the thick beverage and made it halfway through one of the legs. I wished I'd had something different to eat; it felt a little too primal to be using my teeth to tear meat off bones in front of the alien, although, for all I knew, Hollus was stuffing live hamsters into his gullet.

While we ate, Hollus and I watched the videos Abdus had fetched; I'd had the education department deliver a combo VCR-TV unit to my office.

First up was "Arena," an episode of the original *Star Trek* series; I immediately froze the image on a picture of Mr. Spock. "See him?" I said. "He's an alien—a Vulcan."

"He" "looks" "like" "a" "human" "being," said Hollus; he could eat and talk at the same time.

"Notice the ears."

Hollus's eyestalks stopped weaving in and out. "And *that* makes him an alien?"

"Well," I said, "of course it's a human actor playing the part—a guy named Leonard Nimoy. But, yeah, the ears are supposed to suggest alienness; this show was done on a low budget." I paused. "Actually, Spock there is only half-Vulcan; the other half is human."

"How is that possible?"

"His mother was a human; his father was a Vulcan."

"That does not make sense biologically," said Hollus. "It would seem more likely that you could crossbreed a strawberry and a human; at least they evolved on the same planet."

I smiled. "Believe me, I know that. But wait, there's another alien in this episode." I fast-forwarded for a time, then hit the play button again.

"That's a Gorn," I said, pointing to the tailless green reptile with compound eyes wearing a gold tunic. "He's the captain of another starship. Pretty neat, huh? I always loved that one—reminded me of a dinosaur."

"Indeed," said Hollus. "Which means, again, that it is far too terrestrial in appearance."

"Well, it's an actor inside a rubber suit," I said.

Hollus's eyes regarded me as if I were again being Master of the Bleeding Obvious.

We watched the Gorn stagger around for a bit, then I ejected the tape and put in "Journey to Babel." I didn't fast-forward,

52

though; I just let the teaser unfold. "See them?" I said. "Those are Spock's parents. Sarek is a full-blooded Vulcan, and Amanda, the woman there, is a full-blooded human."

"Astonishing," said Hollus. "And humans believe such cross-breeding is possible?"

I shrugged a little. "Well, it's science fiction," I said. "It's entertainment." I fast-forwarded to the diplomatic reception. A stocky snout-nosed alien accosted Sarek: "No, *you*," he snarled. "How do *you* vote, Sarek of Vulcan?"

"That's a Tellarite," I said. Then, remembering: "His name is Gav."

"He looks like one of your pigs," said Hollus. "Yet again, too terrestrial."

I fast-forwarded some more. "That's an Andorian," I said. The screen showed a blue-skinned, white-haired male humanoid, with two thick, segmented antennae emerging from the top of his head.

"What is his name?" asked Hollus.

It was Shras, but for some reason I was embarrassed that I knew that. "I don't remember," I said, then I put in another tape: the special-edition version of *Star Wars,* letterboxed. I fast-forwarded to the cantina sequence. Hollus liked Greedo—Jabba's insectlike henchman who confronted Han Solo—and he liked Hammerhead and a few of the others, but he still felt that humanity had missed the boat on coming up with realistic portrayals of extraterrestrial life. I certainly didn't disagree.

"Still," said Hollus, "your filmmakers did get one thing right."

"What's that?" I asked.

"The diplomatic reception; the scene in the bar. All the aliens shown seem to have about the same level of technology."

I furrowed my brow. "I always thought that was one of the *least* believable things. I mean, the universe is something like twelve billion years old—"

"Actually, it is 13.93422 billion," said Hollus, "measured in Earth years, of course."

53

"Well, fine. The universe is 13.9 billion years old, and Earth is only 4.5 billion years old. There must be planets much, much older than ours, and much, much younger. I'd expect some intelligent races to be millions if not billions of years more advanced than we are, and some to be at least somewhat more primitive."

"A race even a few decades less advanced than you are would not have radio or spaceflight and therefore would be undetectable," said Hollus.

"True. But I'd still expect lots of races to be much more advanced than we are—like, well, like yourself, for instance."

Hollus's eyes looked at each other—an expression of surprise? "We Forhilnors are not greatly advanced beyond your race—perhaps a century at most; certainly no more than that. I expect that within a few decades your physicists will make the breakthrough that will allow you to use fusion to economically accelerate ships to within a tiny fraction of the speed of light."

"Really? Wow. But—but how old is Beta Hydri?" It would be quite a coincidence if it were the same age as Earth's sun.

"About 2.6 billion Earth years."

"A little over half as old as Sol."

"Sol?" said Hollus's left mouth.

"That's what we call our sun, when we want to distinguish it from other stars," I said. "But if Beta Hydri is that young, I'm surprised that you have any vertebrates on your world, let alone any intelligent life."

Hollus considered this. "When did life first emerge on Earth?"

"We certainly had life by 3.8 billion years ago—there are fossils that old—and it may have been here as far back as four billion years ago."

The alien sounded incredulous. "And the first animals with spinal columns appeared just half a billion years ago, no? So it took perhaps as much as 3.5 billion years to go from the origin of life to the first vertebrates?" He bobbed his torso. "Life originated on my world when it was 350 million years old, and vertebrates appeared just 1.8 billion years later."

"I wonder why it took so much longer here?"

"As I told you," said Hollus, "the development of life on both our worlds was manipulated by God. Perhaps his or her goal was to have multiple sapient lifeforms emerge simultaneously."

"Ah," I said dubiously.

"But, even were that not true," said Hollus, "there is another reason for all space-faring races to be comparably advanced."

Something was tickling at the back of my mind, something I'd once seen Carl Sagan explain on TV: the Drake equation. It had several terms, including the rate of star formation, the fraction of stars that might have planets, and so on. By multiplying all the terms together, you were supposed to be able to guesstimate the number of intelligent civilizations that might currently exist in the Milky Way. I can't remember all the terms, but I do remember the final one—because it chilled me when Sagan discussed it.

The final term was the lifetime of a technological civilization: the number of years between the development of radio broadcasting and the extinction of the race. Humans had first started broadcasting in earnest in the 1920s; if the Cold War had turned hot, our tenure as a technological species might have been as little as thirty years.

"You mean the lifetime of a civilization?" I said. "The span before it blows itself up?"

"That is one possibility, I suppose," said Hollus. "Certainly, my own race had a difficult time learning to use nuclear power wisely." The alien paused. "I am given to understand that many humans suffer from mental problems."

I was startled by the apparent change of topic. "Umm, yes. I suppose that's true."

"As do many Forhilnors," said Hollus. "It is another concern: as technology advances, the ability to destroy the entire race becomes more accessible. Eventually, it is in the hands not just of governments but also individuals—some of whom are unbalanced."

That was a staggering thought. A new term in the Drake equation: f-sub-L, the fraction of members of your race who are loony.

The Hollus simulacrum moved a little closer to me. "But that is not the principal issue. I told you that my race, the Forhilnors, had made contact with one other technological race, the Wreeds, prior to meeting you; we actually first met them about sixty years ago—by going to Delta Pavonis and discovering them."

I nodded.

"And I told you that my starship, the *Merelcas,* visited six other star systems, besides the Wreed home one, before arriving here. But what I did not tell you was that each of those six had, at one time, been home to an intelligent race of its own: the star you call Epsilon Indi, the star you call Tau Ceti, the star you call Mu Cassiopeae A, the star you call Eta Cassiopeae A, the star you call Sigma Draconis, and the star you call Groombridge 1618 all once had native intelligent life."

"But they don't anymore?"

"Correct."

"What did you find?" I asked. "Bombed-out ruins?" My mind filled with visions of bizarre alien architecture, twisted and melted and charred by nuclear blasts.

"Never."

"Then what?"

Hollus spread his two arms and bobbed his torso. "Abandoned cities, some immensely old—some so old, they had been deeply buried."

"Abandoned?" I said. "You mean the inhabitants had gone somewhere else?"

The Forhilnor's eyes touched in affirmation.

"Where?"

"That question still vexes."

"Do you know anything else about the other races?"

"A great deal. They left many artifacts and records behind, and in some cases interred or fossilized bodies."

"And?"

"And, at their ends, all were comparably advanced; none had built machines we could not understand. True, the variety of body plans was fascinating, although they all were—what is that phrase humans use?—'life as we know it.' They were all carbon-based DNA lifeforms."

"Really? Are you and the Wreeds also DNA-based?"

"Yes."

"Fascinating."

"Perhaps not," said Hollus. "We believe that DNA is the *only* molecule capable of driving life; no other substance has its properties of self-replication, information storage, and compactibility. DNA's ability to compress into a very small space makes it possible for it to exist in the nucleuses of microscopic cells, even though when stretched out, each DNA molecule is more than a meter long."

I nodded. "In the evolution course I used to teach, we considered whether anything other than DNA could do the job; we never came up with an alternative that was even remotely suitable. Did all the alien DNA use the same four bases: adenine and thymine, guanine and cytosine?"

"Are those these four?" said Hollus. Suddenly, his holoform projector made four chemical formulas float in the air between us in glowing green:

$$C_5H_5N_5$$

$$C_5H_6N_2O_2$$

$$C_5H_5N_5O$$

$$C_4H_5N_3O$$

I peered at them; it'd been a while since I'd done any biochemistry. "Umm, yes. Yes, those are they."

"Then, yes," said Hollus. "Everywhere we have found DNA, it uses those four bases."

"But we've shown in the lab that other bases could be used; we've even made artificial DNA that uses six bases, not four."

"Doubtless extraordinary intervention was required to accomplish that," said Hollus.

"I don't know; I guess." I thought about everything. "Six other worlds," I said, trying to picture them in my mind.

Alien planets.

Dead planets.

"Six other worlds," I said again. "All deserted."

"Correct."

I sought the right word. "That's . . . frightening."

Hollus did not dispute this. "In orbit around Sigma Draconis II," he said, "we found what seemed to be a fleet of starships."

"Do you suppose invaders had wiped out the indigenous life?"

"No," said Hollus. "The starships were clearly built by the same race that had constructed the abandoned cities on the planet below."

"They built starships?"

"Yes."

"And they all left the planet?"

"Apparently."

"But *without* using the starships, which were left behind?"

"Exactly."

"That's . . . mysterious."

"It certainly is."

"What about the fossil records on these planets? Do they have mass extinctions that coincide with ours?"

Hollus's eyestalks moved. "That is difficult to say; if one could easily read fossil records without decades or centuries of searching, I never would have had to reveal myself to you. But as far as we have been able to tell, no, none of the abandoned

ROBERT J. SAWYER

worlds had mass extinctions at 440, 365, 225, 210, and 65 million years ago."

"Were any of those civilizations contemporaneous?"

Hollus's command of English was remarkable, but occasionally it did fail him. "Pardon?"

"Did any of them live at the same time as any of the others?"

"No. The oldest seems to have ended three billion years ago; the most recent, on the third planet of Groombridge 1618, about five thousand years ago. But . . ."

"Yes?"

"But, as I said, all the races seemed to be comparably advanced. Architectural styles varied widely, of course. But, to give you an example, our engineers dismantled one of the orbiting starships we found at Sigma Draconis II; it used different solutions to several problems from the ones we employ, but it was not fundamentally much better—perhaps a few decades beyond what we had developed. That is the way it was for all the races that had abandoned their worlds: they were all only slightly more advanced than the Wreeds or the Forhilnors—or *Homo sapiens,* for that matter."

"And you think this happens to all races? They reach a point where they just leave their home planets?"

"Exactly," said Hollus. "Or else something—perhaps God himself—comes along and takes them away."

5

H ollus's presence was being touted by the ROM's membership department ("Support the museum that attracts visitors from all over the world—and beyond!"), and attendance was up substantially for the first week following the Forhilnor's arrival. But when it became apparent that his shuttle was unlikely to land again and that an alien wasn't going to stride along the sidewalk, up the outside stairs, and through the lobby, the crowds tapered to more normal levels.

I never saw the CSIS agents again. Prime Minister Chrétien did indeed come by the ROM to meet Hollus; Christine Dorati, of course, turned that into quite the photo-op. And several journalists asked Chrétien, for the record, to give his assurance that the alien would be allowed to continue his work unmolested—which was what the *Maclean's* opinion poll said the Canadian people wanted. He did indeed give that assurance, although I suspected CSIS operatives were always still around, lurking just out of view.

On his fourth day in Toronto, Hollus and I were back in the collections room in the basement of the Curatorial Centre. I'd pulled open a metal drawer and was showing him a shale slab containing a beautifully preserved eurypterid. We moved the specimen to a work table, and Hollus used his right eyestalk to look through one of our large magnifiers on an articulated metal arm, with a fluorescent tube encircling the lens. I wondered briefly about the physics of that: the magnified image was being looked at by a simulated eye, and the information was somehow transferred to the real Hollus, in orbit over Ecuador.

I know, I know—I probably should have let it alone. But, dammitall, it had been keeping me up nights ever since Hollus had mentioned it. "How do you know," I said to him at last, "that the universe had a creator?"

Hollus's eyestalks curved to look at me. "The universe was clearly designed; if it has a design, it must therefore have a designer."

I moved my forehead muscles in a way that used to lift my eyebrows. "It looks random to me," I said. "I mean, it's not as if the stars are arranged in geometric patterns."

"There is great beauty in randomness," said Hollus. "But I speak about a much more basic design. This universe has had its fundamental parameters fine-tuned to an almost infinite degree so that it would support life."

I was pretty sure I knew where he was going with this, but I said, "In what way?" anyway; I thought maybe he knew something I didn't—and indeed, to my shock, that was precisely the case.

"Your science knows of four fundamental forces; there are actually five, but you have not yet discovered the fifth. The four forces you know about are gravitation, electromagnetism, the weak nuclear force, and the strong nuclear force; the fifth force is a repulsive one that operates over extremely long distances. The strengths of these forces have wildly varying values, and yet if the values were even slightly different from their current ones, the universe as we know it would not exist, and life could never have formed. Take gravity as an example: were it only somewhat stronger, the universe would have long since collapsed. If it were somewhat weaker, stars and planets never could have coalesced."

"'Somewhat,'" I echoed.

ROBERT J. SAWYER

"For those two scenarios, yes; I am talking about a few orders of magnitude. You wish a better example? Very well. Stars, of course, must strike a balance between the gravitational force of their own mass, which tries to make them collapse, and the electromagnetic force of their own outpouring of light and heat. There is only a narrow range of values in which these forces are in sufficient equilibrium to allow a star to exist. At one extreme blue giants are produced, and at the other red dwarfs form—neither of which are conducive to the origin of life. Fortunately, almost all stars fall in between those two types—specifically because of an apparent numerical coincidence in the values of the fundamental constants in nature. If, for instance, the strength of gravity were different by one part in—give me a second; I must convert to your decimal system—by one part in 10^{40}, this numerical coincidence would be disrupted, and *every* star in the universe would be either a blue giant or a red dwarf; no yellow suns would exist to shine down on Earthlike worlds."

"Really? Just one part in ten to the fortieth?"

"Yes. Likewise the value of the strong nuclear force, which holds the nucleuses of atoms together even though the positively charged protons try to repel each other: if that force were only slightly weaker than it actually is, atoms would never form—the repulsion of protons would keep them from doing so. And if it were only slightly stronger than it actually is, the only atom that could exist would be hydrogen. Either way, we would have a universe devoid of stars and life and planets."

"So you're saying someone *chose* these values?"

"Exactly."

"How do you know that these aren't the only values those constants could possibly have?" I said. "Maybe they are simply that way because they couldn't possibly be anything else."

The alien's round torso bobbed. "An interesting conjecture. But our physicists have proved that other values are indeed theoretically possible. And the odds of the current values arising by chance are one in the number six followed by so many zeros

CALCULATING GOD

that if you could engrave a zero on each neutron and proton in the entire universe, you could still not write out the number in full."

I nodded; I'd heard variations on all this before. It was time to play my trump card. "Maybe all the possible values for those constants do exist," I said, "but in *different* universes. Maybe there are a limitless number of parallel universes, all of which are devoid of life because their physical parameters don't allow it. If that's the case, there's nothing remarkable about us being in this universe, given that it's the only one out of all the possible universes that we *could* be in."

"Ah," said Hollus. "I see . . ."

I folded my arms smugly.

"I see," continued the alien, "the source of your misunderstanding. In the past, the scientists of my world were mostly atheists or agnostics. We have long known of the apparently finely tuned forces that govern our universe; I form the impression that you were already somewhat familiar with them yourself. And that same argument—that there are perhaps an infinite number of universes, manifesting continuums of alternative values for the fundamental constants—was what allowed previous generations of Forhilnor scientists to dismiss the notion of a creator. As you say, if all the possible values exist somewhere, there is nothing noteworthy about the existence of one universe governed by the particular set of values that happens to make life possible.

"But it turns out that there are *no* long-term parallel universes existing simultaneously with this one; there cannot be. The physicists of my world have attained what those of yours presumably currently seek: a grand unified theory, a theory of everything. I could find little on human beliefs about cosmology in your television and radio, but if you hold the belief you just stated, I will guess that your cosmologists are currently at the stage where they consider a hot, inflationary big-bang model to

ROBERT J. SAWYER

be the most likely scenario for the origin of the universe. Is that correct?"

"Yes," I said.

Hollus bobbed. "Forhilnor physicists cherished the same belief—many reputations depended on it—until the fifth interaction, the fifth fundamental force, was discovered; its discovery was related to the energy-production breakthrough that allows us to accelerate ships to within a tiny fraction of lightspeed, despite the relativistic fact that their masses increase enormously as we approach that speed."

Hollus shifted his weight on his six feet, then continued. "The hot, inflationary big-bang model requires a flat universe—one that is neither open nor closed, one that will essentially last an infinite amount of time; it does, however, allow for parallel universes. But accommodating the fifth force required modification of that theory in order to preserve symmetry; from that modification came the coherent, grand unified theory, a quantum theory that embraces all forces including gravity. That grand unified theory has three important provisions.

"First, that this universe is not flat, but rather that it is *closed:* it did indeed start with a big bang and will expand for billions of years more—but it will eventually collapse back down to a singularity in a big crunch.

"Second, that this current cycle of creation follows no more than *eight* previous big-bang/big-crunch oscillations—we are not one in an infinitely long string of universes but, rather, are one of the very few that have ever existed."

"Really?" I said. I was used to cosmology presenting me with infinities or with values that were precisely one. Eight seemed an unusual number, and I said so.

Hollus flexed his legs at their upper joints. "You introduced me to that man named Chen—your staff astronomer. Talk to him; he will likely tell you that even your hot, inflationary big-bang model, with its requirement for a flat universe, allowed for a very limited number of prior oscillations, if any had occurred at all. I suspect he will consider it quite reasonable to learn that this current iteration of reality is one of only a tiny number of universes that have ever existed."

Hollus paused, then continued. "And the third provision of the grand unified theory is this: *no* parallel universes exist simultaneously with ours or any of the previous or subsequent ones, save virtually identical universes with exactly the same physical constants that split briefly from the current one then almost immediately reintegrate with it, thus accounting for certain quantum phenomenons.

"The math to prove all the foregoing is admittedly abstruse, although, ironically, the Wreeds intuitively came to an identical model. But the theory of everything made numerous predictions that have subsequently been confirmed experimentally; it has withstood *every* test it has been put to. And when we found that we could not retreat into the notion that this universe is one of vast number, the argument for intelligent design became central to Forhilnor thought. Since this is one of a maximum of just nine universes that have ever existed, for it to have these highly improbable design parameters implies they were indeed chosen by an intelligence."

"Even if maybe, perhaps, the four—excuse me, the *five*— fundamental forces have seemingly wildly improbable values," I said, "that still is only five separate coincidences, and, although granted it is hugely unlikely, five coincidences could indeed occur by random chance in just nine iterations."

Hollus bobbed. "You have intriguing tenacity," he said. "But it is not just the five forces that have seemingly designed values; many other aspects of the way the universe works appear likewise to have been minutely adjusted."

"For instance?"

"You and I are made up of heavy elements: carbon, oxygen, nitrogen, potassium, iron, and so on. Practically the only elements that existed when the universe was born were hydrogen and helium, in a roughly three-to-one ratio. But in the nuclear furnaces of stars, hydrogen is fused into heavier elements, producing carbon, oxygen, and so on up the periodic table. All of the heavy elements that make up our bodies were forged in the cores of long-dead stars."

"I know. 'We are all star-stuff,' as Carl Sagan used to say."

"Precisely. Indeed, scientists from your world and mine refer to us as carbon-based lifeforms. But the fact that carbon is produced by stars depends critically on the resonance states of the carbon nucleus. To produce carbon, two helium nucleuses must stick together until they are struck by a third such nucleus—three helium nucleuses provide six neutrons and six protons, the recipe for carbon. But if the resonance level of carbon were only four percent lower, such intermediate pair-bonding could not occur, and no carbon would be produced, making organic chemistry impossible." He paused. "But just producing carbon, and other heavy elements, is not enough, of course. Those heavy elements are here on Earth because some fraction of stars—what is the word? When a large star explodes?"

"Supernova," I said.

"Yes. Those heavy elements are here because some fraction of stars become supernovas, spewing their fusion products into interstellar space."

"And you're saying that the fact that stars do go supernova is something that also must have been designed by a god?"

"It is not as simplistic as that." A pause. "Do you know what would happen to Earth if a nearby star became a supernova?"

"If it were close enough, I suppose we'd be fried." In the 1970s, Dale Russell had favored a nearby supernova explosion as the cause of the extinctions at the end of the Cretaceous.

"Exactly. If there had been a local supernova anytime in the last few billion years, you would not be here. Indeed, neither of us would be, since our worlds are quite close together."

"So supernovas can't be too common, and—"

"Correct. But neither can they be too rare. It is shockwaves made by supernova explosions that cause planetary systems to start to coalesce from the dust clouds surrounding other stars. In other words, if there had been no supernovas ever anywhere near your sun, the ten planets that orbit it would never have formed."

"Nine," I said.

"Ten," repeated Hollus firmly. "Keep looking." His eyestalks waved. "Do you see the quandry? Some stars must become supernovas in order to make heavy elements available for the formation of life, but if too many do, they would wipe out any life that got started. Yet if not enough do, there would be precious few planetary systems. Just as with the fundamental physical constants and the resonance levels of carbon, the rate of supernova formation again seems precisely chosen, within a very narrow range of possibly acceptable values; any substantial deviation would mean a universe without life or even planets."

I was struggling for footing, for stability. My head ached. "That could just be a coincidence, too," I said.

"It is either coincidence piled on top of coincidence," said Hollus, "or it is deliberate design. And there is more. Take water, for instance. Every lifeform we know of evolved in water, and all of them require it for their biological processes. And although water seems chemically simple—just two hydrogen atoms bound to an oxygen—it is, in fact, an enormously unusual substance. As you know, most compounds contract as they cool and expand as they heat. Water does this, too, until just before it starts to freeze. It then does something remarkable: it begins to expand, even as it grows colder, so that by the time it does freeze, it is actually *less* dense than it was as a liquid. That is why ice floats instead of sinking, of course. We are so used to seeing that, whether it is ice balls in a beverage or a skin of ice on a pond, that we usually give it no thought. But other substances do not do that: frozen carbon dioxide—what you call dry ice—sinks in liquid carbon dioxide; a lead ingot will sink in a vat of molten lead.

ROBERT J. SAWYER

"But water ice floats—and if it did not, life would be impossible. If lakes and oceans froze from the bottom up, instead of the top down, no sea-floor or lake-bottom ecologies would exist outside equatorial zones. Indeed, once they had started freezing, bodies of water would freeze solid and remain solid forever; it is currents moving unfettered beneath surface ice that promotes melting in the spring—that is why glaciers, which have no such currents beneath them, exist for millennia on dry land adjacent to liquid lakes."

I returned the eurypterid fossil to its drawer. "I grant that water is an unusual substance, but—"

Hollus touched his eyes together. "But this strange expanding-before-freezing is hardly the only remarkable thermal property water has. In fact, it has *seven* different thermal parameters, all of which are unique or nearly so in the chemical world, and all of which independently are necessary for the existence of life. The chances of any of them having the aberrant value it does must be multiplied by the chances of the other six likewise being aberrant. The likelihood of water having these unique thermal properties by chance is almost nil."

"*Almost,*" I said, but my voice was starting to sound hollow, even to me.

Hollus ignored me. "Nor does water's unique nature end with its thermal properties. Of all substances, only liquid selenium has a higher surface tension than does water. And it is water's high surface tension that draws it deeply into cracks in rocks, and, of course, as we have noted, water does the incredible and actually expands as it freezes, breaking those rocks apart. If water had lower surface tension, the process by which soil is formed would not occur. More: if water had higher viscosity, circulatory systems could not evolve—your blood plasma and mine are essentially sea water, but there are no biochemical processes that could fuel a heart that had to pump something substantially more viscous for any appreciable time."

The alien paused. "I could go on," he said, "talking about the remarkable, carefully adjusted parameters that make life possible, but the reality is simply this: if any of them—any in this long chain—were different, there would be no life in this universe. We are either the most incredible fluke imaginable— something far, far more unlikely than you winning your provincial lottery every single week for a century—or the universe and its components were designed, purposefully and with great care, to give rise to life."

I felt a jab of pain in my chest; I ignored it. "It's still just indirect evidence for God's existence," I said.

"You know," said Hollus, "you are in the vast minority, even among your own species. According to something I saw on CNN, there are only 220 million atheists on this planet—out of a population of 6 billion people. That is just three percent of the total."

"The truth in factual matters is not a democratic question," I said. "Most people aren't critical thinkers."

Hollus sounded disappointed. "But *you* are a trained, critical thinker, and I have described to you why God must exist—or, at least, must have at one time existed—in mathematical terms that come as close to certainty as anything in science possibly could. And still you deny his existence."

The pain was growing worse. It would subside, of course.

"Yes," I said. "I deny God's existence."

ROBERT J. SAWYER

6

"ello, Thomas," Dr. Noguchi had begun on that fateful day last October, when I'd come in to discuss the results of the tests he'd ordered. He always called me Thomas instead of Tom. We'd known each other long enough that casual names were surely appropriate, but he liked a little bit of formality, a touch of I'm-the-doctor-and-you're-the-patient distance. "Please sit down."

I did so.

He didn't waste time on a preamble. "It's lung cancer, Thomas."

My pulse increased. My jaw dropped.

"I'm sorry," he said.

A million thoughts ran through my head. He must be mistaken; it must be someone else's file; what am I going to tell Susan? My mouth was suddenly dry. "Are you sure?"

"The cultures from your sputum were absolutely diagnostic," he said. "There is no doubt that it is cancer."

"Is it operable?" I said at last.

"We'll have to determine that. If not, we'll try to treat it with radiation or chemotherapy."

My hand went immediately to my head, touching my hair. "Will—will that work?"

Noguchi smiled reassuringly. "It can be very effective."

Which amounted to a "maybe"—and I didn't want to

hear "maybe." I wanted certainty. "What—what about a transplant?"

Noguchi's voice was soft. "Not that many sets of lungs become available each year. Too few donors."

"I could go to the States," I said tentatively. You read about that all the time in the *Toronto Star,* especially since Harris's cutbacks to the health-care system had begun: Canadians going to the States for medical treatment.

"Makes no difference. There's a shortage of lungs everywhere. And, anyway, it might not do any good; we'll have to see if the cancer has spread."

I wanted to ask, "Am I going to die?" But the question seemed too much, too direct.

"Keep a positive attitude," continued Noguchi. "You work at the museum, right?"

"Uh-huh."

"So you've probably got an excellent benefits package. You're covered for prescription drugs?"

I nodded.

"Good. There's some medication that will be useful. It's not cheap, but if you're covered, you'll be okay. But, as I say, we have to see if the cancer has spread. I'm going to refer you to an oncologist down at St. Mike's. She'll look after you."

I nodded, feeling my world crumbling around me.

Hollus and I had returned to my office. "What you're arguing for," I said, "is a special place in the cosmos for humanity and other lifeforms."

The spiderlike alien maneuvered his bulk to one side of the room. "We *do* occupy a special place," he said.

"Well, I don't know how the development of science went on Beta Hydri III, Hollus, but here on Earth it's followed a pattern of repeatedly dethroning us from any special position. My own

ROBERT J. SAWYER

culture thought our world was at the center of the universe, but that turned out to be wrong. We also thought we had been created full-blown by God in his image, but that turned out to be wrong, too. Every time we believed there was something special about us—or our planet or our sun—science showed that we were misguided."

"But lifeforms like us are indeed special," said the Forhilnor. "For instance, we all mass the same order of magnitude. None of the intelligent species, including those that vacated their worlds, had average adult body masses below fifty kilograms or above 500 kilograms. We all are, more or less, two meters along our longest dimension—indeed, civilized life could not exist much below 1.5 meters in size."

I tried again to lift my eyebrows. "Why on Earth would that be true?"

"It is true everywhere, not just on Earth, because the smallest sustainable fire is about fifty centimeters across, and to manipulate a fire you need to be somewhat bigger than it. Without fire, of course, there is no metallurgy, and therefore no sophisticated technology." A pause, a bob. "Do you not see? We all evolved to be the right size to use fire—and *that* size is poised directly in the logarithmic middle of the universe. At its maximum extension, the universe will be some forty orders of magnitude larger than we are, and its smallest constituent is forty orders of magnitude smaller than we are." Hollus regarded me and bobbed up and down. "We *are* indeed at the center of creation, if only you know how to look at it."

When I started working at the ROM, the entire front part of its second floor was given over to paleontology. The north wing, directly above the gift shops and deli, had always housed the vertebrate-paleontology displays—"the Dinosaur Gallery"— and the south wing had originally housed the invertebrate-paleo gallery; indeed, the words "Museum of Paleontology" are still carved in stone along the top of the wall there.

But the invert gallery had been closed ages ago, and in 1999 the space was reopened to the public as "The Discovery Gallery," precisely the kind of edutainment mind-candy Christine Dorati likes: interactive displays for kids, with almost no real learning going on. The subway-poster ads for the new gallery bore the slogan, "Imagine if the Museum were run by an eight-year-old." As John Lennon once said, it's easy if you try.

Our pride and joy in vert paleo is our duckbilled *Parasaurolophus* skeleton, with its glorious, meter-long head crest. Every specimen you've ever seen anywhere in the world is a cast of our mount. Indeed, even the Discovery Gallery contains a cast of our *Parasaurolophus,* lying on the floor, embedded in fake matrix. Kids whack at it all day long with wooden mallets and chisels, mostly resting their bums on the magnificent skull.

Just out front of the vert-paleo gallery there is an indoor balcony, looking down on the Rotunda, which has a subtle starburst design laid into its marble floor. There's another balcony on the opposite side, out front of the Discovery Gallery. Between the two, above the glass-doored main entrance, are three vertical stained-glass windows.

While the museum was closed to the public, I took Hollus through the vert-paleo gallery. We've got the best collection of hadrosaurs in the world. We've also got a dramatic *Albertosaurus,* a formidable *Chasmosaurus,* two dynamic mounts of *Allosaurus,* an excellent *Stegosaurus,* plus a Pleistocene-mammals display, a wall covered with casts of primate and hominid remains, a La Brea tar-pits exhibit, a standard evolution-of-the-horse sequence, and a wonderful late-Cretaceous underwater diorama, with plesiosaurs, mosasaurs, and ammonites.

I also took Hollus over to the hated Discovery Gallery, where a cast of a *T. rex* looms over the hapless, floor-mounted *Parasaurolophus.* Hollus seemed enchanted by all the fossils.

74

In addition, I showed him a lot of paintings of dinosaurs as they might have looked while alive, and I had Abdus go get a copy of *Jurassic Park* on video so Hollus could watch that.

We also spent a lot of time with crusty old Jonesy, going through the invertebrate-paleo collections; Jonesy's got trilobites up the wazoo.

But, I decided, fair is fair. Hollus had said at the outset that he would share information his people had gathered. It was time to start collecting on that. I asked him to tell me about the evolutionary history of lifeforms on his world.

I'd assumed he was going to send down a book, but he did more.

Much more.

Hollus said he needed some room to do it properly, so we waited until the museum closed for the day. The simulacrum wavered briefly in my office, then disappeared. We found it easier for me to just carry the holoform projector from place to place than for the simulacrum to walk with me through the corridors of the museum, since almost everyone—curator, grad student, janitor, patron—found an excuse to stop us and chat with the alien.

I took the staff elevator down to the main floor, to the wide stone staircase that wound around the Nisga'a totem pole to the basement. Directly below the main Rotunda was what we imaginatively referred to as the Lower Rotunda. This large, open space, painted the color of cream-of-tomato soup, served as the lobby for Theatre ROM, which was located beneath the gift shops of the first floor.

I'd had support staff set up five video cameras on tripods, to record what Hollus was going to show me—I knew that he didn't want people looking over his eight shoulders when he was doing his work; but he understood that when he was giving information to us as payment, we had to make a record of it. I placed the holoform projector in the middle of the wide floor and tapped on it to summon the Forhilnor genie. Hollus reappeared, and I heard his language for the first time as he gave further instructions to the projector. It was like a little song, with Hollus harmonizing with himself.

Suddenly the lobby was replaced with an incredible alien vista. Just as with the simulacrum of Hollus, I couldn't tell that this wasn't real; it was as though I'd been teleported across two dozen light-years to Beta Hydri III.

"This is a simulation, of course," said Hollus, "but we believe it to be accurate, although the coloration of the animals is conjecture. This is how my world appeared seventy million of your years ago, just prior to the most recent mass extinction."

My pulse thundered in my ears. I stomped my feet, feeling the reassuring solidness of the Lower Rotunda's floor, the only evidence that I was still in Toronto.

The sky was as cerulean as Earth's sky, and the clouds were cumulonimbus; the physics of a nitrogen-oxygen atmosphere laden with water vapor were apparently universal. The landscape consisted of gently rolling hills, and there was a large pond, limned by sand, located about where the base of the Nisga'a totem pole really is. The sun was the same pale yellow as Sol and appeared about the same size as our sun did to us. I'd looked up Beta Hydri in a reference book: it was 1.6 times as wide as Sol, and 2.7 times as bright, so the Forhilnor homeworld must have orbited it at a greater distance than Earth orbits our sun.

The plants were all green—chlorophyll, another compound Hollus argued showed signs of intelligent design, was the best chemical for its job no matter what world you were on. The things that served the purpose of leaves were perfectly round and supported from beneath by a central stalk. And instead of having bark over whatever the wood-equivalent was, the trunks were encased in a translucent material, similar to the crystal that covered Hollus's eyes.

Hollus was still visible, standing next to me. Few of the animals I saw seemed to be based on the same body plan as he was, although on those that were, the eight limbs were undifferenti-

76

ated: all were used for locomotion; none for manipulation. But most of the lifeforms seemed to have five limbs, not eight—presumably these were the ectothermic pentapeds Hollus had referred to earlier. Some of the pentapeds had enormously long legs, raising their torsos to great heights. Others had limbs so stubby that the torsos dragged along the ground. I watched, astounded, as one pentaped used its five legs to kick an octoped into unconsciousness, then lowered its torso, which apparently had a mouth on its underside, down onto the body.

Nothing flew in the blue sky, although I did see pentapeds I dubbed "parasols" with membranes stretched between each of their five limbs. They parachuted down from trees, seemingly able to control their descent by moving specific limbs closer together or farther apart; their goal appeared to be to land on the backs of pentapeds or octopeds, killing them with poisonous ventral prongs.

None of the animals I saw had eyestalks like Hollus's; I wondered if they had evolved later specifically to allow animals to see if a parasol was waiting to sail down on them. Evolution was, after all, an arms race.

"It's incredible," I said. "A completely alien ecosystem."

I rather imagine that Hollus was amused. "That is much as I felt when I first arrived here. Even though I had seen other ecosystems, there is nothing more amazing than encountering a different set of lifeforms and seeing how they interact." He paused. "As I said, this is my world as it would have been seventy million of your years ago. When the next extinction event happens, the pentapeds will all be wiped out."

I watched a midsized pentaped attacking a slightly smaller octoped. The blood was every bit as red as terrestrial blood, and the cries of the dying creature, although two toned, coming in alternating anguish from separate mouths, sounded just as terrified.

Not wanting to die was another universal constant, it seemed.

7

I remember coming home last October after getting the initial diagnosis from Dr. Noguchi. I'd pulled my hatchback into the driveway. Susan was already home; on those rare days when I took my car to work, whichever of us got home first turned on the porch light so that the other could tell that there was already a vehicle in the garage. I, of course, had taken my car so I could get to Noguchi's office, over at Finch and Bayview, for my appointment.

I got out of the car. Dead leaves were blowing across our driveway, across our lawn. I went up to the front door, letting myself in. I could hear Faith Hill's "The Kiss" coming from the stereo. I was later than usual getting home, and Susan was busy in the kitchen—I could hear the sounds of pots and pans banging together. I walked through the hardwood-tiled entryway and up the half-flight of steps to the living room; I normally stopped in the den to look at my mail—if Susan got home first, she put my mail on top of the low bookcase just inside the den door—but today I had too much on my mind.

Susan came out of the kitchen and gave me a kiss.

But she knew me well—after all these years, how could she not?

"What's wrong?" she said.

"Where's Ricky?" I asked. I'd have to tell him, too, but it would be easier to first tell Susan.

"At the Nguyens'." The Nguyens lived two doors down; their son Bobby was the same age as Ricky. "What's wrong?"

I was holding the banister at the top of the stairs, still shell-shocked from the diagnosis. I motioned for her to join me on the couch. "Sue," I said once I'd sat down, "I went to see Dr. Noguchi today."

She was looking into my eyes, trying to read messages in them. "Why?"

"That cough of mine. I'd gone last week, and he'd done some tests. He asked me to come in today to discuss the results." I moved closer to her on the couch. "I didn't say anything; it had seemed routine—hardly worth mentioning."

She lifted her eyebrows, her face all concern. "And?"

I sought her hand with my own, took it. Her hand was trembling. I drew in breath, filling my damaged lungs. "I have cancer," I said. "Lung cancer."

Her eyes went wide. "Oh my God," she said, shaken. "What . . . what happens now?" she asked.

I shrugged a little. "More tests. The diagnosis was made based on material in my sputum, but they'll want to do biopsies and other tests to determine . . . determine how far it's spread."

"How?" she said, the syllable quavering.

"How did I get it?" I shrugged. "Noguchi figures it was all the mineral dust I've inhaled over the years."

"God," said Susan, trembling. "My God."

Donald Chen had been with the McLaughlin Planetarium for ten years before it was shut down, but unlike his colleagues, he was still employed. He was transferred internally to the ROM's education-programs department, but the ROM had no permanent facilities devoted to astronomy, so Don had little to do—although the CBC did put his smiling face on the tube every year for the Perseids.

80

Everybody on staff referred to Chen as "the walking dead." He already had an awfully pale complexion—occupational hazard for an astronomer—and it seemed only a matter of time before he would be given the boot from the ROM, as well.

Of course, the entire staff of the museum was intrigued by the presence of Hollus, but Donald Chen had a particular interest. Indeed, he was clearly miffed that the alien had come looking for a paleontologist rather than an astronomer. Chen's original office had been over in the planetarium; his new office, here in the Curatorial Centre, was little more than an upright coffin—but he made frequent excuses to come visit me and Hollus, and I was getting used to his knocks on my door.

Hollus opened the door for me this time. He was now quite good with doors and managed to manipulate the knob with one of his feet, instead of having to turn around to use a hand. Sitting on a chair just outside the door was Bruiser—that's the nickname for Al Brewster, a hulking ROM security guard who was assigned full-time now to the paleobiology department, because of Hollus's visits. And standing next to Bruiser was Donald Chen.

"*Ni hao ma?*" said Hollus to Chen; I'd been lucky enough to be part of the Canada-China Dinosaur Project two decades ago, and had learned passably good Mandarin, so I didn't mind.

"*Hao,*" said Chen. He slipped into my office and closed the door behind him, with a nod to Bruiser. Switching to English, he said, "Hey, Slayer."

"Slayer?" said Hollus, looking first at Chen, then at me.

I coughed. "It's, ah, a nickname."

Chen turned to Hollus. "Tom has been leading the fight against the current museum administration. The *Toronto Star* dubbed him the vampire slayer."

"The *potential* vampire slayer," I corrected. "Dorati is still getting her way most of the time." Chen was carrying an ancient book, written in Chinese judging by the characters on the gold cover; although I could speak the language, reading it at any sophisticated level was beyond me. "What's that?" I said.

"Chinese history," said Chen. "I've been bugging Kung." Kung held the Louise Hawley Stone chair in the Near Eastern and Asian civilizations department, another post-Harris-cutback amalgam. "That's why I wanted to see Hollus."

The Forhilnor tipped his eyestalks, ready to help.

Chen set the heavy book on my desk. "In 1998, a group of astronomers at the Max Planck Institute for Extraterrestrial Physics in Germany announced the discovery of a supernova remnant—what's left behind after a giant star explodes."

"I know about supernovas," said Hollus. "In fact, Dr. Jericho and I were talking about them recently."

"Okay, good," said Chen. "Well, the remnant those guys discovered is very close, maybe 650 light-years away, in the constellation of Vela. They call it RX J0852.0-4622."

"Catchy," said Hollus.

Chen had little sense of humor. He continued on. "The supernova that formed the remnant should have been visible in our skies about the year 1320 A.D. Indeed, it should have outshone the full moon and been visible even during the day." He paused, waiting to see if either of us would dispute this. We didn't, and he went on. "But there is no historical record of it whatsoever; no mention of it has ever been found."

Hollus's eyestalks weaved. "You said it is in Vela? That is a southern constellation, both in the skies of your world and mine. But your world has little population in its southern hemisphere."

"True," said Chen. "In fact, the only terrestrial evidence we've found at all for this supernova is a nitrate spike in Antarctic snow that might be associated with it; similar spikes correlate with other supernovae. But Vela *is* visible from the land of my ancestors; you can see it clearly from southern China. I'd thought if anybody had recorded it, it would be the Chinese." He held up the book. "But there's nothing. Of course, 1320 A.D. was in the middle of the Yuan dynasty."

82   "Ah," I said sagely. "The Yuan."

Chen looked at me as though I were a Philistine. "The Yuan was founded by Kubla Khan in Beijing," he said. "Chinese governments were normally generous in their support of astronomical research, but during that time, science was cut back while the Mongols overrode everything." He paused. "Not unlike what's happening in Ontario right now."

"Not bitter, are we?" I said.

Chen shrugged a little. "That's the only explanation I could think of for why my people didn't record the supernova." He turned to Hollus. "The supernova should have been just as visible from Beta Hydri was it was from here. Do your people have any record of having observed it?"

"I will check," said Hollus. The simulacrum stopped moving; even the torso stopped expanding and contracting. We waited about a minute, and then the giant spider came to life again, Hollus reinhabiting his avatar. "No," he said.

"No record of a supernova 650 years ago?"

"Not in Vela."

"Those are Earth years, of course."

Hollus sounded offended at the suggestion that he might have screwed up. "Of course. The most recent naked-eye supernova observed by either the Forhilnors or the Wreeds was the one in the Large Magellanic Cloud about fifteen years ago. Before that, both races saw one in the constellation you call Serpens, in what would have been very early in your seventeenth century."

Chen nodded. "Kepler's supernova." He looked at me. "It was visible here starting in 1604. It got to be brighter than Jupiter, but you could barely see it during the day." He pursed his lips, thinking. "That's fascinating. Kepler's supernova was nowhere near Earth, or Beta Hydri, or Delta Pavonis, and yet all three worlds saw it and recorded it. Supernova 1987A, of course, wasn't even in this galaxy, and we all recorded it. But the Vela event of circa 1320 was quite nearby. I'd have thought someone would have seen it."

"Perhaps a dust cloud intervened?" said Hollus.

CALCULATING GOD

"There's no dust cloud in the way now," said Chen, "and it would take a cloud either awfully close to the star that blew up or awfully big to obscure the view from Earth *and* Beta Hydri *and* Delta Pavonis. Somebody should have seen this thing."

"Quite a puzzle," said Hollus.

Chen nodded. "Isn't it, though?"

"I would be glad to provide you with what information my kind have gathered about supernovas," said Hollus. "Perhaps it will shed some light on the issue."

I wondered if Hollus was deliberately making a pun.

"That would be great," said Chen.

"I will have some material sent down from the mothership," said Hollus, eyestalks waving.

When I was fourteen, the museum had had a contest for children interested in dinosaurs. The winner would get all sorts of paleontology-related prizes.

If it had been a dinosaur trivia contest, or a test of common knowledge about dinosaurs, or if it had required kids to identify fossils, I would have won, I'm sure.

But it wasn't. It was a contest to make the best dinosaur marionette.

I knew which dinosaur it had to be: *Parasaurolophus,* the ROM's signature mount.

I tried building one out of Plasticine and Styrofoam and wooden dowels.

It was a disaster. The head, with its long crest, kept falling off. I never got it finished. Some fat kid won the contest; I was at the ceremony where he received his prizes, one of which was a sauropod model. He said, "Neat! Brontosaurus!" I was disgusted: even in 1960, no one who knew *anything* about dinosaurs called *Apatosaurus* that.

I did learn one valuable lesson, though.

I learned that you can't choose the ways in which you'll be tested.

Donald Chen and Hollus might have been fascinated by supernovae, but I was more interested in what Hollus and I had been talking about before. Once Don left, I said, "So, Hollus, you guys seem to know an awful lot about DNA."

"I suppose that is true," the alien said.

"What—" My voice had broken a bit; I swallowed and tried again. "What do you know about problems with DNA, about errors in its replication?"

"That is not my field, of course," said Hollus, "but our ship's doctor, Lablok, is reasonably expert in that area."

"And does this Lablok . . ." I swallowed ". . . does this Lablok know anything about, say, cancer?"

"The treatment of cancer is a specialized discipline on our world," said Hollus. "Lablok knows something about it, of course, but—"

"Can you cure cancer?"

"We treat it with radiation and chemicals," said Hollus. "Sometimes these are effective, but often they are not." He sounded rather sad.

"Ah," I said. "The same is true here on Earth." I was quiet for a time; of course, I'd been hoping for a different answer. Oh, well. "Speaking of DNA," I said, at last, "I—I wonder if I might have a sample of yours. If that's not too personal, that is. I'd like to have some studies done on it."

Hollus stretched out an arm. "Help yourself."

I almost fell for it. "You aren't really here. You're just a projection."

Hollus lowered his arm, and his eyestalks did their S-ripple.

"Forgive my sense of humor. But, certainly, if you would like some DNA, you are welcome to it. I will have the shuttle come down with some samples."

"Thanks."

"I can tell you what you will find, though. You will find that my existence is just as unlikely as yours. The degree of complexity in an advanced lifeform simply could not have arisen by chance."

I took a deep breath. I didn't want to argue with the alien, but, dammitall, he was a scientist. He should know better. I swiveled in my chair, turning to face the computer mounted on what had, when I'd started working here, been the return for a typewriter. I've got one of those nifty Microsoft split keyboards; the museum had to provide them to anyone who asked after the staff association started making complaints about liability for carpal-tunnel syndrome.

My computer was a Windows NT system, but I opened a DOS session on it, and typed a command at the prompt. An application began, and it drew a chessboard on the screen.

"That's a standard human game board," I said. "We play two games of strategy on it: chess and checkers."

Hollus touched his eyes together. "I have heard of the former; I understand you used to consider its mastery one of humanity's greatest intellectual achievements—until a computer was able to beat the most-skilled human. You humans do have a tendency to make the definition of intelligence quite elusive."

"I guess," I said. "But, anyway, it's actually something more like checkers I want to talk about." I touched a key. "Here's a random deployment of playing pieces." About a third of the sixty-four squares sprouted circular occupants. "Now, look: each occupied square has eight neighboring squares, including the diagonal corners, right?"

Hollus clinked his eyes together again.

"Now, consider three simple rules: a given square will remain unchanged—either occupied or vacant—if precisely two

ROBERT J. SAWYER

of the neighboring squares are occupied. And if an occupied square has three occupied neighbors, it remains occupied. In all other cases, the square becomes empty if it isn't already, and if it *is* empty, it remains empty. Got it?"

"Yes."

"Okay. Now, let's expand the board. Instead of an 8-by-8 matrix, let's use 400 by 300; on this monitor, that lets every square be represented by a two-by-two pixel cell. We'll show occupied squares by white cells and unoccupied ones by black cells."

I tapped a key, and the checkerboard apparently receded into the distance while at the same time extending to the four corners of the screen. The grid of the board disappeared at this resolution, but the random pattern of lighted and unlighted cells was obvious.

"Now," I said, "let's apply our three rules." I tapped the space bar, and the pattern of dots shifted. "Again," I said, tapping the space bar, and again the pattern shifted. "And once more." Another tap; another reconfiguring of the dots on the screen.

Hollus looked at the monitor and then at me. "So?"

"So this," I said. I tapped another key, and the process began repeating itself automatically: apply the three rules to every piece on the board, redisplay the new configuration, apply the rules again, redisplay the revised configuration, and so on.

It only took a few seconds for the first glider to appear. "See that group of five cells?" I said. "We call that a 'glider,' and—ah, there's another one." I touched the screen, pointing it out. "And another. Watch them move."

And, indeed, they did seem to move, staying a cohesive group as they shifted from position to position across the monitor.

"If you run this simulation long enough," I said, "you'll see all sorts of lifelike patterns; in fact, this game is called Life. It was invented in 1970 by a mathematician named John Conway; I used to use it when I taught evolution at U of T. Conway was astonished by what those three simple rules generated. After enough iterations, something called a 'glider gun' will appear—a structure that shoots out new gliders at regular intervals. And, indeed, glider guns can be created by collisions of thirteen or more gliders, so, in a way, the gliders reproduce themselves. You also get 'eaters,' which can break up passing objects; in the process, the eater gets damaged, but after a few more turns, it repairs itself. The game produces movement, reproduction, eating, growth, the healing of injuries, and more, all from applying those three simple rules to an initially random selection of pieces."

"I do not see the point you are trying to make," said Hollus.

"The point is that life—the apparent complexity of it all— can be generated by very simple rules."

"And these rules you keep iterating represent precisely what?"

"Well, the laws of physics, say . . ."

"No one disputes that seeming order can come out of the application of simple rules. But who wrote the rules? For the universe you are showing me, you mentioned a name—"

"John Conway."

"Yes. Well, John Conway is the god of that universe, and all his simulation proves is that any universe requires a god. Conway was the programmer. God was also a programmer; the laws of physics and physical constants he devised are our universe's source code. The presumed difference between your Mr. Conway and our God is that, as you said, Conway did not know what his source code would produce until he compiled and executed it, and he was therefore astounded by the results. Our creator, one presumes, did have a specific result in mind and wrote code to produce that result. Granted, things have apparently not gone precisely as planned—the mass extinctions seem to suggest that. But, nonetheless, it seems clear that God deliberately designed the universe."

"You really believe that?" I asked.

"Yes," said Hollus, as he watched more gliders dance across my computer screen. "I really do."

8

When I was a boy, I belonged to the Royal Ontario Museum's Saturday Morning Club for three years. It was an incredible experience for a kid like me, fascinated by dinosaurs and snakes and bats and gladiators and mummies. Every Saturday during the school year, we'd go down to the museum, getting in before it opened to the public. We'd congregate in the ROM theater—that's what it was called before some overpriced consultant had decided we should rename it Theatre ROM. It had been quite grotty back then, and upholstered entirely in black; it's since had a face-lift.

The mornings would start off with Mrs. Berlin, who ran the club, showing us a 16 mm movie, usually some short from the National Film Board of Canada. And then we'd head off for a half-day of activities in the museum, not just in the galleries but also behind the scenes. I loved every minute of it and made up my mind that someday I would work at the ROM.

I remember one day we were getting a demonstration from the artist responsible for many of the museum's dinosaur reconstructions. He asked our assembled group what kind of dinosaur a pointed, serrated tooth he was showing us had come from.

"A carnosaur," I'd said at once.

The artist had been impressed. "That's right," he said.

But another kid berated me later. "It's carni*vore,* he said, "n̦ot carnosaur."

Carnosaur was, of course, the correct word: it was the technical name for the group of dinosaurs that included tyrannosaurs and their kin. Most kids don't know that; hell, most adults don't know it.

But I knew it. I'd read it on a placard in the ROM's Dinosaur Gallery.

The original Dinosaur Gallery, that is.

Instead of our current dioramas, that gallery had had specimens mounted so you could walk right around them; velvet ropes kept the public from getting too close. And each specimen had a lengthy, typed explanation in a wooden frame that would take four or five minutes to read.

The centerpiece of the old gallery was a *Corythosaurus,* a huge duckbill standing erect. There was something wonderfully Canadian, although I didn't understand it as such at the time, about the ROM's showcase dinosaur being a placid vegetarian instead of the ravenous *T. rexes* or the fiercely armed *Triceratopses* that were the major mounts at most U.S. museums; indeed, it wasn't until 1999 that the ROM put a *T. rex* cast on display, over in the kid's Discovery Gallery. Still, that ancient *Corythosaurus* mount was wrong. We know now that hadrosaurs almost certainly couldn't stand up like that; they probably spent most of their time as quadrupeds.

Every time I went to the museum as a kid, I made a point of looking at that skeleton, and the others, and reading the placards, and struggling with the vocabulary, and learning as much as I could.

We still have that skeleton at the ROM, tucked to the side of the Cretaceous Alberta diorama, but there's no explanatory text associated with it anymore. Just a small Plexiglas sign that disingenuously glosses over the erroneous stance, and says little else:

ROBERT J. SAWYER

***Corythosaurus Excavatus* Gilmore**

A crested hadrosaur (duck-bill) mounted in an upright alert posture. Upper Cretaceous, Oldman formation (approximately 75 million years), Little Sandhill Creek, near Steveville, Alberta.

Of course, the "new" Dinosaur Gallery was a quarter-century old now. It had opened before Christine Dorati had come to power, but she considered it a model of what our displays should be like: don't bore the audience, don't weigh them down with facts. Just let them gawk.

Christine had a couple of daughters; they were grown now. But I often wondered if, when they were kids, she had been embarrassed at a museum. Perhaps she'd said, "Oh, Mary, that's a *Tyrannosaurus rex.* It lived ten million years ago." And her daughter—or, worse, some smart-aleck kid like I'd been—had corrected her with information that had been written on a lengthy placard. "That's not a tyrannosaur, and it didn't live ten million years ago. It's an *Allosaurus,* and it lived 150 million years ago." But whatever the reason, Christine Dorati hated signage that conveyed information.

I wish we had the money to redo the Dinosaur Gallery again; I'd inherited it in its current condition. But money was scarce these days; the axing of the planetarium was hardly the only cutback.

Still, I wondered how many kids we were inspiring these days.

I wondered—

It wouldn't be my Ricky; that would be too much to ask. Besides, he was still at the stage where he wanted to be a firefighter or a police officer and had evinced no particular interest in science.

Still, when I looked at the tens of thousands of school-aged children who came on field trips to the museum each year, I wondered which if any of them would grow up to follow in my footsteps.

Hollus and I were at an impasse over the interpretation of the game of Life, and so I excused myself, and went to the washroom. As I always did, I opened the faucets on all three sinks, to make some background noise; the public washrooms at the ROM all had faucets controlled by electric eyes, but we didn't have to put up with that indignity in the staff facilities. The running water drowned out the sound as I crouched down in front of one of the toilets and vomited; I tossed my cookies about once a week, thanks to the chemo drugs. It was hard on me; my chest and lungs were already strained. I took a few moments, kneeling there, just to regain my strength, then I stood up, flushed the toilet, and headed to the sinks, washing my hand and turning off all the taps. I kept a bottle of mouthwash at the museum and had brought it in with me; I gargled, trying to kill the foul taste. And, then, at last, I returned to the paleobiology department, smiling at Bruiser as if nothing unusual had happened. I opened the door to my office and went back inside.

To my astonishment, Hollus was reading the newspaper when I came in. He'd picked up my copy of the tabloid *Toronto Sun* from my desk and was holding it in his two six-fingered hands. His eyestalks moved left to right in unison as he read along. I'd expected him to be aware of my presence at once, but maybe the simulacrum wasn't that sensitive. I cleared my throat, tasting a little more unpleasantness as I did so.

"Wel" "come" "back," said Hollus, his eyes now looking at me. He closed the newspaper and faced the front page toward me. The sole headline taking up most of the front page, declared, "Abortion Doc Killed." "I have seen many references to abortion in your media," said Hollus, "but confess to not under-

ROBERT J. SAWYER

standing precisely what it is; the term is bandied about, but never defined—even in the article that apparently relates to this title."

I moved to my chair and took a deep breath, gathering my thoughts, wondering where to begin. I'd read the story myself on the way into work this morning. "Well, um, sometimes human women get pregnant unintentionally. There is a procedure that can be done to terminate the fetus, putting an end to the pregnancy; it's called an abortion. It's, ah, somewhat controversial, and because of that it's often done in special clinics rather than at regular hospitals. Religious fundamentalists disapprove strongly of abortion—they consider it a form of murder—and some extremists have taken to using bombs to blow up abortion clinics. Last week, a clinic was blown up in Buffalo—that's a city just over the border in New York State. And yesterday, one was blown up in Etobicoke, which is part of Toronto. The doctor who owned the clinic was inside at the time, and he was killed."

Hollus looked at me for the longest time. "These—what did you call them? Fundamentalist extremists? These fundamentalist extremists believe it is wrong to kill even an unborn child?"

"Yes."

It was hard to discern tone in Hollus's speech, what with his voice bouncing between two mouths, but he sounded incredulous, at least to me. "And they demonstrate their disapproval over this by murdering adults?"

I nodded slightly. "Apparently."

Hollus was quiet for a few moments longer, his spherical torso bobbing slowly up and down. "Among my people," he said, "we have a concept called"—and his twin mouths sang two discordant notes. "It refers to incongruities, to events or words that convey the opposite of the intended meaning."

"We have a similar concept. We call it irony."

His eyes turned to the newspaper again. "Apparently not all humans understand it."

9

I've never smoked. So why do I have lung cancer?

It's actually, so I've learned, somewhat common among paleontologists, geologists, and mineralogists of my generation. I was right, in a way, when I attributed my cough to the dusty environment I worked in. We often use tools that pulverize rocks, creating a lot of fine dust, which—

But lung cancer takes a long time to develop, and I've been working in paleontology labs for thirty years. These days, I almost always wear a mask; our consciousness has been raised, and almost everyone does so when doing that kind of work. But, still, over the decades, I'd breathed in more than my share of rock dust, not to mention asbestos fibers as well as fiberglass filaments while making casts.

And now I'm paying for it.

Some of Susan's and my friends said we should sue— perhaps the museum, perhaps the Ontario government (my ultimate employer). Surely my workplace could have been made safer; surely I should have been given better safety instruction; surely—

It was a natural reaction. Someone should pay for such an injustice. Tom Jericho: he's a nice guy, good husband, good father, gives to charity . . . maybe not as much as he should, but some, each month. And he was always there to lend a hand when someone was moving or painting their house. And now good old Tom had cancer.

Yes, surely someone should pay, they thought.

But the last thing I wanted to do was waste time on litigation. So, no, I wasn't going to sue.

Still, I had lung cancer; I had to deal with that.

And there was an irony here.

Some of what Hollus was saying about what he took as proof for God's existence wasn't new to me. That stuff about the fundamental constants was sometimes referred to as the anthropic cosmological principle; I'd touched on it in my evolution course. He was certainly right that the universe, superficially at least, seemed designed for life. As Sir Fred Hoyle said in 1981, "A common-sense interpretation of the facts suggests that a superintellect has monkeyed with physics, as well as with chemistry and biology, and that there are no blind forces worth speaking about in nature. The numbers one calculates from the facts seem to me so overwhelming as to put this conclusion almost beyond question." But, then again, Sir Fred championed a lot of notions the rest of the scientific community balked at.

Still, as Hollus and I continued to talk, he brought up cilia—although he called them "ciliums;" he always had trouble with Latin plurals. Cilia are the hairlike extensions from cells that are capable of rhythmic motion; they are present in many types of human cells, and, he said, in the cells of Forhilnors and Wreeds, too. Humans who believed that not just the universe but life itself had been intelligently designed often cited cilia. The tiny motors that allow the fibers to move are enormously complex, and the intelligent-design proponents say they are irreducibly complex: there is no way they could have evolved through a series of incremental steps. Like a mousetrap, a cilium needs all of its various parts to work; take away any element and it becomes useless junk—just as without the spring, or the holding bar, or the platform, or the hammer, or the catch, a mousetrap does nothing at all. It was indeed a conundrum to explain how cilia had evolved through the accumulation of gradual changes, which is supposed to be how evolution works.

96

Well, among other places, cilia are found on the single layer of cells that line the bronchi. They beat in unison, moving mucus out of the lungs—mucous containing particles that have been accidentally inhaled, getting them out before cancers can begin.

If the cilia are destroyed, though, by exposure to asbestos, tobacco smoke, or other substances, the lungs can no longer keep themselves clean. The only other mechanism for dislodging phlegm and moving it upward is coughing—persistent, racking coughing. Such coughing isn't as effective, though; carcinogens stay longer in the lungs, and tumors form. The persistent coughing sometimes damages the surface of the tumor, adding blood to the sputum; as in my case, that is often the first symptom of lung cancer.

If Hollus and the humans who shared his beliefs were right, cilia had been designed by some master engineer.

If so, then maybe that's the son of a bitch who should be sued.

"My friend over at the university has got a preliminary report on your DNA," I said to Hollus, a few days after he'd provided the sample I had asked for; I'd missed the landing of the shuttle again, but a Forhilnor who wasn't Hollus had dropped off the specimen with Raghubir, along with the Forhilnor data on supernovae Hollus had promised to give to Donald Chen.

"And?"

At some point, I would ask him what governed which mouth he would use when he was only going to utter a single syllable. "And she doesn't believe it's extraterrestrial in origin."

Hollus shifted on his six feet; he always found it cramped in my office. "Of course it is. I confess it is not my own DNA; Lablok extracted it from herself. But she is a Forhilnor, too."

"My friend identified hundreds of genes that seem to be the

same as those in life from this planet. The gene that creates hemoglobin, for instance."

"There are only a limited number of possible chemicals that can be used to carry oxygen in the bloodstream."

"I guess she was expecting something more—well, alien."

"I am as alien a being as you are every likely to encounter," said Hollus. "That is, the difference between your body plan and mine is as great as we have ever seen. There are practical engineering constraints on how weird life can get, after all, even"—and here he raised one of his six-fingered hands and did a Vulcan salute—"if your filmmakers seem incapable of coming close to the variety possible."

"I suppose," I said.

Hollus bobbed. "The minimum number of genes required for life is about 300," he said. "But that quantity is sufficient only for truly primitive creatures; most eukaryotic cells share a core group of about three thousand genes—you find them in everything from single-celled lifeforms to elaborate animals like ourselves, and they are the same, or almost the same, on every world we have looked at. On top of that, there are 4,000 additional genes that are shared by all multicellular lifeforms, which encode proteins for cell-to-cell adhesion, signaling between cells, and so on. There are thousands more shared by all animals with internal skeletons. And thousands more beyond that are shared by all warm-blooded animals. Of course, if your friend keeps searching, she will find tens of thousands of genes in Forhilnor DNA that have no counterparts in Earthly lifeforms, although, naturally, it is easier to match genes than to find unfamiliar ones. But there really are only a few possible solutions to the problems posed by life, and they recur on world after world."

I shook my head. "I wouldn't have expected life from Beta Hydri to use the same genetic code as life on Earth does, let alone any of the same genes. I mean, there are even some variations in the code here: out of the sixty-four codons, four have different meanings in mitochondrial DNA than they do in nuclear DNA."

"All lifeforms we have examined share essentially the same genetic code. It surprised us at first, as well."

"But it just doesn't make sense," I said. "Amino acids come in two isomers, left- and right-handed, but all life on Earth uses only the left-handed versions. For starters, it should be a fifty-fifty shot for any two ecosystems to both use the same orientation. And there should be only a one-in-four chance that three ecosystems—yours, mine, and the Wreeds'—would use the same one."

"Indeed," said Hollus.

"And even just taking the left-handed kind, there are still over a hundred different amino acids—but life on Earth only uses twenty of them. What are the chances that life on other worlds would use those exact same twenty?"

"Pretty darn remote."

I smiled at Hollus; I'd expected him to give me a precise statistical answer. "Pretty darn remote indeed," I said.

"But the choice is not random; God designed it that way."

I let out a long sigh. "I just can't buy that," I said.

"I know," said Hollus, sounding as though he despaired for my ignorance. "Look," he said after a time, "I am not a mystic. I believe in God because it makes scientific sense for me to do so; indeed, I suspect God exists in this universe *because* of science."

My head was starting to hurt. "How's that?"

"As I said earlier, our universe is closed—it will eventually collapse back down in a big crunch. A similar event happened after billions of years in the universe that preceded this one—and with billions of years, who knows what phenomenal things science might make possible? Why, it might even make it possible for an intelligence, or data patterns representing it, to survive a big crunch and exist again in the next cycle of creation. Such an entity might even have science sufficient to allow it to influence the parameters for the next cycle, creating a designer universe into which that entity itself will be reborn already armed with billions of years worth of knowledge and wisdom."

I shook my head; I'd expected something better than a riff on "it's turtles all the way down." "Even if that's so," I said, "that hardly solves the problem of whether or not God exists. You're just pushing the creation of life back one step farther. How did life start in the universe before this one?" I frowned. "If you can't explain that, you haven't explained anything."

"I do not believe that the being who is our God was ever alive," said Hollus, "in the sense of being a biological entity. I suspect this is the first universe in which biology and evolution have ever taken place."

"Then what is it, this God-being?"

"I see no evidence here on Earth that you have yet achieved artificial intelligence."

That seemed a *non sequitur* to me, but I nodded. "That's right, although a lot of people are working on it."

"We do have self-aware machines. My starship, the *Merelcas,* is one such. And what we have discovered is this: intelligence is an *emergent* property—it appears spontaneously in systems of sufficient order and complexity. I suspect that the being which is now the God of this universe was a noncorporeal intelligence that arose through chance fluctuations in a previous universe devoid of biology. I believe this being, existing in isolation, sought to make sure that the next universe would teem with in-dependent, self-reproducing life. It seems unlikely that biology could have started in *any* randomly generated universe on its own, but a localized space-time matrix of sufficient complexity to develop sentience could reasonably be expected to arise by chance after only a few billion years of quantum fluctuations, especially in universes unlike this one in which the five funda-mental forces have less divergent relative strengths." He paused. "The suggestion that essentially a scientist created our current universe would explain the long-standing philosophical conun-drum of why this universe is indeed comprehensible to the scientific mind; why Forhilnor and human abstractions, such as mathematics and induction and aesthetics, are applicable to the nature of the reality. Our universe is scientifically understandable *because* it was created by a vastly advanced intelligence who used the tools of science."

It was staggering to think that intelligence could arise more easily than life itself could—and yet we really didn't have a good definition of intelligence; every time a computer seemed to succeed at duplicating it, we simply said that that's not what we meant by the term. "God as a scientist," I said, tasting the thought. "Well, I guess any sufficiently advanced technology is indistinguishable from magic."

"Pithy," said Hollus. "You should write that down."

"I don't think it's original to me. But what you're proposing is just that—a proposal. It doesn't prove the existence of your God."

Hollus bobbed his torso. "And just what sort of evidence would convince you?"

I thought about that for a while, then shrugged. "A smoking gun," I said.

Hollus's eyes moved to their maximum separation. "A what?"

"My favorite genre of fiction is murder mysteries, and—"

"I am astounded that humans take pleasure in reading about killing," said Hollus.

"No, no," I said. "You've got it wrong. We don't enjoy reading about killing; we enjoy reading about justice—about a criminal, no matter how clever, being proved guilty of the crime. And the best proof in a real murder case is to find the suspect holding the smoking gun—actually holding the weapon used to commit the crime."

"Ah," said Hollus.

"A smoking gun is incontrovertible evidence. And that's what I want: indisputable proof."

"There is no indisputable proof for the big bang," said Hollus. "And there is none for evolution. And yet you accept those.

Why hold the question of whether there is a creator to a higher standard?"

I didn't have a good answer for that. "All I know," I said, "is that it will take overwhelming evidence to convince me."

"I believe you have already been given overwhelming evidence," said Hollus.

I touched my head, feeling the smoothness where my hair used to be.

Hollus was right: we do accept evolution without absolute proof. Sure, it seems clear that dogs are descended from wolves. Our ancestors apparently domesticated them, breeding out the fierceness, breeding in companionability, eventually turning the Ice Age *Canis lupus pallipes* into *Canis familiaris,* the modern pooch with its 300 sundry breeds.

Dogs and wolves can't jointly reproduce anymore, or, at least, if they do, the offspring are sterile: canines and lupines are different species. If that's the way it really happened—if human breeding turned Akela into Rover, creating a new species—then one of the basic tenets of evolution has been demonstrated: new species can be created from old ones.

But we can't *prove* the evolution of the dog. And in all the thousands of years we have been breeding dogs since, producing all those myriad kinds, we have not managed to create a new canine species: a Chihuahua can still mate with a Great Dane, and a pit bull can hump a poodle—and both unions can bring forth fertile young. No matter how much we try to emphasize their differences, they are still *Canis familiaris.* And we've never created a new species of cat or rat or elephant, of corn or coconut or cactus. That natural selection can produce changes within a type is disputed by no one, not even the staunchest creationist. But that it can transform one species into another— that, in fact, has never been observed.

ROBERT J. SAWYER

In the vertebrate-paleontology gallery at the ROM, we've got a long diorama filled with horse skeletons, starting with *Hyracotherium* from the Eocene, then *Mesohippus* from the Oligocene, *Merychippus* and *Pliohippus* from the Pliocene, then *Equus shoshonensis* from the Pleistocene, and finally today's *Equus caballus,* represented by a modern quarter horse and a Shetland pony.

It sure as hell *looks* like evolution is happening: the number of toes reduce from *Hyracotherium*'s four on the front feet and three on the rear until there's only one, in the form of a hoof; the teeth grow longer and longer, an apparent adaptation for eating tough grasses; the animals (excepting the pony) get progressively larger. I pass that display constantly; it's part of the background of my life. Rarely do I give it any thought, although often enough I've interpreted it when conducting VIP tours of the gallery.

One species giving rise to the next in an endless pageant of mutations, of adaptations to ever-changing conditions.

I accept that readily.

I accept that because Darwin's theory makes sense.

So why don't I also accept Hollus's theory?

Extraordinary claims require extraordinary proof. That had been Carl Sagan's mantra when confronted by UFO nuts.

Well, guess what, Carl? The aliens are here—in Toronto, in L.A., in Burundi, in Pakistan, in China. The proof is inescapable. They are here.

And what about Hollus's God? What about the proof for an intelligent designer? The Forhilnors and Wreeds had more concrete evidence, it seemed, for that than I had for evolution, the intellectual framework upon which I'd built my life, my career.

But . . . but . . .

Extraordinary claims. Surely they *must* be held to a higher standard. Surely the proof should be monumental, irrefutable.

Of course it should be.

Of course.

10

Susan had come with me last October when I'd gone down to St. Michael's Hospital to meet the oncologist, Katarina Kohl.

It was a terrifying experience, for both of us.

First, Dr. Kohl conducted a bronchoscopic examination. She passed a tube ending in a camera through my mouth into the airway subdivisions of each lung, in hopes of getting at the tumor and collecting a sample. But the tumor was unreachable. And so she performed a needle biopsy, pushing a fine needle through my chest wall directly into the tumor, guided by x rays. Although there had been no doubt, based on the cells I'd coughed up with my phlegm, that I had cancer, this specimen would nonetheless confirm the diagnosis.

Still, if the tumor was isolated, and we knew where it was, it could be surgically removed. But before opening my chest to do so, another test was required: a mediastinoscopy. Dr. Kohl made a short incision just above my breast bone, cutting down to the trachea. She then passed a camera tube through the incision and pushed it down along the outside of my windpipe to inspect the lymph nodes near each lung. More material was removed for inspection.

And, at last, she told Susan and me what she'd found.

We were devastated by the news. I couldn't catch my breath, and even though I was sitting down when Kohl showed us the test results, I thought I might lose my balance. The cancer had spread to my lymph nodes; surgery would be pointless.

Kohl gave Susan and me a few moments to compose ourselves. The oncologist had seen it a hundred times, a thousand times, living corpses looking at her, horror on their faces, fear in their eyes, wanting her to say she was just kidding, it was all a mistake, the equipment had malfunctioned, there was still hope.

But she said none of that.

There'd been a cancellation for two hours hence; a CAT scan would be possible that very day.

I didn't ask why whoever had had the appointment had failed to keep it. Perhaps he or she had died in the interim. The entire cancer ward was filled with ghosts. Susan and I waited, silently. She tried to read some of the outdated magazines; I kept staring into space, my mind racing, eddying.

I knew about CAT scans—computerized axial tomography. I'd seen lots of them done. From time to time, one or another of Toronto's hospitals will let us scan an interesting fossil when the equipment isn't being otherwise used. It's an effective way to examine specimens that are too fragile to remove from the matrix they're encased in; it's also a great way to see the interior structures. We've done some wonderful work on *Lambeosaurus* skulls and *Eucentrosaurus* eggs. I knew all about the procedure—but I'd never had it done to myself before. My hands were sweating. I kept feeling like I was going to throw up, even though none of the tests should have made me nauseous. I was frightened—more frightened than I'd ever been in my life. The only time I'd been even close to this nervous was while Susan and I were waiting for word about whether we were going to get to adopt Ricky. We had sat by the phone, and every time it rang our hearts jumped. But we'd been waiting for good news, then . . .

A CAT scan is painless, and a little radiation could hardly do me any harm now. I lay down on the white pallet, and the technician slid my body into the scanning tunnel, producing images that showed the extent of my lung cancer.

The substantial extent . . .

I'd always been a student, a learner—and so had Susan, for that matter. But the facts and figures came in a dizzying flurry that day, disjointed, complex, too much to absorb, too much to believe. Kohl was detached—she'd given these lectures a thousand times before, a tenured prof, bored, tired.

But to us, to all those who sat in the same vinyl-covered chairs Susan and I sat in then, those who had struggled to take it all in, to understand, to comprehend—to us it was terrifying. My heart was pounding, a splitting headache; no amount of the warm water the specialist kept offering would slake my thirst; my hands—hands that had carefully chiseled embryonic dinosaur bones from shattered eggs; hands that had removed limestone overburden covering fossilized feathers; hands that had been my livelihood, the tools of my trade—shook like leaves in a breeze.

Lung cancer, said the oncologist in even tones, as if discussing the features of the latest sport-utility vehicle or VCR, is one of the most deadly forms of cancer because it usually isn't detected early, and by the time it is, it has often extensively metastasized to lymph nodes in the torso and neck, to the pleural membrane lining the lungs and chest, and to the liver, adrenal glands, and bones.

I wanted her to keep it abstract, theoretical. Just some general comments, mere context.

But no. No. She pressed on; she made her point. It was all relevant to me, to my future.

Yes, lung cancer often metastasizes extensively.

And mine had done precisely that.

I asked the question I'd been dying to ask, the question I'd been afraid to hear the answer to, the question that was paramount, that defined everything—*everything*—in my universe from that moment on. How long? How long?

CALCULATING GOD

Kohl, at last a human being and not a robot, failed for a moment to meet my eyes. The average survival time after diagnosis, she said, is nine months without treatment. Chemotherapy might buy me a little more time, but the kind of lung cancer I had was called adenocarcinoma—a new word, a handful of syllables I would come to know as well as my own name, syllables, indeed, more defining of who I was and what would become of me than "Thomas David Jericho" had ever been. Even with treatment, only one in eight adenocarcinoma patients are alive five years after diagnosis, and most were gone—that's the word she used: "gone," as though we'd slipped out to the corner store for a loaf of bread, as though we'd called it a night, turned in, gotta get up early tomorrow—most were gone much sooner than that.

It was like an explosion, rocking everything Susan and I had ever known.

The clock had started on that autumn day.

The countdown had begun.

I had only a year or so left to live.

ROBERT J. SAWYER

11

H ollus and I went down into the Lower Rotunda each evening, after the museum closed to the public. As payment for what I'd let him see, he continued to present recreations of various periods from Beta Hydri III's geologic past, and I recorded all of these on video.

Maybe it was because my own life was coming to an end, but after a while, I yearned to see something else. Hollus had mentioned the six worlds apparently abandoned by their inhabitants. I wanted to see them, see the most recent artifacts on these alien worlds—the last things the inhabitants had built before they disappeared.

What he showed me was amazing.

First was Epsilon Indi Prime. On its southern continent, there is a huge square, enclosed by walls. The walls are made of giant, roughly hewn granite blocks each more than 8 meters on a side. The area they enclose, almost 500 meters across, is filled with rubble: gargantuan, jagged hunks of broken concrete. Even if one could climb the walls, the vast field of rubble would be imposingly barren. No animal or vehicle could traverse it without great difficulty, and nothing could ever be made to grow there.

Then there's Tau Ceti II. In the middle of a barren landscape, the long-gone inhabitants had made a disk of fused black stone more than 2,000 meters across and, judging by its edge, more than 5 meters thick. The black surface absorbs heat from its sun, making it incredibly hot; flesh would blister trying to walk across it, and the soles of shoes would melt.

The surface of Mu Cassiopeae A Prime reveals no sign of its former inhabitants; everything has been buried by 2.4 million years of erosion. But Hollus showed me a computer-generated model of what the starship *Merelcas*'s sensors had revealed beneath the layers of sediment: a vast plain filled with towering, twisted spires, spikes, and other jagged forms, and beneath that, a vault or chamber, forever hidden from view. That planet had once had a very large moon—proportionately, much larger than Luna is in relation to Earth—but it now sported a glorious system of rings instead. Hollus said they'd determined the ring system was also 2.4 million years old—in other words, it had come into existence at the same time the Cassiopeians had vanished.

I had him show me the rest of the planet. There were archipelagos in the seas—islands spread out like pearls on a string—and the eastern shoreline of the largest continent closely matched the western shoreline of the next largest: telltale signs of a world that had been undergoing plate tectonics.

"They blew up their own moon," I said, surprising myself with the insight. "They wanted to put an end to its tidal forces churning their planet's core; they wanted to shut off plate tectonics."

"Why?" asked Hollus, sounding intrigued by my notion.

"To prevent the vault they'd built from ever being subducted," I said. Continental drift causes crustal rocks to be recycled, with old ones pushed down into the mantle and new ones forming from magma welling up at sea-floor trenches.

"But we had assumed the vault was for the storage of nuclear waste," said Hollus. "Subduction would actually be the best way to get rid of it."

I nodded. The monuments he'd shown me here and on Tau Ceti II and Epsilon Indi Prime were indeed reminiscent of designs I'd seen proposed for nuclear-waste sites on Earth: artificial landscapes so foreboding that no one would ever dig there.

"Did you find any inscriptions or messages related to nuclear waste?" I said. The plans for Earth's waste sites all involved symbolic communication indicating the sort of dangerous materials being stored, so that any future inhabitants of the area would understand what had been buried. The proposed iconography ranged from human faces showing expressions of illness or disgust, indicating that the area was poisonous, to diagrams using atomic numbers to note specifically what elements were interred.

"No," said Hollus. "Nothing like that. Not in the most recent sites, at least—the ones that I have been showing you from just before the races disappeared."

"Well, I suppose they could have wanted the sites to go undisturbed for millions of years—for so long that whatever intelligences that later discovered them might not even be of the same species as those who had buried the waste beneath the warning landscapes. It's one thing to try to communicate the idea of poison or sickness to members of your own species—we humans associate closed eyes, frowning mouths, and protruding tongues with poisoning—but it might be quite another to try to do it across species boundaries, especially when you know nothing about the species that might succeed you."

"You are not integrating," said Hollus. "Most radioactive waste has a half-life of less than a hundred thousand years. By the time a new sapient species has emerged, there would be virtually nothing dangerous left."

I frowned. "Still, they do look a lot like nuclear-waste storage sites. And, well, if the natives of the planets departed to go somewhere else, maybe they felt it was appropriate to bury their garbage before leaving."

Hollus sounded dubious. "But why then would the Cassiopeians want to stop subduction? As I said, that is the best way to get rid of nuclear waste—even better than firing it off into space. If the spaceship you are using explodes, you can end up with nuclear contamination spread over half your world, but if the waste is carried down into the mantle, it is gone for good. That is, in fact, what my own race ended up doing with its nuclear waste."

"Well, then, maybe they buried something else beneath those warning landscapes," I said. "Something so dangerous, they wanted to make sure that it would never be uncovered, so that it could never come after them. Maybe the Cassiopeians were afraid if the vault was subducted, its walls would melt and whatever—whatever *beast* perhaps—they'd imprisoned within might escape. And then, all these races, even after burying whatever they were afraid of, left their homeworlds, putting as much distance as possible between themselves and whatever it was they'd left behind."

"I'm thinking of going to church this Sunday," Susan had said last October, shortly after our first appointment with Dr. Kohl.

We'd been sitting in our living room, me on the couch, she on the matching chair. I'd nodded. "You usually do."

"I know, but—well, with everything that's happened. With . . . "

"I'll be all right," I said.

"Are you sure?"

I nodded again. "You go to church every Sunday. That shouldn't change. Dr. Kohl said we should try to keep our lives as normal as possible."

I wasn't sure what I'd do with the time—but I'd find plenty. At some point, I'd have to call my brother Bill in Vancouver and let him know what was happening. But Vancouver was three hours behind Toronto, and Bill didn't get home from work until late. If I called in what was the early evening his time, I'd end up speaking to his new wife Marilyn—and she could talk your ear

ROBERT J. SAWYER

off. I wasn't up for that. But Bill, and his kids from his previous marriage, were the only family I had; our parents had passed away a couple of years ago.

Susan was thinking; her lips were pursed. Her brown eyes briefly met mine, then looked at the floor. "You—you could come with me, if you want."

I exhaled noisily. It had always been something of a sore point between us. Susan had gone to church regularly her whole life. She knew when she married me that that was not something I did. I spent my Sunday mornings surfing the web and watching *This Week with Sam Donaldson and Cokie Roberts*. I'd made it plain to her when we started dating that I wouldn't be comfortable going to church. It would be too hypocritical, I said— an insult to those who believed.

Now, though, she clearly felt things had changed. Perhaps she expected me to want to pray, to want to make my peace with my maker.

"Maybe," I said, but I'm sure we both knew it wasn't going to happen.

It never rains but it pours.

Dealing with my cancer, of course, took a lot of my time. And Hollus's visits were now taking up most of the rest of it. But I had other responsibilities, too. I'd arranged for the special exhibition at the ROM of fossils from the Burgess Shale, and although we'd had the grand opening months ago, I still had a lot of administrative work related to it.

Charles Walcott of the Smithsonian discovered the Burgess Shale fossils in 1909 in the Burgess Pass through British Columbia's Rocky Mountains; he excavated there until 1917. Starting in 1975 and continuing for the next two decades, the ROM's own Desmond Collins began an ongoing and extremely fruitful series of new Burgess Shale excavations, uncovering additional

113

collecting fields and harvesting thousands of new specimens. In 1981, UNESCO named the Burgess Pass its eighty-sixth World Heritage site, in the same class as the pyramids of Egypt and the Grand Canyon.

The fossils date back to the middle Cambrian Period, 520 million years ago. The shale, which represents a mud slide from the Laurentian shelf that rapidly buried everything living on the sea floor, is so fine grained that it preserved impressions even of soft body parts. A huge diversity of lifeforms is recorded there, including many complex types that some paleontologists, including our own Jonesy, argue don't fit into any modern group. They appeared, existed briefly, then died out, as if nature were trying out all sorts of different body plans to see which ones worked best.

Why had this "Cambrian explosion" of diversity occurred? Life had already existed on Earth for perhaps 3.5 billion years, but, during all that time, it had taken very simple forms. What had caused so much complexity, and so much variety, to suddenly appear?

Davidson and Cameron at CalTech and Peterson at UCLA have argued that the reason for the simplicity prior to the Cambrian explosion was, well, simple: until that time, fertilized cells were severely limited in the number of times they could divide; ten or so divisions seemed to be the maximum. And ten divisions yields just 1,024 cells, producing quite small, and quite unsophisticated, creatures.

But at the beginning of the Cambrian, that ten-division barrier was smashed by the development of a new type of cell, still seen in some living organisms; these cells could divide many more times and were used to define the morphological space— the fundamental body shape—of all sorts of new organisms. (Although Earth had been four billion years old when that happened, the same breakthrough—smashing the ten-division limit—apparently occurred on Hollus's homeworld when it was just two billion years old; at that point life there also stopped spinning its wheels and started evolving in earnest.)

ROBERT J. SAWYER

Earth's Burgess Shale contains our direct ancestor *Pikaia,* the first animal with a notochord, from which the spinal column later evolved. Still, almost all the animal fossils from there are clearly invertebrates, and so a special exhibition of such fossils probably should have been organized by the ROM's senior invertebrate paleontologist, Caleb Jones.

But Jonesy was set to retire in a few months—no one had yet remarked, to me at least, on the fact that the ROM was going to lose its two most senior paleontologists almost simultaneously— and I was the one who had the personal relationship with the people at the Smithsonian, where Walcott's Burgess fossils had ended up before Canada had put laws in place protecting its antiquities. I also helped organize an ongoing series of public lectures to accompany the exhibition; most would be given by our own staff (including Jonesy), but we had also arranged for Stephen Jay Gould, whose book *Wonderful Life* is about the Burgess Shale fossils, to come up from Harvard and give a talk. The exhibition was proving to be a big moneymaker for the ROM; such shows always got us lots of free media coverage and so drew in the crowds.

I'd been excited about the exhibition when I'd first proposed it, and even more excited when it had been approved and the Smithsonian had come on board, agreeing to pool its fossils with ours for a joint show.

But now—

Now, with the cancer—

Now it was just an irritation, an inconvenience.

Yet another thing on my plate.

Yet another demand on my all-too-limited time.

Telling Ricky was the hardest.

You know, if I'd been like my dad—if I'd been content with a bachelor's degree and a regular nine-to-five—things would have been different. I'd probably have fathered my first child in my early twenties—and so, by the time I was the age I am now, that child would be in his thirties, and maybe even have kids of his own.

But I wasn't my dad.

I'd received my bachelor's in 1968, when I was twenty-two.

And my master's in 1970, when I was twenty-four.

And my Ph.D. when I was twenty-eight.

And then there was a postdoc at Berkeley.

And another at the University of Calgary.

And by that time I was thirty-four.

And making peanuts.

And, somehow, not meeting anyone.

And working late at the museum, night after night.

And then, before I knew it, I was forty and unmarried and without children.

Susan Kowalski and I had met at the University of Toronto's Hart House in 1966; we'd both been in the Drama Club. I wasn't an actor—but I had a fascination with theatrical lighting; I guess that's one of the reasons I like museology. Susan had performed in plays, although I suppose, in retrospect, that she'd never been particularly skilled at it. I'd always thought she was fabulous, but the best notices she ever got in the *Varsity* were that she was "competent" as Nurse in *Romeo and Juliet,* and that she "adequately essayed" Jocasta in *Oedipus Rex.* Anyway, we'd dated for a time, but then I headed off to the States for grad school—she'd understood that I had to go away to continue my studies, that my dream depended on it.

I'd thought of her fondly over the years, but never imagined I'd see her again. But I ended up back in Toronto, and, with my mind always on the past and never enough on the future, I finally decided when the big four-o rolled around that I needed some financial advice if I was ever going to be able to retire, and who should the accountant I ended up seeing be but Susan. Her last name had become DeSantis, legacy of a brief, failed marriage

ROBERT J. SAWYER

a decade and a half ago. We rekindled the old relationship and tied the knot a year later. And although she was forty-one then, and there were risks, we decided to have a baby. We tried for five years. Susan got pregnant once in that time, but she miscarried.

And so, at last, we decided to adopt. But that took a couple of years, too. Still, finally, we did have a son. Richard Blaine Jericho was now six years old.

He would not be out of the house by the time his father died.

He would not even be out of grade school.

Susan sat him down on the couch, and I knelt down by him.

"Hey, sport," I said. I took his little hand.

"Daddy." He squirmed a bit and didn't meet my eyes. Maybe he thought he was in trouble.

I was quiet for a few moments. I'd given a lot of thought to what I was going to say, but now the words I'd planned seemed completely inadequate.

"How you feelin', sport?" I asked.

"'Kay."

I glanced at Susan. "Well," I said, "Daddy isn't feeling so good."

Ricky looked at me.

"In fact," I said slowly, "Daddy's pretty sick." I let the words sink in.

We'd never lied to Ricky about anything. He knew he was adopted. We'd always told him that Santa Claus was just a story. And when he'd asked where babies came from, we'd told him that, too. Now, though, I wished we had perhaps taken a different route—that we hadn't always come clean with him.

Of course, he'd know soon enough. He'd see the changes—see me lose my hair, see me lose weight, hear me get up and vomit in the middle of the night, maybe . . .

Maybe even hear me cry when I thought he wasn't around.

"How sick?" asked Ricky.

"Very sick," I said.

He looked at me some more. I nodded: I wasn't kidding.

"Why?" asked Ricky.

Susan and I exchanged a glance. That was the same question I'd been asking myself. "I don't know," I said.

"Was it something you ate?"

I shook my head.

"Were you bad?"

It was an unexpected question. I thought about it for a few moments. "No," I said. "I don't think so."

We were all quiet for a time. Finally, Ricky spoke softly. "You're not going to die, are you, Daddy?"

I'd meant to tell him the truth, unvarnished. I'd meant to level with him. But, when the moment came, I had to give him more hope than Dr. Kohl had given me.

"Maybe," I said. Just maybe.

"But . . . " Ricky's voice was small. "But I don't want you to die."

I squeezed his hand. "I don't want to die, either, but . . . but it's like when Mommy and I make you clean your room. Sometimes we have to do things we don't want to do."

"I'll be good," he said. "I'll always be good, if you just don't die."

My heart hurt. Bargaining. One of the stages.

"I really don't have any choice in any of this," I said. "I wish I did, but I don't."

He was blinking a lot; soon the tears would come.

"I love you, Daddy."

"And I love you, too."

"What—what will happen to Mommy and me?"

"Don't worry, sport. You'll still live here. You won't have to worry about money. There's plenty of insurance."

Ricky looked at me, clearly not understanding.

"Don't die, Daddy," he said. "Please don't die."

I drew him close, and Susan put her arms around both of us.

ROBERT J. SAWYER

12

A s much as cancer frightened me as a victim, it fascinated me as a biologist.

Proto-oncogenes—the normal genes that have the potential to trigger cancer—exist in all mammals and birds. Indeed, *every* proto-oncogene identified to date is present in both mammals and birds. Now, birds evolved from dinosaurs which evolved from thecodonts which evolved from primitive diapsids which evolved from captorhinomorphs, the first true reptiles. Meanwhile, mammals evolved from therapsids which evolved from pelycosaurs which evolved from primitive synapsids which also evolved from captorhinomorphs. Since captorhinomorphs, the common ancestor, date back to the Pennsylvanian, almost 300 million years ago, the shared genes must have existed at least that long (and, indeed, we've found cancerous fossil bones that confirm that the big C existed at least as far back as the Jurassic).

In a way, it's not surprising that these genes *are* shared: proto-oncogenes are related to controlling cell division or organ growth; I suspect we'll eventually discover that the complete suite of them is common to all vertebrates, and, indeed, possibly to all animals.

The potential for cancer, it seems, is woven into the very fabric of life.

Hollus was intrigued by cladistics—the study of how shared features imply common ancestry; it was the principal tool for evolutionary studies on his world. It seemed appropriate, therefore, to show him our hadrosaurs—a clade if ever there was one.

It was Tuesday—the ROM's slowest day—and it was almost closing time. Hollus disappeared, and I worked my way through the museum over to the Dinosaur Gallery, carrying the holoform projector in my pocket. The gallery consists of two long halls, joined at their far ends; the entrance and the exit are side by side. I went in the exit and headed down. There was no one else present; several P.A. announcements about the imminent closing had moved the patrons out. At the far end of this hall is our hadrosaur room, painted with russet and golden horizontal stripes, representing sandstone from the Alberta badlands. The room contains three terrific wall mounts. I stood in front of the middle one, a duckbill, which the placard still called *Kritosaurus* even though we'd known for more than a decade that it was probably really a *Gryposaurus;* maybe my successor would find the time and money to update the gallery's signage. The specimen, which had been collected by Parks during the ROM's first field season in 1918, is lovely, with the ribs still in matrix and the stiffening tendons along the tail beautifully ossified.

Hollus wavered into existence, and I started talking about how the bodies of hadrosaurs were virtually indistinguishable from each other and that only the presence or absence of cranial crests, and the shapes of those crests, made it possible to tell the different genera apart. Just as I was working up a head of steam about this, a boy, maybe twelve years old, came into the room. He entered from the opposite side I had, coming out of the dimly lit Cretaceous-seas diorama. The boy was Caucasian but had epicanthic folds and a slack jaw, and his tongue protruded a bit from his mouth. He didn't say anything; he just kept staring at the Forhilnor.

ROBERT J. SAWYER

"Hell" "oh," said Hollus.

The boy smiled, apparently delighted to hear the alien speak. "Hello," he said back at us, slowly and deliberately.

A breathless woman rounded the corner, joining us in the Hadrosaur room. She let out a little yelp at the sight of Hollus and hurried over to the boy, taking his soft, chubby hand. "Eddie!" she said. "I've been looking all over for you." She turned to us. "I'm sorry if he was disturbing you."

Hollus said, "He" "was" "not."

The P.A. came on. "Ladies and gentlemen, the museum is now closed. Would all patrons please immediately go to the front exit . . . "

The woman pulled Eddie, who kept looking back over his shoulder at us, down through the rest of the Dinosaur Gallery.

Hollus turned to me. "That child was unlike any I have seen."

"He has Down syndrome," I said. "It retards mental and physical development."

"What causes it?"

"The presence of an extra chromosome twenty-one; all chromosomes should come in pairs, but sometimes a third one gets mixed in."

Hollus's eyestalks moved. "We have a similar condition, although it is almost always screened for in the womb. In our case, a chromosome pair forms without telomeres at one end; the two strands join at that end, making a chromosome twice as long as normal. The result is a complete loss of linguistic ability, many spatial-perception difficulties, and an early death." He paused. "Still, the resilience of life amazes me. It is remarkable that something as significant as an entire extra chromosome, or two chromosomes joining into one, does not prevent the organism from functioning." Hollus was still looking in the direction the child had disappeared. "That boy," he said. "Will his life be cut short, too?"

"Probably. Down syndrome has that effect."

"That is sad," said Hollus.

I was quiet for a time. There was a little alcove to one side of the room in which an ancient slide show was playing about how dinosaur fossils form and are excavated. I'd heard its soundtrack a million times, of course. Finally, though, it ended, and since no one had pushed the big red button to start it again, Hollus and I were alone in the silent gallery, only the skeletons for company.

"Hollus," I said at last.

The Forhilnor turned his attention back to me. "Yes?"

"How—how long are you planning to stay here? I mean, how much longer will you need my help?"

"I am sorry," said Hollus. "I have been inconsiderate. If I am taking up too much of your time, merely say so and I shall go."

"No, no, no. It's nothing like that. I'm enjoying this immensely, believe me. But . . . " I blew out air.

"Yes?" said the alien.

"I have something to tell you," I said at last.

"Yes?"

I took another deep breath, then let it out slowly. "I'm telling you this because you have a right to know," I said, pausing again, wondering how to continue. "I know that when you came to the museum, you simply asked to see a paleontologist—any paleontologist. You didn't seek me out in particular. Indeed, you could have gone to a different museum—Phil Currie at the Tyrrell or Mike Brett-Surman at the Smithsonian would have loved to have had you show up on their doorsteps."

I fell silent. Hollus continued to look at me patiently.

"I'm sorry," I said. "I should have told you this earlier." I inhaled again, held the air in as long as I could. "Hollus, I'm dying."

The alien repeated the word, as though somehow he'd missed it in his study of English. "Dying?"

"I have incurable cancer. I have only a matter of months to live."

ROBERT J. SAWYER

Hollus went silent for several seconds. Then his left mouth said, "I," but nothing more came for a time. At last, he started again. "Is it permissible to express regret at such a circumstance?"

I nodded.

"I" "am" "sorry," said his mouths. He was silent for a few seconds. "My own mother died of cancer; it is a terrible disease."

I certainly couldn't argue with that. "I know you still have a lot of research to do," I said. "If you'd prefer to work with somebody else, I'll understand."

"No," said Hollus. "No. We are a team."

I felt my chest constricting. "Thank you," I said.

Hollus looked at me a moment longer, then gestured at the wall-mounted hadrosaurs, the reason we'd come down here. "Please, Tom," he said. That was the first time he'd ever called me by my first name. "Let us continue with our work."

13

Whenever I encountered a new lifeform on Earth, I tried to imagine its ancestors—an occupational hazard, I guess. The same thing happened when Hollus finally introduced me to a Wreed; Wreeds were apparently shy, but I asked to meet one as part of the payment for examining our collections.

We used the conference room on the fifth floor of the Curatorial Centre; again, a series of video cameras were set up to record the event. I placed the holoform projector on the long mahogany table, next to the speaker phone. Hollus sang to it in his language, and suddenly there was a second alien in the room.

Humans, of course, evolved from fishes; our arms were originally pectoral fins (and our fingers originally the supporting bones that gave those fins stiffness), and our legs started out as pelvic fins.

Wreeds almost certainly started out as an aquatic form, as well. The Wreed that stood before me had two legs, but four arms, equally spaced around the top of a torso shaped like an inverted pear. But the four arms perhaps traced ancestry back not just to pectoral fins but also to asymmetrical dorsal and ventral fins. Those ancient pectoral fins had perhaps had four stiffening struts, for the left and right hands now had four fingers apiece (two central fingers and two mutually opposable thumbs). The front hand—presumably derived from the ventral fin—had nine fingers. And the back hand, which I supposed had descended from a dorsal fin, had, when I finally got a look at it, six thick fingers.

The Wreed had no head, and, as far as I could tell, it didn't have eyes or a nose, either. There was a glossy black strip running around the circumference of the upper torso; I had no idea what it was for. And there were areas with complicated folding of skin on either side of the front and back arms; I guessed that these might be ears.

Wreed skin was covered with the same material that had evolved on Earth in many spiders and insects, all mammals, a few birds, and even a few ancient reptiles: hair. There was about a centimeter of reddish-brown fur covering most of the Wreed's upper torso and the arms down to the elbows; the lower torso, the forearms, and the legs were naked, showing blue-gray leathery skin.

The only clothing the Wreed wore was a wide belt that encircled the narrow lower part of its torso; it was held up by the being's knobby hips. The belt reminded me of Batman's utility belt—it was even the same bright yellow, and it was lined with what I presumed were storage pouches. Instead of the bat emblem on the buckle, though, it sported a bright red pinwheel.

"Thomas Jericho," said Hollus, "this is T'kna."

"Hello," I said. "Welcome to Earth."

Wreeds, like humans, used a single orifice for speaking and eating; the mouth was located in a depression at the top of the torso. For several seconds T'kna made noises that sounded like rocks banging around inside a clothes dryer. Once the mouth stopped moving, there was a brief silence, then a deep, synthesized voice emerged from the thing's belt. It said: "Is one animate to speak as for the inanimate?"

I looked at Hollus, baffled by the Wreed's words. "Animate for the inanimate?" I said.

The Forhilnor clinked his eyes. "He is expressing surprise that you are welcoming him to the planet. Wreeds do not generalize from their species to their world. Try welcoming him on behalf of humanity instead."

"Ah," I said. I turned back to the Wreed. "As a human, I welcome you."

More tumbling rocks, then the synthesized voice: "Were you not human, would you welcome me still?"

"Umm . . . "

"The correct answer is yes," said Hollus.

"Yes," I said.

The Wreed spoke in its own language again, then the computer translated the words. "Then welcomed I am, and pleased to be here that is here and here that is there."

Hollus bobbed up and down. "That is a reference to the virtual-reality interface. He is happy to be here, but he acknowledges that he is really still on board the mothership, of course."

"Of course," I repeated. I was almost afraid to speak again. "Did you—um—did you have a good trip to Earth?"

"In which sense do you use 'good'?" said the synthesized voice.

I looked at Hollus again.

"He knows you employ the term *good* to mean many things, including moral, pleasant, and expensive."

"Expensive?" I said.

"'The good china,'" said Hollus. "'Good jewelry.'"

These darned aliens knew my own language better than I did. I turned my attention to the Wreed again. "I mean, did you have a pleasant trip?"

"No," he said.

Hollus interpreted again. "Wreeds only live for about thirty Earth years. Because of that, they prefer to travel in cryofreeze, a form of artificially suspended animation."

"Oh," I said. "So it wasn't a bad trip—he just wasn't aware of it, right?"

"That is right," said Hollus.

I tried to think of something to say. After all this time with

127

my Forhilnor friend, I'd grown used to having flowing conversations with an alien. "So, ah, how do you like it here? What do you think of Earth?"

"Much water," said the Wreed. "Large moon, aesthetically pleasing. Air too moist, though; unpleasantly sticky."

Now we were getting somewhere; I at least understood all that—although if he thought Toronto's air was sticky now, in spring, he had a real treat for him coming in August. "Are you interested in fossils, like Hollus is?"

Tossing gravel, then: "Everything fascinates."

I paused for a moment, deciding if I wanted to ask the question. Then I figured, why not? "Do you believe in God?" I asked.

"Do you believe in sand?" asked the Wreed. "Do you believe in electromagnetism?"

"That is a yes," said Hollus, trying to be helpful. "Wreeds often speak in rhetorical questions, but they have no notion of sarcasm, so do not take offense."

"More significant is whether God believes in me," said T'kna.

"How do you mean?" I asked. My head was starting to hurt.

The Wreed also seemed to be struggling with what to say; his mouth parts worked, but no sound emanated from them. At last he made sounds in his language, and the translator said, "God observes; wavefronts collapse. God's chosen people are those whose existence he/she/it validates by observing."

That one I was able to puzzle out even without Hollus playing interpreter. Quantum physics held that events don't take on concrete reality until they are observed by a conscious entity. That's all well and good, except how did the first concrete reality emerge? Some humans have used the requirements of quantum physics as an argument for the existence of a conscious observer who has been present since the beginning of time. "Ah," I said.

128

"Many possible futures," said T'kna, wriggling all his fingers simultaneously, as if to suggest the profusion. "From all that are possible, he/she/it chooses one to observe."

I got that, too—but it hit me hard. When Deep Blue beat Garry Kasparov at chess, it did so by seeing all the possible positions the chess pieces might have not just at the next turn but also at the one after that and the one after that, and so on.

If God existed, did he see all the possible next moves for all his playing pieces? Did he see right now that I might step forward, or cough, or scratch my bum, or say something that could ruin human-Wreed relations for all time? Did he simultaneously see that a little girl in China might walk to the right or the left or tip her head up to look at the moon? Did he also see an old man in Africa who might give a little boy a piece of advice that would change the child's life forever, or might not do so, leaving the youngster to figure things out for himself?

We could easily demonstrate that the universe does split, at least briefly, as it considers multiple possible paths: single photons interact with the alternate-universe versions of themselves as they pass simultaneously through multiple slits, producing interference patterns. Was that action of photons the sign of God thinking, the ghostly remnants of him having considered all the possible futures? Did God see all the conceivable actions for all conscious lifeforms—six billion humans, eight billion Forhilnors (as Hollus had told me at one point), fifty-seven million Wreeds, plus presumably countless other thinking beings throughout the universe—and did he calculate the game, the real game of Life, through all the panoply of possible moves for each player?

"You are suggesting," I said, "that God chooses moment by moment which present reality he wants to observe, and, by so doing, has built up a concrete history timeslice by timeslice, frame by frame?"

"Such must be the case," said the translated voice.

I looked at the strange, many-fingered Wreed and the bulky, spiderlike Forhilnor, standing there with me, a hairless (more so

129

than some these days), bipedal ape. I wondered if God was happy with the way his game was going.

"And now," said T'kna, through the translator, "reciprocity of interrogatives."

His turn to ask a question. Fair enough. "Be my guest," I said.

The convoluted skin on either side of his front arm wriggled up and down; I guessed this "ear shrug" was the Wreed way of saying "Pardon me?" "I mean go ahead. Ask your question."

"The same, reversed," said the Wreed.

"He means——," began Hollus.

"He means, Do I believe in God?" I said, understanding that he was throwing my question back at me. I paused, then: "It's my belief that even if God exists, he or she is utterly indifferent to what happens to any of us."

"You are wrong," said T'kna. "You should structure your life around God's existence."

"Umm, and what exactly would that entail?"

"Devoting half your waking life to attempts to communicate with him/her/it."

Hollus bent his four front-most legs, tipping his torso toward me. "You can understand why you do not often see Wreeds," he said in soft voices.

"There are some humans who devote that much of their time to prayer," I said, "but I'm not one of them."

"Prayer it is not," said the translator. "We desire nothing material from God; we wish merely to speak with him/her/it. And you should do the same; only one foolish would fail to spend considerable time trying to communicate with a God whose existence has been proved."

I'd encountered evangelical humans before—possibly more than my share, since my public talks on evolution often earned their wrath. When I was younger, I used to occasionally argue with them, but these days, I normally just smile politely and walk away.

ROBERT J. SAWYER

But Hollus responded for me. "Tom has cancer," he said. I was miffed; I'd expected him to keep that confidential, but, then again, the idea that medical matters are private might be uniquely human.

"Sorrow," said T'kna. He touched his belt buckle with the red pinwheel on it.

"There are lots of devoutly religious humans who have died horrible deaths from cancer and other diseases. How do you explain that? Hell, how do you explain the *existence* of cancer? What kind of god would create such a disease?"

"He/she/it may not have created it," said the deep, translated voice. "Cancer may have arisen spontaneously in one or multiple possible timeslices. But the future does not happen one at a time. Nor are there an infinite number of possibilities from which God may choose. The specific deployment of reality that included cancer, presumably undesirable, must have also contained something much desired."

"So he had to take the good with the bad?" I said.

"Conceivably," said T'kna.

"Doesn't sound like much of a god to me," I said.

"Humans are unique in believing in divine omnipotence and omniscience," said T'kna. "The true God is not a form idealized; he/she/it is real and therefore, by definition, imperfect; only an abstraction can be free of flaws. And since God *is* imperfect, there will be suffering."

An interesting notion, I had to admit. The Wreed made some more rattling sounds, and, after a bit, the translator spoke again. "The Forhilnors were surprised that we had any sophisticated cosmological science. But we had always known of the creation and destruction of virtual particles in what you call a vacuum. Just as the fallacy of a perfect God hampered your theology, so the fallacy of a perfect vacuum hampered your cosmology, for to argue that a vacuum is nothingness and that this nothingness is real is to argue that something exists which is nothing at all. There are no perfect vacuums; there is no perfect God. And

131

your suffering requires no more explanation than that unavoidable imperfection."

"But imperfection only explains why suffering begins," I said. "Once your God became aware that someone was suffering, if he did have the power to stop it, then surely, as a moral being, he would have to do so."

"If God is indeed aware of your illness and has done nothing," said T'kna's computer-generated voice, "then other concerns mandate that he/she/it let it run its course."

That was too much for me. "Damn you," I snapped. "I vomit *blood*. I have a six-year-old boy who is scared out of his mind—a boy who is going to have to grow up without a father. I have a wife who is going to be a widow before next summer. What other concerns could possibly outweigh those?"

The Wreed seemed agitated, flexing its legs as if ready to run, presumably an instinctive reaction to a threat. But, of course, he wasn't really here; he was safely aboard the mothership. After a moment, he calmed down. "Do you a direct answer desire?" asked T'kna.

I blew out air, trying to calm down; I'd forgotten about the cameras and now felt rather embarrassed. I guess I wasn't cut out to be Earth's ambassador. I glanced at Hollus. His eyestalks had stopped weaving; I'd seen them do that before when he was startled—my outburst had upset him, too.

"I'm sorry," I said. I inhaled deeply, then let it out slowly. "Yes," I said, nodding slightly. "I want an honest answer."

The Wreed rotated 180 degrees, so that its back was facing me—that's when I first got a glimpse of its rear hand. I later learned that if a Wreed faced you with its opposite side, it was about to say something particularly candid. His yellow belt had an identical buckle on its back, and he touched it. "This symbolizes my religion," he said. "A galaxy of blood—a galaxy of life." He paused. "If God did not directly create cancer, then to berate him/her/it for its existence is unjust. And if he/she/it did create it, then he/she/it did so because it is *necessary*. Your death

ROBERT J. SAWYER

may serve no purpose for yourself or your family. But if it does serve some purpose in the creator's plan, you should be grateful that, regardless of what pain you might feel, you are part of something that does have meaning."

"I don't feel grateful," I said. "I feel cursed."

The Wreed did something astonishing. It turned back around and reached out with its nine-fingered hand. My skin tingled as the force fields making up the avatar's arm touched my own hand. The nine fingers squeezed gently. "Since your cancer is unavoidable," said the synthesized voice, "perhaps you would find more peace if you believed what I believe rather than what you believe."

I had no answer for that.

"And now," said T'kna, "I must disengage; time it is again to attempt to communicate with God."

The Wreed wavered and vanished.

I merely wavered.

14

A *reconstruction . . .*

Half a city away, down by the shore of Lake Ontario, Cooter Falsey was sitting in a dingy motel room's overstuffed easy chair, hugging his knees and whimpering softly. "That wasn't supposed to happen," he said, over and over, almost as if it were a mantra, a prayer. "That wasn't supposed to happen."

Falsey was twenty-six, thin, blond, with a crew cut and teeth that should have received braces but never had.

J. D. Ewell sat down on the bed, facing Falsey. He was ten years older than Cooter, with a pinched face and longer dark hair. "Listen to me," he said gently. Then, more forcefully: "Listen to me!"

Falsey looked up, his eyes red.

"There," said Ewell. "That's better."

"He's dead," said Falsey. "That man on the radio said it: the doctor is dead."

Ewell shrugged. "An eye for an eye, you know?"

"I never wanted to kill anybody," said Falsey.

"I know," said Ewell. "But that doctor, he was doing the devil's work. You know that, Cooter. God will forgive you."

Falsey seemed to consider this. "You think?"

"Of course," said Ewell. "You and me, we'll pray for His forgiveness. And He'll grant it, you know He will."

"What'll happen to us if they catch us here?"

"Nobody's going to catch us, Cooter. Don't you worry about that."

"When can we go home?" Falsey said. "I don't like being in a foreign country. It was bad enough coming up to Buffalo, but at least that was the States. If we get caught, who knows what the Canucks will do to us. They might never let us go home."

Ewell thought about mentioning that at least Canada had no death penalty, but decided not to. Instead, he said, "We can't go back across the border yet. You heard the news report: they've already figured it was the same guys who did that clinic in Buffalo. Best we stay up here for a piece."

"I want to go home," said Falsey.

"Trust me," said Ewell. "It's better we stay awhile." He paused, wondering if it was time to broach the topic yet. "Besides, there's one more job we've got to do up here."

"I don't want to kill anybody again. I won't—I can't do that, J. D. I can't."

"I know," said Ewell. He reached out, stroked Falsey's arm. "I know. But you won't have to, I promise."

"You don't know that," said Falsey. "You can't be sure."

"Yes, I can," said Ewell. "You don't have to worry about killing anybody this time—because this time what we're going after is already dead."

"Well, *that* was a baffling conversation," I said, turning to Hollus after the Wreed had disappeared from the conference room.

Hollus's eyestalks did an S-ripple. "You can see why I like talking to you so much, Tom. At least I can understand you."

"T'kna's voice was translated, it seemed, by a computer."

"Yes," said Hollus. "Wreeds do not speak in a linear fashion. Rather, the words are woven together in a complex way that is

ROBERT J. SAWYER

utterly nonintuitive to us. The computer has to wait until they have finished speaking, then try to decipher their meaning."

I thought about this. "Is it something like those word puzzles? You know, the ones in which we write 'he himself,' but decode it as the word 'he' is adjacent to the word 'himself,' and read that as 'he is beside himself,' and then take that metaphorically to mean 'he was in a state of extreme excitement or agitation.'"

"I have not encountered such puzzles, but, yes, I suppose they are vaguely similar," said Hollus, "but with much more complex thoughts, and much more intricate relationships between the words. Context sensitivity is extremely important to the Wreeds; words mean entirely different things depending on where they are positioned. They also have a language full of synonyms that seem to mean exactly the same things, but only one of which is appropriate at any given time. It took us years to learn to communicate verbally with Wreeds; only a few of my people—and I am not one of them—can do it without a computer's aid. But even beyond the mere syntactic structures, Wreeds are different from humans and Forhilnors. They fundamentally do not think the same way we do."

"What's different about it?" I asked.

"Did you notice their digits?" asked Hollus.

"You mean their fingers? Yes. I counted twenty-three."

"You counted them, yes," said the Forhilnor. "That is what I had to do the first time I met a Wreed, too. But a Wreed would not have had to count. It would have simply known there were twenty-three."

"Well, they *are* its fingers . . . ," I said.

"No, no, no. It would not have had to count because it can perceive that level of cardinality at a glance." He bounced his torso. "It is amusing," he said, "but I have perhaps studied more human psychology than you have—not that it is my field, but . . . " He paused again. "That is another non-Wreed concept: the idea of having a specialized field of endeavor."

"You're making about as much sense as T'kna did," I said, shaking my head.

"You are correct; sorry. Let me attempt this passage again. I *have* studied human psychology—as much as one can from monitoring your radio and TV broadcasts. You said you counted twenty-three fingers on T'kna, and doubtless you did. You mentally said to yourself, one, two, three, *et cetera, et cetera,* all the way up to twenty-three. And, if you are like me, you probably had to redo the counting, just to be sure you had not got it wrong the first time."

I nodded; I had indeed done that.

"Well, if I showed you one object—one rock, say—you would not have to count it. You would just perceive its cardinality: you would know there was one object. The same thing happens with two objects. You just look at the pair of rocks and in a single glance, without any processing, you perceive that there are two of them present. You can do the same with three, four, or five items, if you are an average human. It is only when confronted with six or more items that you actually start counting them."

"How do you know this?"

"I watched a program about it on the Discovery Channel."

"All right. But how was this originally determined?"

"With tests to see how fast humans could count objects. If you are shown one, two, three, four, or five objects, you can answer the question about how many objects are present in roughly the same amount of time. Only for six or more objects does it take more time, and the amount of time it takes to report the tally goes up by an equal increment for every additional item present."

"I never knew that," I said.

"Live and learn," said Hollus. "Members of my species can usually perceive cardinality up to six—a slight improvement over what you can do. But the Wreeds shunt us completely away from the center; the typical Wreed can perceive cardinality up to forty-six, although some individuals can do it as high as sixty-nine."

"Really? But what happens when there are more items? Do they have to count them all, starting with item one?"

"No. Wreeds *cannot* count. They literally do not know how. Either they perceive the cardinality, or they do not. They have separate words for the numerals one to forty-six, and then they simply have a word that means 'many.'"

"But you said some of them can perceive higher numbers?"

"Yes, but they cannot articulate the total; they literally do not have the vocabulary for it. Those Wreeds who can perceive larger cardinalities obviously have a competitive advantage. One might offer to swap fifty-two domesticated animals for sixty-eight domesticated animals, and the other, less-gifted Wreed, knowing only that they are both large quantities would have no way to evaluate the fairness of the trade. Wreed priests almost always have a higher-than-normal ability to do this."

"Real cardinals of the church," I said.

Hollus got the pun. His eyestalks rippled as he said, "Exactly."

"Why do you suppose they never developed counting?"

"Our brains have only those abilities that evolution gave them. For the ancestors of your kind and mine, there were real-world, survival-oriented advantages to knowing how to determine quantities greater than five or six: if there are seven angry members of your species blocking your way on the left, and eight on the right, your chances, although slim, are still better with going to the left. If you have ten members of your tribe including yourself, and your job has been to gather fruit for dinner, you better come back with ten pieces, or you will make an enemy. Indeed, fetching just nine pieces will likely mean you yourself will have to forgo your fruit in order to placate the others, resulting in your having expended effort with no personal benefit.

"But Wreeds never form permanent groups larger than twenty

or so individuals—a quantity they can perceive as a gestalt. And if there are forty-nine enemies to your left and fifty on your right, the difference is immaterial; you are doomed either way." He paused. "Indeed, to use a human metaphor, one could say that nature dealt the Wreeds a lousy hand—or, actually, *four* lousy hands. You have ten fingers, which is a fine number: it lends itself to math, since it is an even number and can be divided into halves, fifths, and tenths; it is also the sum of the first four whole numbers: one plus two plus three plus four equals ten. We Forhilnors did well, too. We count by stomping our feet, and we have six of those—also an even number, and one that suggests halves, thirds, and sixths. And it is the sum of the first three whole numbers: one plus two plus three equals six. Again, a mental basis for mathematics.

"But the Wreeds have twenty-three fingers, and twenty-three is a prime number; it does not suggest any fractions other than twenty-thirds, a divisor too large for most real-world applications. And it is not the sum of any continuous sequence of whole numbers. Twenty-one and twenty-eight are the sums of the first six and first seven whole numbers, respectively; twenty-three has no such significance. With the arrangement of digits they have, they simply never developed counting or the kind of math we perform."

"Fascinating," I said.

"It is indeed," said Hollus. "More: you must have noticed T'kna's eye."

That surprised me. "Actually, no. He didn't seem to have any eyes."

"He has precisely one—that moist, black strip around the top of his torso. It is one long eye that perceives a complete 360-degree circle. A fascinating structure: the Wreed retina is layered with photoreceptive sheets that rapidly alternate in a staggered sequence between transparency and opacity. These sheets are stacked to a depth of more than a centimeter, providing sharp images at all focal lengths simultaneously."

140

"Eyes have evolved dozens of times in Earth's history," I said. "Insects and cephalopods and oysters and vertebrates and many others all developed eyes independently of each other. But I've never heard of an arrangement like that."

"Nor had we until we met the Wreeds," said Hollus. "But the structure of their eye also has an impact on the way they think. To stick with mathematics a moment longer, consider the basic model for all digital computers, whether made by humans or Forhilnors; it is the model, according to a documentary I saw on PBS, that you call the Turing machine."

The Turing machine is simply an infinitely long strip of paper tape divided into squares, coupled with a print/erase head that can move left, right, or remain motionless and can either print a symbol in a square or erase the symbol already there. By programming movements and actions for the print/erase head, any computable problem can be solved. I nodded for Hollus to go on.

"The Wreed eye sees a complete, all-around panorama, and it requires no focusing—all objects are perceived with equal clarity at all times. You humans and we Forhilnors use the words *concentrate* and *focus* to describe both setting one's attention and the act of thinking; you concentrate on an issue, you focus on a problem. Wreeds do neither; they perceive the world holistically, for they are physiologically incapable of focusing on one thing. Oh, they can prioritize in an intuitive sense: the predator up close is more important than the blade of grass far away. But the Turing machine is based on a kind of thought that is foreign to them: the print head is where all attention is concentrated; it is the focus of the operation. Wreeds never developed digital computers. They do, however, have analog computers and are adept at empirically modeling phenomenons, as well as understanding what factors go into producing them—but they cannot put forward a mathematical model. To put it another way, they can predict without explaining—their logic is intuitive, not deductive."

141

"Amazing," I said. "I'd have been inclined to think that mathematics would be the one thing we'd share with any other intelligent lifeform."

"That was our assumption, too. And, of course, the Wreeds have been disadvantaged in some ways by their lack of math. Radio eluded them—which is why despite all the listening your SETI projects have done to Delta Pavonis, they were never detected. My race was monumentally surprised to find a technological civilization when our first starship arrived there."

"Well, maybe Wreeds aren't really intelligent," I said.

"They are. They build the most beautiful cities out of the clay that covers most of their world. Urban planning is an art form for them; they see the whole metropolis as one cohesive entity. In fact, in many ways, they are more intelligent than we are. Well, perhaps that is an overstatement; let us say they are *differently* intelligent. The closest we come to having a common ground is in our use of aesthetics to evaluate scientific theories. You and I agree that the most beautiful theory is probably the correct one; we look for elegance in the way nature works. Wreeds share that, but understanding what constitutes beauty is much more innate in them; it lets them discern which of several theories is correct without testing them mathematically. Their sense of beauty also seems to have something to do with why they are so good at matters that perplex us."

"Such as?"

"Such as ethics and morality. There is no crime in Wreed society, and they seem able to solve the most vexing moral quandaries with ease."

"For example? What insights do they have on moral issues?"

"Well," said Hollus, "one of the simplest is that honor does not have to be defended."

"A lot of humans would disagree with that."

"None that are at peace with themselves, I suspect."

I thought about that, then shrugged. Maybe he was right. "What else?"

ROBERT J. SAWYER

"You tell me. Present an example of a moral quandary, and I will try to tell you how a Wreed would resolve it."

I scratched my head. "Well, okay—okay, how about this? My brother Bill got married recently for the second time. Now, his new wife Marilyn is quite lovely, I think—"

"The Wreeds would say you should not attempt to mate with your brother's spouse."

I laughed. "Oh, I know that. But that's not the question. I think Marilyn is lovely, but, well, she's quite curvy—*zaftig,* even. And she doesn't exercise. Now, Bill keeps bugging Marilyn to go to the gym. Meanwhile, Marilyn wants him to stop picking on her, saying he should accept her the way she is. And Bill says, 'Well, you know, if *I* should accept your not exercising, then *you* should accept my wanting to change you—since wanting to change people is a fundamental part of *my* character.' Get it? And, of course, Bill says his comments are selfless, motivated by genuine concern for Marilyn's health." I paused. The whole thing gives me a headache whenever I think about it; I always end up wanting to say, "Norman, coordinate!" I looked at Hollus. "So who is right?"

"Neither," said Hollus, at once.

"Neither?" I repeated.

"Exactly. That is an easy one, from a Wreed point of view; because they do not do math, they never treat moral questions as a zero-sum game in which someone must win and someone else must lose. God, the Wreeds would say, wants us to love others as they are *and* also to struggle to help them fulfill their potential—both should happen simultaneously. Indeed, a core Wreed belief is that our individual purpose in life is to help *others* become great. Your brother should not vocalize his displeasure at his wife's weight, but, until he attains that ideal of silence, his wife should ignore the comments; learning to ignore things is one of the great paths to inner peace, say the Wreeds. Meanwhile, though, if you are in a loving relationship, and your partner has grown dependent on you, you have an obligation to protect your own health by wearing safety belts in vehicles, by eating well, by exercising, and so on—that is Marilyn's moral obligation to Bill."

I frowned, digesting this. "Well, I guess that does make sense." Not that I could think of any way to communicate it to either Bill or Marilyn. "Still, what about something controversial. You saw that newspaper article about the bombed abortion clinic."

"The Wreeds would say that violence is not a solution."

"I agree. But there are lots of nonviolent people on both sides of the abortion issue."

"What are the two sides?" asked Hollus.

"They call themselves 'pro-life' and 'pro-choice.' The pro-lifers believe every conception has a right to fulfillment. The pro-choicers believe that women should have the right to control their reproductive processes. So who is correct?"

Hollus's eyestalks weaved with unusual speed. "Again, it is neither." He paused. "I hope I am not giving offense—it has never been my desire to be critical of your race. But it does astound me that you have both tattoo parlors and abortion clinics. The former—businesses devoted to permanently altering one's appearance—imply that humans can predict what they will want decades in the future. The latter—facilities to terminate pregnancies—imply that humans often change their minds over timeframes as short as a few months."

"Well, many pregnancies are unintentional. People have sex because it's fun; they do it even when they don't wish to procreate."

"Do you not have methods of contraception? If you do not, I am sure Lablok could devise some for you."

"No, no. We have many methods of birth control."

"Are they effective?" asked Hollus.

"Yes."

"Are they painful?"

ROBERT J. SAWYER

"Painful? No."

"The Wreeds would say that abortion, then, should simply not be a moral issue because simple precautions would obviate the need to discuss it at all, except in a handful of unusual cases. If one can easily choose not to get pregnant, then surely that is the proper exercising of choice. If you can avoid a difficult moral problem, such as when life begins, then why not simply do so?"

"But there are cases of rape and incest."

"Incest?"

"Mating within one's own family."

"Ah. But surely these are exceptional occurrences. And possibly the best moral lesson my own people have learned during our association with the Wreeds is that general principles should not be based on exceptional cases. That one insight has enormously simplified our legal system."

"Well, then, what *do* you do in exceptional cases? What should you do in the case of a rape resulting in pregnancy?"

"Obviously, the woman had no chance to proactively exercise her reproductive rights via contraception; therefore, clearly she should be permitted to regain control of her own biology as fully and completely as she desires. In such cases, abortion is obviously an acceptable option; in others, birth control is clearly the preferred route."

"But there are humans who believe artificial birth control is immoral."

Hollus's eyes looked briefly at each other, then they resumed their normal oscillating. "You humans do seem to go out of your way to manufacture moral issues. There is nothing immoral about contraception." He paused. "But these are easy examples of Wreed thinking. When we get into more complex areas, I am afraid their responses do not make much sense to us; they sound like gibberish—our brains apparently are not wired to appreciate what they are saying. Philosophy departments at the

Forhilnor equivalents of what you call universities had little status until we met the Wreeds; they are now extremely busy, trying to decipher complex Wreed thought."

I considered all of this. "And with minds geared for ethics and for discerning underlying beauty, the Wreeds have decided that God really does exist?"

Hollus flexed his six legs at both their upper and lower knees. "Yes."

I'm not an overly arrogant man. I don't insist that people refer to me as Doctor Jericho, and I try to keep my opinions to myself. But, still, I always felt I had a good grip on reality, an accurate view of the world.

And my world, even before I was stricken with cancer, did not include a god.

But I'd now met not one but two different alien lifeforms, two different beings from worlds more advanced than my own. And both of these advanced creatures believed the universe was created, believed it showed clear evidence of intelligent design. Why did this surprise me so much? Why had I assumed that such thoughts would be, well, *alien* to any advanced being?

Since ancient times, the philosophers' secret has always been this: *we* know that God does not exist, or, at least, if he does, he's utterly indifferent to our individual affairs—but we can't let the rabble know that; it's the fear of God, the threat of divine punishment and the promise of divine reward, that keeps in line those too unsophisticated to work out questions of morality on their own.

But in an advanced race, with universal literacy and material desires fulfilled through the power of technology, surely *everyone* is a philosopher—everyone is privy to the ancient, once-guarded truth, everyone knows that God is just a story, just a myth, and we can drop the pretense, dispensing with religion.

Of course, it's possible to enjoy the traditions of a religion—the ceremonies, the ties with the past—without believing in

God. After all, as one of my Jewish friends has been known to observe, the only Jews who survived World War II were either now atheists or hadn't been paying attention.

But, in fact, there are millions of Jews who believe—really believe—in God (or G-d); indeed, secular Zionist Judaism was on the wane while formal observance was rising. And there are millions of Christians who believe in the holy threefer of, as one of my Catholic friends occasionally quipped, Big Daddy, Junior, and the Spook. And there are millions of Muslims who embraced the Qur'an as the revealed word of God.

Indeed, even here, at the dawn of the century following the one in which we'd discovered DNA and quantum physics and nuclear fission and in which we'd invented computers and spaceships and lasers, ninety-six percent of the world's population still really believed in a supreme being—and the percentage was rising, not falling.

So, again, why was I so surprised that Hollus believed in God? That an alien from a culture a century or two more advanced than my own hadn't shucked off the last vestiges of the supernatural? Even if he hadn't had a grand unified theory to justify his beliefs, why should it be so outlandish that he wasn't an atheist?

I'd never questioned whether I was right or wrong when confronted by obviously deluded creationists. I'd never doubted my convictions when assailed by fundamentalists. But here I was, meeting with creatures from other stars, and the fact that they had been able to come to me while I had no way of going to see them made blindingly obvious which of us was intellectually superior.

And these aliens believed what I hadn't since childhood.

They believed an intelligent designer had made the universe.

15

T here are two reasons why a patient might wish to undergo chemotherapy," Katarina Kohl had said to Susan and me, shortly after my diagnosis. "The first is in hopes of eliminating the cancer." She looked at me, then at Susan, then back again at me. "But I will tell you the truth: the chances of eliminating your cancer are small, Tom. Lung cancer is only rarely cured."

"Well, then I don't want chemo," I said at once. "I don't want what's left of my life to be spent suffering through that."

Dr. Kohl pursed her lips. "It is certainly your decision to make," she said. Then, nodding at Susan, "Both of you. But there are many misconceptions about chemo. It can also be palliative—that's the second reason you might consider it."

My mouth formed the word *palliative*. Dr. Kohl nodded. "You may very well experience a lot of pain in the months to come, Tom. Chemotherapy can reduce the severity of the pain by reducing the size of the tumors."

"What would you do, if you were me?" I asked.

Kohl shrugged a little. "If this were the States—if you were uninsured and had to pay for the chemotherapy treatments yourself, perhaps you might want to forgo them and live with the pain—although of course, either way, I will be prescribing analgesics to help with that. I like to use a platinum compound when dealing with non-small-cell lung cancer, and those compounds are quite expensive. But since OHIP will pay the entire cost of the treatments, I would advise you to have them. We'd use a platinum in combination with vinblastine, etoposide, or mitomycin-C. The platinum drugs have to be administered in hospital, but they're the best bet with lung cancer."

"What about side effects?" I asked.

"There can be nausea. You may lose some or all of your hair."

"I want to keep working as long as I can," I said.

"The chemo can help; it won't significantly extend your life, but it may make it more productive."

Ricky was in school full days now, and Susan had her job. If I could continue to work, even a few months longer, that would be better than having to be home, requiring constant care.

"Don't make your decision right now," said Dr. Kohl. "Think about it." She gave us some pamphlets to read.

Hollus believed in God.

T'kna believed in God.

And me?

"Maybe I'm getting hung up on the word *God*," I said to Hollus, once we were back in my office. "Certainly, if you want to propose that evolution on Earth was interfered with by an outside source, I can't say you are wrong. After all, you yourself told me that there were intelligent aliens in this part of the galaxy as much as three billion years ago."

"The race from Eta Cassiopeae A III, yes."

"Aren't those the ones who blew up their moon?"

"No; that was the race of Mu Cassiopeae A Prime, 5.5 light-years from Eta Cassiopeae."

"Okay. Well, the beings from Eta Cassiopeae—let's call them Etans—had a technological civilization three billion years ago,

ROBERT J. SAWYER

back when life was just beginning on my world. Surely the Etans could have come here then."

"You are glossing over a lot of time," said Hollus, "for you said life had existed here for at least eight hundred million, if not a full billion, years prior to three billion years ago."

"Well, yes, but—"

"And, of course, my own sun, Beta Hydri, had not even formed that long ago; as I told you before, it is only 2.6 billion years old, so no one from Eta Cassiopeae could have ever visited it."

"Well, maybe it wasn't the Etans, then—but beings from some other star could have come here, or gone to your world, or to the Wreed world. All the actions you ascribe to God could have been the doing of advanced aliens."

"There are two problems with your argument," said Hollus, politely. "First, of course, even if you dispense with the need for a god in recent events—events of the last few billion years; events after other conscious observers had emerged in this universe—you have done nothing to dispense with the need for a designer who set the relative strengths of the five fundamental forces, who designed the thermal and other properties of water, and so on. And therefore what you are doing is contrary to the razor of Occam you spoke of: you are increasing, not reducing, the number of entities that have influenced your existence—one unavoidable god to create the universe, and then optional lesser beings who subsequently became interested in manipulating the development of life.

"Second," continued Hollus, "you must remember the timing of the mass extinctions apparently orchestrated to occur simultaneously on our three worlds: the oldest was 440 million years ago; the most recent, 65 million years. That is a span of 375 million years—and yet, as we have found, the lifespan of an intelligent race, measured from the point at which it develops radio, is apparently no more than a couple of hundred years before it either destroys itself or disappears."

CALCULATING GOD

My mind raced, careened. "All right," I said at last. "Maybe the fundamental parameters *were* tweaked to create a universe that could give rise to life."

"There is no supposition involved," said Hollus. "The universe was clearly designed to be biogenerative."

"All right. But if we accept that, surely simply creating life can't be the sole goal. You must believe your putative designer wanted not just life, but *intelligent* life. Unintelligent life is really nothing more than complex chemistry. It's only when it becomes sapient that life really gets interesting."

"That is a strange thing for someone who studies dinosaurs to say," observed Hollus.

"Not really. After all, the dinosaurs disappeared sixty-five million years ago. It's only because of the advent of intelligence that we know they ever existed." I paused. "But you are touching on the point I'm trying to make." I stopped again, searching for the appropriate metaphor. "Do you cook?"

"Cook? You mean make food from raw materials?"

"Yes."

"No."

"Well, I do, or at least I used to. And there are things that you simply can't make by throwing in all the ingredients together at the beginning. If you want to cook them, you have to intervene halfway through."

Hollus thought about this. "So you are suggesting there is no way the creator could have achieved intelligent life without direct intervention? Many who are religious would object to that notion, for occasional intervention implies a God who is usually absent from the universe."

"I'm not implying anything," I said. "I'm just analyzing the assumptions inherent in your beliefs. Look, the dinosaurs dominated this planet for far more time than mammals have, and yet they never achieved anything even remotely like real intelligence. Although their brains got slightly bigger over time, even the most intelligent dinosaur that ever lived"—I picked up Phil

ROBERT J. SAWYER

Currie's *Troödon* skull, now on a shelf behind my desk—"was no more intelligent than the dumbest mammal. In fact, there was no way they could *ever* become substantially more intelligent. The part of the mammalian brain in which intelligence resides doesn't exist in reptiles." I paused. "You told me that the creatures that were dominant on your planet until sixty-five million years ago—those pentapeds—were also dumb brutes, and you said that a similar situation existed on Delta Pavonis."

"Yes."

"And that your ancestors at that time were like my ancestors and the ancestors of the Wreeds: small creatures, living at the margins of the ecosystem."

"That is correct," said Hollus.

"But those ancestors *did* have brains capable of evolving intelligence," I said. "My ancestors were crepuscular: they were active at twilight. And so they developed big eyes and sophisticated visual cortices. And, of course, the brain power to process the resulting images."

"You are suggesting that the infrastructure for intelligence can only arise in those animals at the—what was your phrase?—at the margins of an ecosystem? Animals forced to forage at night?"

"Perhaps. And if that's so, then intelligence can only come to fruition if the dominant, dumb animals are wiped out."

"I suppose," said Hollus. "But—oh, I see. I see. You are saying conditions that might give rise to life, and even the beginnings of intelligence, could be coded into the very design of the universe, but there is no way to bring intelligence to the fore, to let it flourish and develop, without direct intervention."

To my own surprise, I said, "That's my proposal, yes."

"That explains the extinctions sixty-five million years ago. But what about the earlier extinctions?"

"Who knows? Presumably they were also required to move the ecosystem toward the eventual development of intelligence. On Earth, the end-of-the-Permian extinctions helped clear the way for mammallike reptiles—the ancestors of mammals. Their ability to regulate body temperature was perhaps irrelevant in the benign climate that existed until the worldwide glaciation that caused those extinctions. But during a glacial event, even a primitive thermal-regulatory ability would be an asset—and I rather suspect that the true warm-bloodedness, which evolved from that capability, is another prerequisite for intelligence. So the Permian extinction was a way to substantially increase the percentage of nascent endotherms, making sure they weren't outcompeted and eliminated from the gene pool."

"But how could the creator force an ice age?" asked Hollus.

"Well, if we assume he lobbed an asteroid at each of our worlds to end the Cretaceous, he could have broken up an asteroid or two in orbit to form rings around each of the planets at the end of the Permian. A ring like that, properly tilted, could substantially shade the planet, lowering its temperature enough to bring on massive glaciation. Or he could have generated a dust cloud that enveloped all of this part of the galaxy, shading all the planets—yours, mine, and the Wreeds'—simultaneously."

"And the other mass extinctions?" asked Hollus.

"More fine tuning along the way. The one in the Triassic, for instance, allowed the dinosaurs, or their counterparts, to come into ascendancy on the three worlds. Without dinosaurs dominating the ecosystem, mammals—or the endothermic octopeds on Beta Hydri III, and the live-birthers like T'kna on Delta Pavonis II—would never have been forced into the crepuscular existence that fostered the development of bigger brains. It takes wits to eke out a living when you're not the dominant form."

It was strange to hear the giant spider play devil's advocate. "But the only direct evidence," he said, "for the creator having manipulated the evolution of life once it got started is the coincidences in the dates of the mass extinctions on Beta Hydri III, Delta Pavonis II, and Sol III. Yes, possibly, the creator did simi-

ROBERT J. SAWYER

larly manipulate the development of life on the six abandoned worlds we visited, but we could find no unequivocal evidence of that."

"Well, perhaps intelligence *can* develop in this universe through happenstance," I said. "Even by random chance, asteroids do crash into planets every ten million years or so. But you'll never get *multiple* intelligent species existing simultaneously unless you jigger the timetable—and not just once, but several times. To invoke the cooking metaphor, sure, maybe a salad could appear on its own by random chance—wind blowing enough vegetable matter together, say. And maybe a steak might appear on its own—lightning hitting a cow just the right way. And you might end up with wine—grapes that had accumulated in one place and had fermented. But there's just no way to get it all to come together simultaneously—a glass of wine, a salad, and a steak—without lots of intervention. The same might be true of getting multiple sentient lifeforms to appear simultaneously."

"But that raises the question of why God wants multiple sapients at the same time," said the alien.

I scratched my chin. "That *is* a good question."

"It is indeed," said Hollus.

We contemplated this for a time, but neither of us had a good answer. It was almost 5:00 P.M. "Hollus?" I said.

"Yes?"

"I have a favor to ask."

His eyestalks stopped moving. "Yes?"

"I would like you to come home with me. I mean, let me take the holoform projector back to my house and have you appear there."

"To what purpose?"

"It's . . . it's what humans do. We have friends over for dinner. You could meet my family."

"Friends . . . ," said Hollus.

155

Suddenly I felt like an idiot. I was a primitive being next to Hollus; even if his psychology permitted him to feel affection for others, surely he had no warm feelings toward me. I was just a means to an end.

"I'm sorry," I said. "I didn't mean to impose."

"You are not imposing," Hollus said. "I am pleased that you feel for me what I feel for you." His eyestalks danced. "I would very much like to meet your family and visit your home."

I was surprised to find my eyes misting over. "Thank you," I said. "Thank you very much." I paused. "Of course, I could have them come here, if you prefer. We don't have to go to my house."

"No," said Hollus. "I would like to do that. Your family consists of your mate Susan, correct?" He'd heard me talk to her on the phone several times now.

"Yes. And my son Ricky." I turned the little picture frame on my desk around so that Hollus could see him.

The eyestalks converged on the frame. "His countenance is not similar to yours."

"He's adopted," I said with a little shrug. "He's not my biological child."

"Ah," said Hollus. "I would enjoy meeting them both. Is tonight too soon?"

I smiled. Ricky would love this. "Tonight is just perfect," I said.

ROBERT J. SAWYER

16

C ooter Falsey's eyebrows knit in confusion as he looked at J. D. Ewell. "What do you mean, what we're going after is already dead?"

Ewell was still sitting on the edge of the motel bed. "They've got a museum here in Toronto, and it's got some special fossils on display. Those fossils are a lie, says Reverend Millet. A blasphemy. And they'll be showing those fossils to that great big spider alien."

"Yeah?" said Falsey.

"This world is a testament to God's handiwork. And those fossils, they either are fakes or the work of the devil. Creatures with five eyes! Creatures with spikes sticking out everywhere! You've never seen the like. And scientists are telling the aliens that those things are real."

"All fossils are fake," said Falsey. "Created by God to test the faith of the weak."

"You and I know that. And it's bad enough the atheists are able to teach our kids about fossils in schools, but now they are showing them to aliens, making those aliens think we believe the lie of evolution. The aliens are being led to believe that we humans *don't* believe in God. We've got to make it clear that those godless scientists aren't speaking for the majority."

"So . . . ," said Falsey, inviting Ewell to continue.

"So, Reverend Millett, he wants us to destroy those fossils. The Bogus Shale, he calls them. They're on special display here, and then they're supposed to travel down to Washington, but that won't happen. We're going to put an end to the Bogus Shale once and for all, so those aliens will know that we don't care about such things."

"I don't want anyone to get hurt," said Falsey.

"No one will."

"What about the alien? Doesn't one of them spend a lot of time at the museum. We'll be in a powerful lot of trouble if we hurt him."

"Don't you read the papers? He's not really there; that's just a projection."

"But what about the people who go to the museum? They may be misguided, looking on all them fossils, but they aren't evil like those abortion docs."

"Don't worry," said Ewell. "We'll do it on a Sunday night, after the museum has closed."

I called Susan and Ricky and told them to prepare for a very special guest; Susan could do miracles with three hours' notice. I worked on my journal for a time, then left the museum. I'd taken to wearing a floppy Tilley hat and sunglasses to disguise my appearance for the short walk from the staff entrance to the subway station; the UFO nuts still seemed to mostly congregate out in front of the ROM's main entrance, quite some distance away. So far, none of them had intercepted me—and by the time I came out this evening, they all seemed to have gone home, anyway. I went down into the subway station and boarded a silver train.

When we pulled into Dundas station, a young man with a wispy blond beard entered the train. He was the right age to be a student at Ryerson; that university's campus was just north of Dundas. The young man was wearing a green sweatshirt covered with white lettering that said:

ROBERT J. SAWYER

I smiled; the provincial parliament buildings were at Queen's Park, of course. Everyone, it seemed, was taking shots at Premier Harris these days.

When I finally arrived at the house on Ellerslie, I gathered my wife and son, and we went into the living room. I opened my briefcase and put the dodecahedron that was the holoform projector on the coffee table. Then I sat on the couch. Ricky scrambled up next to me. Susan perched herself on the arm of the love seat. I looked at the blue clock on the VCR. It was 7:59 P.M.; Hollus had agreed to join us at 8:00.

We waited, with Ricky fidgeting. The projector always made a two-toned bleep when turning on, but so far, it was dead silent.

8:00.

8:01.

8:02.

I knew the VCR clock was right; we had a Sony unit that picked up a time signal over the cable. I reached over to the coffee table and adjusted the dodecahedron's position slightly, as if that would make any difference.

8:03.

8:04.

"Well," said Susan, generally to the room. "I should go make the salad."

Ricky and I continued to wait.

At 8:10, Ricky said, "What a ripoff."

"I'm sorry, sport," I said. "I guess something came up." I couldn't believe that Hollus had let me down. A lot of things are forgivable; making a man look bad in the eyes of his son isn't one of them.

"Can I go watch TV until it's time for dinner?" Ricky asked.

We normally let Ricky watch only one hour of TV a night, 159 and he'd already done that. But I couldn't disappoint him again. "Sure," I said.

Ricky got up. I let out a heavy sigh.

He'd said we were friends.

Ah, well. I stood up, picked up the projector, weighed it in my hand, then put it back in my briefcase, and—

A sound, from the back door. I closed my briefcase and headed off to investigate. Our back door opened onto a wooden deck that my brother-in-law Tad and I had built five summers ago. I opened the vertical blinds over the sliding glass door, and—

It was Hollus, standing on my deck.

I removed the security rod along the base of the glass door and slid the door open. "Hollus!" I said.

Susan had appeared behind me, wondering what I was up to. I turned to look at her; she'd seen Hollus and other Forhilnors often enough on TV, but her mouth was now agape.

"Come in," I said. "Come in."

Hollus managed to squeeze through the doorway, although it was a tight fit. He had changed for dinner; he was now wearing a wine-colored cloth, fastened with a polished slice out of a geode. "Why didn't you appear inside?" I asked. "Why project yourself outside?"

Hollus's eyestalks moved. There was something subtly different about the way he looked. Maybe it was just the lighting, from a halogen torchiere lamp; I was used to seeing him under the fluorescent panels we have at the museum.

"You invited me to your home," he said.

"Yes, but—"

Suddenly, I felt his hand upon my arm. I'd touched him before, felt the static tingle of the force fields that composed his projection. This was different. His flesh was solid, warm.

"So I came," he said. "But—I am sorry; I have been out there for a quarter of an hour, trying to figure out how to let you

160

know that I had arrived. I had heard of doorbells, but could not find the button."

"There isn't one at the back door," I said. My eyes were wide. "You're here. In the flesh."

"Yes."

"But—" I peered behind him. There *was* something large in the backyard; I couldn't quite make out its form in the gathering darkness.

"I have been studying your planet for a year," Hollus said. "Surely you must have suspected we had ways to reach your planet's surface without attracting undo attention." He paused. "You invited me for dinner, did you not? I cannot enjoy your food via telepresence."

I was amazed, thrilled. I turned to look at Susan, then realized I'd forgotten to introduce her. "Hollus, I'd like you to meet my wife, Susan Jericho."

"Hell," "oh," said the Forhilnor.

Susan was quiet for a few seconds, stunned. Then she said, "Hello."

"Thank you for allowing me to visit your home," Hollus said.

Susan smiled, then looked rather pointedly at me. "If I'd had more advance notice, I could have cleaned the place up."

"It is lovely as is," said Hollus. His eyestalks swiveled, taking in the room. "Great care has obviously gone into the selection of each piece of furniture so that it complements the others." Susan normally couldn't stand spiders, but the big guy was clearly charming the pants off her.

In the bright light of the torchiere, I noticed tiny studs, like little diamonds, set into his bubble-wrap skin at each of the two joints in his limbs, and the three joints in his fingers. And a full row of them ran along each of his eyestalks. "Is that jewelry?" I said. "If I knew you were interested in such things, I'd have shown you the gem collections at the ROM. We've got some fabulous diamonds, rubies, and opals."

"What?" said Hollus. And then, realizing, his eyestalks did their S-ripple again. "No, no, no. The crystals are the implants for the virtual-reality interface; they are what allow the telepresence simulacrum to mimic my moves."

"Oh," I said. I turned around and shouted out Ricky's name. My son came bounding up the stairs from the basement. He started to head to the dining room, thinking I'd called him for dinner. But then he caught sight of me and Susan and Hollus. His eyes went wider than I'd ever seen them. He came over to me, and I put an arm around his shoulders.

"Hollus," I said, "I'd like you to meet my son Rick."

"Hell" "oh," said Hollus.

I looked down at my boy. "Ricky, what do you say?"

Ricky's eyes were still wide as he looked at the alien. "Cool!"

We hadn't expected Hollus to show up for dinner in the flesh. Our dining-room table was a long rectangle, with a removable leaf in the middle. The table itself was dark wood, but it was covered with a white tablecloth. There really wasn't much room for the Forhilnor. I had Susan help me move the sideboard out of the way to free up some space.

I realized I'd never seen Hollus sit down; his avatar obviously didn't need to, but I thought the real Hollus might be more comfortable if he had some support. "Is there anything I can do to make you more comfortable?" I asked.

Hollus looked around. He spotted the ottoman in the living room, positioned in front of the love seat. "Could I use that?" he said. "The little stool?"

"Sure."

Hollus moved into the living room. With a six-year-old boy around, we didn't have any breakables out, which was a good thing. Hollus bumped the coffee table and the couch on his way; our furniture wasn't spread out enough for a being of his pro-

ROBERT J. SAWYER

portions. He brought back the ottoman, placed it by the table, then stepped over it, so that his round torso was directly above the circular stool. He then lowered his torso down onto it. "There," he said, sounding content.

Susan looked quite uncomfortable. "I'm sorry, Hollus. I didn't think you were actually, really coming. I have no idea whether what I made is something you can eat."

"What did you make?"

"A salad—lettuce, cherry tomatoes, diced celery, bits of carrot, croutons, and an oil-and-vinegar dressing."

"I can eat that."

"And lamb chops."

"They are cooked?"

Susan smiled. "Yes."

"I can eat that, too, if you can provide me with about a liter of room-temperature water to go with it."

"Certainly," she said.

"I'll get it," I said. I went to the kitchen and filled a pitcher with tap water.

"I've also made milk shakes for Tom and Ricky."

"This is the bovine mammary secretion?" asked Hollus.

"Yes."

"If it is not rude to do so, I will not partake."

I smiled, and Ricky, Susan, and I took our places at the table. Susan brought the salad bowl out and passed it to me. I used the serving forks to move some to my plate, then loaded some onto Ricky's. I then put some on Hollus's plate.

"I have brought my own utensils," he said. "I hope that is not rude."

"Not at all," I said. Even after my trips to China, I was still one of those who always had to ask for a knife and fork in a Chinese restaurant. Hollus pulled two devices that looked a bit like corkscrews from the folds of the cloth wrapped around his torso.

"Do you say grace?" asked Hollus.

The question startled me. "Not normally."

"I have seen it on television."

"Some families do it," I said. Those that have things to be thankful for.

Hollus used one of his corkscrews to stab some lettuce, and he conveyed it to the orifice on top of his circular body. I'd watched him make the motions of eating before, but had never seen him actually do it. It was a noisy process; his dentition made a snapping sound as it worked. I suppose only his speaking orifices were miked when he used his avatar; I presumed that was why I'd never heard the sound before.

"Is the salad okay?" I asked him.

Hollus continued to transfer it into his eating orifice while he spoke; I guessed that Forhilnors never choked to death while dining. "It is fine, thank you," he said.

Ricky spoke up. "Why do you talk like that?" he asked. My son imitated Hollus by speaking in turns out of the left and right sides of his mouth. "It" "is" "fine" "thank" "you."

"Ricky!" said Susan, embarrassed that our son had forgotten his manners.

But Hollus didn't seem to mind the question. "One thing that humans and my people share is a divided brain," he said. "You have a left and right hemisphere, and so do we. We hold that consciousness is the result of the interplay of the two hemispheres; I believe humans have some similar theories. In cases where the hemispheres have been severed due to injury, so that they function independently, whole sentences come out of a single speaking orifice, but much less complex thoughts are expressed."

"Oh," said Ricky, going back to his salad.

"That's fascinating," I said. Coordinating speech between partially autonomous brain halves must be difficult; maybe that was why Hollus was apparently incapable of using contractions. "I wonder if we had two mouths, whether humans would alternate words or syllables between them as well."

164

"You seem to rely less on left-right integration than we Forhilnors do," Hollus said. "I understand that in cases of a severed *corpus callosum,* humans can still walk."

"I think that's right, yes."

"We cannot," Hollus said. "Each half of the brain controls three legs, on the corresponding side of the body. All our legs have to work together, or we topple over, and—"

"My daddy is going to die," said Ricky, looking down at his salad plate.

My heart jumped. Susan looked shocked.

Hollus put down his eating utensils. "Yes, he told me. I am very sorry about that."

"Can you help him?" asked Ricky, looking now at the alien.

"I am sorry," said Hollus. "There is nothing I can do."

"But you're from space and stuff," said Ricky.

Hollus's eyestalks stopped moving. "Yes, I am."

"So you should know things."

"I know some things," he said. "But I do not know how to cure cancer. My own mother died from it."

Ricky regarded the alien with great interest. He looked like he wanted to offer a word of comfort to the alien, but he clearly had no idea what to say.

Susan stood up and brought the lamb chops and mint jelly in from the kitchen.

We ate in silence.

I realized that an opportunity had presented itself that wasn't likely to be repeated.

Hollus was here in the flesh.

After dinner, I asked him down to the den. He had some trouble negotiating the half-flight of stairs, but he managed.

I went to a two-drawer filing cabinet and pulled out a sheaf of papers. "It's normal for people to write a document called a 165 will to indicate how one's personal effects should be distributed after death," I said. "Naturally, I'm leaving almost everything to Susan and Ricky, although I'm also making some bequests to charities: the Canadian Cancer Society, the ROM, a couple of others. There are also a few things going to my brother, his children, and one or two other relatives." I paused. "I—I've been thinking of amending my will to leave something to you, Hollus, but—well, it seemed pointless. I mean, you won't likely be around after I'm gone, and, well, usually you're not really here, anyway. But tonight . . . "

"Tonight," agreed Hollus, "it is the real me."

I held out the sheaf of papers. "It's probably simplest if I just give you this now. It's the typescript for my book *Canadian Dinosaurs*. These days, people write books on computers, but that one was banged out on a manual typewriter. It doesn't have any real value, and the information is now very much out of date, but it's my little contribution to the popular literature about dinosaurs, and, well, I'd like you to have it—one paleontologist to another." I shrugged a little. "Something to remember me by."

The alien took the papers. His eyestalks weaved in and out. "Your family will not want this?"

"They have copies of the finished book."

He unwrapped a portion of the cloth around his torso, revealing a large plastic carrying pouch. The manuscript pages fit in with room to spare. "Thank you," he said.

There was silence between us. At last, I said, "No, Hollus—thank you. For everything." And I reached out and touched the alien's arm.

ROBERT J. SAWYER

17

I sat in our living room, late that night, after Hollus had returned to his starship. I'd taken two pain pills, and I was letting them settle before I went to bed—the nausea sometimes made it hard to keep the pills down.

Maybe, I thought, the Forhilnor was right. Maybe there was no smoking gun that I would accept. He said it was all there, right in front of my eyes.

There are none so blind as those who will not see; besides the Twenty-ninth Scroll, that's one of my favorite bits of religious writing.

But I wasn't blind, dammit. I had a critical eye, a skeptic's eye, the eye of a scientist.

It stunned me that life on assorted worlds all used the same genetic code. Of course, Fred Hoyle had suggested that Earth—and presumably other planets—were seeded with bacterial life that drifted in from space; if all the worlds Hollus had visited were seeded from the same source, the genetic code would, of course, be the same.

But even if Hoyle's theory isn't true—and it's really not a very satisfying theory, since it simply pushes the origin of life off to some other locale that we can't easily examine—maybe there were good reasons why only those twenty amino acids were suitable for life.

As Hollus and I had discussed before, DNA has four letters in its alphabet: A, C, G, and T, for adenine, cytosine, guanine, and thymine, the bases that form the rungs of its spiral ladder.

Okay—a four-letter alphabet. But how long are the words in the genetic language? Well, the purpose of that language is to specify sequences of amino acids, the building blocks of proteins, and, as I said, there are twenty different aminos used by life. Obviously, you can't uniquely identify each of those twenty with words just one letter long: a four-letter alphabet only provides four different one-letter words. And you couldn't do it with words two letters long: there are only sixteen possible two-letter words in a language that has just four characters. But if you use three-letter words, ah, then you've got an embarrassment of riches, a William F. Buckley–style biochem vocabulary of a whopping sixty-four words. Set aside twenty to name each amino acid, and two more for punctuation marks—one for starting transcription and another for stopping. That means only twenty-two of the sixty-four possible words are needed for DNA to do its work. If a god had designed the genetic code, he must have looked at the surplus vocabulary and wondered what to do with it.

It seems to me that such a being would have considered two possibilities. One was to leave the remaining forty-two sequences undefined, just as there are letter sequences in real languages that don't form valid words. That way, if one of those sequences cropped up in a string of DNA, you'd know that a mistake had occurred in copying—a genetic typo, turning the valid code A-T-A into, say, the gibberish A-T-C. That would be a clear, useful signal that something had gone wrong.

The other alternative would be to live with the fact that copying errors were going to occur, but try to reduce their impact by adding synonyms to the genetic language. Instead of having one word for each amino acid, you could have three words that mean the same thing. That would use up sixty of the possible words; you could then have two words that mean start and two more that mean stop, rounding out the DNA dictionary. If you tried to group the synonyms logically, you could help

ROBERT J. SAWYER

guard against transcription errors: if A-G-A, A-G-C, and A-G-G all meant the same thing, and you could only clearly read the first two letters, you'd still have a good shot at guessing what the word meant even without knowing the third letter.

In fact, DNA *does* use synonyms. And if there were three synonyms to specify each amino acid, one might look at the code and say, yup, someone had carefully thought this out. But two amino acids—leucine and serine—are specified by six synonyms each, and others by four, three, two, or even just one: poor tryptophan is specified only by the word T-G-G.

Meanwhile, the code A-T-G can mean either the amino acid methionine (and there are no other genetic words for it) or, depending on context, it can be the punctuation mark for "start transcription" (which also has no other synonyms). Why on Earth—or anyplace else—would an intelligent designer make such a hodgepodge? Why require context sensitivity to determine meaning when there were enough words available to avoid having to do that?

And what about the variations in the genetic code? As I'd told Hollus, the code used by mitochondrial DNA differs slightly from that used by the DNA in the nucleus.

Well, in 1982, Lynn Margulis had suggested that mitochondria—cellular organelles responsible for energy production—had started out as separate bacterial forms, living in symbiosis with the ancestors of our cells, and that eventually these separate forms were co-opted into our cells, becoming part of them. Maybe . . . God, it was a long time since I'd done any serious biochemistry . . . but maybe the mitochondrial and nuclear genetic codes had indeed originally been identical, but, when the symbiosis began, evolution favored mutations that allowed for a few changes in the mitochondrial genetic code; with two sets of DNA existing within the same cell, maybe these few changes served as a way to distinguish the two forms, preventing accidental mingling.

I hadn't mentioned it to Hollus, but there were also some minor differences in the genetic code employed by ciliated protozoans—if I remember correctly, three codons have different meanings for them. But . . . I was blue-skying; I knew that . . . but some said that cilia, those irreducibly complex organelles whose death had brought about my own lung cancer, had started out as discrete organisms, as well. Maybe those ciliated protozoa that had a variant genetic code were descended from some cilia who had been in symbiosis with other cells in the past, developing genetic-code variations for the same safety-net reasons mitochondria had but, unlike the cilia we still retained, had subsequently broken off the symbiosis and returned to stand-alone life.

It was a possibility, anyway.

Still, when I'd been a kid in Scarborough, we'd shared a back fence with a woman named Mrs. Lansbury. She was very religious—a "Holy Roller," my dad would say—and was always trying to persuade my parents to let her take me to church on Sundays. I never went, of course, but I do remember her favorite expression: the Lord works in mysterious ways.

Perhaps so. But I found it hard to believe he would work in shoddy, haphazard ones.

And yet—

And yet what was it Hollus had said about Wreed language? It, too, relies on context sensitivity and the unusual use of synonyms. Maybe at some Chomsky-esque level, I just wasn't wired properly to see the elegance in the genetic code. Maybe T'kna and his kin found it perfectly reasonable, perfectly elegant.

Maybe.

Suddenly the cat was out of the bag.

I hadn't said a word to anyone about the *Merelcas*'s mission being, at least in part, to look for God. And I was pretty sure the gorillas in Burundi had been mum on the topic. But all at once, everyone knew.

ROBERT J. SAWYER

There was a row of newspaper boxes by the entrance to North York Centre subway station. The headline on today's *Toronto Star* said, "Aliens Have Proof of God's Existence." The headline on the *Globe and Mail* proclaimed, "God a Scientific Fact, Say ETs." The *National Post* declared, "Universe Had a Creator." And the *Toronto Sun* proclaimed just two giant words, filling most of its front page: "God lives!"

Usually I grabbed the *Sun* for light reading on the way to work, but for in-depth coverage, nothing beats the *Mop and Pail;* I dropped coins into the gray box and took a copy. And I stood there, in the crisp April air, reading everything above the fold.

A Hindu woman in Brussels had asked Salbanda, the Forhilnor spokesperson who met periodically with the media, the simple, direct question of whether he believes in any gods.

And he'd answered—at length.

And of course, cosmologists all over the planet, including Stephen Hawking and Alan Guth, were quickly interviewed to find out if what the Forhilnor had said made sense.

Religious leaders were jockeying for position. The Vatican— with rather a history of backing the wrong horse in scientific debates—was reserving comment, saying only that the pope would address the issue soon. The Wilayat al-Faqih in Iran denounced the alien's words. Pat Robertson was calling for more donations, to help his organization study the claims. The moderator of the United Church of Canada embraced the revelations, saying that science and faith were indeed reconcilable. A Hindu leader, whose name, I noted, was spelled two different ways in the same article, declared the alien's statements to be perfectly compatible with Hindu belief. Meanwhile, the ROM's own Caleb Jones pointed out, on behalf of CSICOP, that there was no need to read anything mystical or supernatural into any of the Forhilnor's words.

When I arrived at the ROM, the usual round of UFO nuts had been joined by several different religious groups—some in robes, some holding candles, some chanting, some kneeling in prayer. There were also several police officers, making sure that staff members—including but by no means limited to myself—made it safely into the museum; once the main doors opened for the day, they'd extend the same courtesy to patrons.

Laser-printed leaflets were blowing down the sidewalk; one that caught my eye showed Hollus, or another Forhilnor, with his eyestalks exaggerated to look like a devil's horns.

I entered the museum and made it up to my office. Hollus wavered into existence a short time later. "I have been thinking about the people who blew up the abortion clinic," he said. "You said they were religious fundamentalists."

"Well, one presumes so, yes. They haven't been caught yet."

"No smoking gun," said Hollus.

I smiled. "Exactly."

"But if they are, as you suspect, religious people, why is that relevant?"

"Blowing up an abortion clinic is an attempt to protest a perceived moral outrage."

"And . . . ?" said Hollus.

"Well, on Earth, the concept of God is inextricably linked to issues of morality."

Hollus listened.

"In fact, three of our principal religions share the same Ten Commandments, supposedly handed down by God."

Susan once quipped that the only piece of scripture I knew was the Lawgiver's Twenty-ninth Scroll:

> Beware the beast Man, for he is the devil's
> pawn. Alone among God's primates, he kills
> for sport, or lust, or greed. Yea, he will murder
> his brother to possess his brother's land. Let
> him not breed in great numbers, for he will
> make a desert of his home and yours. Shun

172

him. Drive him back into his jungle lair, for
he is the harbinger of death.

It's what Cornelius read to Taylor near the end of *Planet of the Apes*. Powerful words, and, like Dr. Zaius, I've always tried to live by their injunction. But Susan isn't quite right. Back when I was a student at U of T, lo those many years ago, I occasionally audited classes by Northrop Frye, the great teacher of English; I also snuck into lectures given by Marshall McLuhan and Robertson Davies, the other two members of U of T's internationally acclaimed humanities triumvirate. It was heady, listening to such staggering intellects. Frye contended that you could not appreciate English literature without knowing the Bible. Perhaps he was right; I'd once made it through about half the Old Testament and had skimmed the color-coded "actual words of Jesus" in a King James version I'd bought at the campus bookstore.

But, basically, what Susan said was true. I didn't know the Bible well, and I didn't know the Qur'an or any other holy book at all.

"And these Ten Commandments are?" asked Hollus.

"Umm, well, thou shalt not kill. Thou shalt not commit adultery. Thou shalt not . . . umm, something about an ass."

"I see," said Hollus. "But as far as we have been able to determine, the creator has never communicated directly with anyone. Indeed, the Wreeds—who, as you know, spend half their lives actively seeking such communication—claim no success. I am not sure how such commandments would be passed on to any lifeform."

"Well, if I remember the movie correctly, God wrote them with a finger of fire on stone tablets."

"There is a movie of this event? Would that not be your smoking gun?"

I smiled. "The movie is a drama, a story. The Ten Command-

CALCULATING GOD

ments were supposedly handed down thousands of years ago, but the movie was made about half a century ago."

"Oh."

"Still, many humans believe that they *are* in direct or indirect communication with God—that he listens to prayers."

"They are delusional," said Hollus. His eyestalks came to rest. "Forgive me," he said. "I know you are dying. Have you been moved to pray?"

"No. But my wife Susan does."

"Her prayers have not been answered."

"No," I said softly. "They haven't."

"How do members of your species reconcile the act of prayer with the reality that most prayers go unanswered?"

I shrugged a little. "We say things like 'Everything happens for a reason.'"

"Ah, the Wreed philosophy," said Hollus.

"My little boy asked me if I'd done something wrong—if that's why I'd gotten cancer."

"And *did* you do something wrong?"

"Well, I've never smoked, but I suppose my diet could have been better."

"But did you do anything morally wrong? Those Ten Commandments you mentioned—did you break any of those?"

"To be honest, I don't even know what all ten are. But I don't think I've ever done anything horrible. I've never committed murder. I've never cheated on my wife. I've never stolen anything—at least not as an adult. I've never—" Thoughts of Gordon Small, and events of three decades past, came to mind. "Besides, I can't believe a caring God would punish anyone, no matter what the transgression, with what I'm going through."

"'A caring God,'" repeated Hollus. "I have also heard the phrases 'a loving God,' and 'a compassionate God.'" His eyestalks locked on me. "I think you humans apply too many adjectives to the creator."

174

"But you're the ones who believe that God has a purpose for us," I said.

"I believe the creator may have a specific reason for wanting a universe that has life in it, and, indeed, as you say, for wanting multiple sentiences to emerge simultaneously. But it seems clear beyond dispute that the creator takes no interest in specific individuals."

"And that's the generally held opinion amongst members of your race?" I asked.

"Yes."

"Then what is the source of Forhilnor morality? How do you tell right from wrong?"

Hollus paused, either searching for an answer or considering whether he wanted to answer at all. Finally, he said, "My race has a violent past," he said, "not unlike your own. We are capable of feats of great savagery—indeed, we do not need weapons to easily kill another member of our own kind. The right things to do are those that keep our violence in abeyance; the wrong things are those that bring it to the fore." He shifted his weight, redeploying his six feet. "Our race has not fought a war for three generations; since we have the capability to destroy our world, this is a good thing."

"I wonder if violence is innate in all intelligent species," I said. "Evolution is driven by struggles for dominance. I've heard it suggested that no herbivore could ever develop intelligence because it doesn't take any cunning to sneak up on a leaf."

"It does create an odd dynamic," said Hollus. "Violence is required for intelligence, intelligence gives rise to the ability to destroy one's species, and only through intelligence can one overcome the violence that gave rise to that intelligence."

"We'd call that a Catch-22," I said. "Maybe we create the idea of a caring God and morality to foster self-preservation. Perhaps any race that doesn't have morality, that doesn't suppress its violent urges in a desire to please a god, is doomed to destroy itself once it gets the technology to do so."

"An interesting thought," said Hollus. "Belief in God conferring a survival advantage. Evolution would then select for it."

"Does your race still worry about destroying itself?" I asked.

Hollus bobbed, but I think it was a gesture of negation, not affirmation. "We have a unified planetary government, and much tolerance for diversity. We have eliminated hunger and want. There is little reason for us to come into conflict with each other anymore."

"I wish I could say the same thing about my world," I said. "Since this planet was fortunate enough to have life arise on it, it would be a shame to see it snuffed out because of our own stupidity."

"Life did not arise here," said Hollus.

"What?" I was completely lost.

"I do not believe that there was a biogenerative event in Earth's past; I do not believe life began here."

"You mean it drifted here from deep space? Fred Hoyle's panspermia hypothesis?"

"Possibly. But I suspect it is more likely that it began relatively locally, on Sol IV."

"Sol—you mean Mars?"

"Yes."

"How would it get here from there?"

"On meteors."

I frowned. "Well, there've been a couple of Martian meteorites found over the years that some said had fossils in them. But they've been pretty thoroughly discredited."

"It would only take one."

"I suppose. But why don't you think life is native to this planet?"

"You said you thought life had emerged on this world as much as four billion years ago. But that early in your solar system's history, this planet was still routinely undergoing extinction-level impact events, as large comets and asteroids frequently slammed into it. It is extremely unlikely that conditions suitable for life could have been maintained during that period."

"Well, Mars is no older than Earth, and surely it was undergoing bombardment, too."

"Oh, doubtless so," said Hollus. "But although Mars clearly had running water in its past—its surface today is really quite impressive to stand upon; the erosion features are incredible—it never had large or deep oceans like those here on Earth. If an asteroid hits land, heat from the impact might raise temperatures for a matter of months. But if it hits water, which, after all, covers most of Earth's surface now as well as billions of years ago, the heat would be retained, raising the planet's temperature for decades or even centuries. Mars would have had a stable environment for the development of life perhaps as much as half a billion years before Earth did."

"And then some of it was transferred here, on meteors?"

"Exactly. About one thirty-sixth of all the material that gets knocked off Mars by meteor impacts should eventually be swept up by Earth, and many forms of microbes can survive freezing. It neatly explains why full-fledged life is recorded in the oldest rocks here, even though the environment was too volatile for it to develop domestically."

"Wow," I said, well aware that my response wasn't adequate. "I suppose one meteor with life on it might have made it here. After all, every lifeform on this planet shares a single common ancestor."

Hollus sounded astonished. "All life on this planet shares one common ancestor?"

"Of course."

"How do you know that?"

"We compare the genetic material of different lifeforms, and, judging by how much it diverges, we can tell how long ago they had an ancestor in common. For instance, you've seen Old George, the stuffed chimpanzee we have in the Budongo Rain Forest diorama?"

"Yes."

"Well, humans and chimps differ genetically by only 1.4 percent."

"If you will forgive me for saying so, it does not seem right to stuff and display so close a relative."

"We don't do that anymore," I said. "That mount is more than eighty years old." I decided not to mention the stuffed Australian aborigine they used to have on display at the American Museum of Natural History. "In fact, it's largely through genetic studies that the concept of ape rights gained credence."

"And such studies show all life on this planet to have a common ancestor?"

"Of course."

"Incredible. On both Beta Hydri and Delta Pavonis, we believe there were multiple biogenerative events. Life on my world, for instance, arose at least six times during an initial 300-million-year period." He paused. "What is the highest level in your hierarchical biological classification system?"

"Kingdom," I said. "We generally recognize five: Animalia, Plantae, Fungi, Monera, and Protista."

"Animalia are the animals? And Plantae the plants?"

"Yes."

"All animals are grouped together? Likewise all plants?"

"Yes."

"Fascinating." His spherical torso bobbed deeply. "On my world, we have a level above that, consisting of the six—well, 'domains' might be an appropriate translation—the six domains from the six separate creation events; separate kinds of animals and plants exist in each. For instance, our pentapeds and octopeds are, in fact, completely unrelated; cladistic studies have demonstrated that they share no common ancestor."

178   "Really? Still, you should be able to use the DNA technique

I described to determine evolutionary relationships amongst members of the same domain."

"The domains have commingled over the eons," Hollus said. "The genome of my own species contains genetic material from all six domains."

"How is that possible? As you said about Spock, the idea of members of different species—even from the same domain—having offspring is ludicrous."

"We believe viruses played a substantial role over millions of years in moving genetic material across domain boundaries."

I thought about that. It had been suggested on Earth that unnecessary material transferred into lifeforms by viruses accounted for much of the junk DNA—the ninety percent of the human genome that did not code for protein synthesis. And, of course, geneticists today were deliberately transferring cow genes into potatoes and so on.

"All six domains are based on DNA?" I asked.

"As I have said, every complex lifeform that we have discovered is based on DNA," said Hollus. "But with DNA crossing domains throughout our history, the kind of comparative study you suggest is not something we have had much success with. Animals that are clearly very closely related, based on the gross details of body form, may have significant recent intrusions of new DNA from another domain, which would make the percentage of deviation between the two species deceptively large."

"Interesting," I said. A thought occurred to me, too crazy to voice out loud. If, as Hollus said, DNA was universally used in all lifeforms, and the genetic code was the same everywhere, and lifeforms even from different domains could incorporate each other's DNA, then why couldn't lifeforms from different *worlds* do the same thing?

Maybe Spock wasn't so improbable after all.

18

I t wasn't yet Sunday night, but J. D. Ewell and Cooter Falsey visited the ROM anyway, to familiarize themselves with the museum's layout.

"Nine dollars to get in!" exclaimed Falsey once they'd crossed through the Rotunda to the admissions desk, and he'd had a chance to consult the appropriate sign.

"They're just *Canadian* dollars," said Ewell. "It's like a buck and a half U.S." He reached into his wallet and pulled out two of the garish purple Canadian ten-dollar bills he'd gotten as change from his U.S. fifty for last night's dinner at the Red Lobster. He gave them to the middle-aged woman behind the desk, and she handed him back a receipt, a two-toned two-dollar Canadian coin, and two rectangular plastic clips that said "ROM" on them, with a little crown above the central "O." Ewell stared at them.

"You attach them to your shirt," said the woman, helpfully. "They show you've paid."

"Ah," said Ewell, handing one to Falsey and clipping the other one on.

The woman gave them a glossy brochure. "Here's a map of the galleries," she said. "And there's a coatroom over there." She pointed to her right.

"Thank you kindly," said Ewell.

They stepped forward. A dark-skinned man wearing a brown turban and a security officer's blue blazer, white shirt, and red tie, was standing at the top of the four wide steps that led out of the Rotunda. "Where's the Bogus Shale?" asked Ewell.

The guard smiled, as if Ewell had said something funny. "Back there; the entrance is by the coat check."

Ewell nodded, but Falsey had continued going forward. Just ahead, two giant staircases rounded out onto this level, one on the left and one on the right. It was easy to see that each set of stone steps went up three floors, and the one on the right continued down into the basement. Each staircase encircled a huge totem pole of dark wood. Falsey had stopped by one of the totems and was staring up. The pole rose all the way to the ceiling and was topped by a carved eagle. The wood was devoid of paint, and had long vertical cracks in it.

"Will you look at that?" said Falsey.

Ewell glanced at it. Pagan symbols of a heathen people. "Come on," he said.

The two walked back through the Rotunda. Next to the coat check was a set of open glass doors, with a carved-stone sign above them that said Garfield Weston Exhibition Hall; there were wheat sheaves on either side of the Weston name. Above this was a dark-blue fabric banner proclaiming in white letters:

TREASURES OF THE BURGESS SHALE
Fossils from the Cambrian Explosion

Along the sides of the doors were logos and names of the corporate sponsors who had made the exhibition possible, including Bank of Montreal, Abitibi-Price, Bell Canada, and the *Toronto Sun*.

Falsey and Ewell entered the gallery. A mural depicting a supposedly ancient ocean bottom dominated one wall, with all sorts of bizarre critters swimming around. Display cases with angled glass tops lined the other walls and a central room divider.

"Look," said Ewell, pointing.

Falsey nodded. The cases jutted out from the walls; there was space underneath each one. Explosives could easily be planted there—but they'd probably be spotted, if not by adults, certainly by little kids.

There were perhaps a hundred people milling around, looking at the fossils or listening to video presentations about their discovery. Ewell pulled a small, spiral-bound notebook out of his hip pocket and began making notes. He walked through the gallery, counting the number of cases—there were twenty-six. Falsey, meanwhile, discreetly noted the three security cameras, two that were fixed, and one that panned back and forth. They would present a problem—but not an insurmountable one.

Ewell didn't care what the fossils themselves looked like, but young Falsey did. He examined each case in turn. They contained slabs of gray shale held in place by little Plexiglas posts. It would be a tricky problem; although shales could shatter if dropped, they could also be quite strong. Unless the explosions were designed just right, the display cases might be damaged but the rocks with their bizarre fossils might escape unscathed.

"Mommy," said a little boy, "what are those?" Falsey looked at where the child was pointing. At the back of the room were two large models: one showed a creature with numerous stiltlike legs and waving tentacles coming off its back. The other showed a creature walking on tubular legs with a forest of spikes rising up from its body.

The child's mother, a pretty woman in her twenties, peered at a placard, then explained for her son. "Well, dear, see, they weren't quite sure how this creature looked, because it's so strange. Originally, they couldn't even tell which way was up, so it's been modeled two different ways here."

The child seemed satisfied by the answer, but Falsey had to fight to keep from speaking. The fossil was an obvious lie, a test of faith. That it didn't look right no matter which way you put it was proof that it had never really been alive. It tore his heart out to see a young mind being led astray by all this trickery.

183

Falsey and Ewell spent an hour in the gallery, completely familiarizing themselves with it. Falsey sketched the contents of each display case so that he knew exactly how the fossils were deployed within. Ewell noted the alarm systems—they were obvious if you knew what you were looking for.

And when they were done, they exited the museum. Outside, there was a large group of people, many sporting buttons depicting the traditional big-headed black-eyed gray alien; they'd been there when Falsey and Ewell had entered, too—UFO nuts and religious fanatics, waiting for a glimpse of the alien or its ship.

Falsey bought a tiny, oily bag of popcorn from a street vendor. He ate some and tossed the rest, kernel by kernel, at the numerous pigeons that were waddling along the sidewalk.

"Well," said Ewell, "what do you think?"

Falsey shook his head. "No place to hide bombs. And no guarantee that even if we could hide them that the rock slabs would be damaged by the explosions."

Ewell nodded reluctantly, as if he'd been forced to the same conclusion. "It means we'll have to take direct action," he said.

"I'm afraid so." Falsey turned and faced the imposing stone facade of the museum, with its wide steps leading up to the glass entrance doors and the triptych of stained-glass windows rising up above those doors.

"Too bad we didn't get to see the alien," Falsey said.

Ewell nodded, sharing Cooter's disappointment. "The aliens may believe in God, but they haven't yet found Christ. Imagine if we could be the ones to introduce them to the Savior . . ."

"That would be glorious," said Falsey, his eyes wide. "Absolutely glorious."

Ewell pulled out the city map they'd been using. "Well," he said, "it looks like if we take the subway four stops south, that will put us purty near the place where they tape *The Red Green Show*." He tapped the large red square labeled "CBC Broadcasting Ctr."

Falsey smiled, all thoughts of greater glory temporarily banned

ROBERT J. SAWYER

from his mind. They both loved *The Red Green Show* and had been surprised to learn it was made here in Canada. There was a taping tonight, and tickets were free. "Let's go," he said. They walked over to the entrance stairwell and descended below the street.

All right, I'll admit it. There's one good thing about dying: it causes you to be introspective. As Samuel Johnson said, "When a man knows he is to be hanged in a fortnight, it concentrates his mind wonderfully."

I knew why I was resisting the notion of intelligent design so much—why almost all evolutionists do. We had fought for more than a century against creationists, against fools who believed that the Earth was made in 4004 B.C. during six literal twenty-four-hour days; that fossils, if they had any validity at all, were remnants of Noah's flood; that a deceptive God had created the universe with starlight already *en route* to us, giving the illusion of great distances and great age.

The popular account was that Thomas Henry Huxley had slain Bishop "Soapy Sam" Wilberforce in the great evolution debate. And Clarence Darrow, so I'd been taught, had buried William Jennings Bryan during the Scopes trial. But the battle had only begun with them. Others kept coming, spewing garbage under the guise of so-called creation science, forcing evolution out of the classroom, even today, even here at the beginning of the twenty-first century, trying to force a literal, fundamentalist interpretation of the Bible into the mainstream.

We'd fought the good fight, Stephen Jay Gould, Richard Dawkins, and even me, to a lesser extent—I didn't have the soapbox of the other two, but I'd debated my share of creationists at the Royal Ontario Museum and U of T. And twenty years ago, the ROM's own Chris McGowan had written a crackerjack book called *In the Beginning: A Scientist Shows Why the Cre-*

ationists Are Wrong. But I remember a friend of mine—a guy who teaches philosophy—pointing out the arrogance of that subtitle: one man was going to show why all the creationists everywhere were benighted. Maybe we could be forgiven our siege mentality, though. Polls in the United States showed that even today, less than a quarter of the population believed in evolution.

To grant that there had been any guiding intelligence, at any point, would open the floodgates. We'd struggled so long, and so hard, and some of us had even been jailed for the sake of the cause, that to allow for even a moment the possibility of an intelligent designer would be tantamount to raising the white flag. The media, we'd felt sure, would have a field day, ignorance would reign supreme, and not only would Johnny be unable to read, he wouldn't know any real science, either.

In retrospect, maybe we should have been more open, maybe we should have considered other possibilities, maybe we should not have glossed so readily over the rough spots in Darwin's theory, but the cost, it had always seemed, was too high.

The Forhilnors weren't creationists, of course—no more so, really, than were any scientists who accepted the big bang, with its definite creation point (something Einstein had found so abhorrent to common sense that he'd made what he regarded as the "greatest blunder" of his life, cooking his equations for relativity to avoid the universe ever having a beginning).

And now the floodgates *were* open. Now everyone, everywhere, was talking about creation, and the big bang, and the previous cycles of existence, and the fudging of fundamental constants, and intelligent design.

And the charges were running high against evolutionists and biochemists and cosmologists and paleontologists, claiming that we'd known—or at least had an inkling—that perhaps all this might be true, and that we'd deliberately suppressed it, rejecting papers submitted to journals on these topics, and ridiculing those who had published such ideas in the popular press, lumping anyone who supported the anthropic cosmological principle

ROBERT J. SAWYER

in with the obviously deluded fundamentalist young-Earth creationists.

Of course, phone calls poured in requesting interviews with me—approximately one every three minutes, according to the logs from the ROM's switchboard. I'd told Dana, the departmental assistant, that unless the Dalai Lama or the pope called, not to bother me. I'd been joking, but representatives of both were on the phone to the ROM within twenty-four hours of Salbanda's revelations in Brussels.

As much as I wanted to dive publicly into the fray, I couldn't. I didn't have the time to spare.

I stood bending over my desk, trying to sort through the papers on it. There was a request from the AMNH for a copy of that paper I'd done on *Nanshiungosaurus;* a proposed budget for the paleobiology department that had to be approved by me before the end of the week; a letter from a high-school student who wanted to become a paleontologist and was looking for career advice; employee-evaluation forms for Dana; an invitation to give a lecture in Berlin; galley proofs of that introduction I wrote for Danilova and Tamasaki's handbook; two article manuscripts for the *JVP* that I'd agreed to referee; two quotes on the resin we needed; a requisition form that I had to fill out to get the damned lighting for the *Camptosaurus* in the Dinosaur Gallery fixed; a copy of my own book that had been sent to me for an autograph; seven—no, eight—unanswered letters on other topics; my own expense-claim form for the previous quarter that had to be filled out; the departmental long-distance bill, with calls that no one had yet owned up to highlighted in yellow.

It was too much. I sat down, turned to my computer, tapped the E-mail icon. Seventy-three new messages waiting; Christ, I didn't have time to even begin to wade through that many.

Just then, Dana stuck her head through the door. "Tom, I really need those vacation schedules approved."

"I know," I said. "I'll get to it."

"As soon as you can, please," she said.

"I said I'll get to it!"

She looked startled. I don't think I'd ever snapped at her before. But she disappeared out into the corridor before I could apologize.

Maybe I should have just dispensed with or delegated all my administrative duties, but, well, if I stepped down as department head, surely my successor would claim the right to be Hollus's guide. Besides, I couldn't leave everything a mess; I had to wrap things up, complete as much as I could, before . . .

Before . . .

I sighed and turned away from the computer, looking again at the piles of stuff on my desk.

There wasn't enough time, dammitall. There just wasn't enough time.

ROBERT J. SAWYER

19

Many employees have no idea how much their bosses make, but I knew to the penny what Christine Dorati was pulling down. The law in Ontario required public disclosures of all civil-service salaries of over a hundred thousand Canadian dollars per year; the ROM had just four staff members who fell into that category. Christine made $179,952 last year, plus $18,168 in taxable benefits—and she had an office that reflected that stature. Despite my complaints about the way Christine ran the museum, I understood that it was necessary for her to have such an office. She had to entertain potential donors there, as well as government bigwigs who could boost or slash our budget on a whim.

I'd been sitting in my office, waiting for my pain pills to settle, when I'd gotten the call saying Christine wanted to see me. Walking was a good way to get the pills to stay down, so I didn't mind. I headed off to her office.

"Hi, Christine," I said, after Indira let me pass into the inner sanctum. "You wanted to see me?"

Christine was looking at something on the web; she raised a hand to tell me to be patient a moment longer. Beautiful textiles hung from her office walls. There was a suit of armor behind Christine's desk; ever since our Armour Court—which I'd always thought had been a rather popular exhibit—had been scrubbed to make room for one of Christine's trademark feed-them-pablum displays, we'd had more suits of armor than we knew what to do with. Christine also had a stuffed passenger pigeon (the ROM's Centre for Biodiversity and Conservation Biology—the slapped-together catchall formed by merging the old ichthyology, herpetology, mammalogy, and ornithology departments—had about twenty of them). She also had a cluster of quartz crystals as big as a large microwave oven, salvaged from the old Geology Gallery; a beautiful jade Buddha, about the size of a basketball; an Egyptian canopic jar; and, of course, a dinosaur skull—a fiberglass cast from a *Lambeosaurus*. The blade-shaped crest on the duckbill's head at one end of the room nicely balanced the double-headed ax held by the suit of armor at the other.

Christine clicked her mouse, minimizing her browser window, and at last gave me her full attention. She gestured with an open palm toward one of the three leather-upholstered swivel chairs that faced her desk. I took the middle one, feeling a certain trepidation as I did so; Christine had a policy of never offering a seat if the meeting was to be wrapped up quickly.

"Hello, Tom," she said. She made a solicitous face. "How are you feeling?"

I shrugged a little; there wasn't much to say. "As well as can be expected, I suppose."

"Are you in much pain?"

"It comes and goes," I said. "I've got some pills that help."

"Good," she said. She was quiet for a time; that was abnormal for Christine, who usually seemed to be in a great hurry. Finally, she spoke again. "How's Suzanne doing? She holding up all right?"

I didn't correct her on my wife's name. "She's managing. There's a support group that meets at the Richmond Hill Public Library; she goes to meetings there once a week."

"I'm sure they're a comfort to her."

I said nothing.

"And Richie? How's he?"

Two in a row was too much. "It's Ricky," I said.

"Ah, sorry. How's he doing?"

I shrugged again. "He's frightened. But he's a brave kid."

Christine gestured toward me, as if that only made sense given who Ricky's father was. I tipped my head in thanks at the unspoken compliment. She was silent a moment longer, then: "I've been talking to Petroff, over in H.R. He says you're fully covered. You could go on long-term-disability leave and receive eighty-five percent of your salary."

I blinked and thought carefully about my next words. "I'm not sure it's your place to be discussing my insurance situation with anyone."

Christine raised both hands, palms out. "Oh, I didn't discuss you in particular; I just asked about the general case of an employee with a ter— with a serious illness." She'd started to say "terminal," of course, but hadn't been able to bring herself to use the word. Then she smiled. "And you're covered. You don't have to work anymore."

"I know that. But I *want* to work."

"Wouldn't you rather be spending your time with Suzanne and Rich—Ricky?"

"Susan has her own job, and Ricky's in grade one; he's in school full days."

"Still, Tom, I think . . . Isn't it time you faced facts? You're not able to bring a hundred percent to your job anymore. Isn't it time you took some leave?"

I was in pain, as always, and that just made it harder to control my temper. "I don't want to take any leave," I said. "I want to work. Damn it, Christine, my oncologist says it's *good* for me to be coming to work every day."

Christine shook her head, as if saddened that I was unable to see the big picture. "Tom, I've got to think of what's best for the museum." She took a deep breath. "You must know Lillian Kong."

"Of course."

"Well, you know that she quit as curator of fossil vertebrates at the Canadian Museum of Nature to—"

191

"To protest government cutbacks in spending on museums; yes, I know. She went to Indiana University."

"Exactly. But I've heard through the grapevine that she's not happy there, either. I think I could entice her to join us here at the ROM, if I move quickly. I know the Museum of the Rockies wants her, too, so she's certainly not going to be available for long, and . . ."

She trailed off, waiting for me to complete her thought for her. I crossed my arms in front of my chest but said nothing. She looked disappointed that she'd have to spell it out. "And, well, Tom, you *are* going to be leaving us."

A tired old joke drifted through my mind: Old curators never die; they just become part of their collections. "I can still do useful work."

"The chances of me being able to get someone as qualified as Kong a year from now are slim."

Lillian Kong was a damn fine paleontologist; she'd done some amazing work on ceratopsians and had received enormous amounts of press, including being on the cover of *Newsweek* and *Maclean's* for her contributions to the dinosaur-bird controversy. But, like Christine, she was a dumb-downer: the Canadian Museum of Nature's displays had become cloyingly populist, and not very informative, under her. She'd doubtless be an ally in Christine's desire to make the ROM into an "attraction," and indeed would agree to put pressure on Hollus to do public programming, something I'd steadfastly refused to do.

"Christine, don't make me go."

"Oh, you wouldn't necessarily have to go. You could stay on, doing research. We owe you that."

"But I would have to step down as department head."

"Well, the Museum of the Rockies *is* offering her a very senior position; I won't be able to entice her here with anything less than—than—"

"Than my job," I said. "And you can't afford to pay both of us."

ROBERT J. SAWYER

"You could go on disability leave, but still come in to show her the ropes."

"If you've been talking to Petroff, you know that's not true. The insurance company won't pay me unless I declare that I'm too sick to work. Now, yes, they've made clear that in terminal cases, they won't argue the point. If I say I'm too sick, they'll believe me—but I cannot come into the office and still receive benefits."

"Getting a scholar of Lillian's stature would be great for the museum," Christine said.

"She's hardly the only option you'll have to replace me," I said. "When I have to leave, you can promote Darlene, or—or make an offer to Ralph Chapman; get him to bring his applied-morphometrics lab here. That would be a real coup."

Christine spread her arms. It was all bigger than her. "I'm sorry, Tom. Really I am."

I folded my arms across my chest. "This doesn't have anything to do with finding the best paleontologist. This has to do with our disagreements over how you've been running this museum."

Christine did a credible job of sounding wounded. "Tom, you do me a disservice."

"I doubt that," I said. "And—and, besides, what's Hollus going to do?"

"Well, I'm sure he'll want to continue his research," said Christine.

"We've been working together. He trusts me."

"He'll work just fine with Lillian."

"No, he won't," I said. "We're a . . ." I felt silly saying it. "We're a team."

"He simply needs a competent paleontologist as his guide, and, well, forgive me, Tom, but surely you recognize that it should be someone who will be around for years to come, someone who can document everything he or she has learned from the alien."

193

"I'm keeping a meticulous journal," I said. "I'm writing everything down."

"Nonetheless, for the sake of the museum—"

I was growing more angry—and more bold. "I could go to any museum or university with a decent fossil collection, and Hollus would come with me. I could get an offer from anywhere I wanted, and, with an alien along for the ride, no one would care about my health."

"Tom, be reasonable."

I don't have to be reasonable, I thought. No one going through what I'm going through has to be reasonable. "It's nonnegotiable," I said. "If I go, so does Hollus."

Christine made a show of studying the woodgrain on her desktop, tracing it with her index finger. "I wonder how Hollus would react if I told him you were using him this way."

I stuck out my chin. "I wonder how he'd react if I told him how you are treating me."

We both sat in silence for a time. Finally, I said, "If there's nothing else, I'll be getting back to my work." I made an effort not to stress the final word.

Christine sat motionless, and I got up and left, pain slicing through me, although, of course, I refused to let it show.

20

I stormed back to my office. Hollus had been looking at endocranial casts in my absence; spurred on by my earlier comments, he was now exploring the rise of intelligence in mammals after the K/T boundary. I was never sure if I was reading his body language correctly, but he seemed to have no trouble reading mine. "You" "seem" "upset," he said.

"Dr. Dorati—the museum's director, remember her?" He'd met her several times now, including when the prime minister had shown up. "She's trying to force me to go on long-term disability leave. She wants me out."

"Why?"

"I'm the potential vampire slayer, remember? I'm an opponent of hers politically here at the museum. She has taken the ROM in a direction a number of us long-time curators object to. And now she sees an opportunity to replace me with someone who agrees with her views."

"But disability leave . . . surely that relates to your illness?"

"There's no other way for her to force me out."

"What is the nature of your dispute?"

"I believe the museum should be a place of scholarship and it should provide as much information as possible about each of its displays. She believes the museum should be a tourist attraction and should not intimidate laypeople with a lot of facts, figures, and fancy words."

"And this issue is important?"

I was taken aback by the question. It had *seemed* important when I'd started fighting Christine over it three years ago. I'd even called it, in an interview in the *Toronto Star* about all the brouhaha at the ROM, "the fight of my life." But that was before Dr. Noguchi had shown me the dark spot on my x ray, before I'd started feeling the pain, before the chemotherapy, before . . .

"I don't know," I said, honestly.

"I am sorry to hear of your difficulties," said Hollus.

I chewed my lower lip. I had no right to say any of this. "I told Dr. Dorati that you would leave if she forced me out."

Hollus was quiet for a long time. Back on Beta Hydri III, he had been an academic of some sort himself; he doubtless understood the prestige his presence brought to the ROM. But perhaps I'd offended him enormously, making him a pawn in a political game. He could surely see ahead several moves, surely knew that this might become ugly. I'd gone too far; I knew that.

And yet—

And yet, who could blame me? Christine was going to win regardless. All too soon, she would win.

Hollus pointed at my desk set. "You have used that device before to communicate with others in this building," he said.

"My phone? Yes."

"Can you connect to Dr. Dorati?"

"Umm, yes, but—"

"Do so."

I hesitated for a moment, then lifted the handset and tapped out Christine's three-digit extension.

"Dorati," said Christine's voice.

I tried to hand Hollus the handset. "I cannot use that," he said. Of course he couldn't; he had two separate mouths. I touched the speaker-phone key and nodded for him to go ahead.

"Dr. Dorati, this is Hollus deten stak Jaton." It was the first time I'd heard the Forhilnor's full name. "I am grateful for your hospitality in letting me do research here, but I am contacting

ROBERT J. SAWYER

you to inform you that Thomas Jericho is an integral part of my work, and if he leaves this museum, I will follow him wherever he goes."

There was a stony silence for several seconds. "I see," said Christine's voice.

"Terminate the connection," Hollus said to me. I clicked the phone off.

My heart fluttered; I had no idea if what Hollus had just done was the right thing. But I was deeply moved by his support. "Thank you," I said.

The Forhilnor flexed both his upper and lower knees. "Dr. Dorati was all on the left."

"All on the left?"

"Sorry. I mean what she did was wrong, in my view. Intervening was the least I could do."

"I thought it was wrong, too," I said. "But—well, I thought maybe my telling her you would go if I went was wrong, also."

I was silent for a time, and at last Hollus replied. "So much of what is right and wrong is difficult to determine," he said. "I probably would have performed similarly, had I been in your place." He bobbed. "I do sometimes wish I had a Wreed's insight into these matters."

"You'd mentioned that before," I said. "Why do Wreeds have an easier time than we do with questions of morality?"

Hollus shifted slightly from foot to foot. "The Wreeds are freed from the burden of ratiocination—of the kind of logic you and I undertake. Although math may confound them, thinking about philosophical questions, about the meaning of life, about ethics and morality, confounds *us*. We have an intuitive sense of right and wrong, but every theory of morality we come up with fails. You showed me those *Star Trek* movies . . ."

I had indeed; he'd been intrigued enough by the episodes we'd looked at to want to watch the first three classic *Trek* films. "Yes," I said.

"There was one in which the impossible hybrid died."

197

"*The Wrath of Khan*," I said.

"Yes. In it, much was made of the notion that 'the needs of the many outweigh the needs of the few, or the one.' We Forhilnors have similar sentiments. It is an attempt to apply mathematics— something we are good at—to ethics, something we are not good at. But such attempts always fail us. In the film in which the hybrid was reborn—"

"*The Search for Spock*," I said.

His eyeballs clicked together. "In that one, we learn that the first formulation was flawed, and in fact 'the needs of the one outweigh the needs of the many.' It seemed intuitively right that the fellow with the fake hair and the others should have been willing to sacrifice their lives to save one unrelated comrade, even though it defied mathematical logic. And yet this happens all the time: many human societies and all Forhilnor ones are democratic; they are committed to the principle that each individual has identical worth. Indeed, I have seen the great phrase devised by your neighbors to the south: 'We hold these truths to be self-evident, that all men are created equal.' And yet the people who wrote those words were slave owners, oblivious to the irony—to use a word you have taught me—of that fact."

"True," I said.

"Many human and Forhilnor scientists have tried to reduce altruism to genetic imperatives, suggesting that the degree of sacrifice we are willing to make for another is directly proportional to how much genetic material we share. You or I, say these scientists, would not necessarily let ourselves die in order to save one sibling or child, but we should consider it an even trade if our death would save two siblings or children, since between them they have the same quantity of our genes as we ourselves possess. And we would surely sacrifice ourselves to save three siblings or children, since that quantity represents a greater concentration of our genetic material than our own bodies contain."

"I would die to save Ricky," I said.

He gestured at the picture on my desk, the frame's cardboard back once again facing him. "And yet, if I understand what you have said, Ricky is not your natural son."

"That's right. His birth parents didn't want him."

"Which confounds on two levels: that parents could choose to reject their healthy offspring and that nonparents could choose to adopt another's child. And of course there are many good people who, in defiance of genetic logic, have chosen not to have children. There simply is no formula that successfully describes the range of Forhilnor or human choices in the areas of altruism and sacrifice; you cannot reduce these issues to mathematics."

I thought about that; certainly, Hollus intervening on my behalf with Christine was altruistic, but it obviously had nothing whatsoever to do with favoring a genetic relative. "I guess," I said.

"But," said Hollus, "our friends the Wreeds, because they never developed traditional math, never find themselves vexed by such matters."

"Well, they certainly vex me," I said. "Over the years, I've often lain in bed, trying to sort out moral quandaries." The old dyslexic agnostic insomniac joke came to mind: lying awake at night, wondering if there is a dog. "I mean, where *does* morality come from? We know it's wrong to steal, and—" I paused. "You do know that, right? I mean, Forhilnors have a taboo against theft?"

"Yes, although it is not innate; Forhilnor children will take anything they can reach."

"It's the same with human kids. But we grow up to realize that theft is wrong, and yet . . . and yet *why* do we feel it's wrong? If it increases reproductive success, shouldn't evolution have favored it? For that matter, we think infidelity is wrong, but I could obviously increase my reproductive success by impregnating multiple females. If theft is advantageous for everyone who succeeds at it, and adultery is a good strategy, at least for males, for increasing presence in the gene pool, why do we feel they are wrong? Shouldn't the only morality that evolution produces be the kind Bill Clinton had—being sorry you got caught?"

Hollus's eyestalks weaved in and out more quickly than usual. "I have no answer," he said. "We struggle to find solutions to moral questions, but they always defeat us. Preeminent thinkers, both human and Forhilnor, have devoted themselves to asking what is the meaning of life and how do we know when something is morally wrong. But despite centuries of effort, no progress has been made. The questions are as beyond us as 'What is two plus two?' is beyond a Wreed."

I shook my head in disbelief. "I still find it incredible that they can't simply see that two objects and two additional objects is equivalent to four objects."

The Forhilnor tipped his body toward me by flexing the lower knees on three of his legs. "And they find it incredible that we cannot see the underlying truths of moral issues." He paused. "Our minds do chunking: we break problems down into manageable bits. If we wonder how a planet stays in orbit about its sun, we can ask numerous simpler questions—how does a rock stay on the ground; why is the sun at the center of the solar system—and by solving those, we can confidently answer the larger question. But the problems of ethics and morality and the meaning of life are apparently irreducible, like the ciliums in cells: there are no component parts that are tractable in isolation."

"You mean to say that being a scientist, a logician, like—well, like you or me—is fundamentally incompatible with being at peace over moral and spiritual issues?"

"Some succeed at both—but they usually do it by compartmentalizing. Science is given responsibility for certain matters; religion for others. But for those looking for a single, overarching worldview, there is little peace. A mind is wired for one or the other, but not both."

Pascal's wager came to mind: it was safer, he said, to bet on the existence of God, even if he doesn't exist, than to risk the eternal damnation of being wrong. Pascal, of course, had been a mathematician; he'd had a logical, rational, number-crunching mind, a human mind. Old Blaise had had no choice in the kind of brain he had; it had been bequeathed to him by evolution, just as mine had.

But if I'd had a choice?

If I could trade some bafflement in factual matters for certitude about questions of ethics, would I do so? Which is more important: knowing the precise phylogenetic relationships between all the various branches on the evolutionary bush or knowing the meaning of life?

Hollus departed for the day, wavering and disappearing, leaving me alone with my books and fossils and unfinished work.

I found myself thinking about the things I wanted to do one last time before I died. At this stage, I realized I had a greater desire to repeat previous pleasurable experiences than to have new ones.

Some of the things I wanted to do again were obvious, of course: make love to my wife, hug my son, see my brother Bill.

And there were the less obvious—the things that were unique to me. I wanted to go to the Octagon again, my favorite steak-house in Thornhill, the place where I'd proposed to Susan. Yes, even with the nausea caused by the chemotherapy, I wanted to do that once more.

And I wanted to watch *Casablanca* again. *Here's looking at you, kid* . . .

I wanted to see the Blue Jays win the World Series one more time . . . but I suppose there wasn't much chance of that.

I wanted to go back to Drumheller and walk amongst the hoodoos, drinking in the Badlands at twilight with coyotes howling in the background and fossil shards scattered all around.

I wanted to visit my old neighborhood, out in Scarborough. I wanted to walk the streets of my youth, gaze at my parents' old house or stand in the yard of William Lyon Mackenzie King Public School, and let memories of friends from decades past wash over me.

I wanted to dust off my old ham-radio set, and listen—just listen—to voices in the night from all around the world.

But, most of all, I wanted to go up with Ricky and Susan to our cottage on Otter Lake, and sit on the dock after dark, late enough in the summer that the mosquitoes and black flies would be gone, and watch the moon rise, its pitted face reflecting in the calm water, and listen to the haunting call of a loon and the sound of the odd fish jumping up out of the lake, and lean back in my lounge chair, and clasp my hands behind my head, and breathe out a contented sigh, and feel no pain at all.

ROBERT J. SAWYER

21

So far, Susan had said nothing related to Salbanda's widely publicized comments about the universe having had a creator—a creator who, apparently, on at least five occasions, had directly intervened in the development of intelligent life.

But, finally, we did have to have the conversation. It's one I'd never anticipated. I'd humored my wife, indulging her faith, even agreeing to be married in a traditional church service. But I'd always quietly known that I was the enlightened one, I was in the right, I was the one who really knew how things worked.

Susan and I were sitting out back on the deck. It was an abnormally warm April evening. She was going to take Ricky to his swimming lesson this evening; sometimes I took him, and sometimes we went together, but tonight I had other plans. Ricky was up in his room, changing.

"Had Hollus told you he was searching for God?" asked Susan, looking down at her mug of coffee.

I nodded.

"And you didn't say anything to me?"

"Well, I . . ." I trailed off. "No. No, I didn't."

"I would have loved to have talked to him about that."

"I'm sorry," I said.

"So the Forhilnors are religious," she said, summing it all up, at least for her.

But I had to protest; I *had* to. "Hollus and his colleagues believe the universe was intelligently designed. But they don't worship God."

"They don't pray?" asked Susan.

"No. Well, the Wreeds spend half of each day in meditation, attempting to communicate with God telepathically, but—"

"That sounds like prayer to me."

"They say they don't want anything from God."

Susan was quiet for a moment; we rarely talked about religion, and for a good reason. "Prayer isn't about asking for things; it's not like visiting a department-store Santa Claus."

I shrugged; I guess I really didn't know much about the topic.

"Do the Forhilnors believe in souls? In an afterlife?"

The question surprised me; I'd never thought about it. "I honestly don't know."

"Maybe you should ask Hollus."

I nodded. Maybe I should.

"You know that I believe in souls," she said simply.

"I know."

That's as far as she went with the thought, though. She didn't ask me to go to church with her again; she'd asked once, a while ago, and that was fine. But she wouldn't push. If attending St. George's was helping her get through all this, then that was great. But we each had to cope with it in our own way.

Ricky came through the sliding glass door, out onto the deck. "Hey, sport," I said. "Give your dad a kiss."

He came over and kissed my cheek. Then he patted my face with his little hand. "I like it better this way," he said. I think he was trying to cheer me up; he'd never liked the sandpaper roughness of the five o'clock shadow I used to get. I smiled at him.

Susan got up and kissed me, too.

And my wife and my son headed off.

ROBERT J. SAWYER

With Ricky and Sue off at the Douglas Snow Aquatic Centre, four blocks away, I was all alone. I went back into the house and set up our video camera—an indulgence, a Christmas gift we'd given to each other a few years back—on a tripod in the den.

I turned on the camera, moved to the chair behind the desk, and sat down. "Hello, Ricky," I said. And then I smiled apologetically. "I'm going to ask your mother not to show you this tape for ten years, so I guess you're sixteen now. I'm sure you don't go by 'Ricky,' anymore. Maybe you're a 'Rick,' or maybe you've decided 'Richard' suits you better. So—so maybe I'll just call you 'son.'"

I paused. "I'm sure you've seen plenty of pictures of me; your mom was always taking snapshots. Maybe you even have some memories of me—I sure hope you do. I remember a few things from when I was six or seven . . . maybe an hour or two total." I paused again. If he *did* remember me, I hoped it was as I looked before the cancer, back when I had hair, when I wasn't so gaunt. Indeed, I should have made this tape as soon as I was diagnosed—certainly before I'd gone through chemotherapy.

"So you have me at a disadvantage," I said. "You know what I look like, but I find myself wondering what you look like— what sort of man you've grown into." I smiled. "You were a little small for your age when you were six—but so much can change in ten years. When I was your age—the age you are now, sixteen—I had grown a scraggly beard. There was only one other guy in my school who had one; it was, I guess, an act of youthful rebellion." I shifted a bit in my chair.

"Anyway," I said, "I'm sure you've grown up to be a fine man—I know your mother wouldn't have let it turn out any other way. I'm sorry I wasn't there for you. I would have loved to have taught you how to tie a tie, how to shave, how to throw a football, how to drink a glass of wine. I don't know what interests you've pursued. Sports? School theater? Whatever they are, you know I would have been in the audience as often as I could."

I paused. "I guess you're wrestling with what you want to do in life. I know you'll find happiness and success whatever you choose. If you want, there should be plenty of money for you to go to university for as long as you like—right through to a doctorate, if that's what you want. Do whatever will make you happy, of course, but I will tell you that I have greatly enjoyed the rewards of an academic life; maybe it won't be for you, but if you *are* contemplating it, I do recommend it. I've traveled the world over, I'm reasonably well paid, and I get an enormous amount of flexibility in my time. I say that just in case you were wondering if your dad was happy in his job; yes, I was—very much so. And that's the most important thing. If I have one piece of career advice to give you, it's this: don't worry about how much money you'll make. Pick something that you'll enjoy doing; you only go around once in life."

I paused again. "But, really, there's not much advice I can give you." A smile. "Heck, when I was your age, the last thing I wanted was advice from my dad." And then I shrugged a little. "Still, I will say this: please don't smoke. Believe me, son, nothing is worth risking going through what I've been going through. I wasn't a smoker—I'm sure you mom has told you that—but that is the way most people get lung cancer. Please, I beg you; don't risk this."

I glanced at the clock on the wall; there was plenty of time left—on the tape, at least.

"You're probably curious about my relationship with Hollus, the Forhilnor." I shrugged. "Frankly, I'm curious about it, too. I suppose if you remember anything from your childhood, it's the night he came to visit our house. You know that was the real Hollus? Not a projection? Well, it was. You, me, and your mother were the first humans to actually meet a Forhilnor in the flesh. Besides this tape, I'm also leaving you a copy of the journal I've been keeping about my experiences with Hollus. Maybe someday you, or somebody else, will put together a book about all this. Of course, there will be gaps that have to be filled in—I'm

ROBERT J. SAWYER

sure there are relevant things going on that I don't know about—but the notes I've made should give you a good start.

"Anyway, about my relationship with Hollus, all I know is this: I like him and I think he likes me. There's a saying that an unexamined life is not worth living; getting cancer caused me to examine my life, but I think getting to know Hollus has caused me to examine what it means to be human." I shrugged a little, acknowledging that what I was about to say was the sort of thing people didn't normally say aloud. "And I guess what it means is this: to be human is to be *fragile*. We are easily hurt, and not just physically. We are easily hurt emotionally, too. So, as you move through life, my son, try not to hurt others." I lifted my shoulders again. "That's it; that's the advice I have for you." It wasn't nearly enough, I knew; there was no way to make up for a lost decade with a few bromides. Ricky already had become the man he was going to be . . . without my help.

"There's one final thing I want you to know," I said. "Never doubt this for a moment, Richard Blaine Jericho. You had a father once, and he loved you. Always remember that."

I got up, shut off the video camera, and stood there in the den, my sanctuary.

22

I t had come to me while sleeping, doubtless because of the recording I'd made for Ricky: a version of me that would live on after my body had died. I was so excited, I got up and went downstairs to tap repeatedly on the holoform dodecahedron, in hopes of summoning Hollus. But he didn't come; I had to wait until he appeared in my office of his own volition the next day.

"Hollus," I said, as soon as his image had stabilized, "I think I know what they've buried beneath those warning landscapes on all those dead worlds."

Hollus locked his eyes on me.

"It's not nuclear waste," I said. "As you said, there are no markings related to nuclear waste, and no need to worry about such things over million-year timeframes. No, they buried something they wanted to *preserve* forever, not something they wanted to get rid of. That's why the Cassiopeians went so far as to shut off plate tectonics on their world by blowing up their moon—they wanted to be sure what they had in their subterranean vault never subducted."

"Perhaps," said Hollus. "But what would they want to preserve so carefully while at the same time trying to frighten anyone away from digging it up?"

"Themselves," I said.

"You propose something like a bomb shelter? Seismic soundings suggest there is not enough volume in the vault on Mu Cassiopeae A Prime to house more than a small number of individuals."

"No, no," I said. "I think they're *all* down there. Millions, billions; whatever their entire population was. I think they scanned their brains and uploaded themselves into a computer world—and the actual hardware generating that world, the machines they didn't want anyone messing with, are stored beneath those horrendous landscapes."

"Scanned . . . ," said Hollus's left mouth, and "scanned . . . ," ruminated his right. "But we only found three worlds with artificial landscapes designed to frighten off the curious," he said. "The other worlds we visited—Eta Cassiopeae A III, Sigma Draconis II, and Groombridge 1618 III—had simply been vacated."

"On those worlds, the computer hardware may have been shot into space. Or else those races may have decided that the best way to avoid detection was simply to do nothing at all. Even a warning marker attracts the curious; maybe they decided to hide their computing hardware with no indication of where it is."

"But why would entire races do that?" asked Hollus. "Why give up physical existence?"

That was a no-brainer for me. "How old are you?" I asked.

"In subjective Earth years? Forty-seven."

That surprised me. For some reason, I'd expected Hollus to be older than I was. "And how long will you live?"

"Perhaps another eighty years, assuming an accident does not befall me."

"So a typical Forhilnor lifespan is a hundred and thirty years?"

"For females, yes. Males live about ten years longer."

"So, um—my God—so you're female?"

"Yes."

I was stunned. "I hadn't been aware of that. Your voice—it's rather deep."

"That is just the way Forhilnor voices are—male or female."

"I think I'll go on calling you 'he,' if that's okay."

"I am no longer offended by it," said Hollus. "You may continue to do so."

"Anyway," I said, "you'll live a total of about a hundred and thirty years. Me, I'm fifty-four right now; if it weren't for the adenocarcinoma, I'd live another twenty-odd years, if not thirty or forty."

Hollus's eyestalks moved.

"But that's it. And, again, even if I didn't have cancer, a lot of that time would be in declining health." I paused. "Do Forhilnors age gracefully?"

"A poet on my world once said, 'It is all eclipsing moons'—a metaphor that means much the same as your expression 'it is all downhill'—from the moment you are born. Forhilnor bodies and minds deteriorate over time, too."

"Well, if you could assume a virtual existence—if you could live inside a computer—starting in the prime of youth, you could go on forever, without any deterioration."

"Immortality has always been a dream of my people," Hollus admitted.

"Mine, too. In fact, many preachers use a promise of life everlasting, albeit in some other realm, as their main inducement for good behavior. But although we've extended our life spans a great deal through improved health care, we are nowhere near immortal."

"Nor are we," said Hollus. "Nor are the Wreeds. But both they and we harbor hopes of making eternal life possible."

"We thought we'd made a breakthrough a few years ago when we discovered how to put the end caps back on DNA." Chromosomes have little protective bits at their ends, like the plastic-wrapped tips of shoelaces; every time a chromosome divides, the tips—called telomeres—are shortened. After enough divisions, the tips are completely gone, and the chromosome can't divide anymore.

"We discovered that, too," said Hollus, "almost a hundred

211

years ago. But although replacing telomeres can make individual cells divide forever in the laboratory, it does not work in an integrated organism. When an organism reaches a critical mass of cells, division either halts after a set number of repeats, just as if the telomeres had been diminished, or reproduction becomes uncontrolled, and tumors form." His eyestalks dipped. "As you know, I lost my own mother to cancer of the *vostirrarl*, an organ that serves much the same function for us as does the marrow in your bones."

"Leukemia," I said softly. "We call cancer of the marrow leukemia."

Hollus was quiet for a time.

Yes, I could surely understand the appeal.

To be uploaded.

To be divorced from the physical.

To live without tumors, without pain.

If the opportunity were presented to me, would I do it?

In a minute.

"It's certainly a great incentive to give up physical existence," I said. "Living forever in the good health of youth." I looked at Hollus, who was standing on just five legs; he seemed to be giving the sixth a rest. "In which case, perhaps your people have nothing to fear. Presumably, soon enough your race will develop the same ability—it seems every race does. And then, if your people want, they will . . . will *transcend* into a new form of existence."

Hollus said nothing for several seconds. "I am not sure that I would look forward to that," he said.

"It must be very tempting, if race after race has chosen that route."

"I suppose," said Hollus. "My people have been making considerable progress in brain-scanning technology—it is somewhat more difficult for us than it will be for your people, since our brains are in the centers of our bodies and since the integration of the two halves will doubtless pose some problems.

ROBERT J. SAWYER

Still, I imagine we will be able to upload a combined Forhilnor consciousness within a few decades." He paused. "But this does explain the phenomenon I observed in those science-fiction videos you showed me: why alien races that encounter each other in the flesh are always at about the same technological level. There is, it seems, a narrow window between when interstellar flight is developed and when a race ceases to have corporeal existence. It also explains why the search for extraterrestrial intelligence via radio telescopes usually fails; again, there is only a short time between the development of radio and the abandonment of its use."

"But, as far as you've been able to determine, none of the races you're aware of, except our three, have existed simultaneously." I paused. "Our races—the three of us—may be the first chance the galaxy has ever had for a . . . a planetary federation."

"Interesting thought," said Hollus. "Do you suppose that is why God intervened on our worlds? To bring us to technological sophistication simultaneously so that we could form some sort of alliance?"

"Possibly," I said. "Although I'm not sure what that would accomplish. I mean, it might be good for our races, but what does it do for the creator?"

Hollus lowered his sixth foot. "That is a very good question," he said at last.

Later that night, after we'd put Ricky to bed, and I'd read to him for a bit, Susan and I were sitting on the couch in the living room. I had my arm draped around her shoulders, and she had her head resting on my chest.

"Have you ever thought about the future?" I asked her. I lifted my arm a little bit. "I don't mean the near future." I'm sure she'd been giving that much thought. "I mean the far future—thousands, or even millions, of years from now."

I couldn't see Susan's face. I hoped she was smiling. "I won't be around to see that."

I was quiet for a moment; I didn't know if I really wanted to broach this topic. "But what if there was a way," I said. "A way to live forever."

Susan was sharp; that's one of the reasons I'd married her. "Has Hollus offered you that? Immortality?"

I shook my head. "No. He doesn't have any better idea of how to make it work than we do. But his race has found evidence of six other species that seem to have perhaps discovered immortality . . . of a sort."

She shifted slightly against my chest. "Oh?"

"They seem to have . . . well, the word we've been using is 'transcended' into another level of existence . . . presumably by uploading themselves into computers."

"That's hardly 'living forever.' You might as well be a corpse preserved in formaldehyde."

"We presume the uploaded beings continue to exist within the computer, acting and reacting and interacting. Indeed, they might not even be able to tell that they don't have material existence anymore; the sensory experience might be comparable to, or better than, what we're used to."

She sounded incredulous. "And you say whole races have done this?"

"That's my theory, yes."

"And you think the individual consciousnesses continue on forever inside the computers?"

"It's possible."

"Which means . . . which means you wouldn't have to die?"

"Well, the flesh-and-blood me would die, of course, and I would have no continuity with the uploaded version once the scan had been made. But the uploaded version would remember having been me, and would go on after I'd died. As far as it—or those interacting with it—would be concerned, it would be me. So, yes, if we had access to the technology, in a very real sense I wouldn't have to die. I assume that one of the big reasons for people uploading themselves was to overcome the limitations imposed by growing old or ill."

"This isn't on the table?" asked Susan. Her heart was pounding; I could feel it. "You really haven't been offered this?"

"No," I said. "Neither the Forhilnors nor the Wreeds know how to do it—and, for that matter, we're only assuming that this is what really happened to the other races. It seems that every intelligent species either destroys itself shortly after discovering nuclear weapons, or that it survives maybe a hundred and fifty years longer, but then decides to transcend."

Susan lifted her shoulders. "If it *were* on the table—if it was something you were being offered right now—my response might be different. You know that . . ." She trailed off, but I knew she'd been about to say that she'd do anything to keep from losing me. I squeezed her hand.

"But," she continued, "if it weren't for that, if it weren't for what we're facing, I'd say no. I can't imagine it being something I'd want."

"You'd live forever," I said.

"No, I'd *exist* forever. That's not the same thing."

"It could all be simulated, of course. Every aspect of life."

"If it isn't real," said Susan, "it isn't the same."

"You wouldn't be able to tell that it wasn't real."

"Perhaps not," Susan said. "But I'd *know* it wasn't, and that would make all the difference."

I shrugged a little. "Ricky seems just as happy playing Nintendo baseball as he is playing the real game—in fact, he plays the computer version more often; I don't think his generation is going to have the conceptual problems with this that we do." I paused. "A virtual existence does have its appeals. You wouldn't have to grow old. You wouldn't have to die."

"I like growing and changing." She frowned. "I mean, sure, I sometimes wish I still had the body I'd had when I was eighteen, but I'm mostly content."

"Civilization after civilization seems to decide to do this."

Susan frowned. "You say they either upload themselves or blow themselves up?"

"Apparently. Hollus said his people faced the same sort of nuclear crisis we're still facing."

"Maybe they decide they have no choice but to trade reality for a simulation, then. If, say, the U.S. and China were to go to war, we'd all probably die, and the human race would be over. But if this were all a simulation, and things went bad, you could just reset the simulation and go on existing. Maybe unreal existence is the only long-term hope for violent races."

That was certainly an intriguing thought. Maybe you didn't outgrow your desire to blow each other up. Maybe it was inevitable that some nation, or some group of terrorists, or just some lunatic, would do it; as Hollus had said, the ability to destroy life on a massive scale becomes cheaper, more portable, and more readily available as time goes by. If there was no way to put the genie back in the bottle—whether it's nuclear bombs, biological weaponry, or some other tool of mass destruction—then perhaps races transcend just as soon as they can, because it's the only safe thing to do.

"I wonder what humanity will choose when the time comes?" I said. "Presumably, we'll have the technology within a century." No need to state it dramatically; Susan and I were in the same boat on timeframes that long. "You and I won't live to see it, but Ricky might. I wonder what they will choose to do?"

Susan was quiet for a few moments. She then started shaking her head slowly back and forth. "I'd love for my son to live forever, but . . . but I hope he, and everyone, chooses normal existence."

I thought about that—about the pain of skinned knees and broken hearts and broken bones; about the risks flesh was susceptible to; about what I'd been going through.

I doubted there was any way to reverse the decision. If you copied whatever you were into a computer, you presumably couldn't go back. If the biological version of you continued on, it would have a separate existence from the moment the scan was made. There'd be no way to reintegrate the two versions later on; it would be like trying to force identical twins to inhabit a single body.

There were no intelligent lifeforms left on any of those six worlds Hollus's starship had explored. Perhaps all races terminated the biological versions of themselves once the electronic ones were created. Indeed, perhaps that was the only sensible thing to do, preventing any possibility of terrorist disruptions of the virtual world. Of course, at least on Earth, there were those who would never agree to be voluntarily uploaded— the Amish, Luddites, and others. But they might be scanned surreptitiously, moving them into a virtual world indistinguishable from the one they'd left, rather than leaving any flesh-and-blood beings around whose descendants might vandalize the computers.

I wondered if any of the races that had transcended regretted their decision?

Susan and I got ready for bed. She eventually drifted off to sleep, but I lay awake, staring at the dark ceiling, envying the Wreeds.

Shortly after I'd been diagnosed, I'd walked the few blocks from the ROM to the Chapters flagship store on Bloor Street and had bought Elisabeth Kübler-Ross's *On Death and Dying*. She outlined the five stages of coming to terms with death: denial and isolation, anger, bargaining, depression, and acceptance; by my own reckoning I was now well into number five, although there were occasional days on which I felt as though I was still mired in number four. Nonetheless, almost everyone went through the stages in the same sequence. Was it surprising, then, that there were stages whole species went through?

Hunter-gatherer.

Agriculture or animal husbandry.

Metallurgy.

217

Cities.

Monotheism.

An age of discovery.

An age of reason.

Atomic energy.

Space travel.

An information revolution.

A flirtation with interstellar voyaging.

And then—

And then—

And then something else.

As a Darwinian, I've spent countless hours explaining to laypeople that evolution doesn't have a goal, that life is an ever-branching bush, a pageant of shifting adaptations.

But now, perhaps, it seemed as though there *was* a goal, a final result.

The end of biology.

The end of pain.

The end of death.

I was, on some visceral level—an appropriate metaphor, invoking guts and biology and humanity—dead-set against the idea of giving up corporeal existence. Virtual reality was nothing but air guitar writ large. My life had meaning *because* it was real. Oh, I'm sure I could use a virtual-reality device to send me on simulated digs, and I could find simulated fossils, including even breakthrough specimens (such as, oh, I don't know, say, a sequence showing in a thousand graduated steps the change from one species into another . . .). But it would be meaningless, pointless; I'd just be a glider shooting out of a gun. There'd be no thrill of discovery—the fossils would be there simply because I *wanted* them to be there. And they would contribute nothing to our real knowledge of evolution. I never know in advance what I will find on a dig—no one knows. But whatever I do find has to fit into that vast mosaic of facts discovered by Buckland and Cuvier and Mantell and Dollo and von Huene and

ROBERT J. SAWYER

Cope and Marsh and the Sternbergs and Lambe and Park and Andrews and Colbert and the older Russell and the younger, unrelated Russell and Ostrom and Jensen and Bakker and Horner and Weishampel and Dodson and Dong and Zheng and Sereno and Chatterjee and Currie and Brett-Surman and all the rest, pioneers and my contemporaries. It was real; it was part of the shared universe.

But now, here I was spending most of my time with a virtual-reality simulation. Yes, there was a real flesh-and-blood Hollus somewhere, and yes, I'd even met him. But most of my interactions were with something computer-generated, a cyberghost. One could easily get sucked into an artificial world. Yes, one surely could.

I hugged my wife, savoring reality.

23

I hadn't slept well last night or the night before, and I guess the fatigue was getting to me. I'd tried—I had really tried—to be stoic about what I was going through, to keep a stiff upper lip. But today—

Today . . .

It was the golden hour, the hour between the beginning of work at 9:00 A.M. and the opening of the museum to the public at 10:00. Hollus and I were looking at the special exhibit of Burgess Shale fossils: *Opabinia* and *Sanctacaris* and *Wiwaxia* and *Anomalocaris* and *Hallucigenia*, lifeforms so bizarre they defied easy categorization.

And the fossils made me think of Stephen Jay Gould's book about the Burgess fauna, *Wonderful Life*.

And that made me think about the movie Gould was alluding to, the Jimmy Stewart classic, the Yuletide favorite.

And *that* made me think about how much I valued *my* life . . . my real, actual, flesh-and-blood existence.

"Hollus," I said, tentatively, softly.

His twin eyestalks had been staring at *Opabinia's* cluster of five eyes, so unlike anything else in Earth's past. He swiveled the stalks to look at me.

"Hollus," I said again, "I *know* your race is more advanced than mine."

He was motionless.

"And, well, you *must* know things that we don't."

"True."

"I—you've met my wife Susan. You've met Ricky."

He touched his eyes together. "You have a pleasant family," he said.

"I—I don't want to leave them, Hollus. I don't want Ricky to grow up without a father. I don't want Susan to be alone."

"That is unfortunate," agreed the Forhilnor.

"There *must* be something you can do—something you can do to save me."

"I am sorry, Tom. I really am. But as I said to your son, there is nothing."

"Okay," I said. "Okay, look, I know how these things work. You've got some sort of noninterference directive, right? You're not allowed to change anything here. I understand that, but—"

"There really is no such directive," Hollus said. "I would help you if I could."

"But you've *got* to know how to cure cancer. With everything you know about DNA and how life works—you've got to know how to cure something as simple as cancer."

"Cancer plagues my people, too. I told you that."

"And the Wreeds? What about the Wreeds?"

"Them as well. Cancer is, well, a fact of life."

"Please," I said. "Please."

"There is nothing I can do."

"You *have* to," I said. My voice was growing more strident; I hated the way it sounded—but I couldn't stop. "You have to."

"I *am* sorry," said the alien.

Suddenly I was shouting, my words echoing off the glass display cases. "Damn it, Hollus. God damn it. I'd help you if I could. Why won't you help me?"

Hollus was silent.

"I've got a wife. And a son."

The Forhilnor's twin voices acknowledged this. "I" "know."

"So help me, damn you. *Help me!* I don't want to die."

222

"I do not want you to die, either," said Hollus. "You are my friend."

"You're not my friend!" I shouted. "If you were my friend, you would help me."

I expected him to wink out, expected the holographic projection to shut off, leaving me alone with the ancient, dead remnants of the Cambrian explosion. But Hollus stayed with me, calmly waiting, while I broke down and cried.

Hollus had disappeared for the day around 4:20 in the afternoon, but I stayed late, working in my office. I was ashamed of myself, disgusted at my performance.

The end was coming; I'd known it for months.

Why couldn't I be more brave? Why couldn't I face it with more dignity?

It was time to wrap things up. I knew that.

Gordon Small and I hadn't spoken for thirty years. We had been good friends in childhood, living on the same street in Scarborough, but we'd had a falling out at university. He felt I had wronged him horribly; I felt he had wronged me horribly. For the first ten years or so after our big fight, I probably thought about him at least once a month. I was still furious about what he'd done to me, and, as I would lie in bed at night, my mind cycling through all the things it could possibly be upset about, Gordon would come up.

There was a lot of other unfinished business in my life, of course—relationships of all sorts that should be concluded or repaired. I knew that I'd never get around to some of them.

For instance, there was Nicole, the girl I'd stood up the night of our high-school prom. I'd never been able to tell her why—that my father had gotten drunk and had pushed my mother down the stairs, and that I'd spent that night with her in the emergency department at Scarborough General. How could I tell Nicole that? In retrospect, of course, perhaps I should have just said that my mother had had a fall, and I'd had to take her to the hospital, but Nicole was my girlfriend, and she might have wanted to come to see my mother, so instead I lied and said I'd had car trouble, and I was caught in that lie, and I never was able to explain to her what really happened.

Then there was Bjorn Amundsen, who had borrowed a hundred dollars from me at university but had never repaid it. I knew he was poor; I knew he wasn't getting help from his parents, the way I was; I knew he'd been turned down for a scholarship. He needed the hundred more than I did; indeed, he *always* needed it more than I did, and was never able to pay it back. Stupidly, I'd once made a comment about him being a bad risk. He took to avoiding me rather than have to admit that he could not repay the loan. I'd always thought you couldn't put a price on friendship, but, in that case, it turned out that I could—and it was a measly hundred bucks. I'd love to apologize to Bjorn, but I had no idea what had become of him.

And there was Paul Kurusu, a Japanese student in my high school, who once, in a fit of anger, I'd called a racist name—the only time in my life I'd ever done that. He'd looked at me with such hurt; he'd heard similar names from others, of course, but I was supposed to be his friend. I had no idea what had come over me, and I'd always wanted to tell him how sorry I was. But how do you bring something like that up three decades later?

But Gordon Small was one I had to make peace with. I couldn't—couldn't go to my grave with that unresolved. Gordon had moved to Boston in the early '80s. I called directory assistance. There were three Gordon Smalls listed for Boston, but only one had the middle initial *P*—and Philip, it came back to me, had been Gordon's middle name.

I jotted down the number, dialed nine again for an outside line, dialed my long-distance billing code, then keyed in Gordon's number. A girl's voice answered. "Hello?"

ROBERT J. SAWYER

"Hello," I said. "May I please speak to Gordon Small?"

"Just a second," said the girl. Then she shouted out, "Grandpa!"

Grandpa. He was a grandfather now—a grandfather at fifty-four. This was ridiculous; so much time had passed. I was about to put down the handset when a voice came from the speaker. "Hello?"

Two syllables, that's all—but I recognized him at once. The sound brought a flood of memories rushing back.

"Gord," I said, "it's Tom Jericho."

There was startled silence for a few seconds, and then, frosty, "Ah."

He didn't slam down the phone, at least. Maybe he was thinking that someone had died—a mutual friend, someone he'd want to know about, someone who meant enough to both of us that I'd set aside our differences to let him know about the funeral, someone from the old gang, the old neighborhood.

But he didn't say anything else. Just "ah." And then he waited for me to get on with it.

Gordon was in the States now, and I knew the American media well: once an alien had appeared on U.S. soil—there was that Forhilnor who had been haunting the San Francisco courts, and another visiting the psychiatric hospital in Charleston—no mention would be made of anything outside of America; if Gordon knew about Hollus and me, he gave no sign.

I'd rehearsed what I'd wanted to say, of course, but his tone—the coldness, the hostility—left me tongue-tied. Finally, I blurted out, "I'm sorry."

He could have taken that any number of ways: sorry to bother you, sorry to have interrupted what you were doing, sorry to hear about whatever your current sadness is, sorry that an old friend is dead—or, of course, as I meant it: sorry for what had happened, for the wedge we'd driven between ourselves all those decades past. But he wasn't going to make this easy for me. "For what?" he said.

I exhaled, probably quite noisily, into the mouthpiece. "Gord, we used to be friends."

"Until you betrayed me, yes."

That's the way it was going to be, then. There was no reciprocity; no sense that we had each wronged the other. It was all my fault, entirely my doing.

I felt anger bubbling within me; for a moment, I wanted to lash out, tell him how what he had done had made me feel, tell him how I'd cried—literally cried—in rage and frustration and agony after our friendship had disintegrated.

I closed my eyes for a moment, calming myself. I'd made this call to bring closure, not to restart an old fight. I felt pain in my chest; stress always magnified it. "I'm sorry," I said again. "It's bothered me, Gord. Year after year. I never should have done what I did."

"That's for damn sure," he said.

I couldn't take all the blame, though; there was still pride, or something akin to it, in me. "I was hoping," I said, "that we might apologize to each other."

But Gordon deflected that idea. "Why are you calling? After all these years?"

I didn't want to tell him the truth: "Well, Gord-o, it's like this: I'll be dead soon, and . . ."

No. No, I couldn't say that. "I just wanted to clean up some old business."

"It's a little late for that," said Gordon.

No, I thought. Next year would be too late. But, while we're alive, it's not too late.

"Was that your granddaughter who answered the phone?" I said.

"Yes."

"I have a six-year-old boy. His name is Ricky—Richard Blaine Jericho." I let the name hang in the air. Gordon had been a big *Casablanca* fan, too; I thought perhaps hearing the name

ROBERT J. SAWYER

might soften him. But if he were smiling, I couldn't tell over the phone.

He said nothing, so I asked, "How are you doing, Gord?"

"Fine," he said. "Married for thirty-two years; two sons and three grandkids." I waited for him to invite reciprocity; a simple "You?" would have done it. But he didn't.

"Well, that's all I wanted to say," I said. "Just that I'm sorry; that I wish things had never gone the way they did." It was too much to add, "that I wish we were still friends," so I didn't. Instead, I said, "I hope—I hope the rest of your life is terrific, Gord."

"Thanks," he said. And then, after a pause that seemed interminable, "Yours, too."

My voice was going to break if I stayed on the phone much longer. "Thank you," I said. And then, "Goodbye."

"Goodbye, Tom."

And the phone went dead.

24

Our house on Ellerslie was almost fifty years old. We'd upgraded it with central air conditioning, a second bathroom, and the deck Tad and I had built a few summers back. It was a good home, full of memories.

But at the moment, I was all alone in it—and that was strange.

It seemed that I was hardly ever alone anymore. Hollus was with me a lot at work, and when he wasn't around, the other paleontologists or grad students were milling about. And except for church, Susan almost never left me alone at home anymore. Whether she was trying to make the most of what time we had left, or was simply afraid that I had deteriorated so much that I couldn't get along without her for even a few hours, I don't know.

But it was rare for me to be at home alone, with neither her nor Ricky around.

I wasn't sure what I wanted to do.

I could watch TV, but . . .

But, God, how much of my life had I wasted watching television? A couple of hours every night—that would be 700 hours a year. Times forty years; my family had gotten its first black-and-white TV in 1960. That's 28,000 hours, or . . .

My God.

That's three years.

In three years, Ricky will be nine. I'd give anything to see that. I'd give anything to have those three years back.

No, no, I wasn't going to watch TV.

I could read a book. I always regretted that I didn't spend more time reading for pleasure. Oh, I spent an hour and a half every day on the subway perusing scientific monographs and printouts of work-related newsgroups, trying to keep up, but it had been a long time since I'd cracked open a good novel. I'd gotten both John Irving's a *A Widow for One Year* and Terence M. Green's *A Witness to Life* for Christmas. So, yes, I could start either one this evening. But who knew when I might get to finish it? I was going to have enough uncompleted business left on my plate as it was.

It used to be when Susan was out that I'd order a pizza, a big, hot, massive pie from Dante's, which one local newspaper had given an award for the heaviest pizza—a Dante's with Schneider's pepperoni, so spicy it would still be on your breath two days hence. Susan didn't like Dante's—too filling, too hot—so when she was around, we ordered more pedestrian pies from that Toronto institution, Pizza Pizza.

But the chemotherapy had robbed me of much of my appetite; I couldn't face anyone's pizza tonight.

I could watch a porno film; we had a few on tape, bought as a lark years ago and rarely viewed. But no. The chemo had killed most of that desire, too, sad to say.

I sat down on the couch and stared at the mantelpiece above the fireplace, lined with little framed pictures: Susan and me on our wedding day; Susan cradling Ricky in her arms, shortly after we'd adopted him; me in the Alberta badlands, holding a pick; the black-and-white author photo from my one published book, *Canadian Dinosaurs;* my parents, about forty years ago; Susan's dad, scowling as usual; all three of us—me, Susan, and Ricky—in the pose we'd used one year on our Christmas cards.

My family.

My life.

I leaned back. The upholstery on the couch was worn; we'd

230

bought it just after we'd gotten married. Still, it should have lasted longer than this . . .

I was all alone.

The chance might not come again.

But I couldn't. I couldn't.

I'd spent my whole life being a rationalist, a secular humanist, a scientist.

They say Carl Sagan maintained his atheism right until the end. Even as he lay dying, he didn't recant, didn't admit any possibility of there ever being a personal God who cared one way or the other whether he lived or died.

And yet—

And yet, I had read his novel *Contact.* I'd seen the movie, too, for that matter, but the movie watered down the message of the novel. The book was unambiguous: it said that the universe had been designed, created to order by a vast sentience. The novel concluded with the words, "There is an intelligence that antedates the universe." Sagan may not have believed in the God of the Bible, but he at least allowed the possibility of a creator.

Or did he? Carl was no more obliged to believe what he wrote in his sole work of fiction than George Lucas was required to believe in the Force.

Stephen Jay Gould had fought cancer, too; he'd been diagnosed with abdominal mesothelioma in July 1982. He'd been lucky; he'd won. Gould, like Richard Dawkins, argued for a purely Darwinian view of nature—even if the two of them couldn't agree on the precise details of what that view was. But if religion had helped Gould get through his illness, he never said. Still, after his recovery, he'd written a new book, *Rocks of Ages: Science and Religion in the Fullness of Life,* which argued for the scientific and the spiritual being two separate realms, two "nonoverlapping magisteria"—a typical bit of Gouldish bafflegab. Clearly, though, larger questions had preoccupied him during his bout with the big C.

And now it was my turn.

231

Sagan had apparently remained stalwart until the end. Gould seemed perhaps to have wavered, but he'd ultimately returned to his old self, the perfect rationalist.

And me?

Sagan hadn't had to contend with visits from an alien whose grand unified theory pointed toward the existence of a creator.

Gould hadn't known of the advanced lifeforms from Beta Hydri and Delta Pavonis who believed in God.

But I did.

Many years ago, I'd read a book called *The Search for God at Harvard*. I was more intrigued by the title than by the actual contents, which told of the experiences of Ari Goldman, a *New York Times* journalist who spent a year enrolled in the Harvard Divinity School. If I wanted to search for fossils from the Cambrian explosion, I'd go to Yoho National Park; if I wanted to search for dinosaur eggshell fragments, I'd go to Montana or Mongolia. Most things require you to go to them, but God—God, if he is ubiquitous—should be something you could search for anywhere: at Harvard, at the Royal Ontario Museum, at a Pizza Hut in Kenya.

Indeed, it seemed to me if Hollus was correct, you should be able to reach out, anywhere, at any time, and sort of grab hold of a handful of space just the right way, and peel back the flap in front of you, revealing the machinery of God behind.

Pay no attention to that man behind the curtain . . .

And I hadn't. I'd ignored him utterly.

But now, right now, I was alone.

Or . . .

Christ, I never had thoughts like this. Am I weaker than Sagan? Weaker than Gould?

I'd met them both over the years; Carl had lectured at U of T, and we invited Stephen up to the ROM every time he had a new book out; he was coming again in a few weeks to speak in conjunction with the Burgess Shale exhibition. I'd been surprised at how tall Carl was, but Stephen was every bit the little round guy they'd drawn him as on *The Simpsons*.

232

Physically, neither looked stronger than I—than I used to be. But now, now perhaps I *was* weaker than either of them.

God damn it, I didn't want to die.

Old paleontologists never die, the joke goes. But they sure are petrified by death.

I got up off the couch. The living-room rug was pretty much obstacle-free; Ricky was getting better about putting his toys away.

It shouldn't matter where you do it.

I looked out the living-room window. Ellerslie was a great, old street up in what had been called Willowdale when I was a kid; it was lined by mature trees. A passerby would have to make a real effort to see in.

Still . . .

I walked over, closed the brown drapes. The room darkened. I threw the wall switch that controlled one of the torchiere floor lamps. A glance at the glowing blue clock on the VCR: I still had time before Susan and Ricky got home.

Did I want to do this?

There was no place for a creator in the curriculum I'd taught at U of T. The ROM was one of the most eclectic museums in the world, but, despite that ceiling mosaic proclaiming the museum's mission to be "that all men may know His work," there was no specific gallery devoted to God.

Of course not, the founders of the ROM would have said. The creator is everywhere.

Everywhere.

Even here.

I blew out air, exhaling my last bit of resistance to the idea.

And I knelt down, on the carpet, by the fireplace, the pictures of my family staring blindly at what I was doing.

I knelt down.

And I began to pray.

"God," I said.

The word echoed softly inside the brick fireplace.

I repeated it. "God?" A question that time, an invitation for a response.

There was none, of course. Why should God care that I'm dying of cancer? Millions of people worldwide were battling one form or another of that ancient foe at this very moment, and some of them were much younger than I. Surely children in leukemia wards should command his attention first.

Still, I tried again, a third uttering of the word I'd only ever used as a curse. "God?"

There was no sign, and indeed there never would be. Isn't that what faith is all about?

"God, if Hollus is right—if the Wreeds and Forhilnors are correct, and you designed the universe piece by piece, fundamental constant by fundamental constant—then couldn't you have avoided this? What possible good does cancer do anyone?"

The Lord works in mysterious ways. Mrs. Lansbury had always said that. Everything happens for a purpose.

Such bull. Such unmitigated crap. I felt my stomach knotting. Cancer didn't happen for any purpose. It tore people apart; if a god did create life, then he's a shoddy workman, churning out flawed, self-destructing products.

"God, I wish—I wish you had decided to do some things differently."

That's as far as I could go. Susan had said prayer wasn't about asking for things—and I couldn't bring myself to ask for mercy, ask not to die, ask to get to see my son graduate from university, ask to be there to grow old with my wife.

Just then, the front swung open. I'd been lost in thought, obviously, or else I would have likely heard Susan jostling her keys as she worked the lock.

I felt myself going beet red. "Found it!" I exclaimed, as if to myself, making a show of picking up some invisible lost object. I rose to my feet and smiled sheepishly at my beautiful wife and my handsome, young son.

But I hadn't found anything at all.

ROBERT J. SAWYER

25

I n 1997, Stephen Pinker came to the ROM to promote his new book, *How the Mind Works*. I attended the fascinating lecture he gave. Among other things, he pointed out that humans, even across cultural boundaries, use consistent metaphors in speech. Arguments are always battles. He won; I lost; he beat me; she attacked every point; he made me defend my position; I had to retreat.

Love affairs are patients or diseases. They have a sick relationship; he got over her; she's got it bad for him; it broke his heart.

Ideas are food. Food for thought; something to chew on; his suggestion left a bad taste in my mouth; I couldn't stomach the notion; a delicious irony; the idea kept me going.

Virtue, meanwhile, is *up*, presumably related to our erect posture. He's an upstanding citizen; that act is beneath me; I wouldn't sink so low; he took the high road; I tried to come up to his standards.

Still, it wasn't until I met Hollus that I realized how uniquely human those ways of thinking were. Hollus had done an excellent job of mastering English, and he did often use human metaphors. But from time to time, I glimpsed what I presumed was the true Forhilnor way of thinking behind his speech.

For Hollus, love was astronomical—two individuals

coming to know each other so well that their movements could be predicted with absolute precision. "Rising love" meant that the affection would be there tomorrow, just as surely as the sun would come up. "A new constellation" was new love between old friends—seeing a pattern amongst the stars that had always been there, but had heretofore eluded detection.

And morality was based on the integration of thought: "that thought alternates well," referring to a notion that causes significant switching back and forth between his two mouths. An immoral thought was one that came only from one side: "He was all on the left with that." A half-brained idea wasn't a stupid one to Hollus; it was an evil one. And although Forhilnors spoke as we do of having "second thoughts," they used the phrase to mean that the other brain-half had finally kicked in, bringing the individual back to a moral position.

As Hollus had intimated the night he came to my house for dinner, Forhilnors alternated words or syllables between two mouths because their brains, like ours, consisted of two lobes, and their consciousness came even more than ours did from the interplay between those two lobes. Humans often speak of a crazy person as someone who has lost it—"it" presumably being his or her grip on reality. Forhilnors didn't use that metaphor, but they did share our one about the struggle "to keep it together," although in their case "it" referred directly to the ongoing effort to integrate the two halves of the brain; healthy Forhilnors like Hollus always overlapped the syllables of their names—the "lus" beginning from his right mouth before the "Hol" had ended from his left—communicating to those around them that their brain-halves were safely integrated.

Still, Hollus had told me that high-speed photography showed that their eyestalks didn't actually move as mirror images of each other. Rather, one always took the lead and the other followed a fraction of a second later. Which eyestalk led—and which half of the brain was in control—varied from mo-

ROBERT J. SAWYER

ment to moment; the study of which lobe initiated which actions was at the center of Forhilnor psychology.

Because Susan had put the question in my mind, I had indeed asked Hollus whether he believed in souls. Most modern Forhilnors, himself included, did not, but what Forhilnor myths there were about life-after-death had grown out of their split-brain psychology. In their past, most Forhilnor religions had held that each individual possessed not one but two souls, one for each half of the body. Their conception of an afterlife consisted of two possible destinations, a heaven (although it was not as blissful as the Judeo-Christian one—"even in heaven, the rains must fall" was a Forhilnor platitude) and a hell (although it was not a place of torture or suffering; theirs had never been a vengeful god). Forhilnors were not creatures of extremes—having so many limbs perhaps led them to view things as more balanced (I never saw Hollus more astonished than when I stood on one leg to check to see if there was something on the bottom of my shoe; he was amazed I didn't fall over).

Anyway, the two Forhilnor souls could each go to heaven, each to hell, or one could go far and the other farther (the post-mortal realms were not "up" and "down"—again, a human notion of opposite extremes). If both souls went to the same place, even if it were hell, it was a better afterlife than if they were split up, for in the splitting whatever personality had been manifest in the being's physical form would be lost. A split-soul person was truly dead; whatever he had been was gone for good.

So there was a part of Hollus that was baffled by my fear of death. "You humans believe you have but a single, integrated soul," he said. We were in the collections room, examining mammallike reptiles from South Africa. "So what do you fear? Under your mythology, you will retain your identity even after death. Surely you do not worry about going to your hell, do you? You are not an evil person."

"I don't believe in souls, or an afterlife."

CALCULATING GOD

"Ah, good," said Hollus. "It surprised me that in this late stage of your race's development, so many humans still link the concept of a deity with the notion of they themselves having an immortal soul; the one surely does not require the other."

I'd never quite thought about it that way. Maybe Hollus's God was the ultimate Copernican-style dethroning: yes, a creator exists, but its creations don't have souls. "Still," I said, "even if I did believe in the afterlife my wife's religion describes, I'm not sure that I'm a good enough person to make it into heaven. The bar might be set awfully high."

"The bar?"

"A metaphor; it refers to high-jumping, a human sport. The higher the bar you have to jump over is set, the harder it is to do."

"Ah. Our comparable metaphor is one of narrowing passages. Still, you must know that the fear of death is irrational; death comes to everyone."

It was all clinical for him; he wasn't the one with only a handful of months left. "I know that," I said, perhaps too harshly. I took a deep, calming breath. He *was* my friend; there was no need to be short with him. "I don't exactly fear death," I lied. "I just don't want it to come so soon." A pause. "It still surprises me that you haven't conquered death." I wasn't fishing; really, I wasn't.

"More human thinking," said Hollus. "Death as an opponent."

I should show him *The Seventh Seal*—either that, or *Bill and Ted's Bogus Journey*. "Regardless," I said, "I would have expected you to have managed to prolong your lives more."

"We have. The average age of death prior to our development of antibiotics was half what it is now; prior to the development of drugs to unclog arteries, it was only three-quarters of what it is now."

"Yes, but—" I paused, trying to think of how to make my point. "I saw a doctor interviewed on CTV not too long ago. He said that the first human who is going to live forever has probably already been born. We've been assuming that we can conquer—sorry, that we can *avoid*—death, that there's nothing theoretically impossible about living forever."

"I am not sure that I would want to live in a world in which the only certain thing was taxes," said Hollus, his eyestalks doing their S-ripple. "Besides, my children are my immortality."

I blinked. "You have children?" I said. Why had I never asked him—*her*—about that?

"Yes," Hollus said. "A son and a daughter." And then, in a startlingly human act, the alien said, "Would you like to see pictures of them?"

I nodded. The holoform projector buzzed slightly, and suddenly two more Forhilnors were in the collections room with us, life-size but unmoving. "That is my son Kassold," Hollus said, indicating the one on the left. "And my daughter Pealdon."

"They are all grown up?" I asked; Pealdon and Kassold seemed to be about the same size as Hollus.

"Yes. Pealdon is a—what would you call it? One who works in the theater; she tells performers which interpretations will be allowed."

"A director," I said.

"A director, yes; part of the reason I wished to view some of your movies was to improve my sense of how human drama compared with Forhilnor plays. And my son Kassold is—a psychiatrist, I suppose. He treats disorders of the Forhilnor mind."

"I'm sure you're very proud of them," I said.

Hollus bobbed up and down. "You have no idea," the alien said.

Hollus had disappeared during the middle of the afternoon; he—no, *she:* for Pete's sake, she was a *mother*—she'd said she needed to attend to some other research. I used the time to dig

CALCULATING GOD

through the layers of paperwork on my desk and to reflect a little on what I'd done yesterday. Alan Dershowitz, one of my favorite columnists, once said, "It is while praying that I experience my greatest doubts about God, and it is while looking at the stars that I make the leap of faith." I wondered if—

The holoform projector bleeped twice. It startled me; I hadn't expected to see Hollus again today, but here she was, wavering back into existence in my office—and she looked more excited than I'd ever seen her before: eyestalks weaving rapidly, and her spherical torso bobbing as though it were being dribbled by an invisible hand.

"The last star we visited before coming here," Hollus said as soon as her image had stabilized, "was Groombridge 1618, some sixteen light-years from here. The second planet of that star once had a civilization, like the other worlds we had visited. But the inhabitants were gone."

I smiled. "Welcome back."

"What? Yes, yes. Thank you. But we have now found them. We have found the missing inhabitants."

"Just now? How?"

"Whenever we discovered a planet that had apparently been abandoned, we did a scan of its entire sky. The assumption is simple: if the inhabitants had vacated their world, they might have done so via starship. And the starship would likely be taking the shortest path between the planet and wherever it was going, meaning that its fusion exhaust—assuming it *is* powered by fusion—might be aimed back toward the home planet. We checked in the direction of every F, G, and K-class star within seventy terrestrial light-years of Groombridge, looking for an artificial fusion signature overlapping one of those stars' own spectra."

"And you found something?"

"No. No, we never did. Until yesterday. We had saved the whole scan in our computers, of course. I retrieved that scan

240

and wrote a program to do a wider search through it, checking *every* star of *every* type, out to five hundred light-years—Forhilnor light-years that is, about seven hundred and twenty terrestrial ones. And the program found it: a fusion exhaust in a direct line between Groombridge and the star Alpha Orionis."

That would be the brightest star in Orion, which is—"Betelgeuse?" I said. "You mean Betelgeuse? But that's a red supergiant, isn't it?" I'd seen the star countless times in the winter skies; it formed the left shoulder of Orion, my favorite constellation—I think the name was even Arabic for "shoulder of the hunter."

"Betelgeuse, yes," said Hollus.

"Surely no one would relocate to such a star. It can't possibly have habitable planets."

"That is exactly what we thought. Betelgeuse is the largest star visible in the night sky from any of our three worlds; if it were placed where Earth's sun is now, its outer rim would extend well past the orbit of Mars. It is also much cooler than Sol, Delta Pavonis, or Beta Hydri; that is why it only glows red, of course."

"How far away is Betelgeuse?" I asked.

"Four hundred and twenty-nine terrestrial light-years from Sol—and roughly the same from Groombridge 1618, of course."

"That's a heck of a long way."

"It is just one half of one percent of our galaxy's diameter."

"Still," I said, "I can't imagine why they'd send a ship there."

"Nor can we. Betelgeuse is a prime candidate to go supernova; it is not suitable at all for a colony."

"Then why go there?"

"We do not know. Of course, it is possible that the ship is headed to some destination on the other side of Betelgeuse, or that it plans to use Betelgeuse either as a refueling stop—it might be easy to harvest hydrogen from the attenuated outer atmosphere of a low-density red supergiant. And, of course, the

CALCULATING GOD

ship may wish to use Betelgeuse as a gravitational slingshot, giving it a speed boost as it angles off to some other destination."

"Did you find evidence that the people from Groombridge had sent out other starships?"

"No. But if any of them had changed course even slightly, so that their fusion exhaust did not aim back toward the home planet, we would not be able to detect them."

"How long ago was the ark launched? And how long until it gets to Betelgeuse?"

"Judging interstellar distances is very difficult, especially without a long baseline for measuring parallax. The ark has been under way for at least 5,000 years—they apparently never developed the near-light-speed fusion engines we have—and it is certainly more than five-sixths of the way to Betelgeuse." She paused for a moment, her torso bobbing up and down the way it did when she was excited. "But do you see, Tom? Maybe what you proposed happened on the other five worlds we visited; maybe their inhabitants did upload themselves into computers. But the Groombridge natives did not do that. They have built an ark; they are still alive. And that ark lacks the speed of our own ships; it would be possible for us to overtake it. Meaning—" she bobbed some more—"there is another race for us to meet."

ROBERT J. SAWYER

26

T he ROM had closed to the public at 6:00; Hollus and I were now walking alone again through the Burgess Shale exhibition.

"I have noticed," the alien said, "that many of the fossils you have on display are casts."

"Well, all of these are real," I said, gesturing at the shales around us. "But, sure, we either trade with other museums, giving them a cast of one of ours that they want in exchange for something we want, or we simply purchase the cast from them." I paused and pointed straight up. "That *T. rex* we've got in the Discovery Gallery is a cast. Meanwhile, our *Parasaurolophus* is our most popular trade; we just finished making a cast of it for a museum in Helsinki."

"I am fascinated by these fossils," said Hollus. "We do not make physical casts, but we do make high-resolution holographic scans of objects of interest." She paused. "Would it be permissible for me to scan these fossils."

"To scan the Burgess Shale specimens?"

"Yes, please," said Hollus. "The process is noninvasive; no damage is done."

I scratched where my right sideburn used to be. "I guess that would be all right, but—" For once I was the savvy businessman. "But, as I said, we usually trade or sell casts of our fossils. What could you give us in return?"

Hollus considered for a moment. "I offer you a similarly scanned library of the counterpart of Beta Hydri's Cambrian explosion."

Bargaining is the third of Elisabeth Kübler-Ross's five stages. That sort of bargaining is usually futile, but at least it had taught me not to easily give up. "I want a comparable scan library of the Delta Pavonis equivalent of the Cambrian explosion, too." Hollus's eyestalks moved in a way I'd learned meant she was about to object, but I pressed on. "After all, you're doubtless going to share the data with the Wreeds, anyway, so they, too, should pay a price for it. And I'll need two copies of your scans, since I'll have to give one to the Smithsonian."

Hollus considered this for a moment, then, eyestalks rippling, she said, "Done."

"How is the scan performed?" I asked.

"Several of us will have to come down here physically with the equipment," said Hollus.

"Really? Wow." I smiled. "It will be good to see you again—in the flesh, I mean. How long will the process take?"

She looked around at the cases, as if estimating the magnitude of the task. "About one of your days, I imagine. Scanning at that level of resolution is time-consuming."

I frowned. "Well, regardless, we'd have to do it when the museum is closed. It's too much of a security risk to have you here in the flesh when we're open to the public. And if it's going to take that long, we'll have to start on a Sunday evening and continue on through Monday, when the museum is closed all day." Mike Harris's latest round of cutbacks had forced us to be open only six days a week. "I suppose there's no reason to wait. How does this Sunday night sound?"

"When is that?" asked Hollus.

"Two days from now."

"Yes," said the alien. "That should work out just fine."

ROBERT J. SAWYER

For me, showering had always simply been a way to quickly get clean—and it was even quicker, now that I had no hair to wash. But for Susan, it was one of her real pleasures. She had to do it quickly on weekdays, but on Saturday mornings, she would spend half an hour or so showering, enjoying the warmth, the wetness, letting the water massage her. While she did so, I lay in bed, staring at the swirls of plaster decorating our bedroom ceiling, thinking. Trying to make sense of it all.

One of my favorite movies is *Inherit the Wind*—the original version, with Spencer Tracy, Frederic March, and Gene Kelly in the roles modeled after Clarence Darrow, William Jennings Bryan, and H. L. Mencken. There's also been a couple of made-for-TV remakes; I'll never understand why they remake *good* movies. Why doesn't somebody go back and remake bad ones, correcting the mistakes? I'd love to see a decent version of *Dune* or *V. I. Warshawski*—or *The Phantom Menace,* for that matter. But they did remake *Inherit the Wind,* first with Jason Robards, Kirk Douglas, and good old Darren McGavin, *The Night Stalker's* Carl Kolchak himself—in fact, come to think of it, Mencken and Kolchak are pretty darn similar . . . except for the vampires.

But I digress again. Christ, I wish I could concentrate better.

I wish the pain would go away.

I wish—God damn it, how I wish—I could be sure that what I'm thinking is coherent, is reasonable, is what I *really* think, and not just the result of pain, or my pain medication, confusing my thoughts.

When I first saw *Inherit the Wind,* I'd laughed smugly at the way Spencer Tracy demolished Fredric March, reducing the fundamentalist to a gibbering idiot on the witness stand. Take *that,* I thought. Take that.

I used to teach evolution at U of T. I said that before, right? When Darwin first proposed his theory, scientists assumed the fossil record would bear it out: that we would see a gradual progression from form to form, with slow changes accumulating over time, until a new species emerged.

But the fossil record *doesn't* show that. Oh, there are transitional forms: *Ichthyostega,* which seems intermediate between fish and amphibians; *Caudipteryx,* a melange of dinosaur and bird; even *Australopithecus,* the quintessential ape-man.

But gradual change? An accumulation of tiny mutations over time? No. Sharks have been sharks for almost four hundred million years; turtles have turted for two hundred million years; snakes have snuck for eighty million years. Indeed, the fossil record is mostly lacking in gradual sequences, in incremental improvements; the only really good vertebrate sequence we've got is that of the horse, which is why just about every large museum has a display of equine evolution like the one here at the ROM.

Stephen Jay Gould and Niles Eldredge responded, putting forth the theory of punctuated equilibria—punky-E, as we say in the evolution biz. Species are stable for long periods of time, and then suddenly, when environmental conditions change, they rapidly evolve into new forms. Ninety percent of me wanted to believe Stephen and Niles, but ten percent felt it was a bit of a semantic trick, word play like Gould's "nonoverlapping magisteria" of religion and science, glossing over a thorny issue, in this case that the fossil record didn't show what Darwin predicted it would, with bafflegab—as though giving a fancy name to the problem was the same as solving it. (Not that Gould was the first to do that: Herbert Spencer's phrase for the engine of evolution—"survival of the fittest"—was nothing more than a circular definition, since fitness was never pinned down more precisely than simply being that which increased the odds of survival.)

Long-term environmental stability? In February, Toronto often has temperatures of twenty degrees Fahrenheit, and the snow can lie hip-deep on the ground. The air is so dry that skin flakes off and lips crack open. Without a bulky sweater and a down-filled parka, a scarf and a tuque, you could easily die from exposure.

246

Six months later, in August, temperatures in the nineties are common, and breaking one hundred is not unheard of. The air is so laden with humidity that just standing still is enough to cause sweat to pour out of you; the sun is so bright that even a few minutes without my clip-ons and a hat brings on a splitting headache, and the radio often urges the elderly and those with heart conditions to stay indoors.

The theory of punctuated equilibria says the environment stays stable for extended periods of time. In much of the world, the environment isn't stable for *months* at a time.

But I soldiered on; we all did—all of us who taught evolution. We incorporated punky-E into our lesson plans, and we shook our heads condescendingly when naïve students asked us about missing links.

It wasn't the first time we'd been smug. Evolutionists had arrogantly folded their arms across their chests back in 1953 when Harold Urey and Stanley Miller created amino acids by putting an electric discharge through a primordial soup—what they thought, then, Earth's early atmosphere might have been like. Why, we were halfway to creating life in a jar, we thought; the final triumph of evolutionary theory, the proof that it had all started through simple, natural processes. If we zapped the soup just right, full-fledged self-replicating organisms might appear.

Except they never did. We still don't know how to go from amino acids to self-replication. And we look at the cell under electron microscopes, we see things Darwin never dreamed of, mechanisms like the cilia that turn out to be so incredibly complex in their own right that it's almost impossible to see how they might have evolved in the step-by-single-step fashion that evolution allows, mechanisms that seemed to have been created full-blown with all their complex, moving parts.

But, well, we ignored the biochemical argument, too—and with equal smugness. I remember old Jonesy handing me an article out of his *Skeptical Inquirer* once, in which Martin Gardner tried to tear apart Michael Behe, the Lehigh University profes-

247

sor who wrote *Darwin's Black Box: The Biochemical Challenge to Evolution,* a strongly presented case for intelligent design. The name Behe, Gardner wasted no time pointing out, rhymes with "tee-hee," a titter, a giggle, a joke, nothing to take seriously. Just because we couldn't at the moment see the sequence of steps that might have given rise to cilia—or to the cascade sequence that causes blood to clot, or to the complexity of the human eye, or to the ATP-driven system of cellular metabolism—didn't mean that such sequences hadn't occurred.

And, of course, we kept arguing that the universe *had* to be teeming with life—that there was nothing remarkable about Earth, that it was, in fact, *mediocre,* that planets like it were, well, as common as the dirt after which we'd named our own world.

But then, in 1988, the first extrasolar planet was discovered, orbiting the star HD 114762. Of course, back then we didn't think it was a planet; we thought maybe it was a brown-dwarf star. After all, it was nine times as heavy as Jupiter, and it orbited HD 114762 closer than Mercury orbits our sun. But in 1995, another extrasolar planet was discovered, this one at least half as big as Jupiter, and also orbiting its parent, the star 51 Pegasi, closer than Mercury came to Sol. And then more and more were found, all from solar systems unlike our own.

In our solar system, the gas giants—Jupiter, Saturn, Uranus, and Neptune—orbit far away from the central star, and the inner planets are small, rocky worlds. Rather than being a normal planetary system, ours was beginning to look like a freak. And yet the layout of bodies in our system seemed to be crucial to developing and sustaining life. Without the gravitational effects of our giant moon—almost a sister planet, formed early on when an asteroid slammed into our still-molten world—Earth would wobble in an unstable fashion, and our atmosphere would be crushingly dense, like that of Venus. And without Jupiter, patrolling the border between the inner and outer solar

ROBERT J. SAWYER

system, sweeping up wayward comets and asteroids with its immense gravity, our world would have been hit far more frequently by such objects. A bolide impact apparently almost wiped out all life on Earth sixty-five million years ago; we could not have withstood more frequent bombardment.

Of course, Hollus's solar system apparently resembled ours, as did the Wreed system. But, nonetheless, systems like Sol's were extraordinary; the exception, not the rule. And cells aren't simple; they are enormously complex. And the fossil record, fascinating but frustrating thing that it is, shows evolution proceeding by leaps rather than by the accumulation of gradual changes.

I've spent my whole adult life being an uncompromising neo-Darwinian evolutionist. I certainly don't want to issue a deathbed retraction.

And yet—

And yet perhaps, as Hollus believes, there *is* more to the puzzle of life.

I *know* evolution happens; I know it for a fact. I've seen the fossils, seen the DNA studies that say that we and chimps have 98.6 percent of our genetic material in common, and therefore must have had a recent common ancestor.

Proceeding by leaps . . .

By . . . perhaps, maybe . . . by *quantum* leaps.

Newton's seventeenth-century laws of physics are mostly correct; you can use them to reliably predict all sorts of things. We didn't discard them; rather, in the twentieth century, we subsumed them into a new, more comprehensive physics, a physics of relativity and quantum mechanics.

Evolution is a nineteenth-century notion, outlined in Darwin's 1859 book, a book called, in full, *On the Origin of Species by Means of Natural Selection, or the Preservation of Favoured Races in the Struggle for Life*. But the more we learn, the more natural selection seems inadequate on its own as a mechanism

249

for the creation of new species; even our best attempts at artificial, intelligently guided selection apparently aren't up to the task—all dogs are still *Canis familiaris*.

And now it's the start of the twenty-first century. Surely it's not unreasonable to think that Darwin's ideas, like Newton's before them, will be subsumed into a greater whole, a more comprehensive understanding?

Damn it!

God damn it.

I hate it when the pain comes like that—like a knife, slicing into me.

I reached over onto my cluttered night table. Where are my pills? Where are they?

ROBERT J. SAWYER

27

Rhonda Weir, short, stocky, silver-haired, was a detective for the Toronto Police. Her phone rang at 1:11 P.M. on Sunday afternoon. She picked up the handset and said, "Detective Weir."

"Hello," said a raspy man's voice at the other end of the phone, sounding somewhat exasperated. "I hope I've got the right person this time; I've been transferred several times."

"What can I do for you?" asked Rhonda.

"My name is Constantin Kalipedes," said the voice. "I'm the weekend manager at the Lakeshore Inn in Etobicoke. One of my housekeepers just found a gun in one of the rooms."

"What kind of gun?"

"A pistol. And she also found an empty gun case, the kind you'd use to carry one of those—what do you call it?—one of those assault weapons."

"Has the guest checked out?"

"Guests, plural. And no. They've got a reservation through Wednesday morning."

"What are their names?"

"One is J. D. Ewell; the other, C. Falsey. They have Arkansas license plates."

"You took down the plate number?"

"No, but they wrote it themselves on the registration card." He read the string of characters to Rhonda.

"Did the maid finish cleaning the room?"

"No. I had her stop as soon as she found the gun."

"Good man," said Rhonda. "What's your address?"

He told her.

"I'll be there in"—she looked at her watch, then calculated; traffic should be light on a Sunday afternoon—"twenty minutes. If this Ewell or Falsey return, stall them if you can, but don't put yourself at risk, understood?"

"Yes."

"I'm on my way."

The Lakeshore Inn was, not surprisingly, on Lakeshore Boulevard. Rhonda Weir and her partner, Hank Li, parked their unmarked car in front of the entrance. Hank checked the license plates on the cars to the left, and Rhonda looked at those on the ones to the right. Six were American—two from Michigan, two from New York, and one each from Minnesota and Illinois—but none were from Arkansas. A little rain was falling; there would doubtless be more later. The air was pungent with ozone.

Constantin Kalipedes turned out to be an old, paunchy Greek, with a stubble of gray beard. He led Rhonda and Hank along a row of units, past door after door, until they came to an open one. There they found the East Indian woman who was his housekeeper, and he brought her with them to room 118. Kalipedes got out his pass key, but Rhonda had him hand it over; she opened the door herself, turning the knob with the key so as not to disturb any fingerprints that might be on it. It was a fairly shabby room, with two framed prints hanging crookedly, and powder-blue wallpaper peeling at the seams. There were two double beds, one of which had beside it the sort of oxygen bottle that a person who suffered from sleep apnea needed. Both beds were disheveled; the maid obviously hadn't gotten to them by the time she'd made her discovery.

ROBERT J. SAWYER

"Where's the gun?" asked Rhonda.

The young woman stepped into the room and pointed. The gun was lying on the floor, beside a suitcase. "I had to move the suitcase," she said with a lilting accent, "to get at the outlet, so I could plug in the vacuum cleaner. It must not have been closed all the way, and the gun tumbled out. Behind it was that wooden case." She pointed.

"A Glock 9mm," said Hank, glancing at the handgun. Rhonda looked at the case. It had a specially cut black foam-rubber inlay, just the right size to hold an Intertec Tec-9 carbine, a nasty beast—essentially a submachine gun—about the length of a man's forearm. Possession of the handgun was illegal in Canada, but more disturbing was that Falsey and Ewell had left it behind, opting for the Tec-9 instead, a weapon banned now even in the U.S. because of its thirty-two-round clip. Rhonda put her hands on her hips and slowly surveyed the room. There were two ashtrays; it was a smoking room. It had data jacks for hooking up a modem, but there was no sign of a portable computer. She stepped into the bathroom. Two straight razors and a can of foam. Two toothbrushes, one of them badly chewed.

Back in the main room, she noticed a black-covered Bible sitting on one of the night tables.

"Probable cause?" said Rhonda to her partner.

"I'd say," said Hank.

Kalipedes was looking at them. "What does that mean?"

"It means," said Rhonda, "there's enough superficial evidence to indicate that a crime has been or is about to be committed to allow us to thoroughly search this room without first obtaining a warrant. You're welcome to remain and watch—in fact, we encourage you to do so." The department had been sued more than once by people who had claimed that valuables had disappeared during a search.

Kalipedes nodded, but he turned to the chambermaid. "Back to work," he said. She scurried out the door.

253

Rhonda pulled out a handkerchief and used it held between two fingers to open the drawer in one of the night tables. It had another Bible in it, this one bound in red—typical Gideon issue. She crossed over to the other night table. She pulled a pen out of her pocket and used it to flip open the cover of the black bible. It wasn't a Gideon one, and on the inside front cover it said "C. Falsey" in red ink. She glanced at the submachine-gun case. "Our Bible boy needs to reread the part about swords into plowshares, I think."

Hank grunted in response as he used his own pen to fan out the papers on the dresser. "Look at this," he said, after a moment.

Rhonda came over. Hank had revealed an unfolded city map of Toronto. Taking care to handle only the edges, Hank turned it over and pointed to the segment that would have been the cover had the map been folded up. It had a Barnes and Noble price sticker on it—an American bookstore chain, with no outlets in Canada. Falsey and Ewell had presumably brought the map with them from Arkansas. Hank gingerly flipped it over again. It was a full-color map with all sorts of symbols and markings. It took a moment before Rhonda noticed the simple circle drawn in ballpoint pen at Kipling and Horner, less than two kilometers from the spot they were currently at.

"Mr. Kalipedes," called Rhonda. She motioned for him to come over, and he did so. "This is your neighborhood, sir. Can you tell me what's at the intersection of Kipling and Horner?"

He scratched his chin with its grizzled stubble. "A Mac's Milk, a Mr. Submarine, a dry cleaner's. Oh yeah—and that clinic that was blown up a while ago."

Rhonda and Hank exchanged glances. "Are you sure?" asked Rhonda.

"Of course," said Kalipedes.

"Jesus Christ," said Hank, realizing the magnitude of it all. "Jesus Christ."

They hurriedly scanned the map, looking for any other markings. There were three more. One was a circle drawn in pencil around a building shown by a red rectangle on Bloor Street. Rhonda didn't have to ask anyone what that was. It was typeset in italics right on the map: *Royal Ont. Museum*.

Also circled were the SkyDome—the stadium where the Blue Jays play—and the CBC Broadcasting Centre, a few blocks north of the SkyDome.

"Tourist attractions," said Rhonda.

"Except they took a semiautomatic weapon," said Hank.

"The Jays playing today?"

"Yup. Milwaukee is in town."

"Anything happening at the CBC?"

"On a Sunday? I know they do a live show from the lobby there in the mornings; I'm not sure about the afternoons." Hank looked at the map. "Besides, maybe they went somewhere other than these places. They didn't take the map with them, after all."

"Still . . . "

Hank didn't need the consequences spelled out. "Yeah."

"We'll take the ROM—they've got that alien visiting there," said Rhonda.

"It's not really there," said Hank. "It's just a transmission from the mothership."

Rhonda snorted, conveying that she knew that. She pulled a cellular phone out of her jacket pocket. "I'll get teams sent to the CBC and SkyDome, and I'll call for a couple of uniforms to wait here in case Falsey and Ewell return."

Susan gave me a lift to Downsview subway station about three-thirty in the afternoon; it was cloudy, the sky bruised, a storm threatening. Ricky was spending the rest of the day with the Nguyens—my young son was developing quite a taste for Vietnamese food.

The subways were slow and infrequent on Sundays; I'd save time on my trip downtown by starting at Downsview at the north end of the Spadina line rather than at North York Centre. I gave my wife a kiss goodbye—and she held the kiss for a long time. I smiled at her. And she smiled back.

I then took the paper bag with the sandwiches she'd packed for me and headed into the station, riding the long escalator down into the subterranean world.

Rhonda Weir and Hank Li had got descriptions of Falsey and Ewell from Kalipedes. Kalipedes didn't know which was which, but one was mid-twenties, blond, scrawny, maybe five-eight, with an overbite and a crew cut; the other was mid-thirties, three or four inches taller, narrow face, and had brown hair. Both had accents from the southern States. And, of course, one of them might well be carrying a Tec-9 submachine gun, perhaps hidden under a coat. Although the museum was crowded on Sundays—it was a favorite place for divorced fathers to take their kids—there was still a good chance that Rhonda or Hank would be able to spot them.

They parked their car in the small lot at the Bora Laskin Law Library, on the south side of the planetarium building, then walked over to the ROM, entering through the main doors and making their way over to Raghubir Singh.

Rhonda flashed her badge and described whom she and Hank were looking for.

"They were here before," said Raghubir. "A few days ago. Two Americans with southern accents. I remember them because one of them called the Burgess Shale 'the Bogus Shale.' I told my wife about that when I got home—she got quite a kick out of it."

Rhonda sighed. "Well, it's unlikely that they're back, then.

Still, it's the only lead we've got. We'll look around, if that's okay."

"Of course," said Raghubir. He radioed the other security guards, getting them to join in the search.

Rhonda pulled out her cellular again. "Weir," she said. "The suspects were here at the ROM last week; still we're going to have a look around on the off chance that they've come back, but I'd concentrate our forces at SkyDome and the CBC."

I arrived at the museum about 4:30 P.M., entered through the staff entrance, and made my way up to the Burgess Shale exhibition, just to have a final look around, to make sure everything was okay before the arrival of Hollus and company.

Rhonda Weir, Hank Li, and Raghubir Singh met up in the Rotunda at 4:45. "No luck," said Rhonda. "You?"

Hank shook his head. "I'd forgotten how big this place was. Even if they had come back here, they could be anywhere."

"None of my people found them, either," said Raghubir. "A lot of patrons carry their coats in the museum. We used to have a free coat check, but that was before the cutbacks." He shrugged. "People don't like having to pay."

Rhonda looked at her watch. "It's almost closing time."

"The school-group entrance is locked on weekends," said Raghubir. He pointed at the bank of glass doors beneath the stained-glass windows. "They'll have to go out through the main doors."

Rhonda frowned. "They probably aren't even here. But let's wait outside and see if we can spot them leaving."

Hank nodded and the two detectives headed through the

glass-doored vestibule. It looked like it was about to rain. Rhonda used her cellular again. "Any update?" she asked.

A sergeant's voice crackled over the phone. "They're definitely not at the CBC Broadcasting Centre."

"My money's on SkyDome," said Rhonda, into the phone. "Ours, too."

"We'll head down there." She put the phone away.

Hank looked up at the dark sky. "I hope we get there in time to see them close the stadium roof," he said.

J. D. Ewell and Cooter Falsey were leaning against a tomato-soup-colored wall in the Lower Rotunda; Falsey was wearing a Toronto Blue Jays cap that he'd bought yesterday when they took in a game at SkyDome. A prerecorded male voice with a Jamaican accent came over the public-address system: "Ladies and gentlemen, the museum is now closed. Would all patrons please immediately go to the front exit. Many thanks for visiting us, and do come again. Ladies and gentlemen, the museum is now closed. Would—"

Falsey flashed Ewell a grin.

Theatre ROM had four double doors that gave access to it, and these were often left unlocked. Curious patrons sometimes stuck their heads in the doors, but if no programming was going on, all they saw was a large darkened room.

Ewell and Falsey waited until the Lower Rotunda was empty, then walked down the nine steps into the theater. They stood still for a moment, letting their eyes adjust. Although the theater had no windows, there was still some light: the red glow of EXIT signs, light seeping in under the doors, a large illuminated analog clock on the wall above the doors, red LEDs from smoke detectors, and lights from a control panel or some such coming from the five little windows of the projection booth above the entrance.

ROBERT J. SAWYER

Earlier in the day, Falsey and Ewell had sat through a seemingly endless film about a little wooden carving of a canoe with a male Native Canadian figure in it traveling down various waterways. But they didn't pay much attention to the movie. Instead, they'd examined the physical structure of the theater: the presence of a stage in front of the movie screen, the number of rows of chairs, the position of the aisles, and the location of the staircases leading up to the stage.

Now they quickly made their way in the dark down the gently sloping left-hand aisle, found one of the staircases leading to the stage, climbed the steps, slipped behind the large movie screen, which hung from the roof, and entered the backstage area.

There was more light back there. A small washroom was at one side, and someone had left the light on in it and the door ajar. There were several mismatched chairs behind the screen, and the usual hodgepodge of lighting equipment, microphone stands, anaconda-like ropes hanging from the ceiling, and lots of dust.

Ewell dropped his jacket, revealing the small submachine gun he'd had concealed under it. Tired of lugging it around, he placed the gun on the floor, then sat in one of the chairs.

Falsey took a different chair, intertwined his fingers behind his head, and leaned back, waiting patiently.

t was now 10:00 P.M. and traffic here, downtown, had dwindled to almost nothing. Hollus's shuttle dropped silently from the sky, and landed not as it had the first time, out front of the planetarium, but rather behind the museum, along Philosopher's Walk, a grassy U of T parkette that snaked from Varsity Stadium over toward Hart House. Although the shuttle's descent had doubtless been observed by some, at least the ship wasn't in open view from the street.

Christine Dorati had insisted on being here for the arrival of the aliens. We'd talked about the best way to handle security and had decided that simply keeping everything quiet made the most sense; if we asked for police or military support, that would have just drawn crowds. By this late date, we only had a handful of nut cases hanging around the museum, and none were ever seen this late at night—it was public knowledge that Hollus and I kept normal business hours.

Things had been strained between us ever since Christine had tried to oust me, but I rather suspected, looking at me today, that she knew the end was getting near regardless. I still avoided mirrors, but I could see the reactions other people were having to me: the forced, insincere comments about me looking well, looking fit, the handshakes that were free of pressure, lest my bones might shatter, the involuntary ever-so-slight shaking of heads as people who hadn't seen me for weeks caught sight of my current state. Christine was going to get her way soon enough.

We'd watched the shuttle land while standing in the alley-way between the ROM and planetarium; Philosopher's Walk was not the sort of place you wanted to hang around after dark. Hollus, a second Forhilnor, and two Wreeds quickly emerged from the black, wedge-shaped ship. Hollus was wearing the same bright-blue winding cloth she'd worn when we first met; the other Forhilnor was clad in a black-and-gold cloth. All four aliens were carrying pieces of elaborate-looking equipment. I walked over to greet them, then quickly hustled the group down the alleyway and into the museum through the staff entrance. That entrance was at street level, which really was the museum's basement (the main public entrance had all those outdoor steps leading up to it, putting it really most of a story above street level). A security guard was on duty there, reading a magazine instead of looking at the constantly changing black-and-white images from the security cameras.

"Better turn off the alarms," said Christine to the guard. "If we've got to be in here all night, I'm sure we'll be wandering around to various parts of the building." The guard nodded and pushed some buttons on a console in front of him.

We headed into the museum, most of which was dark. The Wreeds were both wearing yellow utility belts like the ones I'd seen before, but they were also wearing something else: strange harnesses that crisscrossed between their four arms. "What's that?" I asked Hollus, pointing at one of them.

"A repulsor-field generator; it helps them walk around here. The gravity on Earth is higher than that on the Wreed home-world."

We took the elevator up to the first floor—it took two carloads to transport everyone, as only one Forhilnor could fit in at a time. I went with the first group; Hollus, who had seen me operate elevators repeatedly came up in the second (she had said getting Wreeds to understand that floors might be represented

ROBERT J. SAWYER

by numbers would have taken too long to explain). The two Wreeds were particularly impressed by the giant totem poles made of western red cedar. They quickly scooted all the way up to the third floor on the staircases that wrapped around the poles, then returned to the main floor. I then led everyone across the Rotunda to the Garfield Weston Exhibition Hall. As we walked along, Hollus had both mouths going a mile a minute, singing in her native language. She was presumably playing tour guide to the other Forhilnor and the Wreeds.

I was intrigued by the second Forhilnor, whose name, I was told, was Barbulkan. He was larger than Hollus and had one discolored limb.

The locks were at the bases of the double glass doors. I bent over, grunting as I did so, used my key to unlock them, then pulled the doors until they clicked into their open positions. I then stepped in and turned on the lights. The others followed me into the hall. The two Wreeds conferred quietly. After a few moments they seemed to reach an agreement. Of course, they didn't have to turn to talk to somebody behind them, but one of them was obviously now saying something to Hollus: it made rock-grinding sounds, which, a moment later, were translated into the musical Forhilnor language.

Hollus moved over to stand next to me. "They are ready to set up the equipment for the first case."

I moved forward and used another key on the display case, unlocking the angled glass cover and swinging it up. The hinge locked into place at the maximally open position. There was no chance of the glass sheet coming crashing down while people worked inside—museums might not have always taken appropriate precautions to safeguard their employees in the past, but they did do so now.

The scanner consisted of a large metal stand with a dozen or so complex-looking articulated arms coming off it, each one ending in a translucent sphere about the size of a softball. One of the Wreeds was working on deploying the arms—some above the case, some below, more on either side—while the other Wreed made numerous adjustments to an illuminated control panel attached to the supporting stand. He seemed displeased with the results being displayed, and continued to fiddle with the controls.

"It is delicate work," said Hollus. Her compatriot stood silently next to her. "Scanning at this resolution demands a minimum of vibrations." She paused. "I hope we will not have problems with the subway trains."

"They'll stop running for the night soon," Christine said. "And although you can feel the trains go by downstairs in the Theatre ROM, I've never really noticed them making the rest of the museum vibrate."

"We will probably be fine," said Hollus. "But we should also refrain from using the elevator while the scans are being made."

The other Forhilnor sang something, and Hollus said, "Excuse us," to Christine and me. The two of them scuttled across the gallery and helped move another piece of equipment. It was clear that operating the scanner wasn't Hollus's field, but she was useful as an extra set of hands.

"Extraordinary," said Christine, looking at the aliens milling about the gallery.

I wasn't inclined to make small talk with her, but, well, she *was* my boss. "Aren't they?" I said, without much feeling.

"You know," she said, "I never really believed in aliens. I mean, I know what you biologists say: there's nothing special about the Earth, there should be life everywhere, yatitty-yatitty-ya. But still, down deep, I thought we were alone in the universe."

I decided not to contradict her about whether there was anything special about out planet. "I'm glad they're here," I said. "I'm glad they came to visit us."

Christine yawned expansively—quite a sight with her horsey mouth, although she tried to hide it behind the back

264

of her hand. It *was* getting late—and we'd only just begun. "Sorry," she said when she was done. "I just wish there was some way to get Hollus to do some public programming here. We could—"

At that moment, Hollus rejoined us. "They are ready to do the first scan," she said. "The equipment will run on its own, and it would be better if we all left the room to avoid vibrations."

I nodded, and the six of us headed out into the Rotunda. "How long will the scan take?"

"About forty-three minutes for the first case," said Hollus.

"Well," said Christine, "no point just standing around. Why don't we go have a look at some Far Eastern artifacts?" Those galleries were also on the first floor, rather close to our current location.

Hollus spoke to the three other aliens, presumably to get their consent. "That would be fine," she said, turning back to us.

I let Christine take the lead; it was her museum, after all. We crossed the Rotunda diagonally again, passed the totem poles, and entered the T. T. Tsui Galleries of Chinese Art (named for the Hong Kong businessperson whose donation had made them possible); the ROM had the finest collection of Chinese artifacts in the western world. We passed through the galleries, with their cases full of ceramics, bronzes, and jades, and entered the Chinese Tomb area. For decades, the tomb had been located outside, exposed to Toronto's weather, but now it was here, on the first floor of the ROM's terrace galleries. The outside wall was glass, looking out on a slick, wet Bloor Street; a Pizza Hut and McDonald's faced in from the other side of the road. The roof was tented skylights; raindrops beat against them.

The tomb components—two giant arches, two stone camels, two giant human figures, and the huge tumulus dome—had no velvet ropes around them. The other Forhilnor, Barbulkan, reached out to touch the carvings on the nearer archway with

CALCULATING GOD

his six-fingered hand. I imagined that if you did a lot of work via telepresence, getting to really touch things with your own flesh-and-blood fingers was a special thrill.

"These tomb pieces," said Christine, standing by one of the stone camels, "were purchased by the museum in 1919 and 1920 from George Crofts, a British fur trader and art dealer stationed in Tianjin. They supposedly come from the tomb complex at Fengtaizhuang in Hebei province and are said to belong to the famous Ming-dynasty general Zu Dashou, who died in 1656 A.D."

The aliens murmured among themselves. They were clearly fascinated; maybe they didn't build monuments to their own dead.

"Chinese society at this time was shaped by the idea that the universe was a highly ordered place," continued Christine. "The tomb and tomb figures here reflect this idea of a structured cosmos, and—"

At first I thought it was thunder.

But that wasn't it.

A sound was ripping through the tomb area, echoing loudly off the stone walls.

A sound I'd only ever heard before on TV and in the movies.

The sound of rapid gunfire.

Foolishly, we ran from the tomb toward the sound. The Forhilnors easily outpaced us humans, and the Wreeds brought up the rear. We hurried through the T. T. Tsui Galleries and out into the darkened Rotunda.

The sound was coming from the Garfield Weston Exhibition Hall—from the Burgess Shale exhibit. I couldn't imagine who was being shot at: besides the security guard at the staff entrance, we were the only people in the building.

Christine had a cellular phone with her; she'd already flipped it open and was presumably dialing 9-1-1. Another volley of gunfire split the air, and here, closer, I was able to discern an additional, more familiar sound: rock shattering. I suddenly real-

266

ized what was happening. Somebody was shooting at the price-less, half-billion-year-old Burgess Shale fossils.

The gunfire stopped just as the Wreeds were arriving in the Rotunda. We had hardly been quiet: Christine was talking into her cellular, our footfalls had echoed in the galleries, and the Wreeds, utterly mystified—maybe they had never developed projectile weapons—were chatting animatedly to each other despite my attempts to shush them.

Even partially deafened by the sound of their own gunfire, the people shooting up the fossils evidently heard the sounds we had made. First one and then another emerged from the Exhibition Hall. The one who came out first was covered with wood chips and rock fragments, and he was holding some sort of semiautomatic weapon—a submachine gun, maybe. He aimed it at us.

That, at last, was enough to get us to do the sensible thing. We froze. But I glanced over at Christine and made a questioning face, silently asking whether she'd gotten through to the 9-1-1 operator. She nodded yes, and tipped the case of her cellular just enough so that I could see by its glowing faceplate that she was still connected. Thank God the emergency operator had had the good sense to fall silent as soon as Christine had.

"Holy God," said the man holding the gun. He half turned to face his younger partner, who had a crew cut. "Holy God, will you look at them things?" He had an accent from the southern U.S.

"Aliens," said the man with the crew cut, as if trying on the word for size; he had a similar accent. Then, a moment later, deciding that the word indeed fit, he said it again, more forcefully. "Aliens."

I took a half-step forward. "They're projections, of course," I said. "They're not really here."

The Forhilnors and Wreeds might have different ways from humans, but at least they weren't fool enough to contradict me.

"Who are you?" asked the man with the gun. "What are you doing here?"

"I'm Thomas Jericho," I said. "I'm the head of the paleobiology department here at"—I raised my voice as much as I dared, hoping the 9-1-1 operator would pick up my words, in case Christine hadn't yet conveyed to him or her where we were—"the Royal Ontario Museum." Of course, by this point the museum's own overnight security guard must have realized something was up and had presumably also called the cops.

"No one should be here this time of night," said the man with the crew cut.

"We were taking some photographs," I said. "We wanted to do it when the museum was empty."

Maybe twenty meters separated our group from the two of them. There might have been a third or fourth intruder inside the exhibit hall, but I'd seen no sign of that.

"What, may I ask, are you doing?" asked Christine.

"Who are you?" asked the man with the gun.

"Dr. Christine Dorati. I'm the director of the museum. What are you doing?"

The two men looked at each other. The guy with the crew cut shrugged. "We're destroying those lying fossils." He looked at the aliens. "You aliens, y'all have come to Earth, but you're listening to the wrong people. These *scientists*"—he almost spat the word—"are lying to you, with their fossils and all. This world is six thousand years old, the Lord created it in just six days, and we are his chosen people."

"Oh, God," I said, invoking the entity they believed in but I did not. I looked at Christine. "Creationists."

The man with the submachine gun was growing impatient. "Enough," he said. He aimed the gun at Christine. "Drop that phone."

She did so; it hit the marble floor with a clang and its flip-down mouthpiece broke free.

"We came here to do a job of work," said the man with the

gun. "Y'all are going to lie down on the ground, and I'm going to finish that work. Cooter, cover them." He returned to the gallery.

The other man reached into his jacket pocket and pulled out a pistol. He aimed it at us. "Y'all heard the man," he said. "Lie down."

Christine lowered herself to the ground. Hollus and the other Forhilnor hunkered down in a way I'd never seen before, lowering their spherical torsos enough that they touched the floor. The two Wreeds just stood there, either baffled or perhaps physiologically incapable of lying down.

And I did not lie down, either. I was terrified—no doubt about it. My heart was pounding, and I could feel sweat on my forehead. But these fossils were priceless, dammitall—among the most important in the entire world. And I was the one who had arranged for them to all be on public display in one place.

I took a step forward. "Please," I said.

More staccato gunfire from inside the gallery. It was almost as if the bullets were tearing into me; I could picture the shales shattering, the remains of *Opabinia* and *Wiwaxia* and *Anomalocaris* and *Canadia* that had survived 500 million years exploding into clouds of dust.

"Don't," I said, genuine pleading in my voice. "Don't do that."

"Stay back," said the short-haired man. "You just stay where you are."

I took in air through my mouth; I didn't want to die—but I was going to, regardless. Whether it happened tonight or a few months from now, it was going to happen. I took another step forward. "If you believe in the Bible," I said, "then you've got to believe in the Ten Commandments. And one of them"—I knew I'd have made a more convincing argument if I'd known which one—"says 'Thou shalt not kill.' " I took another couple of steps toward him. "You may want to destroy those fossils, but I can't believe that you'd kill me."

269

"I will," said the man.

More bursts of gunfire, counterpointed by the sounds of breaking glass and shattering rock. My chest felt like it was going to explode. "No," I said, "you won't. God wouldn't forgive you for that."

He jabbed the gun in my direction; we were maybe fifteen meters apart. "I've already killed," he said. It sounded like a confession, and there was what seemed to be genuine anguish in his voice. "That clinic; that doctor . . . "

More gunfire, echoing and reverberating.

My God, I thought. The abortion-clinic bombers . . .

I swallowed deeply. "That was an accident," I said, guessing. "You can't shoot me in cold blood."

"I'll do it," said the man the other one had called Cooter. "So help me, I'll do it. Now you stay back!"

If only Hollus *weren't* here in the flesh. If she were present as her holographic projection, she could manipulate solid object without having to worry about being harmed by the bullets. But she was all too real, and all too vulnerable—as were the other extraterrestrials.

Suddenly, I became conscious of the sound of sirens growing closer and closer, barely audible here, inside the museum. Cooter must have heard them, too. He turned his head and called out to his partner, "The cops!"

The other man reemerged from the temporary-exhibitions gallery. I wondered how many of the fossils he'd managed to destroy. He cocked his head, listening. At first he didn't seem to be able to hear the sirens; doubtless the gunfire still echoed in his ears. But a moment later he nodded and gestured with his submachine gun for us to start moving. Christine got to her feet; the two Forhilnors lifted their torsos off the ground.

"We're getting out of here," said the man. "Each of you put your hands up."

I lifted my arms; so did Christine. Hollus and the other

270

Forhilnor exchanged a glance, then each lifted their two arms, as well. The Wreeds followed suit a moment later, each lifting all four arms and splaying all twenty-three fingers. The man who wasn't Cooter—he was taller and older than Cooter—ushered us farther into the darkened Rotunda. From there we had a clear view out the glass-doored vestibule. Five uniformed Emergency Task Force officers were beetling up the outside stairs to the museum's glass entrance. Two were brandishing heavy guns. One had a bullhorn. "This is the police," called that cop, the sound distorted as it passed through the two layers of glass. "We have the building surrounded. Come out with your hands up."

The man with the submachine gun gestured for us to keep moving. The four aliens were bringing up the rear, forming a wall between us humans on the inside and the police on the outside. I wished now that I hadn't told Hollus to land her shuttle out back on Philosopher's Walk. If the cops had seen the shuttle, they might have realized that the aliens weren't the holographic projections they'd read about in the newspapers but instead were the real thing. As it stood, some hotshot might assume that he could pick off the two armed men standing behind the aliens by shooting through the projections.

We made it out of the Rotunda, up the four steps to the marble landing between the two stairwells, each with its central totem pole, and then—

And then everything went to hell.

Coming quietly up the stairwell on our right from the basement was a uniformed ETF officer, wearing a bulletproof vest and brandishing an assault weapon. The cops had cleverly made a public stand outside the main entrance while sending a contingent up through the staff entrance from the alleyway between the ROM and the planetarium.

"*J. D.,*" shouted the man with the buzz cut, catching sight of the cop, "*look!*"

J. D. swung his gun and opened fire. The cop was blown back-

CALCULATING GOD

ward, down the wide stone steps, his bulletproof vest being put to the test as it erupted in numerous places, bleeding out white fabric stuffing.

While J. D. was distracted, the cops on the front steps had somehow opened one door—the one at the far left, as they faced it, the one that was designed for wheelchair access; perhaps the ROM security guard had given them the key. Two cops, safe behind riot shields, were now inside the vestibule. The inner doors didn't lock—there was no need for that. One of the officers reached forward and must have touched the red button that operated the door for handicapped patrons. It swung slowly open. The cops were silhouetted by streetlamps and the revolving red lights of their vehicles out on the street.

"Stop where you are," shouted J. D. across the Rotunda, its wide diameter separating our motley group from the cops. "We have hostages."

The cop with the bullhorn was one of those now inside, and he felt compelled to keep using it. "We know the aliens aren't real," he said, his words reverberating in the darkened, domed Rotunda. "Put your hands up and come out."

J. D. jerked his large gun at me. "Tell them who you are."

With the shape my lungs were in, it was hard for me to shout, but I cupped my hands around my mouth and did the best I could. "I'm Thomas Jericho," I said. "I'm a curator here." I pointed at Christine. "This is Christine Dorati. She's the museum's director and president."

J. D. shouted. "We get safe passage out of here, or these two die."

The two cops hunkered down behind their riot shields. After a few moments of consultation, the bullhorn erupted again. "What are your terms?"

Even I knew he was stalling. Cooter looked first at the southern staircase, which led up, and then at the northern staircase, which led both up and down. He must have thought he saw something move—it could have been a mouse; a giant, old building like the museum has plenty of them. He fired a shot down the northern staircase. It hit the stone steps, jagged shards went flying, and—

And one of them hit Barbulkan, the second Forhilnor—

And Barbulkan's left mouth made a sound like *"Ooof!"* and his right mouth went *"Hup!"*

And a carnation of bright-red blood exploded from one of his legs, and a flap of bubble-wrap skin hung loose from where the stone fragment had hit—

And Cooter said, "Holy God!"

And J. D. turned around, and he said, "Sweet Jesus."

And they both apparently realized it at the same moment. The aliens weren't projections; they weren't holograms.

They were real.

And suddenly they knew they had the most valuable hostages in the history of the world.

J. D. stepped backward, moving behind the group; he'd apparently realized he'd been insufficently covering the four aliens. "Are you all real?" he said

The aliens were silent. My heart was jumping. J. D. aimed his submachine gun at the left leg of one of the Wreeds. "One burst from this gun will blow your leg right off." He let this sink in for a moment. "I ask again, are you real?"

Hollus spoke up. "They" "are" "real." "We" "all" "are."

A satisfied smile spread across J. D.'s face. He shouted to the police. "The aliens aren't projections," he said. "They're real. We've got *six* hostages here. I want all of you cops to withdraw. At the first sign of any trick, I will kill one of the hostages—and it won't be a human."

"You don't want to be a murderer," called the cop over the megaphone.

"I *won't* be a murderer," J. D. shouted back. "Murder is the killing of another human being. You won't be able to find anything to charge me with. Now, withdraw fully and completely, or these aliens die."

273

"One hostage will do as well as six," called the same cop. "Let five of them go, and we'll talk."

J. D. and Cooter looked at each other. Six hostages *was* an unwieldy group; they might have an easier time controlling the situation if they didn't have to worry about so many. On the other hand, by having the six form a circle, with J. D. and Cooter at the center, they could be protected from sharpshooters firing from just about any direction.

"No way," shouted J. D. "You guys—you're like a SWAT team, right? So you must have come here in a van or truck. We want you to back off, far away from the museum, leaving that van with its motor running and the keys in it. We'll drive it to the airport, along with as many of the aliens as will fit, and we want a plane waiting there to take us"—he faltered—"well, to take us wherever we decide to go."

"We can't do that," said the cop through his megaphone.

J. D. shrugged a little. "I will kill one hostage sixty seconds from now, if y'all are still here." He turned to the man with the crew cut. "Cooter?"

Cooter nodded, looked at his watch, and started counting down. "Sixty. Fifty-nine. Fifty-eight."

The cop with the bullhorn turned around and spoke to someone behind him. I could see him pointing, presumable indicating the direction to which his force should withdraw on foot.

"Fifty-six. Fifty-five. Fifty-four."

Hollus's eyestalks had stopped weaving in and out and had instead locked at their maximum separation. I'd seen her do that before when she had heard something that interested her. Whatever it was, I hadn't heard it yet.

"Fifty-two. Fifty-one. Fifty."

The cops were moving out of the glass vestibule, but they were making a lot of noise about it. The one with the bullhorn kept speaking. "All right," he said. "All right. We're withdrawing." His magnified voice echoed through the Rotunda. "We're backing away."

ROBERT J. SAWYER

It seemed to me he was talking unnecessarily, but—

But then I heard the sound Hollus had heard: a faint rumbling. The elevator, to our left, was descending in its shaft; someone had called it down to the lower level. The cop with the bullhorn was deliberately trying to drown out the sound.

"Forty-one. Forty. Thirty-nine."

It would be suicide, I thought, for whoever would get in the car; J. D. could blow away the occupant as soon as the metal doors split down the middle and started to slide away.

"Thirty-one. Thirty. Twenty-nine."

"We're leaving," shouted the cop. "We're going."

The elevator was coming back up now. Above the doors was a row of square indicator lights—B, 1, 2, 3—indicating which floor the car was currently on. I dared steal a glance at it. The "1" had just winked out, and, a moment later, the "2" lit up. Brilliant! Either whoever was in the elevator had known about the balconies on the second floor, overlooking the Rotunda, or else the ROM's own security guard, who must have let the police in, had told him.

"Eighteen. Seventeen. Sixteen."

As the "2" lit up, I did my part to muffle the sound of the elevator doors opening by coughing loudly; if there was one thing I did well these days, it was cough.

The "2" was staying lit; the doors must have opened by now, but J. D. and Cooter hadn't heard them. Still, presumably one or more armed cops had now exited onto the second floor—the one that housed the Dinosaur and Discovery Galleries.

"Thirteen. Twelve. Eleven."

"All right," called the ETF officer with the megaphone. "All right. We're leaving." At this distance I couldn't tell if he was making eye contact with the officers on the darkened balcony. We were still by the elevator; I didn't dare tip my eyes up, lest I give away the presence of the people on the floor above.

"Nine. Eight. Seven."

The cops moved out of the vestibule, exiting into the dark

275

night. I watched them sink from view as they headed down the stone steps to the sidewalk.

"Six. Five. Four."

The red lights from the roofs of the cruisers that had been sweeping through the Rotunda started to pull away; one set of lights—presumably from the ETF van—continued to rotate.

"Three. Two. One."

I looked at Christine. She nodded almost imperceptibly; she knew what was happening, too.

"Zero!" said Cooter.

"All, right," said J. D. "Let's move out."

I'd spent much of the last seven months worrying about what it was going to be like to die—but I hadn't thought that I would see someone else die before I did. My heart was pounding like the jackhammers we use to break up overburden. J. D., I figured, had only seconds to live.

He arranged us in a semicircle, as if we were a biological shield for him and Cooter. "Move," he said, and although my back was to him I was sure he was swinging his large gun left and right, preparing to fire in an arc if need be.

I started walking forward; Christine, the Forhilnors, and the Wreeds followed suit. We stepped out from under the overhang that shielded the area by the elevator, went down the four steps into the Rotunda proper, and started crossing the wide marble floor leading toward the entryway.

I swear I felt the splash against my bald head first, and only then heard the deafening shot from above. I swung around. It was difficult to make out what I was seeing; the only light in the Rotunda was what was spilling in from the George Weston gallery and from the street through the glass-doored vestibule and the stained-glass windows above it. J. D.'s head was open, like a melon, and blood had gone everywhere, including onto me and the aliens. His corpse jerked forward, toward me, and his submachine gun went skittering across the floor.

276

A second shot rang out almost on top of the first, but it hadn't quite been synchronized; perhaps in the darkened balcony above, the two officers—there seemed to be at least that many up there—hadn't been able to see each other. Short-haired Cooter moved his head just in time, and he was suddenly diving forward, trying to retrieve J. D.'s gun.

A Wreed was in the way; Cooter knocked him over. With the alien splayed out and flailing around, the sharpshooters apparently couldn't clearly see Cooter.

I was in shock; I could feel J. D.'s blood dripping down to my neck. Suddenly the Wreed who was still standing flew up into the air. I knew it had been wearing a device to help it walk comfortably under Earth's gravity; I hadn't realized that it was strong enough to let him fly.

The other Forhilnor kicked the large gun, sending it spinning farther out into the Rotunda. Cooter continued to scramble toward it. The Wreed who had fallen was pulling himself to his feet. Meanwhile, the flying Wreed had now risen three meters off the ground.

Cooter had made it to the gun and rolled onto his side, shooting up into the darkened balconies. He pumped the trigger repeatedly, spraying out an arc of lead. The bullets hit ninety-year-old stone carvings, sending debris raining down upon us.

The other Wreed took to the air as well. I tried to get behind one of the freestanding wall segments that partially defined the edges of the Rotunda. Hollus was moving quickly—but going in the opposite direction, and soon, to my astonishment, she had reached the taller of the two totem poles. She flexed her six legs and leapt the short distance from the staircase onto the pole, wrapping her various limbs about it. And then she started shimmying at a great clip up the totem. Soon she was out of sight; she could go all the way to the third floor. I was glad she was apparently safe.

"All right," shouted Cooter in his accented voice, as he aimed the submachine gun at Christine, the second Forhilnor, and me in turn. His voice was edged with panic. "All right, y'all. Nobody move."

There were cops back in the vestibule now, cops up on the balcony, two Wreeds flying around the Rotunda like crazed angels, one Forhilnor standing on one side of me, Christine standing on the other, and the corpse of J. D. exsanguinating all over the marble starburst of the Rotunda's floor, making it slick.

"Give it up," said Christine to Cooter. "Can't you see you're surrounded?"

"Shut up!" shouted Cooter. He was clearly at a loss without J.D. "Just shut the hell up."

And then, to my astonishment, I heard a familiar two-toned bleep. The holoform projector, which, as always, I had in a pocket, was signaling that it was about to come on.

Cooter had backed under the overhang of the balcony; he could no longer see the sharpshooters, meaning they could no longer see him. An image of Hollus wavered into existence, full-blown, almost indistinguishable from the real thing. Cooter turned around; he was panicked and didn't seem to notice that the missing Forhilnor had suddenly rejoined us.

"Cooter," said the Hollus simulacrum, boldly stepping forward. "My name is Hollus." Cooter immediately aimed the submachine gun at her, but the Forhilnor continued to close the distance between them. We all started falling back. I could see that the police in the vestibule were confused; Hollus had apparently interposed himself between them and Cooter. "You have not shot anyone yet," said Hollus, the words like the beating of twin hearts. "You saw what happened to your associate; do not let the same fate befall you."

I made motions with my hands that I hoped the others could see in the dark: I wanted them to fan out so that none of us were along the same line that connected Cooter and Hollus.

"Give me the weapon," said Hollus. She was now four meters

from Cooter. "Relinquish it and we will all depart from here alive."

"Back off!" cried Cooter.

Hollus continued to approach. "Give me the weapon," she said again.

Cooter shook his head violently. "All we wanted to do was show you aliens that what these scientists were telling you wasn't the truth."

"I understand that," said Hollus, taking another step forward. "And I will gladly listen to you. Just give me the weapon."

"I know you believe in God," said Cooter. "But you haven't yet been saved."

"I will listen to anything you wish to say," said Hollus, inching forward, "but only after you relinquish the weapon."

"Make all the cops leave," said Cooter.

"They are not going to leave." Another six-legged increment toward the man.

"Don't come any closer, or I'll shoot," said Cooter.

"You do not want to shoot anyone," said Hollus, still advancing, "least of all a fellow believer."

"I swear I'll kill you."

"You will not," said Hollus, closing the gap even more.

"Stay back! I'm warning you!"

The six round feet moved forward again.

"God forgive me," said Cooter and—

—and he squeezed the trigger.

And bullets erupted from the gun—

And they entered the Hollus simulacrum—

And the force fields that composed the simulated body slowed the bullets down, retarding their motion more and more, until they emerged from the other side. They continued to fly across the Rotunda, traveling another two meters or so in parabolic paths that brought them clattering to the stone floor.

The simulacrum moved forward, reaching out with its force-field arms to grab the submachine gun by the muzzle, which surely was now so hot that no flesh-and-blood being could have managed to hold it.

The real Hollus, upstairs, presumably on the third floor, yanked her arms back, and her simulacrum, down here in the lobby, yanked its arms back, too. And Cooter, startled that the being he'd just filled with bullets was not dead, let go of the gun. The avatar spun around and quickly retreated.

The police surged in through the vestibule and—

It was unnecessary now. Totally unnecessary.

One of the cops squeezed off a round.

And Cooter staggered backward, his mouth a wide, perfect "O" of surprise. He hit a wall segment and slumped down in the dark, a trail of blood like a claw mark following him to the floor.

And his head lolled to one side.

And he went to meet his maker.

ROBERT J. SAWYER

29

The cops questioned Christine and me for hours, but they had let the four aliens immediately return to the mothership so that Barbulkan's wound could be treated. I finally took a cab home—thirty dollars, with tip—and was up for another two hours telling Susan all about what had happened.

"My God," she said, over and over again. "My God, you could have been killed."

"Hollus saved me. She saved everyone."

"I'm going to give that great big spider a huge hug if I ever get the chance," said Susan, smiling.

I smiled, too, and kissed her. But I was exhausted by this point—absolutely bone-weary. My vision was blurring, and I felt lightheaded. "I'm sorry, sweetheart," I said, "but I have got to get some sleep."

She nodded, kissed me again, and we headed up to our room.

I slept until 10:00 Monday morning. The shootout had occurred too late to make the morning papers, but Susan told me that both *Breakfast Television* and *Canada A.M.* had led with the story. She'd stayed home from the office to be there for me when I awoke. Ricky was already off to school by the time I crawled out of bed.

I finally managed to make it into the ROM by noon. Fortunately, since it was indeed Monday, the museum was closed to the public, giving the facilities division a chance to clean things up; they were still mopping the Rotunda's marble floor when I got there. Meanwhile, Jonesy and all his preparators were in Garfield Weston Hall, salvaging everything they could from the shattered shales. Several paleontologists were flying up from the Smithsonian, too, to lend a hand; they were expected before the end of the day.

I made it up to my office and collapsed into my chair, rubbing my temples, trying to banish the headache I'd woken up with. Shortly after I sat down, the holoform projector bleeped, and the Hollus simulacrum wavered into existence.

I rose from my chair, my head pounding as I did so. "How are you?" I asked, concerned.

The Forhilnor's torso bobbed. "Distressed. I did not sleep well, despite medication given me by my ship's doctor."

I nodded sympathetically. "I didn't sleep well, either; I kept hearing gunshots echo through my head." I frowned and sat back down. "They say there's going to be an inquest. The cops probably didn't have to kill Cooter."

Hollus's eyestalks moved in a way I'd never seen them do before. "I have limited sympathy for him," she said. "He injured Barbulkan and tried to kill me." She paused. "How extensive was the damage to the Burgess Shale fossils?"

I shook my head slowly. "Everything in the first five cases was destroyed," I said, "including the one you were scanning." I felt nauseous contemplating the loss; not only were they some of the world's most important fossils, but they had also been some of the best preserved, hauntingly beautiful creatures, almost extraterrestrial in appearance. Harming them was barbarous, a sacrilege. "Of course, the fossils were insured," I said, "so there will be a lot of money coming to both the ROM and the Smithsonian, but the specimens are irreplaceable."

"In a way it is fortunate," said Hollus. "Presumably they started shooting with the case we were scanning specifically because its glass cover was open. The scans were partially com-

282

pleted, so at least a few of the specimens can be recovered. I will have reconstructions made for you."

I nodded, knowing no matter how realistic and accurate the reconstructions might be, they would never be the same as the originals. "Thank you."

"It is a terrible loss," Hollus said. "I have never seen fossils of that quality on any other world. They were really quite—"

She broke off in mid-sentence, and her simulacrum froze in place, as if the real Hollus, the one in synchronous orbit aboard the mothership, had been distracted by something happening up there.

"Hollus?" I said, not really concerned; one of her shipmates was probably just asking her a question.

"Just a moment," she replied, the simulacrum moving again. I heard a few songs in the Forhilnor language as she communicated with somebody else, and then the simulacrum froze once more.

I sighed impatiently. This was worse than Call Waiting: you still had the damned simulacrum taking up most of your office. I picked up a magazine off my desk—the latest *New Scientist;* the departmental copy started its circulation with me and worked its way down through the ranks. I'd only just opened its cover when the Hollus avatar started moving again. "Terrible news," she said, one word per mouth, her voices oddly attenuated. "I— my God, it is terrible news."

I dropped the magazine. "What?"

Hollus's eyestalks were swinging back and forth. "Our mothership does not have to contend with the scattering of light by your planet's atmosphere; even during daytime, the *Merelcas's* sensors can still clearly see the stars. And one of those stars . . . "

I leaned forward in my chair. "Yes? Yes?"

"One of those stars has begun its conversion to a—what is the word, again? When a massive star explodes?"

"A supernova?" I said.

"Yes."

"Wow." I remembered all the excitement around the planetarium back in 1987 when the U of T's Ian Shelton discovered the supernova in the Large Magellanic Cloud. "That's great."

"It is *not* great," said Hollus. "The star that has begun to explode is Alpha Orionis."

"Betelgeuse?" I said. "Betelgeuse has started going supernova?"

"That is correct."

"Are you sure?"

"There can be no doubt," said the Forhilnor, her two voices sounding quite shaky. "It is already shining with more than a million times its normal brightness, and its luminosity is still increasing.

"My God," I said. "I—I should phone Donald Chen. He'll know who to notify. There's a central bureau for astronomical telegrams, or some such thing . . . " I picked up my phone and dialed Chen's extension. He answered on the third ring; one more and his voice mail would have picked up.

"Don," I said, "it's Tom Jericho. Hollus here tells me that Betelgeuse has just gone supernova."

There was silence for a few moments. "Betelgeuse is—*was*—a prime candidate to go supernova," he said. "But no one knew precisely when it would happen." A pause, and then, earnestly, as if he just realized something: "Did Hollus say Betelgeuse? Alpha Orionis?"

"Yes."

"Look, is Hollus sure? Absolutely sure?"

"Yes, she says she's positive."

"Damn," said Chen into his phone's mouthpiece, but I don't think he was really talking to me. "Damn."

"What?" I said.

Chen's voice sounded strained. "I've been going over that supernova data Hollus sent down, particularly as related to gamma-ray output. For the last supernova, the one in 1987, we had lousy data; it happened before we had any dedicated gamma-ray observation satellites—Compton didn't go up until 1991. The only gamma-ray data we had for Supernova 1987A was from the Solar Maximum Mission satellite, and it wasn't designed for extragalactic observations."

"So?"

"So the gamma-ray output of a supernova is much greater than we'd thought; Hollus's data proves that."

"And?" I said. "What does that mean?" I looked over at Hollus, who was bobbing extremely rapidly; I'd never seen her so upset.

Chen let out a long sigh, the sound rumbling across the phone line. "It means that our atmosphere is going to be ionized. It means that the ozone layer is going to be depleted." He paused. "It means that we're all going to die."

Ricky Jericho was many kilometers north of the ROM, in the playground at Churchill Public School. It was the middle of the ninety-minute lunch break; some of his classmates went home for lunch, but Ricky ate at school in a room where they let the kids watch *The Flintstones* on CFTO. After he'd finished his bologna sandwich and apple, he'd gone out into the grassy yard. Various teachers were walking around, breaking up fights, cooing over skinned knees, and doing all the other things teachers had to do. Ricky looked at the sky. Something was shining brightly up there.

He made his way past the jungle gym and found his teacher. "Miss Cohan," he said, tugging at her skirt. "What's that?"

She used a hand to shield her eyes as she looked up in the direction he was pointing. "That's just an airplane, Ricky."

Ricky Jericho wasn't one to contradict his teachers lightly. But he shook his head. "No, it's not," he said. "It can't be. It's not moving."

285

My mind was swirling, and my intestines were knotting. A new day was dawning, not just in Toronto, but for the entire Milky Way. In fact, even observers in far-distant galaxies would surely see the growing brightness once sufficient time had elapsed for the light to reach them. It beggared the imagination. Betelgeuse was indeed going supernova.

I put Don on the speaker phone, and he and Hollus conversed back and forth, with me interjecting the occasional worried question. What was happening, I gathered, was this: in every active star, hydrogen and helium undergo fusion, producing successively heavier elements. But, if the star is sufficiently massive, when the fusion chain reaches iron, energy starts being absorbed rather than released, causing a ferrous core to build up. The star grows too dense to support itself: the outward explosive thrust of its internal fusion no longer counteracts the huge pull of its own gravity. The core collapses into degenerate matter—atomic nuclei crushed together, forming a volume only twenty kilometers across but with a mass many times that of Sol. And when infalling hydrogen and helium from the outer layers of the star suddenly hit this new, hard surface, they fuse instantly. The fusion blast and the shockwave of the collision propagate back out, blowing off the star's gaseous atmosphere and releasing a torrent of radio noise, light, heat, x rays, cosmic rays, and neutrinos—a deadly sleet pouring out in all directions, an expanding spherical shell of death and destruction shining brighter than all the other stars in the galaxy combined: a supernova.

And that, apparently, was happening right now to Betelgeuse. Its diameter was expanding rapidly; within days, it would be bigger than Earth's entire solar system.

Earth would be protected for a time: our atmosphere would keep the initial onslaught from reaching the ground. But there was more coming. Much more.

ROBERT J. SAWYER

I'd tuned the radio in my office to CFTR, an all-news station. As reports started appearing on Earth's TV and radio stations, some people rushed to caves and mine shafts. It wouldn't make any difference. The end of the world was coming—and with a bang, not a whimper.

Those Forhilnors and Wreeds currently visiting Earth, perhaps along with a few human passengers, might escape, at least for a time; they could maneuver their starship to keep the bulk of the planet between themselves and Betelgeuse, acting as a shield of stone and iron almost thirteen thousand kilometers thick. But there was no way they could outrun the expanding shell of death; it would take the *Merelcas* a full year to accelerate to close to the speed of light.

But even if that ship could escape, the Forhilnor and Wreed homeworlds could not; they would soon be facing the same onslaught, the same scourge. The asteroids that hit Sol III and Beta Hydri III and Delta Pavonis II sixty-five million years ago were minor blows in comparison, mere flesh wounds from which the ecosystems rebounded within a matter of decades.

But there would be no rebounding this time. This would be the *sixth* great extinction, felt equally on all three worlds. And whether biology had started in this solar system on Mars rather than Earth, whether it really had arisen multiple times on the Forhilnor world, whether the Wreeds even knew that it *was* the sixth extinction, didn't matter.

For this would also be the *last* great extinction, the concluding chapter, a wiping clean of the slate, the final turn in the game of Life.

30

What do you do in the last moments of your life? Unlike most of the six billion humans who had just received a death sentence, I actually had been preparing for my own demise. But I'd expected it to come at a more dilatory pace, with me in a hospital bed, accompanied by Susan, maybe my brother Bill, a few friends, and perhaps even brave little Ricky.

But the explosion of Betelgeuse was utterly unheralded; we didn't see it coming. Oh, as Hollus had said earlier, we knew Betelgeuse would doubtless eventually go supernova, but there was no reason to expect it to happen right now.

Toronto's subway system was jammed already, according to the radio reports. People were going down into the stations, into the subway cars, hoping that they would be protected by being underground. They were refusing to vacate the trains, even at the ends of the lines.

And the roads outside the ROM had already turned into parking lots, total gridlock. I wanted to be with family just as much as everyone else did, but there didn't seem to be any way to manage it. I tried repeatedly calling Susan's office, but all I got were busy signals.

Of course, death wouldn't be instantaneous. There would be weeks, or even months, before the ecosystem collapsed. Right now, Earth's ozone layer was protecting us from the high-energy photons, and, of course, the sleet of bulky charged particles, traveling slower than the speed of light, hadn't arrived yet. But soon enough the onslaught from Betelgeuse would strip off the ozone layer, and hard radiation both from that exploding star and from our own sun would reach the ground, breaking down living tissue. Surely I would be able to reunite with my wife and son before the end. But for now, it seemed, my company would be the simulacrum of an alien being.

The first blast from Betelgeuse had already disrupted the satellite-based long-distance telephone network, and so I guess I shouldn't have been surprised to see the avatar wink in and out of existence periodically, as the electromagnetic cacophony from Orion interfered with the communication between the real Hollus over Ecuador and her holographic stand-in here in Toronto.

"I wish I could be with Susan," I said, looking at the Forhilnor across my desk, cluttered with unfinished business.

To my astonishment, Hollus actually raised her voices— something I'd never heard her do before. "At least you will likely get to see your family before the end. You think *you* are far from home? I cannot even contact my children. If Betelgeuse is hitting Earth with this sort of force, it will slam Beta Hydri III, as well. I cannot even radio a goodbye to Kassold and Pealdon; not only is there too much interference, but the radio signal would not reach them for twenty-four years."

"I'm sorry," I said. "I wasn't thinking."

"No, you were not," she snapped again, holographic spittle actually flying from her left mouth. But after a moment, she calmed down a little. "Apologies," she said. "It is just that I love my children so much. To know that they—that my entire race— is dying . . ."

I looked at my friend. She'd been away from her world for so long already—out of touch with what was going on back home for years now. Her son and daughter were grown when she left on her grand tour of eight star systems, but now—now, they

290

were likely middle aged, perhaps even biologically older than Hollus herself was, for she had traveled at relativistic speeds during much of her journey.

It was worse than that, actually, come to think of it. Betelgeuse was in Earth's northern sky; Beta Hydri in its southern one—which meant that Earth was between the two stars. It would be several years before the brightening of Betelgeuse would be visible from Beta Hyrdi III—but there was no way to get a warning to that world; nothing could reach it faster than the angry photons from Betelgeuse that were already on their way.

Hollus was visibly trying to regain her composure. "Come," she said at last, her torso bobbing slowly, deliberately. "We might as well go outside and look at the spectacle."

And we did, taking the elevator down and exiting through the staff entrance. We stood outdoors on the same patch of concrete that Hollus's shuttle had originally landed on.

For all I knew, the Forhilnor and her colleagues were indeed positioning their starship for maximum safety. But the simulacrum of her stood with me, out front of the ROM, in the shadow of the abandoned planetarium dome, staring up. Even most of the passersby were looking up at the cerulean bowl rather than at the weird, spiderlike alien.

Betelgeuse was clearly visible as we looked out over the street toward Queen's Park; it was about a third of the way up the southeastern sky. It was disquieting to see a star shining during daylight. I tried to imagine the rest of Orion's splayed form against the blue backdrop but had no idea how it would be oriented at this time of day.

Other staff members and patrons exited the museum, as well, joining the gathering crowd on the side of the road. And, after a few minutes, astronomer Donald Chen, the walking dead, came out of the staff entrance and headed over to join us, more of the walking dead.

The Hubble Space Telescope had, of course, been immediately trained on Betelgeuse. Much better pictures were being obtained by Hollus's starship, the *Merelcas,* and these were broadcast down to be freely shared with the people of Earth. Even before the star had started to expand, the mothership's telescopes had been able to resolve Betelgeuse into a red disk marred by cooler sun spots and speckled with hotter convective patches, all surrounded by a magnificent ruddy corona.

But now that diaphanous outer atmosphere had been blown off in a phenomenal explosion, and the star itself was expanding rapidly, swelling to many times its normal diameter—although since Betelgeuse was a variable star, it was hard to say precisely what its normal diameter was. But, still, it had never before reached anywhere near *these* proportions. A yellow-white shell of superheated gas, a lethal plasma, was expanding outward from the spreading disk, hurtling in all directions.

From the ground, in the light of day, all we could see was a bright point of light, flaring and flickering.

But the starship's telescopes showed more.

Much more.

Incredibly more.

Through them, one could see another explosion rocking the star—it actually shifted slightly in the telescopes' fields of view—and more plasma spewing into space.

And then what appeared to be a small vertical rip—jagged-edged, its sides limned with piercing blue-white energy—opened up a short distance to the right of the star. The rip grew longer, more jagged, and then—

—and then a substance darker than space itself started to pour through the rip, flowing out of it. It was viscous, almost as if tar were oozing through from the other side, but . . .

But, of course, there was no "other side"—no way a hole could appear in the wall of the universe, my fantasy about grabbing hold of space itself and peeling it aside like a tent flap notwithstanding. The universe, by definition, was self-contained. If the blackness wasn't coming from outside, then the rip must be a tunnel, a wormhole, a join, a warp, a stargate, a shortcut—*something* connecting two points in the cosmos.

The black mass continued to flow out. It had definite edges; stars winked into invisibility as its perimeter passed over them. Assuming it really was near Betelgeuse, it must have been huge; the rip would have been more than a hundred million kilometers in length, and the object pouring out of it several times that in diameter. Of course, since the thing was utterly, overwhelmingly black, neither radiating nor reflecting any light, it had no spectrum to analyze for Doppler shifts, and there would be no easy way to do a parallactic study to determine the object's distance.

Shortly, the entire mass had passed out of the rip. It had a palmate structure—a central blob with six distinct appendages. No sooner was it free than the rift in space closed up and disappeared.

Dying Betelgeuse was contracting again, falling in upon itself. What had happened so far, said Donald Chen, was just the preamble. When the infalling gas hit the iron core for a second time, the star would *really* blow up, flaring so brightly that even we—four hundred light-years distant—shouldn't look directly at it.

The black object was moving through the firmament by *rolling* like a spiked wheel, as if—it couldn't be; no, it couldn't—as if its six extensions were somehow gaining purchase on the very fabric of space. The object was moving toward the contracting disk of Betelgeuse. The perspective was tricky to work out—it wasn't until one of the limbs of the blackness touched, then covered, the edge of the disk that it became clear that the object was at least slightly closer to Earth than Betelgeuse was.

As the star continued to collapse behind it, the blackness further interposed itself between here and there, until in short order it had completely eclipsed Betelgeuse. From the ground, all we could see was that the superbright star had disappeared; Sol no longer had a rival in the daytime sky. Through the *Merelcas*'s telescopes, though, the black form was clearly visible, a multiarmed inkblot against the background dusting of stars. And then—

And then Betelgeuse must have done as Chen said it would, exploding behind the blackness, with more energy than a hundred million suns. As seen from worlds on the opposite side, the great star must have flared enormously, an eruption of blinding light and searing heat, accompanied by screams of radio noise. But from Earth's perspective—

From Earth's perspective, all that was hidden. Still, the inkblot seemed to surge forward, toward the telescopes' eyes, as if it had been punched from behind, its central blob expanding to fill more of the field of view as it was hurtled closer. The six arms, meanwhile, were blown backward, like the tentacles of a jet-propelled squid seen head on.

Whatever this object was, it bore the brunt of the explosion, shielding Earth—and presumably the Forhilnor and Wreed homeworlds, too—from the onslaught that otherwise would have destroyed each world's ozone layer.

Standing outside the ROM, we didn't know what had happened—not yet, not then. But slowly realization dawned, even if the supernova didn't. The three homeworlds were going to be spared, somehow.

Life would go on. Incredibly, thankfully, miraculously, life would go on.

At least for some.

ROBERT J. SAWYER

31

I did finally make it home that night; word filtered down to those in the subways that, somehow, the disaster had been averted. By eight in the evening I was able to get a packed train heading south to Union station; I took it, even though I had to stand all the way home. I wanted to see Susan, to see Ricky.

Susan hugged me so hard it hurt, and Ricky hugged me, too, and we all moved to the couch and Ricky sat in my lap, and we hugged some more, a family.

Eventually Susan and I put Ricky to bed, and I kissed him good night, my boy, my son, whom I loved with all my heart. As with so much that was impinging on his life lately, he was too young to understand what had happened today.

Susan and I settled back onto the couch, and at 10:00 P.M., we watched the images taken by the *Merelcas*'s telescopes, broadcast as the lead story on *The National*. Peter Mansbridge looked more dour than usual as he went on about the close call Earth had had today. After showing the footage, the ROM's Donald Chen joined him in the studio—the CBC Broadcasting Centre was more or less due south of the museum—to explain in detail what had happened, and to confirm that the black *anomaly* (that was the word Don used) was still interposed between Earth and Betelgeuse, shielding us.

Mansbridge concluded the interview by saying,

"Sometimes we get lucky, I guess." He turned to the camera. "In other news today—"

But there was no other news—none that mattered in the slightest, none that could compare with what had happened this afternoon.

"Sometimes we get lucky," Mansbridge had said. I put an arm around Susan, pulled her close to me, felt the warmth of her body, smelled the fragrance of her shampoo. I thought of her, and, for once, not of how little time we had left together, but of all the wonderful times we'd had in the past.

Mansbridge was right. Sometimes we do indeed get lucky.

It came to me the next day, on the subway on the way down to the Museum; full-blown, a revelation, it came to me.

It was more than an hour after I got to my office before the Hollus avatar appeared. I fidgeted the entire time, waiting for her.

"Good morning, Tom," she said. "I wish to apologize for the harshness of my words yesterday. They were—"

"Don't worry about it," I said. "We all go a little nuts when we first realize we might be dying." I didn't pause, didn't allow her to take back control of the conversation. "Forget that. But look, something hit me this morning, while I was riding the subway, packed up there with all those other people. What about the ark? What about that ship sent from Groombridge 1618 to Betelgeuse?"

"Surely the ark was incinerated," said Hollus. She sounded sad. "The first spasm of the dying star would have accomplished that."

"No," I said. "No, that's not what happened." I shook my head, still stunned by the enormity of it. "Damn it, I should have realized that earlier—and *he* should have, too."

"Who?" said Hollus.

296

I didn't answer her—not yet. "The natives of Groombridge didn't abandon their planet," I said. "They transcended into a virtual realm, just like all the others."

"We found no warning landscape on the surface of their world," said Hollus. "And why, then, would they send a ship to Betelgeuse? Do you propose that it contained a splinter group who did not wish to transcend?"

"No one would go to Betelgeuse to live there; as you said, it's just not suitable. And four hundred light-years is an awfully long way to travel just to get a gravitational boost. No, I'm sure the craft you detected had no crew or passengers; all of the Groombridge natives are still back on their home planet, uploaded into a virtual-reality world. What the Groombridge natives sent to Betelgeuse was an unmanned ship containing a catalyst of some sort—something to *trigger* the supernova explosion."

Hollus's eyestalks stopped moving. "Trigger? Why?"

My head was swimming; the thought was almost too much. I looked at the Forhilnor. "To sterilize all the worlds in this part of the galaxy," I said. "To wipe them clean of life. If you were going to bury some computers and then transfer your consciousness into those computers, what would your greatest fear be? Why, that someone would come along and dig up the computers, damaging them or vandalizing them. On many of the worlds your starship visited, warning landscapes were created to scare people away from unearthing what was buried beneath. But on Groombridge, they decided to go one better. They tried to make sure that no one, not even anyone from another nearby star, could possibly come along and interfere with them. They knew Betelgeuse—the biggest star in local space—was eventually going to go supernova. And so they hurried things up by a few millennia, sending a catalyst, a bomb, a device that caused the supernova explosion to happen as soon as it arrived." I paused. "In fact—in fact, that's why you could still see the ship's fusion exhaust, even though it was almost all the way to

CALCULATING GOD

Betelgeuse. Of course, it had never turned around to brake—because it never intended to slow down. Instead, it rammed itself right into the star's heart, setting off the supernova explosion."

"That is—that is monstrous," said Hollus. "It is entirely on one side."

"Damn right it is," I said. "Of course, the Groombridge natives might not have known for sure that any lifeforms existed elsewhere. After all, they reached intelligence in isolation—you said that the ark had been traveling for five thousand years. It might have just seemed a prudent precaution; they weren't certain that they were wiping out any other civilizations." I paused. "Or maybe they just didn't give a damn. Maybe they thought they were God's chosen people and that he had put Betelgeuse right there for them to use in just the way they did."

"They may have indeed believed that," said Hollus, "but you know it is not true."

She was right. I *did* know it. I had seen the smoking gun. I had seen proof good enough even for me. I took a deep breath, trying to calm myself, trying to reign in all the thoughts running through my mind. Of course, it could have been something made by an advanced race; it could have been an artificial nova deflector; it could have been . . .

But at some point, the simplest theory—the theory that proposes the fewest elements—has to be adopted. At some point, you have to stop demanding of *this* question—this one question out of all the others—a higher degree of proof than required for any other theory. At some point—maybe very near the end of one's life—you have to deal with this. At some point, the walls have to come tumbling down.

"You want me to say it?" I said. I found myself shrugging slightly, as though the idea were a sweater that needed to be shifted in order to fit comfortably. "Yes, that was God; that was the creator."

I paused, letting the words float freely for a time, considering whether I wanted to try to recant them.

298

But I didn't. "You said a while ago, Hollus, that you thought God was a being who had somehow survived the previous big crunch, had somehow managed to continue to exist from an earlier cycle of creation. If that's true, he would indeed be a part of the cosmos. Or, if he wasn't until now, maybe he has the ability to become—what's the word the theologians use?—to become *incarnate*. God took on physical form and interposed himself between the exploding star and our three worlds."

And suddenly another thought occurred to me: "In fact, it wasn't the first time he'd done that!" I said. "Remember the Vela supernova from 1320 A.D.—a supernova almost as close as Betelgeuse, a supernova whose remnant is now detectable but nobody saw when it happened, nobody recorded, not the Chinese here on Earth, not anybody else here, not anyone on your planet, not anyone on the Wreed homeworld. This entity intervened then, as well, shielding us from that supernova's radiation. You said it yourself, the first time we talked about God: the rate of supernova formation has to be carefully balanced. Well, if you can't actually prevent supernovas, this is the next best thing."

Hollus's eyestalks moved closer together. She seemed to slump a bit, as if her six legs were having trouble supporting her weight. No doubt the idea that the entity was God had occurred to her before it had to me, but she clearly had not previously thought about what that meant in relation to the Vela supernova. "God does not just cause mass extinctions," said the Forhilnor. "He routinely prevents them, too, when it suits his purpose."

"Incredible, isn't it?" I said, feeling as unsteady as Hollus looked.

"Maybe we should go see," Hollus said. "If we now know where God is, maybe we should go see him."

The idea was staggering, huge. I felt my heart jackhammering again. "But—but what we saw actually happened near Betelgeuse over 400 years ago," I said. "And it would take at least

400 more years for your ship to get there. Why would God hang around for a total of a thousand years?"

"A typical human or Forhilnor lifespan is about a century, which is roughly fifty million minutes," said Hollus. "God is presumably at least as old as the universe, which has existed for 13.9 billion years so far; even if he were near the end of his span, a thousand years for him would be comparable to four minutes for one of us."

"Still, surely he won't waste time waiting for us."

"Perhaps not. Or perhaps he knew his actions would be observed, attracting our attention. Perhaps he will arrange to be present there again—the only location we have ever been able to identify for him—for a rendezvous at the appropriate time. He may leave to take care of other business in the interim, then return. He seems rather mobile; presumably had he known that the Groombridge ark was going to detonate Betelgeuse, he would have simply destroyed the ark before it got there. But once the explosion began, he arrived very quickly—and he could return just as quickly, by the time we get there."

"*If* he wants to meet us. It's a long shot, Hollus."

"Doubtless so. But my crew embarked on this journey to find God; this is the closest we have come, and therefore we must pursue this lead." Her eyestalks regarded me. "You are welcomed to join us on this voyage."

My pulse was racing again, even faster than before. But it could not be for me. "I don't have that much time left," I said softly.

"The *Merelcas* can accelerate to very close to the speed of light in less than one year," said Hollus. "And once at such a speed, most of the distance would be covered in what would seem to be very little time; of course we would need a second year for decelerating, but in a little over two subjective years, we could be at Betelgeuse."

"I don't have two years."

"Well, no," said Hollus. "Not if you stay awake for the trip.

But I believe I told you that the Wreeds travel in suspended animation; we could do the same thing for you, and not take you out of cyrofreeze until we had reached our destination."

My vision blurred. The offer was incredibly tempting, an amazing proposition, an unimaginable gift.

In fact—

In fact, maybe Hollus could freeze me until—"Could you freeze me indefinitely?" I asked. "Eventually, surely there will be a cure for cancer, and—"

"Sorry, no," said Hollus. "There is degradation with the process; although the technique is as safe as a general anesthetic over periods of up to four years, we have never successfully revived anyone after more than ten years in cyrofreeze. It is a convenience for traveling, not a way of moving into the future."

Ah, well; I never quite saw myself following in Walt Disney's frosty footsteps, anyway. But, still, to get to take this journey with Hollus, to fly aboard the *Merelcas* out to see what might really, actually be God . . . it was an incredible notion, an astounding thought.

And, I suddenly realized, it might even be the best thing for Susan and Ricky, sparing them the agony of the last few months of my life.

I told Hollus I'd have to think about it, have to discuss it with my family. Such a tantalizing possibility, such an enticing offer . . . but there were many factors to consider.

I'd said that Cooter had gone to meet his maker—but I didn't really believe that. He had simply died.

But perhaps I *would* meet my maker . . . and while I was still alive.

32

H ollus has offered me a chance to go with her to her next destination," I said to Susan when I got home that night. We were sitting on the living-room couch.

"To Alpha Centauri?" she replied. That had indeed been the next, and last, planned stop on the *Merelcas*'s grand tour before it headed back home to Delta Pavonis and then Beta Hydri.

"No, they've changed their minds. They're going to go to Betelgeuse instead. They're going to go see whatever it is that's out there."

Susan was quiet for a time. "Didn't I read in the *Globe* that Betelgeuse is 400 light-years away?"

I nodded.

"So you couldn't be back for over a *thousand* years?"

"From Earth's point of view, yes."

She was silent some more. After a time, I decided to fill the void. "See, their ship will have to turn around at the halfpoint and face its fusion exhaust toward Betelgeuse. So in just 250 years, the—the entity will see that bright light, and will know that someone is coming. Hollus hopes that he—that it—will wait for us to arrive, or else will come back to meet us."

"The entity?"

I couldn't bring myself to use the other word with her. "The being that interposed itself between us and Betelgeuse."

"You think it's God," said Susan simply. She was the one who went to church. She was the one who knew the Bible. And she'd been listening to me for weeks now, talking over dinner about ultimate origins, first causes, fundamental constants, intelligent design. I hadn't often said the G-word—not around her, at any rate. It had always meant so much more to her than it had to me, and so I'd kept some distance from it, some scientific detachment. But she knew. She knew.

I shrugged a little. "Maybe," I said.

"God," repeated Susan, placing the concept firmly on the table. "And you've got a chance to go see him." She looked at me, her head tilted to one side. "Are they taking anyone else from Earth?"

"A few, ah, individuals, yes." I tried to remember the list. "A severely schizophrenic woman from West Virginia. A silverback gorilla from Burundi. A very old man from China." I shrugged. "They're some of the people the other aliens have bonded with. All of them immediately agreed to go."

Susan looked at me, her expression carefully neutral. "Do you want to go?"

Yes, I thought. Yes, with every fiber of my being. Although I longed for more time with Ricky, I'd rather he remembered me as still somewhat healthy, still able to get around on my own, still able to pick him up. I nodded, not trusting my voice.

"You've got a son," Susan said.

"I know," I said softly.

"And a wife."

"I know," I said again.

"We—we don't want to lose you."

I said it gently. "But you will. All too soon, you will."

"But not yet," said Susan. "Not yet."

We sat silently. My mind roiled.

Susan and I had known each other at university, back in the 1960s. We'd dated, but I'd left, to go to the States, to pursue my dream. She hadn't stood in my way then.

And now here was another dream.

But things were different, incalculably so.

We were married now. We had a child.

If that was all there were to the equation, it would be a no-brainer. If I were healthy, if I were well, there was no way I'd have contemplated leaving them—not even as an idle speculation.

But I wasn't healthy.

I wasn't well. Surely she understood that.

We'd been married in a church, because that's what Susan had wanted, and we'd said the traditional vows, including "Till death do us part." Of course, no one standing there, in a church, affirming those words, ever contemplates cancer; people don't expect the damned crab to scuttle into their lives, dragging torture and calamity behind it.

"Let's think about it some more," I said. "The *Merelcas* isn't leaving for three days."

Susan moved her head slightly, in a tight nod.

"Hollus," I said, the next day, in my office. "I know you and your shipmates must be terribly busy, but—"

"Indeed we are. There is much preparation to be done before leaving for Betelgeuse. And we are involved in considerable moral debate."

"About what?"

"We believe you are correct: the beings of Groombridge 1618 III did try to sterilize all of local space. It is not a thought that would have occurred to either a Forhilnor or a Wreed; forgive me for so saying, but it is something so barbarous, only a human—or, apparently, a Groombridge native—would think of it. We are debating whether to send messages to our homeworlds, advising them of what the beings of Groombridge tried to do."

"That seems like a reasonable thing to do," I said. "Why wouldn't you tell them?"

"The Wreeds are a generally nonviolent race, but, as I have told you, my species is—well, *passionate* would be the kind word. Many Forhilnors would doubtless wish to seek retribution for what was attempted. Groombridge 1618 is thirty-nine light-years from Beta Hydri; we could easily send ships there. Regrettably, the natives left no warning landscape marking their current location—so if we wish to be sure they are exterminated, we might have to destroy their entire world, not just a segment of it. The people of Groombridge never developed the ultra-high-energy fusion technology my race possess; if they had, they surely would have used it to send their bomb to Betelgeuse more quickly. That technology does give us strength enough to destroy a planet."

"Wow," I said. "That *is* a moral dilemma. Are you going to tell your homeworld?"

"We have not decided."

"The Wreeds are the great ethicists. What do they think you should do?"

Hollus was quiet for a time. "They suggest we should use the *Merelcas*'s fusion exhaust to wipe out all life on Beta Hydri III."

"On the Forhilnor homeworld?"

"Yes."

"Good God. Why?"

"They have not made that clear, but I suspect they are being—what is that word again? *Ironic*. If we are willing to destroy those who have been, or might be, a threat to ourselves, then we are no better than the Groombridge natives." Hollus paused. "But I did not mean to burden you with this. You wanted something from me?"

"Well, next to what you've just said, it seems pretty small potatoes."

"Small potatoes?"

"Inconsequential. But, well, I'd like to talk to a Wreed. I've got a moral quandary, and I can't solve it."

Hollus's crystal-covered eyes regarded me. "About whether you will come with us to Betelgeuse?"

I nodded.

"Our friend T'kna is currently involved with his daily attempt to contact God, but he should be available in about an hour. If you can take the holoform projector to a larger room then, I will ask him to join us."

Others, of course, had reached the same conclusion I had: what Donald Chen had neutrally referred to as an "anomaly," and Peter Mansbridge had discreetly dismissed as simple "luck," was being heralded as proof of divine intervention by people all over the world. And of course those people put their own spin on it: what I'd called a smoking gun many were referring to as a miracle.

Still, that was a minority opinion: most people knew nothing about supernovae, and many, including a large contingent in the Muslim world, didn't trust the images supposedly produced by the *Merelcas*'s telescopes. Others claimed that what we'd seen was the devil's work: a fiery glimpse of hell, and then an all-encompassing darkness; some Satanists were now claiming vindication.

Meanwhile, Christian fundamentalists were scouring the Bible, looking for bits of scripture that could be bent to this occasion. Others were invoking predictions by Nostradamus. A Jewish mathematician at the Hebrew University of Jerusalem pointed out that the six-limbed entity was topologically equivalent to a six-pointed Star of David and suggested that what had been seen heralded the arrival of the Messiah. An organization called the Church of Betelgeuse had already set up an elaborate web site. And every bit of pseudoscientific crap about ancient Egyptians and Orion—the constellation in which the supernova happened to have occurred—was being given sensationalist play in the media.

But all that those other people could do was guess.

I had an opportunity to go and see—to find out for sure.

We were back in the conference room on the fifth floor of the Curatorial Centre, but there were no video cameras present this time. It was just me and a tiny alien dodecahedron—and the projections of two extraterrestrial beings.

Hollus stood quietly at one side of the room. T'kna was standing at the other side, the conference table between them. T'kna's utility belt was green today, rather than yellow, but it still sported the same galaxy-of-blood icon.

"Greetings," I said, once the Wreed's projection had stabilized.

The sound of tumbling rocks, then the mechanical voice: "Greetings reciprocated. Of this one you desire something?"

I nodded. "Advice," I said, tipping my head slightly. "Your counsel."

The Wreed was motionless, listening.

"Hollus told you I have terminal cancer," I said.

T'kna touched his belt buckle. "Sorrow expressed again."

"Thanks. But, look, you guys have offered me a chance to go with you to Betelgeuse—to meet whatever is out there."

A pebble hitting the ground. "Yes."

"I will be dead soon. I'm not certain precisely when, but—but surely within a couple of months. Now, should I spend those last few months with my family, or should I go with you? On the one hand, my family wants every minute they can have with me—and, well, I guess I understand that being with me when I . . . when I pass on is part of bringing closure to our relationships. And, of course, I love them greatly, and wish to be with them. But, on the other hand, my condition will deterio-

ROBERT J. SAWYER

rate, becoming an increasing burden on them." I paused. "If we lived in the States, maybe there would be a monetary issue—the last few weeks of one's life, spent in a hospital, can run up enormous bills down there. But here, in Canada, that doesn't figure into the equation; the only factors are the emotional toll, on me and on my family."

I was conscious that I was expressing my problem in mathematical terms—factors, equations, monetary issues—but that's the way the words had come tumbling out, without any preplanning by me. I hoped I wasn't completely baffling the Wreed.

"And of me you ask which choice you should make?" said the translator's voice.

"Yes," I said.

There was the sound of rocks grinding, followed by a brief silence, and then: "The moral choice is obvious," said the Wreed. "It always is."

"And?" I said. "What is the moral choice?"

More sounds of rocks, then: "Morality cannot be handed down from an external source." And here all four of the Wreed's hands touched the inverted pear that was its chest. "It must come from within."

"You're not going to tell me, are you?"

The Wreed wavered and vanished.

That night, while Ricky watched TV in the basement, Susan and I sat again on the couch.

And I told her what I'd decided.

"I'll always love you," I said to Susan.

She closed her eyes. "And I will always love you, too."

No wonder I liked *Casablanca* so much. Would Ilsa Lund go with Victor Laszlo? Or would she stay with Rick Blaine? Would she follow her husband? Or would she follow her heart?

And were there things bigger than her? Bigger than Rick?

Bigger than both of them? Were there other factors to consider, other terms in the equation?

But—let's be honest—was there anything bigger involved in my case? Sure, God might be at the heart of the matter—but if I went, it wouldn't change anything, I'm sure . . . whereas Victor's continued resistance to the Nazis helped save the world.

Still, I'd made my decision.

As difficult as it was, I'd made my decision.

But I'd never know if it was the right one.

I leaned over and kissed Susan, kissed her as if it were the last time.

ROBERT J. SAWYER

33

H i, sport," I said as I came into Ricky's room.

Ricky was sitting at his desk, which had a world map laminated into its surface. He was drawing something with pencil crayons, his tongue sticking out and up from the corner of his mouth in the quintessential childhood look of concentration. "Dad," he said, acknowledging me.

I looked around. The room was messy but not a disaster. Some dirty clothes were on the floor; I usually remonstrated him for that, but would not do so today. He had several small plastic dinosaur skeletons that I'd bought for him, and a talking Qui-Gon Jinn action figure he'd received for Christmas. And books, lots of children's books: our Ricky was going to grow up to be a reader.

"Son," I said, and I waited patiently for him to give me his full attention. He was completing one of the elements of his drawing—it looked like an airplane. I let him do so; I knew how gnawing unfinished business could be. At last he looked up, seeming surprised that I was still there. He lifted his eyebrows questioningly.

"Son," I said again, "you know Daddy's been awfully sick."

Ricky put down his pencil crayon, realizing we were moving onto serious ground. He nodded.

"And," I said, "well, I think you know that I'm not going to get better."

He pursed his lips and nodded bravely. My heart was breaking.

"I'm going to go away," I said. "I'm going to go away with Hollus."

"Can he fix you?" Ricky said. "He said he couldn't, but . . . "

Rick didn't know that Hollus was female, of course, and I hardly wanted to go off on tangents now. "No. No, there's nothing he can do for me. But, well, he's going on a trip, and I want to go with him." I'd been on numerous trips before—to digs, to conferences. Ricky was used to me traveling.

"When will you be coming back?" he asked. And then, his face all cherubic innocence, "Will you bring me something?"

I closed my eyes for a moment. My stomach was churning.

"I, ah, I won't be coming back," I said softly.

Ricky was quiet for a moment, digesting this. "You mean—you mean you're going off to die?"

"I'm so sorry," I said. "I'm so sorry to be leaving you."

"I don't want you to die."

"I don't want to die, either, but . . . but sometimes we don't have any choice in things."

"Can I—I want to go with you."

I smiled sadly. "You can't, Ricky. You have to stay here and go to school. You have to stay here and help Mommy."

"But . . . "

I waited for him to finish, to complete his objection. But he didn't. He simply said, "Don't go, Daddy."

But I *was* going to leave him. Whether this month, on Hollus's starship, or a couple more months down the road, lying in a hospital bed, tubes in my arm and nose and the back of my hand, EKG monitors softly bleeping in the background, nurses and doctors scuttling to and fro. One way or the other, I was going to leave. I had no choice about leaving, but I did have a say in when and how.

"Nothing," I said, "is harder for me than going." There was no point in telling him I wanted him to remember me like this,

ROBERT J. SAWYER

when really I wanted him to remember me as I was a year ago, seventy pounds heavier, with a reasonably full head of hair. But, still, this was better than what I would soon become.

"Then don't go, Daddy."

"I'm sorry, sport. Really, I am."

Ricky was as good as any kid his age at begging and wheedling to get to stay up late, to get a toy he wanted, to get to eat some more candy. But he realized, it seemed, that none of that would work here, and I loved him all the more for his six-year-old wisdom.

"I love you, Daddy," he said, tears coming now.

I bent down, lifting him from his chair, raising him up to my chest, hugging him to me. "I love you, too, son."

Hollus's starship, the *Merelcas,* looked nothing like what I'd expected. I'd grown used to movie spaceships with all sorts of detailing on their hulls. But this ship had a perfectly smooth surface. It consisted of a rectangular block at one end and a perpendicular disk at the other, joined by two long tubular struts. The whole thing was a soft green. I couldn't tell which end was the bow. Indeed, it was impossible to get any sense of its scale; there was nothing that I could recognize—not even any windows. The ship could have been only a few meters long, or kilometers.

"How big is it?" I asked Hollus, who was floating weightlessly next to me.

"About a kilometer," she said. "The block-shaped part is the propulsion module; the struts are crew habitats—one for Forhilnors, the other for Wreeds. And the disk at the end is the common area."

"Thank you again for taking me along," I said. My hands were shaking with excitement. Back in the eighties, there had been some brief talk about someday sending a paleontologist to 313

Mars, and I'd daydreamed that it might be me. But of course they'd want an invertebrate specialist; no one seriously believed that vertebrates had ever inhabited the red planet. If Mars did once have an ecosystem, as Hollus contended, it probably lasted only a few hundred million years, ending when too much atmosphere had bled off into space.

Still, there's a group called the Make-A-Wish Foundation that tries to fulfill final requests of terminally ill children; I don't know if there's a comparable group for terminally ill adults, and, to be honest, I'm not sure what I would have wished for had I been given the chance. But this would do. It would certainly do!

The starship continued to grow on the viewscreen. Hollus had said it had been cloaked, somehow, for more than a year, making it invisible to terrestrial observers, but there was no need for that anymore.

Part of me wished there were windows—both here on the shuttle and on the *Merelcas*. But apparently there were none on either; both had unbroken hulls. Instead, pictures from outside were conveyed to wall-sized viewscreens. I'd loomed in close at one point and couldn't discern any pixels or scan lines or flicker. The screens served just as well as real glass windows would— indeed, were better in many ways. There was no glare whatsoever from their surface, and, of course, they could zoom in to give a closeup, show the view from another camera, or indeed display any information one wanted. Perhaps sometimes the simulation *is* better than the real thing.

We flew closer and closer still. Finally, I could see something on the starship's green hull: some writing, in yellow. There were two lines of it: one in a system of geometric shapes—triangles and squares and circles, some with dots orbiting them—and the other a squiggle that looked vaguely like Arabic. I'd seen markings like the first set on Hollus's holoform projector, so I assumed that was the Forhilnor language; the other must have been the script of the Wreeds. "What's that say?" I asked.

314   "'This end up,'" said Hollus.

I looked at her, mouth agape.

"Sorry," she said. "A little joke. It is the name of the starship."

"Ah," I said. "*Merelcas,* isn't it? What does that mean?"

"'Vengeful Beast of Mass Destruction,'" said Hollus.

I swallowed hard. I guess some part of me had been waiting for one of those "It's a cookbook!" moments. But then Hollus's eyestalks rippled with laughed. "Sorry," she said again. "I could not resist. It means, 'Stellar Voyager,' or words to that effect."

"Kind of bland," I said, hoping I wasn't giving offense.

Hollus's eyestalks moved to their maximum separation. "It was decided by a committee."

I smiled. Just like the name for our Discovery Gallery back at the ROM. I looked again at the starship. While my attention had been diverted, an opening had appeared in its side; I have no idea whether it had irised open or some panel had slip away. The opening was bathed in yellow-white light, and I could see three other black wedge-shaped landers positioned inside.

Our shuttle continued to grow closer.

"Where are the stars?" I asked.

Hollus looked at me.

"I expected to see stars in space."

"Oh," she said. "The glare from Sol and Earth washes them out." She sang a few words in her own language, and stars appeared on the wallscreen. "The computer has now increased each star's apparent brightness enough so that it is visible." She pointed with her left arm. "See that zigzag there? That is Cassiopeia. Just below the central star in the pattern are Mu and Eta Cassiopeae, two of the places I visited before coming here." The indicated stars suddenly had computer-generated circles around them. "And see that smudge below them?" Another circle obligingly appeared. "That is the Andromeda galaxy."

"It's beautiful," I said.

Soon, though, the *Mercelcas* filled the entire field of view. Everything was apparently automatic; except for the occasional sung command, Hollus had done nothing since we entered the shuttle.

There was a clanging sound, conducted through the shuttle's hull, as we connected with a docking adapter on the far wall of the open bay. Hollus kicked off the bulkhead with her six feet and sailed gently toward the door. I tried to follow, but I realized I'd drifted too far from the wall; I couldn't reach out to kick or push off anything.

Hollus recognized my predicament, and her eyestalks moved with laughter again. She maneuvered her way back and reached out a hand to me. I took it. It was indeed the flesh-and-blood Hollus; there was no static tingle. She pushed off the bulkhead again with three of her feet, and we both sailed toward the door, which dutifully opened as we approached it.

Waiting for us were three more Forhilnors and two Wreeds. The Forhilnors would be easy to tell apart—each one had a cloth wrapped around its torso of a different color—but the Wreeds looked awfully similar to each other.

I spent three days exploring the ship. The lighting was all indirect; you couldn't see the fixtures. The walls, and much of the equipment, were cyan. I assumed that to Wreeds and Forhilnors, this color, not too far removed from that of the sky, was considered to be neutral; they used it everywhere humans used beige. I visited the Wreed habitat once, but it had a moldy smell I found unpleasant; I spent most of my time in the common-area module. It contained two concentric centrifuges that spun to simulate gravity; the outer one matched the conditions on Beta Hydri III, and the inner one simulated Delta Pavonis II.

All four of us passengers from Earth—me; Qaiser, the schizophrenic woman; Zhu, the ancient Chinese rice farmer; and Huhn, the silverback gorilla—enjoyed watching the fabulous spectacle of the Earth, a glorious sphere of polished sodalite, receding behind us as the *Merelcas* began its voyage—although Huhn, of course, didn't really understand what he was seeing.

It was less than a day later before we passed the orbit of the

316

moon. My fellow passengers and I were now farther into space than anyone from our planet had ever gone before—and yet we'd only covered less than one ten-billionth of the total distance we were going to traverse.

I tried repeatedly to have conversations with Zhu; he was initially quite wary of me—he later told me I was the first Westerner he'd ever met—but the fact that I spoke Mandarin eventually won him over. Still, I suppose I revealed my ignorance more than a few times in our chats. It was easy for me to understand why I, a scientist, might want to go off to the vicinity of Betelgeuse; it was harder for me to understand why an old peasant farmer would wish to do the same. And Zhu *was* indeed old—he himself wasn't sure what year he'd been born, but I wouldn't have been surprised if it had been prior to the end of the nineteenth century.

"I am going," said Zhu, "in search of Enlightenment." His voice was slow, whispery. "I seek *prajna,* pure and unqualified knowledge." He regarded me through rheumy eyes. "Dandart"— that was the Forhilnor who had bonded with him—"says the universe has undergone a series of births and deaths. So, of course does the individual, until Enlightenment is achieved."

"So it is religion that brings you here?" I asked.

"It is everything," said Zhu, simply.

I smiled. "Let's hope the trip is worth it."

"I am certain it will be," said Zhu, with a peaceful look on his face.

"You're sure this is safe?" I said to Hollus, as we floated down to the room where they would put me in cryogenic freeze.

Her eyestalks rippled. "You are flying through space at what you would refer to as breakneck speed, heading toward a creature who has almost inconceivable strength—and you worry about whether the hibernation process is safe?"

I laughed. "Well, when you put it that way—"

"It is safe; do not worry."

"Don't forget to wake me when we reach Betelgeuse."

Hollus could be perfectly deadpan when she felt like it. I will write myself a little note."

Susan Jericho, now sixty-four, sat in the den in the house on Ellerslie. It had been almost ten years since Tom had left. Of course, if he'd stayed on Earth, he'd have been dead for almost a decade. But instead he was presumably still alive, frozen, suspended, traveling aboard an alien starship, not to be revived for 430 years.

Susan understood all this. But the scale of it gave her a headache—and today was a day for celebrations, not pain. Today was Richard Blaine Jericho's sixteenth birthday.

Susan had given him what he'd wanted most—the promise to pay for driving lessons, and, after he'd received his license, the even bigger promise to buy him a car. There had been a lot of insurance; the cost of the car was a minor concern. Great Canadian Life had tried briefly to renege on paying out; Tom Jericho wasn't really dead, they'd said. But when the media got hold of the story, GCL had taken such a beating that the president of the company had publicly apologized and had personally hand-delivered a half-million-dollar check to Susan and her son.

A birthday was always special, but Susan and Dick—who would have thought that Ricky would grow up wanting to be called that?—would also celebrate again in a month. Dick's birthday had never quite had the proper resonance for Susan, since she hadn't been present when he'd been born. But a month from now, in July, would be the sixteenth anniversary of Dick's adoption, and that was a memory Susan cherished.

When Dick got home from school—he was just finishing grade ten at Northview Heights—Susan had two more presents

318

for him. First was a copy of his father's journal about the time he's spent with Hollus. And second was a copy of the tape Tom had made for his son; she'd had it converted from VHS to DVD.

"Wow," said Dick. He was tall and muscular, and Susan was enormously proud of him. "I never knew Dad made a video."

"He asked me to wait ten years before giving it to you," Susan said. She shrugged a little. "I think he wanted you to be old enough to understand it."

Dick lifted the jewel case, weighing it in his hand, as if he could thus divine its secrets. He was clearly anxious to see it. "Can we watch it now?" he said.

Susan smiled. "Sure."

They went into the living room, and Dick slipped the disk into the player.

And the two of them sat on the couch and watched Tom's gaunt, disease-ravaged form come to life again.

Dick had seen a few pictures of Tom from that time—they were in a scrapbook Susan had kept of the press coverage of Hollus's visit to Earth and Tom's subsequent departure. But he'd never seen what the cancer had done to his father in quite this detail. Susan watch him recoil a bit as the images began.

But soon all that was on Dick's face was attention, rapt attention, as he hung on every word.

At the end, they both wiped tears from their eyes, tears for the man they would always love.

34

Absolute darkness.

And heat, licking at me from all sides.

Was it hell? Was—

But no. No, of course not. I had a splitting headache, but my mind was beginning to focus.

A loud click, and then—

And then the lid of the cryofreeze unit sliding aside. The oblong coffin, made for a Wreed, was set flush into the floor, and Hollus was straddling it, her six feet in stirrups to keep her from floating away, her front legs tipped, and her eyestalks drooping down to look at me.

"Time" "to" "get" "up," "my" "friend," she said.

I knew what you were supposed to say in a situation like this; I'd seen Khan Noonien Singh do it. "How long?" I asked.

"More than four centuries," replied Hollus. "It is now the Earth year 2432."

Just like that, I thought. More than four hundred years gone, passing by without me being aware. Just like that.

They were wise to have installed the cryochambers outside of the centrifuges; I doubt I could have stood up under my own weight yet. Hollus reached down with her right hand, and I reached up with my left to grab it, the simple gold band on my ring finger looking unchanged by the freezing and the passing of time. Hollus helped haul me up out of the black ceramic coffin; she then slipped her feet out of the stirrups and we floated freely.

"The ship has ceased decelerating," she said. "We are almost to what is left of Betelgeuse."

I was naked; for some reason, I was embarrassed to have the alien see me this way. But my clothes were waiting for me; I quickly dressed—a blue Tilley shirt and a pair of soft, khaki-colored pants, veterans of many digs.

My eyes were having trouble focusing, and my mouth was dry. Hollus must have anticipated this; she had a translucent bulb full of water ready to give me. The Forhilnors never chilled their water, but that was fine right now—the last thing I needed was something cold.

"Should I have a checkup?" I asked, after I'd finished squeezing the water into my mouth.

"No," said Hollus. "It is all automatic; your health has been continuously monitored. You are—" She stopped; I'm sure she'd been about to say I was fine, but we both knew that wasn't true. "You are as you were before the freezing."

"My head hurts."

Hollus moved her limbs in an odd way; after a second I realized it was the flexing that would have bobbed her torso had we not been in zero-g. "You will doubtless experience various aches for a day or so; it is natural."

"I wonder how Earth is?" I said.

Hollus sang to the nearest wall monitor. After a few moments, a magnified image appeared: a yellow disk, looking about the size of a quarter held at arm's length. "Your sun," she said. She then she pointed at a duller object, about one-sixth the diameter of Sol. "And that is Jupiter, showing a gibbous face from this perspective." She paused. "At this distance, it is difficult to resolve Earth in visible light, although if you look at a radio image, Earth outshines your sun at many frequencies."

ROBERT J. SAWYER

"Still?" I said. "We're still broadcasting in radio, after all this time?" That would be wonderful. It would mean—

Hollus was quiet for a moment, perhaps surprised that I didn't get it. "I do not know. Earth is 429 light-years behind us; the light reaching us now shows how your solar system looked shortly after we left it."

I nodded sadly. Of course. My heart started pounding, and my vision blurred some more. At first I thought something had gone wrong in reviving me, but that wasn't it.

I was staggered; I hadn't been prepared for how I would feel. I was still alive.

My eyes squinted at the tiny yellow disk, then tipped down to the gold ring encircling my finger. Yes, I was still alive. But my beloved Susan was not. Surely, she was not.

I wondered what kind of life she had made for herself after I'd left. I hoped it had been a happy one.

And Ricky? My son, my wonderful son?

Well, there *was* that doctor I'd heard interviewed on CTV, the one who had said that the first human who would live forever had likely already been born. Maybe Ricky was still alive, and was—what?—438 years old.

But the chances were slim, I supposed. More likely, Ricky had grown up to be whatever sort of man he'd been destined to become, and he had worked and loved, and now . . .

And now was gone.

My son. I had almost certainly outlived him. A father is not supposed to do that.

I felt tears welling in my eyes; tears that had been frozen solid not an hour ago, tears that just sort of pooled there, near their ducts, in the absence of gravity. I wiped them away.

Hollus understood what human tears signified, but she didn't ask me why I was crying. Her own children, Pealdon and Kassold, must surely now be dead, too. She floated patiently next to me.

I wondered if Ricky had left children and grandchildren and great-grandchildren; it shocked me to think that I could easily have fifteen or more generations of descendants now. Perhaps the Jericho name echoed on still . . .

And I wondered whether the Royal Ontario Museum still existed, whether they'd ever reopened the planetarium, or if, in fact, cheap spaceflight for all the people had finally, properly, rendered that the institution redundant.

I wondered if Canada still existed, that great country I loved so much.

More, of course, I wondered if *humanity* still existed, if we had avoided the sting at the end of the Drake equation, avoided blowing ourselves up with nuclear weapons. We'd had them for fifty-odd years before I'd left; could we have resisted using them for eight times longer than that?

Or maybe . . .

It was what the natives of Epsilon Indi had chosen.

And those of Tau Ceti.

Of Mu Cassiopeae A, also.

And of Eta Cassiopeae A.

Those of Sigma Draconis, as well.

And even those amoral beings of Groombridge 1618, the arrogant bastards who had blown up Betelgeuse.

All of them, if I was right, had transcended into a machine realm, a virtual world, a computer-generated paradise.

And by now, with four centuries of additional technological advances, surely *Homo sapiens* had the capability of doing the same.

Perhaps they *had* done it. Perhaps they had.

I looked at Hollus, floating there: the real Hollus, not the simulacrum. My friend, in the flesh.

Maybe humanity had even taken a hint from the natives of Mu Cassiopeae A, blowing up Luna, giving Earth rings to rival those of Saturn; of course, our moon is relatively smaller than the Cassiopeian one and so contributes less to the churning of our mantle. Still, perhaps now a warning landscape was spread out across some geologically stable part of Earth.

I was floating freely again, too far from any wall; I had a tendency to do that. Hollus maneuvered over to me and took my hand in hers.

I hoped we hadn't uploaded. I hoped humanity was, well, still *human*—still warm and biological and real.

But there was no way to know for sure.

And was the entity still there, waiting for us, after more than four centuries?

Yes.

Oh, perhaps it hadn't stuck around all that time; perhaps it had indeed calculated when we would arrive, and had nipped off to take care of other things in the interim. While the *Merelcas* was traversing the 429 light-years at a hair below the speed of light, the view ahead had blueshifted into ultraviolet invisibility; the entity could have been gone for much of that time.

And, of course, perhaps it wasn't really God; perhaps it was just some extremely advanced lifeform, some representative of an ancient, but entirely natural, race. Or maybe it was actually a machine, a massive swarm of nanotechnological entities; there was no reason why advanced technology couldn't look organic.

But where do you draw the line? Something—some*one*—set the fundamental parameters for this universe.

Someone had intervened on at least three worlds over a period of 375 million years, a span two *million* times longer than the couple of centuries intelligent races seem to survive in a corporeal state.

And someone had now saved Earth and Delta Pavonis II and Beta Hydri III from the explosion of a supergiant star, absorbing more energy in a matter of moments than all the other stars in the galaxy were putting out, and doing so without being destroyed in the process.

How do you define God? Must he or she be omniscient? Omnipotent? As the Wreeds say, those are mere abstractions, and possibly unattainable. Must God be defined in a way that places him or her beyond the scope of science?

I'd always believed that there was *nothing* beyond the scope of science.

And I still believe that.

Where *do* you draw the line?

Right here. For me, the answer was right here.

How do you define God?

Like this. A God I could understand, at least potentially, was infinitely more interesting and relevant than one that defied comprehension.

I floated in front of one of the wall screens, Hollus on my left, six more Forhilnors next to her, a string of Wreeds off to my right, and we looked out at him, at it, at the being. It turned out to be about 1.5 billion kilometers wide—roughly the diameter of Jupiter's orbit. And it was so unrelentingly black that I was told that even the glow of the *Merelcas*'s fusion exhaust, which had been facing this way for two centuries of braking, had not reflected back from it.

The entity continued to eclipse Betelgeuse—or whatever was left of it—until we were quite close to it. Then it rolled aside, its six limbs moving like the spokes of a wheel, revealing the vast pink nebula that had formed behind it and the tiny pulsar, the corpse of Betelgeuse, at its heart.

But that was its only acknowledgement of our presence, at least as far as I could tell. I wished again for real windows: maybe if it could see us waving at it, it would respond in kind, moving one of its vast obsidian pseudopods in a slow, majestic arc.

It was maddening: here I was, within spitting distance of

what might well be God, and it seemed as indifferent to me as, well, as it had been when tumors had started to form in my lungs. I'd tried once before to speak to God and had received no reply, but now, dammitall, surely courtesy if nothing else required a response; we had traveled farther than any human or Forhilnor or Wreed ever had before.

But the entity made no attempt at communication—or, at least, none that I, or Zhu, my ancient Chinese fellow traveler, or Qaiser, the schizophrenic woman, or even Huhn, the silverback gorilla, could detect. Nor did the Forhilnors seem to be able to contact it.

But the Wreeds—

The Wreeds, with their radically different minds, their different way of seeing, of thinking—

And with their unshakeable faith . . .

The Wreeds apparently *were* in telepathic communication with the being. After years of trying to talk to God, God was now, it seemed, talking to them, in ways only they could detect. The Wreeds could not articulate what they were being told, just as they couldn't articulate in any comprehensible way the insights about the meaning of life that gave them peace, but nonetheless they started building something in the Wreed centrifuge.

Before it was finished, Lablok, the *Merelcas*'s Forhilnor doctor, recognized what it was, based on its general design principles: a large artificial womb.

The Wreeds took genetic samples from the oldest member of their contingent, a female named K't'ben, and from the oldest Forhilnor, an engineer named Geedas, and—

No, not from me, although I wished it had been; it would have brought completion, closure.

No, the human sample they took was from Zhu, the ancient Chinese rice farmer.

There are forty-six human chromosomes.

There are thirty-two Forhilnor chromosomes.

There are fifty-four Wreed chromosomes . . . not that they know that.

The Wreeds took a Forhilnor cell and vacuumed all the DNA from the nucleus. They then carefully inserted into that cell diploid sets of chromosomes from Geedas and K't'ben and Zhu, chromosomes that had divided so many times already that their telomeres had been reduced to nothing. And this cell, containing the 132 chromosomes from the three different races, was carefully placed into the artificial womb, where it floated in a vat of liquid containing purine and pyrimidine bases.

And then something astonishing happened—something that caused my heart to jump, that caused Hollus's eyestalks to move to their maximum separation. There was a flash of bright light; the *Merelcas*'s sensors revealed that a particle beam had shot out of the precise center of the black entity, passing right through to the artificial womb.

Peering in with a magnifying scanner, the interactions were astonishing.

Chromosomes from the three worlds seemed to seek each other out, joining up into longer strands. Some consisted of two Forhilnor chromosomes joined together, with a Wreed chromosome at the end; Hollus had talked about the Forhilnor equivalent of Down syndrome and of how telomere-lacking chromosomes could join end to end, an innate ability, seemingly useless, even detrimental, but now . . .

Other chains consisted of human chromosomes sandwiched between Forhilnor and Wreed chromosomes. Still others consisted of human chromosomes at either end of a Wreed. A few chains were only two chromosomes long; usually a human and a Forhilnor. And six of the Wreed chromosomes remained unaltered.

It was obvious now that strands of DNA had built into them the ability to do more—much more—than simply die or form tumors after their telomeres had been eliminated. Indeed, telomere-less chromosomes were ready for the long-awaited

328

next step. And now that intelligent lifeforms from multiple worlds had finally, with a little prodding, come into existence simultaneously, these chromosomes were at last able to take that step.

I now understood why cancer existed—why God needed cells that could continue to divide even after their telomeres were exhausted. The tumors in isolated lifeforms were merely an unfortunate side effect; as T'kna had said, "The specific deployment of reality that included cancer, presumably undesirable, must have also contained something much desired." And the much-desired thing was this: the ability to link chromosomes, to join species, to concatenate lifeforms—the biochemical potential to create something new, something *more*.

I dubbed the combined chromosomes *supersomes*.

And they did what regular chromosomes do: they reproduced, unzipping down their entire length, separating into two parts, adding in corresponding bases from the nutrient soup—a cytosine pairing with every guanine; a thymine for every adenine—to fill in their now-missing halves.

Something fascinating happened the first time the supersomes reproduced: the strand got *shorter*. Large sequences of intronic DNA—junk—dropped out during the copying process. Although the supersomes contained three times as much active DNA as did regular chromosomes, the resulting strings were much more compact. The supersomes did not push the theoretical limit of the size for biological cells; indeed, they packed even more information into a smaller space.

And, of course, when the supersomes reproduced, the cell containing them divided, creating two daughter cells.

And then those cells divided.

And on and on.

Prior to the middle of the Cambrian, life had had a fundamental constraint imposed by the fact that fertilized cells could not divide more than ten times, severely limiting the complexity of the resulting organism.

329

Then the Cambrian explosion occurred, and life suddenly got more sophisticated.

But there were still limits. A fetus could grow only so large—baby humans and Wreeds and Forhilnors all massed on the order of five kilograms. Larger babies would have required impossibly wide birth canals; yes, bigger bodies could have accommodated bigger brains via live birth—but much of the additional brain mass would end up being devoted to controlling the larger body. Maybe, just maybe, a whale was as intelligent as a human—but it wasn't *more* intelligent. Life had apparently reached its ultimate level of complexity.

But the supersome-driven fetus continued to grow larger and larger in its artificial womb. We had expected it to stop on its own at some point: oh, a Forhilnor might stumble into life with a double-length chromosome; a human child might survive for a time having three chromosome twenty-ones. But this combination, this wild genetic concoction, this mishmash, was surely too much, surely pushed the limits of the possible too far. Most pregnancies—be they Wreed or Forhilnor or human—spontaneously abort early on as something goes wrong in the embryo's development, usually before the mother is even aware that she's pregnant.

But our fetus, our impossible triple hybrid, did not.

In all three species, ontogeny—the development of the fetus—seems to recapitulate phylogeny—the evolutionary history of that organism. Human embryos develop then discard gills, tails, and other apparent echoes of their evolutionary past.

This fetus was going through stages, too, changing its morphology. It was incredible—like watching the Cambrian explosion play out in front of my own eyes, a hundred different body plans tried and discarded. Radial symmetry, quadrilateral symmetry, bilateral symmetry. Spiracles and gills and lungs and other things none of us recognized. Tails and appendages unnamed, compound eyes and eyestalks, segmented bodies and contiguous ones.

ROBERT J. SAWYER

No one had ever quite figured out what ontogeny apparently recapitulating phylogeny was all about, but it wasn't a real replay of the organism's evolutionary history—that was apparent since the forms didn't match those found in the fossil record. But now its purpose seemed clear: DNA must contain an optimization routine, trying every variation that might be possible before selecting which set of adaptations to express. We were seeing not just terrestrial and Beta Hydrian and Delta Pavonian solutions, but also blendings of all three.

Finally, after four months, the fetus seemed to settle on a body plan, a fundamental architecture different from that of human or Forhilnor or Wreed. The fetus's body consisted of a horseshoe-shaped tube, girdled by a hoop of material from which six limbs depended. There was an internal skeleton, visibly forming through the translucent material of the body, but it was made not of smooth bone but rather of bundles of braided material.

We gave the embryo a name. We called her *Wibadal,* the Forhilnor word for peace.

She was another child I would not live to see grow up.

But, like my own Ricky, I'm sure she would be adopted, cared for, nurtured, if not by the crew of the *Merelcas,* then by the vast, palmate blackness sprawling across the sky.

God was the programmer.

The laws of physics and the fundamental constants were the source code.

The universe was the application, running now for 13.9 billion years, leading up to this moment.

That the ability to transcend, to discard biology, came too soon in a race's life was a bug, a flaw in the design, a complication never intended. But finally, with careful manipulation, the programmer had worked around that bug.

331

And Wibadal?

Wibadal was the output. The point of it all.

I wished her well.

It was the ancient progression, the engine that had always driven evolution. One life ends; another begins.

I went into cryofreeze again, passing the next eleven months with my body, and its degenerations, arrested. But when Wibadal's gestation was finally complete, Hollus reawakened me for what, we both knew, would be the last time.

The Wreeds had announced that today would be the day; the child was now whole and would be removed from the artificial womb. "May she express the best in all of us," said T'kna, the Wreed I'd first met by telepresence all those months—and all those centuries—ago.

Hollus bobbed her torso. "A" said one of her mouths, and "men" concluded the other.

I was groggy from the suspended animation, but I watched in fascination as Wibadal was decanted from the womb. She came into the universe crying, just as I had done, and just as all the billions who had gone before me had.

Hollus and I spent hours simply looking at her, a strange, bizarre form, already half as big as I was.

"I wonder what her life span will be," I said to my Forhilnor friend; perhaps an odd question, but life spans were very much on my mind.

"Who" "knows?" she replied. "The lack of telomeres does not seem to be an impediment for her. Her cells could go on re-producing forever, and—"

She stopped.

"And they *will*," she said after a few moments of reflection. "They will. That entity"—she gestured at the space-faring blackness centered on one of the wall-sized viewing screens—

"survived through the last big crunch and big bang. Wibadal, I suspect, will survive though the next, becoming God to the universe that follows this one."

It was a staggering notion, although perhaps Hollus was right. But I wouldn't live long enough to know for sure.

Wibadal was behind a glass window in a specially built maternity ward with a single circular crib. I tapped on the glass, the way parents on my world had done millions of time before. I tapped, and I waved.

And Wibadal stirred, and waved a stubby, chubby appendage back at me. Maybe the current God had never acknowledged my presence—even when I'd come right up to him, he'd still been indifferent to me—but this god-to-be had noticed me, at least once, at least for a moment.

And, for that moment, I felt no pain.

But soon, the agony was back; it had been growing worse, and I had been growing weaker.

Time was running short.

I wrote a final, long letter to Ricky in case, by some miracle, he was still alive. Hollus transmitted it to Earth for me; it would reach there almost half a millennium hence. I told my son what I'd seen here and how much I loved him.

And then I asked Hollus for a last favor, a final kindness. I asked her for the sort of thing only a good friend could request of another. I asked her to help release me, to help me pass on. I'd brought only a few things with me from Earth, besides my cancer medication and pain pills. But I did bring a biochemistry text with enough information for the *Merelcas*'s doctor to synthesize something that would painlessly and swiftly end my life.

Hollus herself administered the injection, and she sat by my bed, holding my emaciated hand in one of hers, her bubble-wrap skin the last thing I felt.

I told Hollus to write down my final words and transmit them back to Earth, as well, so that Ricky, or whoever was still there, would know what I'd said. As I mused before, perhaps he, 333 or one of my great-to-the-nth grandchildren, might even put together a book about the first contact between an extraterrestrial and someone who, I suppose, was all too human.

I was surprised by what my last thoughts turned out to be. "You know," I said to Hollus, her eyes weaving back and forth, "I remember when I first became fascinated with fossils."

Hollus listened.

"I'd been at the beach," I said, "playing with some rocks, and I was amazed to find a stone shell embedded in one of them. I'd found something then that I'd never even known I'd been looking for." The pain was easing; everything was slipping away. I squeezed the Forhilnor's hand. "I guess I'm a lucky man," I said, feeling peace come over me. "It's happened a second time."

ABOUT THE AUTHOR

Robert J. Sawyer is the best-selling author of eleven previous novels, including *The Terminal Experiment,* which won the Nebula Award for Best Novel of the Year; *Starplex,* which was both a Nebula and Hugo Award finalist; and *Frameshift* and *Factoring Humanity,* both of which were Hugo Award finalists.

Rob has won twenty-one national and international awards for his fiction, including an Arthur Ellis Award from the Crime Writers of Canada; five Aurora Awards (Canada's top honor in SF); five Best Novel HOMer Awards voted on by the 30,000 members of the SF&F Forums on CompuServe; the *Science Fiction Chronicle* Reader Award; and the top SF awards in France (*Le Grand Prix de l'Imaginaire*), Japan (*Seiun*), and Spain (*Premio UPC de Ciencia Ficción,* which he has won twice).

Maclean's: Canada's Weekly Newsmagazine says Rob is "science fiction's northern star—in fact, one of the hottest SF writers anywhere. By any reckoning Sawyer is among the most successful Canadian authors ever." Rob is profiled in *Canadian Who's Who,* has been interviewed more than one hundred times on TV, and has given talks and readings at countless venues, including the Library of Congress. He lives in Thornhill, Ontario (just north of Toronto), with Carolyn Clink, his wife of sixteen years.

For more about Rob and his fiction—including a readers' group discussion guide for this novel—visit his World Wide Web site (called "the largest genre writer's home page in existence" by *Interzone*) at **www.sfwriter.com.**